TIMESCOPE

JOE HARDING

Dedication

> To Mike, who first asked for more.
> The Esther, my sincerest critic.
> And above all to Steve who said:
> "You need to rewrite!"

Copyright Page

Timescope

1

The young boy could not have been more than two or three years old. The older youth was about thirteen, lean and suntanned with straggly hair that reached over his shoulders combining to give an air of wildness and independence. Slung over his shoulders were a deadly-looking bow and a quiver of arrows. His face registered contempt as he gripped the flailing fists of his screaming half-brother; holding him at arm's length until the child's tantrum subsided.

"Why don't you go?" he goaded. "I was here before you and you don't belong here."

The little face was grimy and tear-streaked. He gave a bellow of rage and an ineffectual kick.

Abruptly the look of amused contempt vanished; giving place to an ugly mixture of jealousy and repressed hate.

"What if I kill you?" he demanded. "Then Father will love me again."

In a flash he released the tiny hands, unhitched the weapon and fitted an arrow to the string. Young as the child was, he understood. He stopped in mid-scream and began backing away; his eyes on the bow wide with fear.

"Run," the older lad spat. "Run to Mummy. Like you always do, you whimpering brat!"

The white-haired old man lounging in the shade of a large tent, started up in fear too. For a minute or two he had watched the confrontation between the siblings with curiosity, but now he felt, first alarm, then outright horror at the turn of events. For the bowstring was taut against the arrow-nock, the muscles standing out on the lad's bare arms. The child retreated further from him, then stumbled and fell backwards into the dust; his eyes fastened on the point of the arrow, his breathing racked with terror.

"Run!" the archer shouted in fury. "Get up and run!!"

With a cry the old man dashed towards the assailant.

·

Jon had tried smoking several times when he and Faris were hanging out in the park with the Apostles. Roger Lord regarded Jon with ill-concealed contempt as he gasped and choked, tears running down his face. Then with an attempt at composure Jon handed the cigarette to Faris who drew effortlessly on it. If Roger's approval was going to be won, Jon thought, wiping his streaming nose, it would have to be some other way. As his eyes cleared and his breathing returned to normal, Roger was planning their next moneymaking scheme.

"My old man can shift laptops". His eyes, sunk deeply into his face regarded them in turn. He spat. Years of smoking had given him a noticeable rattle in his chest, and he spat between sentences. Jon had tried spitting too, but it was as unconvincing as his smoking. Oliver Wainwright finished a can of Coke and threw it past Jon and into the dark.

"I'll get laptops." Jon said quietly.

All eyes were on him. Faris nudged him, "Don't be stupid, Jon!" he hissed.

"Sez you!" Roger's bored response irritated Jon further. "Just ask your Mum for a few, will you?"

Like most people Roger assumed that having a mother who was a Member of Parliament meant that he was privileged. Anything he wanted he could get. Easy. Even Faris didn't understand that she was off most days of the week, travelling around, at the London office, abroad, anywhere except home. She probably would give him a laptop if he asked, but that wasn't the point. If Roger needed laptops, Jon would acquire laptops the right way, the only way, he'd nick them like everyone else.

"How many d'you want?" He had no idea where he would acquire one, let alone several laptop computers, but the rest of Roger Cross' mates talked big so why shouldn't he? Roger grunted something inaudible and the gang moved away.

They were wandering down Keswick Avenue away from

the park now. Faris lagged behind with his latest girlfriend. The houses here were palatial, huge front gardens, with full size trees in front and behind. Automatic lights glared at them as they drifted by. Gates operated by key-pads barred many driveways. Oliver ran a stick down one as they passed.

"Shut it will you?" Oliver stopped, startled. This was unlike Roger who wasn't above swearing at the residents or lobbing a stone and legging it himself. Roger took Jon's elbow and steered him into the shadow cast by a streetlamp overhung by a tree.

"See there?" He nodded his head towards a huge house, set back from the road. It stuck out like a sore thumb. Amidst the immaculate gardens and pristine lawns of Keswick Avenue it wept neglect. The front lawn had long overgrown, and near the weed-ridden path was a rusty lawnmower minus its petrol engine. The tall grass grew gleefully through the seized blades. Huge bushes overhung the pavement and the gate was wedged open.   Three of the downstairs windows blazed with light, but the upstairs was shrouded in darkness.

"Who's is that dump?" Oliver wanted to know.

Roger pulled his hood over his head trying to look sinister. "I've been casing this place for a while," he confided, the smell of cigarettes on his breath still strong. "It's a crazy old man and his granddaughter. But they're out quite a bit so it's there for the taking."

"How d'you mean crazy?" Jon had visions of a wild-eyed axe-wielding maniac.

Roger gave a short humourless laugh; "You'll see! Anyway, he's into computers, he's always chucking out the boxes they came in. Top-notch stuff I reckon. Bound to be a few laptops in there." His sunken eyes were on Jon, as if sizing him up.

"I'll do it." Jon said recklessly. "Be a doss, dump like that."

Roger had forgotten how to smile, but he leered in a poor imitation. "Knew you would-mate!"

"Why'd you have to say you'd do it?" Faris grumbled, as

they picked their way along the service road that accessed the huge rear gardens in the avenue. Jon didn't reply. He was wondering the same thing. He glanced at the adjacent houses, bristling with CCTV cameras, spotlights and angry red alarm boxes high up under the eaves.

The back garden was worse. A scented Buddleia bush still wet from the afternoon shower shed chilly droplets down their necks as they passed. It was just past eleven when they ran their fingers along the crumbling paint of the ground floor windowsill.

"Here, try this." Faris had retrieved a scrap of rusty angle iron from the shrubbery. The window gave easily then Jon was into the house. Faris remained outside to keep watch.

Along the hall lay piles of junk, a box of electronic circuit boards and bits of wire; magazines stacked waist-high, their titles dimly visible in the refracted moonlight glimmering through the window Jon had clambered through a minute before: *"Computing solutions," "New Scientist"* and so on.

The whirring sound drew him irresistibly to the slightly open door. What he saw inside made him gasp, he felt momentarily giddy with excitement and apprehension. It was Aladdin's cave. It was Treasure Island: computers, servers, printers, data storage devices and a maze of wiring connecting them together. Like a futuristic library, the shelves bristled with hardware. The roar of the fans undulated on his ears. And all around lay more clutter- empty cases, power supplies, cables snaking away through a serving hatch to a room beyond.

"Faris", Jon called softly over his shoulder, "you just gotta see this!"

There was no answer. Faris had gone. And above the sound of the computers could be heard the keening of a siren.

Jon's chest constricted in fear. For a moment he contemplated fleeing back the way he had come, but the sound of voices from the back garden carried into the house. He would have to find a ground-floor window that opened out onto the side of the property or a place to lie low and make his escape later. Taking a deep breath he entered the computer room, stumbling over the junk, until he came to another door beyond. It opened into a huge high-ceilinged space.

The contrast with the computer room was extraordinary. A faint light came from dimmed ceiling lights, high above in the plaster cornices revealing an immense room. In each corner of the room were hefty loudspeakers, and a few, thick wires ran along the wall. The walls were covered with an irregular soft material that deadened sound, heightening the sensation of a vast space.

The door swung closed behind him muting the whirring roar from the computer room. Jon spotted a window and darted across the room towards it.

A flicker caught his eye, on a huge flat monitor screen mounted about waist height a child dashed across a dusty field near some tents. He had tears streaming down his chubby cheeks. A short distance behind stood an older youth, his face was set in a smile, but there was no kindness in that smile. A bow was gripped expertly in his hand and an arrow drawn to its full length.

Jon sucked in his breath. The film had to be a pirate copy judging by the picture quality. Although the screen was huge, the features of the characters were badly defined. Sections of scenery, bathed in bright sunlight appeared washed-out, and when the child moved rapidly the images lagged and fragmented. All the same there was a compelling realism to the sequence. The point of the arrow flicked from side to side as it traced the child's headlong flight. There could be no doubt the arrow was aimed at the fleeing boy. The boy's yells rang out through the loudspeakers…

"Eeeargh!"

Jon's involuntary cry was of genuine terror. He had assumed this room, like the rest of the house to be empty. But the windows covered by thick velvet curtains allowed none of the dimmed light to escape, hence from outside, it had appeared dark like the rest.

As Jon paused in the middle of the bare wooden floor, a shape that had been motionless by the curtains lurched towards him. The tall, spidery figure wore a headset of dark, flexible rubber. Straps encircled his head, and his eyes and ears were completely shrouded with a single enclosure that wrapped around the front and sides of his face.

He had an explosion of pure white hair that stuck through the straps in a manner reminiscent of an untidy halo, and fell down his forehead like an avalanche. At any other time the sight would have been funny, even ridiculous. But bearing down zombie-like on Jon with its arms extended, as if to strangle him, it was ghastly.

Jon turned, stumbled and fell headlong. Seconds later the apparition crashed down on top of him. They rolled and grappled on the floor, Jon's arms were pinned behind him and his face brutally rammed against the boards.

"You leave him, Ishmael, you hear?" The man's voice was breathless, and he smacked Jon's head down on the floor, momentarily stunning him. "You kill him and I'll kill you, you nasty, vicious…"

Smack!'

Jon tasted blood in his mouth. He had bitten his lip. He tried to yell out, but an arm wrapped around his throat and he was hauled upright. Dimly from the corner of his eye he could see the youth with the bow laughing at the fleeing child, the bow resting now, the arrow point facing the ground. He called something but the little child ran out of the picture.

"I'm…aargh, I'm not Ish… Ish…mel!" gasped Jon, aware that he was being rapidly choked. His throat burned with bile and he felt light-headed. His captor took no notice. A voice in his ear whispered, "Isaac's special, you know that, don't you? You lay a finger on him and you're dead, got it?"

Jon nodded. "An…thing y'say!" he croaked. He wanted to fight back, get out of the clutches of this maniac, throw himself to the police for safety, but right now there simply was no escaping his frenzied grip. Dimly he could hear someone banging on the door, then a female voice crying out;

"Granddad, let him go, you're strangling him!"

The grip relaxed slightly, but not enough to struggle free. Vaguely aware that the arms were being prised loose he slid to the floor, his bruised throat filling with saliva and fresh blood welling up from his lip. Desperate to escape he spun round on the floor and looked up at the two people in the room.

An old man was struggling with the rubber headset. He pulled it away, leaving his hair wilder than ever. His eyes were looking at something much further away, and it took several seconds to refocus on Jon. Even when he did there was incomprehension in his stare that was disturbing. That was it. Jon had had enough and bolted for the door.

"Ishmael, don't go!" his arm shot out and a wiry grip clamped on his forearm. The face was within a few inches of his, but the eyes were still focussed to middle distance. Jon struggled in terror, better the police than this maniac!

"Granddad, he's not Ishmael!" The girl snatched the old man's arm away, her voice a mixture of alarm and impatience. "He's..." she turned to face Jon fully, then her face darkened with horror. "You?" She cried. "What are you doing here?"

"Who is he Naomi?" The old man was now looking directly at Jon, "Do you know him?"

"Yes I do!" She scowled; there was a lot of loathing in three little words. "It's Jon Heath; you know his Mum's the MP."

It took several seconds for Jon to recognise her back. *'Naomi, Naomi, who?* Then he realised that as she had always sat at the front of the classroom, he had only usually seen the back of her head with its untidy chestnut-coloured curls of hair. Yes, the right hand always raised to answer the question first, the eyes always attentive to the teacher, the ghastly, snotty, know-it-all he remembered from school. *'Naomi Avery! That's it:* top of the class in English, Science, Maths and probably every other subject. No! Come to think of it she had had to make do with sharing first place with him for a while before he dropped out.

So Naomi Heath lived here, she had grown up quite a lot, but right now she looked every bit as irritable as he remembered her.

"What's he doing in here?"

Jon noticed that the old man was trembling; this didn't make sense, he was easily strong enough to take care of himself, so what was making him so agitated?

"Oh I can guess!" She did not hide her contempt. "Need money for drugs do you? Can't be bothered to work like normal people?"

"Rubbish!" Jon erupted, although his bruised throat made speaking difficult. "How do you know what I want the money for? It's all the same with you lot, isn't it? You think anyone who doesn't fit your ideas is on drugs, or is going to kill you! You've no idea what life is all about, just as long as you pass exams everything's all right."

"Oh get real!" She snapped back, red-faced. "Who's the one caught breaking in? Not me for one…"

There was another burst of hammering on the door. "Who's that at this time of the afternoon?" muttered the old man.

"It's the Police, Granddad. I came down to tell you. Somebody must've seen him breaking in. I'll go and let them in."

"No!" He almost shrieked, then with an effort controlled himself. "Did you say Heath? Mary Heath?" He turned to Jon. "Is it true? Your mother's the Family Values MP?"

Jon nodded, fascinated. He'd never seen anything like it. The old man looked really scared. His face white, his hands shaking and beads of sweat breaking out on his upper lip.

"It'll never do… there'll be reporters crawling all over the place." He cast his eyes around the huge room. "Keep him in here!" He ordered, "Leave the police to me."

"Granddad," there was a warning note in her voice; "He's broken into our house! The moment you let him go, he's going to go somewhere else or bring his mates back with him."

He peered at Jon. "No, I don't think so he's probably just showing off for a dare. I'll deal with him in a minute." He strode from the room.

"Stay there!" She said abruptly, her mouth a thin gash. Then, "there's blood on your face!"

"I'm not surprised!" Jon burst out.

"Shhh!" She stuffed her hand over his mouth. Through the door could be heard the voices, the police concerned, the old man reassuring. Jon just caught the end of the exchange;

"If you're quite sure, sir!"

"Yes, yes, absolutely. This mess is quite normal, I assure you. I'll check, of course, but I don't think there's any need to stay…"

"Goodnight sir."

More murmuring, then the sound of the door closing gently.

"Right you!" The old man's voice was grim. He glared at Jon, who however, no longer felt intimidated.

"Aren't you going to report me to the police, then?" He saw the old man swallow hard. He moistened his lips then replied;

"No, not this time. I rather hope that I can spare your mother the embarrassment that it would cause."

"Oh, don't worry about that! It would be nothing to the embarrassment you'd have. See this?" Jon shouted, pulling out his lower lip which began bleeding afresh. He turned to Naomi. "He's crazy, that's what he is! He attacked me, half-choked me, rammed my face into the floor, bust my lip open and threatened to kill me. I ought to sue."

The old man shuffled. "I thought you were someone else". Naomi turned savagely on Jon.

"Sue?" she spat. "How dare talk about suing us when you break in and start going through our stuff. Then you whine about being hurt, tough! Now get out while you can!"

The old man, however, had deflated. He shuffled to one of the huge loudspeakers and sat down on it, rubbing the bridge of his nose. "What do you want?" he asked finally.

The question caught Jon by surprise. These computers, all this hardware, and the way in which the old man had been acting it all added up to a very big Secret. What was it all about? The film clip he had seen was disturbing with its implied violence. Were they producing illegal movies? What was going on with the headset and the bizarre behaviour? One thing was certain they did not want him here. So here he would stay!

11

"Ok," he said. He waved his hand around the room. "What's all this for?"

"I can't tell you!" His voice was weak, but resolute.

"Oh, you can!" Said Jon, enjoying his discomfort. He turned towards the door. "Or I'm going to give myself up to the Police. I'll have to tell them what you did to me."

"No, stop... please." He left out a very deep breath. He was still shaking.

"Jon, please understand this, I can't tell you what this is for. Not you or anyone for that matter. I'm not saying this because it's unlawful, or a commercial secret. I can't tell you because if news of this got out, our world would change forever. I mean forever."

Whatever the old man had meant to say, unfortunately he had chosen the worst way to say it. Jon gloated.

"I like change!" He smirked. "There's money in change."

"Oh for crying out loud!" Naomi yelled. "You've no idea what this could do to the world! You, us, everybody would be affected. There would be no privacy, no secrets, nothing. Jon, for pity's sake just forget this and go. Go now whilst you can. Don't make him tell you."

Jon stared at her. Privacy? Secrets? So it was some spying device then! She was angry, sure. But she was frightened as well. Time to turn the screws; find out all he could, then work out what it would be worth. His heart was thumping, his mouth dry. This was Big. Bigger than anything he had ever experienced before. He shook his head.

"Oh no! You shouldn't keep secrets," he smirked.

The old man chewed his knuckles, inspecting Jon, debating what to do. Finally he spoke. "Alright Jon, if you really want to know, I'll tell you. First, give me your earring."

Jon gaped. Was this a trick? The old man put out his hand in an impatient gesture.

"Come on, don't waste my time, just give it here!"

Jon eyed him suspiciously. He had to be mad. There was no other explanation for it.

"You want to know about this stuff?" The hand was stretched out, "Well I need your earring!"

Jon slipped the earring out. It was one he had bought with his birthday money four years ago. Was this a device to distract him?

"But Granddad, it'll take ages to condition..." began the girl.

"No, not a stone this size, and we're only after a short time. I'll put it in now and try conditioning it for about ten minutes. In the meantime, could you get him cleaned up? Oh, and I could use a cup of tea. He seized the earring with its small diamond stud and stumped out of the room.

It was fifteen minutes later when they assembled in the large room. A few cushions had been thrown on the floor facing the huge screen. Jon sat down on one, and Naomi came in clutching a chipped mug.

The old man sauntered in, his face wearing a suppressed grin. *'What is he so pleased about?'* thought Jon. He stood in front of them, like a teacher about to start a lesson.

"Well I think introductions are in order, don't you?" Ignoring the sniff from Naomi he went on.

"Firstly, I am Professor Avery, but 'Prof' usually suffices. And you already know Naomi, my granddaughter." He seemed composed, even relaxed. Jon felt uneasy.

"And you, I believe are Jon Heath, son of Mary Heath, our Member for Parliament."

"Get on with it, old man!" snapped Jon. He glanced at his watch, quarter-past midnight. "Show me what this does."

"Absolutely," the Prof beamed. He twisted a knob on the wall and the lights went out. "It's show time!"

"Here try this!" The voice was Faris's and a length of rusty angle iron was thrust into view. Hands, Jon's and Faris's, levered up at the wooden frame until with a splintering 'crack' the window opened. There was a brief glimpse of Faris, his hands in his pockets then the cluttered corridor came into view.

Jon watched stunned as the recent scene unfolded. He could feel his scalp tingling and shivers running up and down his spine.

Tentatively his hand pushed the door to the adjacent

computer room then he could hear his own voice;

"Faris, you just gotta see this!"

"What is this?" Jon stood up, the blood draining from his face and his heart thudding. Naomi ignored him, but the Professor smiled.

"Oh, don't get cross!" he purred, "There's plenty more where that came from! What were you doing this morning? Let's see shall we?" He turned and tapped a small, black keyboard and the images froze. When they restarted, they were in Jon's bathroom.

A tap was running in the sink. "Terribly wasteful of water!" he heard the Professor mock. *The face in the mirror gazed back at him, then hands reached up to squeeze an area of skin below his ear.* For the first time Jon heard Naomi laugh, a snort of suppressed mirth as the face in the mirror grimaced and the red spot burst. The earring winked in the early morning sunlight as the face in the mirror surveyed the mark left behind. Jon felt as if he would faint.

"Some kinda camera, huh?" He tried to recall what happened next. He didn't need to- the face screwed up, cleared its throat then spat revoltingly into the sink. Jon rushed at the Professor fists raised.

"Just stop it, Ok? I don't know how you managed it but you can stop it now!"

Deftly the Professor snatched Jon's fists twisting back on his arms and pushing him back down on to the cushion. His smile vanished.

"Oh no!" His voice was soft, but clear. "Not by a long chalk. I've hardly started Jon. You just sit there and enjoy the grubby little sideshow that is the last four years of your life. That's when you had that earring wasn't it, just less than four years ago? Let's look at something a bit more serious shall we?"

The boy curled into a foetal position to try to protect himself from the kicks and blows that rained down on him. His anguished cries filled the room. The images were clear, even in the poor light, the sound terribly lifelike.

Roger spat and lit a cigarette. His voice, laced with

expletives was loud and clear.

"OK Jon, I think he's got the message!"

One more kick caught the boy in the stomach. He gasped in pain.

The foot was wearing Jon's old trainers: sitting there he could almost feel the sensation of his toes contacting the boy's ribs. Jon shuddered, the floating sensation that he was going to faint overwhelming him once more.

"How d'you do that?" He asked numbly. He was aware of Naomi's look of shocked disgust. In fact he felt dismayed himself, at the time it had seemed a fitting outcome to a confrontation, a just punishment; viewed again it took on an entirely different perspective. The Professor voiced Jon's unspoken thoughts:

"Four, or was that five to one? Brave chap aren't you?" He straightened up. "I'm not going to tell you right now how we do this, but rest assured, it's not done by camera. I've got many more points of interest; that school fire last February for example; do you want to see it?"

Naomi shook her head, appalled. "You're just rubbish," she observed.

Jon felt nauseous. Was every part of his life open to inspection? It was to do with the earring, obviously, but how? Was the earring fitted with a camera? No, impossible! He took a gulp of tea; the warmth helped him recover his wits.

"Ok, we're quits. I won't tell if you won't..."

The Professor straightened up, folding his arms. "Your mother is running her re-election campaign on the family values ticket, is she not? Whilst I have no doubt she is a very worthy and excellent member of society, I think such a comprehensive record of her son's misdemeanours as this would not only sink her chances of re-election, but probably ruin her career as well." There was silence.

Jon hung his head. His earlier bravado had evaporated. He debated trying to brazen this out, but in his mind he could see the newspaper headlines;

"MP's son appears in court
Jon Heath, only son of Mary Heath, the Member of Parliament, has been made subject to a youth custody order after pleading guilty to a charge of burglary near his home . "

No, better go with the flow right now. The Professor was talking. He leant down so that once more his face was close to Jon's. "I know an awful lot about you, Jon Heath. I have to admit that I don't like much what I see. But I want you where I can see you. This morning at ten o'clock you'll be at our Watford Street Church near the Bus station. It's a wooden building set back from the road ...."

"What Sunday School?" Jon interrupted, aghast. "I'm not going..."

"We call it 'Living Word,'" he replied "But whatever you want to call it, I think you need a better influence than what you've had lately. You'll be there!"

He disappeared into the other room.

Jon felt trapped, but what could he do? The ordeal was at an end for the moment. A few moments later the Professor returned holding a small object in a piece of tissue paper.

"Yours, I believe? Watch out it's cold!"

Jon took the object from him. The earring tumbled out of the tissue paper and onto his palm. He gasped- it was bitterly cold! As he turned to go, a thought struck him.

"That stuff on the screen when I came in," he said, wrapping it up and putting it in his pocket, "the kid with the bow and arrow, and the other one screaming- was that this, er... Time-viewer whatever-you call it thing as well?"

"I call it the Timescope," the Professor said. "Yes, that's what I was viewing when you made your entrance. Why?"

"It's just that the pictures were...terrible. I mean they looked really worn-out compared to those pictures you got of me."

He smiled sweetly. "Jon, those pictures were of things that happened much, much longer ago. They're bound to be a bit dim!"

16

2

Moriah

When Jon awoke, it was to discover that he had slept on his arm. From his shoulder down it was completely numb, swinging around like a sailing boat jib. He massaged it, grimacing as the sensation returned to his fingers. On his bedside table the earring glimmered in the sunlight, he put out his hand and touched it. It was no longer icy cold as it had been when he had been given it back last night.

Last night! The memory returned painfully.

Was it really possible that the old man had simply taken his earring and re-run his recent life in glorious Technicolor and surround sound?

True or not, Jon reflected as the last tingling died from his fingertips, he was in too deep to back out now. If that damning file on his activities was genuine, well he had better play ball with the Professor's contract to attend his stupid church, and thus prevent exposure. He could use the opportunity to find out more about the Timescope. If it were true, well who wouldn't pay well to know about it?

•

Watford Street bordered the shopping centre of town. Buses rumbled to and fro and Jon noted with pride that the bus station wall still bore the Apostles' multi-coloured graffiti mural with their 'cross and honour' tag. That had taken half a night to create and was right in Centre City territory.

To Jon's relief none of the Apostles were anywhere to be seen as he sloped towards the large wooden building, set apart from the rest of the shops and houses on a patch of land behind the station buildings. He knew it well from previous visits. He and Faris had hung out there with Roger and his brother Clive, shouting and swearing at the kids when they went in and out.

There were a surprising number of young people in the building, about thirty young people and four or five adults who were settling down in small groups on cushions on the floor. A buzz of conversation filled the room, two small children were wandering around looking for their friends to sit with, and in the far corner a far younger child was clambering over a lanky youth. As Jon watched, she tripped and fell heavily onto the wooden floor and burst into screams. The lanky youth shifted uneasily, but offered no assistance to the youngster. At that moment Jon saw Naomi emerge from a side room. She scooped up the little girl and cuddled her. The child buried her face in Naomi's neck and the sobs subsided. As Naomi turned away she caught sight of him. In less than a passing glance she made her disapproval of him clear. Jon wavered, contemplating retreat through the open door behind, but before he could move the Professor bore down on him.

"Jon, welcome, come in please." There was none of last night's tension in his voice. He was friendly and relaxed, taking his elbow and shepherding him across the room, introducing him to various people. Questions, quizzical glances, strained smiles; Jon barely heard a thing. He focussed his fury on Naomi's back, but she studiously ignored him.

After a hymn, the Professor sat on a dark oak table at the front and began telling a Bible story. He spent a few minutes recalling the previous week's lesson and asking questions of the group.

Despite himself Jon had to admit that the Professor knew how to capture the interest of his audience. The old man got down from the table and walked around the group, weaving the story as he went. From the audience a younger lad was drawn, and the Professor, affecting a stoop and a bit of a shuffle played the part of Abraham, leaning on the younger lad as they journeyed together. The young lad was too tongue-tied to say much, but appeared at ease with his role as Isaac the son.

"Is this the place?" Abraham asked the lad. The boy nodded eagerly. "Then fetch me firewood for we must do sacrifice here to the LORD!" He commanded.

"Use the books!" Hissed one of the older girls and the young boy immediately seized the box stowed away under the table and strewed the books over the table. Jon watched enthralled as the young lad was laid on the table, and the Professor brandished a small knife taken from the kitchen. He gaped, what sort of things did they do here?

"Imagine you're Isaac!" Called the Professor, breaking off from his storyline for a moment, running his finger up the edge of the blunt knife. "How are you going to feel?" The group shuffled;

"Scared!"

"Terrified!"

"I'd want to get up and run!"

"Jon, how would you feel?" The Professor's eyes were bearing down on him. Jon yawned unconvincingly. "I'd grab the knife, if there's any killing; I'll be the one doing it."

A few younger ones looked scared. An older boy leaned across to a girl who had played the guitar. "What a prat!" he whispered. The Professor affected not to notice.

"Sometimes the toughest person is the one who is prepared to be hurt." His soft voice carried through the quiet room.

After a break the group split into smaller groups and the Professor lead the oldest group into a back room.

The study was based around the journey of Abraham and Isaac to Moriah where God had commanded Abraham to sacrifice Isaac. From the businesslike shuffling of papers and opening of books, it was clear that the routine was well established. Jon sulkily opened the Bible he had been given, upside down and folded his hands contemptuously. Naomi rolled her eyes but the other class members paid no attention at all.

"Prof?" said a nerdy boy. "How old would Ishmael be when this happened?"

Jon sat bolt upright. '*Who?*' He thought.

"Well we know that there was thirteen years between the brothers..." the Prof began, thumbing the pages of his Bible. "And Abraham was one hundred when Isaac was born..."

Jon was listening intently now. His heart was racing. '*Isaac, Ishmael...Ishmael much older than his brother-*'

"Did Ishmael hate Isaac?" Jon blurted out. The Professor

19

gave him a narrow glance, but before he could answer the nerdy boy replied.

"Oh yes he did; we did that last week, Ishmael was such a threat to Isaac that Sarah, that's Isaac's mother had Abraham throw him out of the house! She was afraid he would kill him. Ishmael killing Isaac, I mean," he added, blinking. "Is that a help?"

Jon shrugged. But his mind was racing:

"You leave him, Ishmael, you hear? You kill him and I'll kill you, you nasty, vicious…" It couldn't be… could it?

"Isaac's special- you know that, don't you? You lay a finger on him and you're dead, got it?"

The terrible strength of those fingers around his still-raw throat, a man possessed and now he could guess why! Much, much older images indeed! It was clear what this was all about, he had blundered in on a reconstruction of the very history they had recorded in the pages in front of them. Biblical history being unwound in real time. Was it possible? Why not? Had not the Professor taken an earring from him and together they had inspected the last few months of his existence. Why limit it to a few months? A flood of questions rose in his mind; how could this be done? How far back could the system go? What was the headset all about? Was this all the Professor's invention?

Jon rubbed his sore neck; best keep his mouth shut right now, the less people who knew about this the better.

"How long ago would this have happened?" Jon asked, his mind racing to work out the answer. This was before Christ, so at least two thousand years ago. Two-five? Three thousand?

"Abraham lived about four thousand years ago, that's when England was back in the Stone Age; about the time Stonehenge was built, if that gives you an idea," there was no doubt from the way that the Professor was gazing at him that he knew what Jon suspected.

Jon leaned back in his chair, giddy with anticipation. It couldn't be! But it was! He was party to the invention of all time, the Timescope! Capable of piecing the past together without the people involved having any idea they were being spied upon!

"Is something funny?" The nerdy boy was peering closely at Jon, a worried look creasing his freckles.

"Oh, no!" Jon bit back a huge chuckle that was welling up within. "I was just thinking of Ishmael, you know with his bow and arrow..." He mimed aiming an arrow at the Professor... "Pow!"

"Shall we get on?" Naomi said dryly.

•

During the rest of the morning's study he had felt like a dam had broken and a tsunami had washed over his head. Such potential! Once the notion of the Timescope had taken root in his fertile imagination, it had grown with incredible speed. Who would not pay for a reliable glimpse of the past? He recalled the dreary history lessons: *'research the topic and supply your evidence.'* What evidence? Just opinion based on other people's opinions, with no solid facts. Not any more! Who killed JFK? Now they would know! How did Harold die at the Battle of Hastings? No more room for conjecture! How did Diana die? Now come to think of it...

Of course! Never mind the long past, what about events last week, or yesterday? How many governments would give a fortune to be able to check on the loyalty of their staff, especially in the military or Secret Services? Insurance companies would just love this to sort out accident claims. Or come to that, how many frauds could be committed if it was possible to spy on access codes just a few hours after they had been entered at a keyboard?

Where would he fit into this unfolding scenario? He had absolutely no idea! But keep in with the Professor he must, at all costs, whatever it took.

•

"Have you made a copy of our door key?" Naomi's tone was acid. "Or did we leave a window open?"

21

Jon swallowed the comment, barbs and all. *'Just wait...'* he thought, *'he who laughs last...'*

"I came to speak to the Professor," he kept his tone as civil as possible, "in private!" Out of the corner of his eye he could see the screen, the characters were busily collecting wood to make a fire. A leather water bottle had been unhitched from the donkey and they passed it round. Naomi moved swiftly to the keyboard and after a few furious keystrokes the images vanished. Jon affected not to notice.

The Professor bounded into the room. He punched the air exultantly. "They say *Ja!*" he crowed. "Four hours off-peak every night, weekends included. They wanted to do it for free, I had to insist on payment..."

Naomi was frantically twitching her head towards Jon; Jon shuffled and inspected the wallpaper in minute detail. The Professor, however, seemed unperturbed.

"Jon!" he boomed, "how good to see you again so soon. Can we help you with something? Naomi, the kettle's just boiled..."

"Make a cup of tea!" she finished the sentence for him crossly. Honestly, if tea had never been discovered he would have to have invented a substitute. Even worse than having to skivvy for him, she was curious to find out what Jon wanted now, this late in the evening. Her instinct was to distrust his every motive.

"I...er, came to give you this." Jon held out an envelope to the Professor when she had left the room. "It's, sort of, to pay for the damage to your window. I came to um... apologise for what happened, I guess I..."

The Professor opened the envelope. Inside were some bank notes. He immediately stuffed them back into Jon's hand. "No, there's no need for that! Honestly, I need to get that window replaced anyway. Thank you for the thought. And don't worry about it, we all make a nuisance of ourselves from time to time - me included! "

"No!" Jon pushed the money across firmly. "It's one thing to say you're sorry, but I think you should try to, you know, do something to make up."

It was nothing like the speech Jon had rehearsed, but it gave a much better impression than he had expected. The old man looked visibly moved.

The door opened, Naomi sidled in. At a glance she took in the situation, Jon's sycophantic posture, the banknotes being pressed into her Grandfather's hand. She ground her teeth. Little swine! He knew how to ingratiate himself all right. She banged the door behind her. "Tea's in the pot!" She snapped.

"Splendid! I'll go and pour. Jon, would you stop for a cup with us?"

"So where'd you nick those from?" She hissed when the Prof had gone out to the kitchen? "Some old lady's pension money?"

"Oh shut up!" Jon responded, his face reddening. "I try to even things up but all you do is rubbish me. Call yourself religious? At least he believes me!" He jerked his thumb in the direction of the kitchen.

"You manipulative little beast!" She had to speak quietly because she could hear the Professor coming down the hall. "Suddenly it's anything to get in with him! So what's the object? That's what I want to know!"

"Jon!" The door burst open, propelled by the Professor's foot. In his hands was a tray with tea and biscuits. "Do you remember asking me about the study we had this morning? You seemed quite interested."

Jon's heart leapt, was it really going to be this easy? "Yes, I was hoping you could tell me a bit more- you know why it happened, that sort of thing."

"Sit down," he said, "I can do better than that!" He placed the tray on the floor, and strode to the keyboard in the alcove. "How would you like to see Abraham and Isaac for yourself?"

•

It was slow going. If Jon was expecting to be entertained, he was mistaken. For half an hour they watched the scene as the group pottered around, carrying out tasks like collecting water, tethering the beast, gathering a good supply of wood for the fire, all the sort of things that even an amateur filmmaker would edit out of the movie. But however slow events were proceeding on the screen, his mind was racing to assess what he was seeing. A large slice of his mind discarded the whole thing, it was a con, it had to be! The very notion of being able to view events so remote in the past was absurd. But had not the earring yielded up his own life in terrifying detail only last night?

The slowness of the action spoke volumes it was so authentic. No drama, documentary or television show would ever crawl along at this rate: it would be unthinkable. It had to be real life. Real life, not from the last century, or even the middle-ages. Real life from the dawn of civilisation.

"How can you do this?" Jon asked fascinated.

"Do you want the technical explanation or the short version?" The Prof seemed in an expansive mood. He marched from the room, returning a few moments later clutching an object swathed in tissue paper. Without waiting for an answer he went on:

"I guess it began when a forensic team came to me with a malfunctioned CCTV camera that had recorded a serious crime, the images were there, they just needed, well we got to calling it 'temporal slicing.' Each image needed time tagging and we designed recognition software to reconstruct the images as the camera should have recorded them if it had worked properly. From that research came the idea: if we could do that with a camera, could it work from other materials?"

"Such as?" Jon gazed at the tissue-wrapped item the Professor was holding. He unwrapped it, beaming from ear to ear.

"Stones!" He chortled. "Just ordinary stones! Bricks were OK, but stones, naturally formed in the earth were much better. Even ten years ago we managed to get them to act like a camera; it just needed good image reconstruction software. We could skim off layers of energy, not only light but sound as well, and rebuild scenes as they first impacted on the material."

Jon frowned at the flat, greyish stone he was holding. *'This is a wind-up!'* he thought. *'A total con, he's got nothing here worth having!'* The thought disillusioned him, for a moment he had felt the dizzying sense of discovery. Now he felt depressed. His feelings must have shown on his face, the Professor continued his explanation more earnestly.

"At first it was still images. They were amazing enough, to see an image of the laboratory with the clock on the wall reading ten minutes earlier. Then we got back a few hours, then a whole day! Then we got software fast enough to run sequences, like a video player. What was more, there didn't seem to be any obvious limit to how far back we could go."

"Hang on though!" Jon protested. "This was, what, ten years ago? Why didn't we hear anything then? I mean this is pretty amazing stuff if…"

"If it's true!" He acknowledged Jon's scepticism. "Yes, you're right to disbelieve. Most people did at the time. So why didn't this get anywhere?" He sighed. "Well there was a number of reasons, project funding for one; you see for a good reason the backers of the project were told very little about what we could achieve, so in the end all they could see was a lot of money going into the project and very little, apparently, coming out. Also we locked up the university mainframe for hours on end, which was expensive and annoyed a lot of influential people. Not only that, we had problems with system sensitivity, signal-noise problems, stability, outside interference…"

"But these problems are sorted, I take it?"

"Better than I could have believed possible!" He was triumphant, his extraordinary eyes blazing under his preposterous tufted eyebrows. "It was simply, well a matter of time!" Seeing Jon's arched eyebrows he went on, "computers, as you know have advanced by an extraordinary amount. Year on year, even month on month, bigger and better performance in decreasing processor sizes. Your pocket calculator has more computing power than the combined systems that launched the Apollo moon missions. Today's laptop does the job of a computing resource that would have filled a four-storey building even then! Faster, better, easier, it's a real success story. But best of all is the ability of computers to communicate." He was almost breathless, leading up to his main point.

"Once, we were limited to a local computer doing all our number-crunching. A slow, bulky computer at that. But now we have a global network of powerful, little machines, all talking to each other. One system can do one bit of processing whilst another, the other side of the world does the other. Then they put the results together- hey presto! True teamwork! More computers involved - faster results."

"Not that I can take all the credit!" He added, "the technology was built to my requirements and the hardware is off the shelf. It's the software that really makes it fly!"

"Take the image recognition programs." He was well into his stride now. "That helps focus on the received signals and extract typically human features, such as body heat, upright stance, vocalisations; and so on. It makes it easier for the system to track and reconstruct human beings and to follow them around."

Jon was thinking in a different direction. "You said earlier that you couldn't get funding because you didn't tell the project backers what you were doing. Why didn't you just tell them?"

Behind him he heard Naomi cough, a warning cough he guessed. For the first time the Professor looked uncomfortable. For a few moments it looked as if the torrent of information was going to dry up completely, but after a few more seconds wavering he came to a decision.

"Jon, do you remember Saturday night you wanted to see all this then? And I tried to divert you by saying that this would change the world?"

Jon pretended to think for a moment; in reality the conversation was embedded in his mind- Naomi's exasperated, almost anguished cry: *There would be no privacy, no secrets, nothing. Jon, for pity's sake just forget this and go. Go now whilst you can. Don't make him tell you.'*

"Something about secrets…" the Professor coaxed.

"Yeah, I remember now. So would this really change the world?"

The Professor sat down on the edge of the giant speaker enclosure. Suddenly he looked weary, almost depressed. The fire had gone out of his eyes.

"Jon, you saw what we did to you, how we rewound your life in full detail. There was nothing we couldn't find out about you. There was nowhere we couldn't go. There was no way you could hide from us.

"And that's just the start. Some politicians live pretty grubby lives, but do we really want to know every shocking detail? What about the criminal fraternity? How they would love to view the access codes to the safe deposit box? How the espionage agencies would love to have remote, safe spying, and not only that…"

"Hang on!" Jon felt the need to deflect him from his rant. "You saw my life because of my earring. All I needed to do was take it off and I'm safe. Aren't I?"

The look on the Professor's face was all the answer he needed. He held up the stone.

"This stone was buried in the soil, some six or seven centimetres below the surface. It receives images and sound just as well as your earring does. In fact better because it doesn't move around; the system has a stable reference and we can track away from it and navigate around. We can go miles away from the detector stone if we wish."

Now Jon felt very uneasy.

"So you see, nobody is safe any more and we're at a turning point, Jon!" He said softly. "Ten days ago those images were rough, poorly defined, tatty even. Now look at them!"

Their faces glimmered in the firelight; two servants sitting cross-legged on the sparse grass of the hillside, the young man reaching over and thrusting a stick into the fire. A constellation of sparks leapt into the night sky, twinkling and dancing into oblivion. Nearby the donkey snorted and flapped its ears.

"Where's Abraham?" Naomi was using the keyboard to explore the scene. "Oh, hang on, there he…"

She stopped abruptly. Abraham was on his knees in prayer. His face was raised to the sky and a new moon cast a soft light over the old, old man. Even with the limitations of the system, it was easy to see the tears coursing down his face.

Naomi flushed, mortified. She started to navigate away, but both Jon and the Professor cried out, "no, let's hear what he's saying!"

"Granddad! He's upset, can't you leave him alone?"

"I know, I know," he said impatiently. "But this is important!" He seized the keyboard from her and spun the image back to Abraham. It was clearer now, and they could see that he was some distance from the other three, huddled by some rocks. The Professor dragged a volume control slider up and a voice burst out of the loudspeakers.

"Oh my son… my son!"

"But that's English," objected Jon.

The Professor explained that they were hearing a translation from the original words uttered by Abraham, which were then put into a speech simulator. But the simulator 'listened' to the original speaker and used their vocal patterns to modify the translated speech, so an old man would sound old, a young girl young and feminine, and so on. As time went on the programs became so proficient in their speed and accuracy that it was taken entirely for granted that they were the sounds of the appropriate speaker.

"Oh Isaac, my son!"

The grief in his voice reached across forty centuries. To the right there was a roar of laughter from the other three by the fire, contrasting terribly with Abraham's agony. He fell forward into the shadows and his sobs filled the room.

"I think you're right Na." The Professor closed the program and stood shifting uneasily. "Perhaps it isn't our business." He glanced at his watch. "Jon, would you like to see some more tomorrow?"

Jon, his heart chilled by the sound of a soul in torment, as fresh as it had just happened completely missed the question.

"Oh my son, my son…" the words tolled like a bell in his brain. He stared at the dark screen. Once more a river of shivers flowed down his spine.

"Jon?"

"Eh? Oh yes, absolutely!"

•

As she got ready for bed, Naomi fished around in the bedside drawer. Downstairs her tireless guardian was 'doing some tweaking'.

There it was! Battered, but recognisable. The face was younger, the ears unpierced, the hair a respectable length. Despite the difference of four years and a lot of attitude, Jon Heath looked back at her. His face was frozen in time from the moment the teacher had taken the snap on a field trip. It was the look of a precocious, cheeky adolescent, the same lad who had unknowingly turned her stomach to blancmange in year seven. The teacher had not noticed one picture missing from the pile on the table. Neither had the subject of the photo noticed the way the colour rose in her cheeks when he was near her, or the effort she had made to do something with her hair, or the way she had casually asked his advice on a lab procedure, or the myriad little ways she had struggled with the cloudburst of unfamiliar and scary feelings just the thought of him touched off in her.

Naomi stared at the photograph. It was so absurd! Could she really have held a candle secretly for such a toe rag? Even if his project and exam results had in many cases topped hers, she had shown that it was staying power that mattered! Where was he now? A sad, pathetic basket case headed for the juvenile courts!

For a few seconds more she gazed at the photo, then with a small cry she tore it in half, then in halves again, then into smaller and smaller pieces until it was in shreds.

"Where you belong!" She savagely flung the pieces in the bin.

3

Roger Lord's driving was far from smooth. The bass beat of the music playing in the car resonated the air of the quiet street like some monstrous heartbeat, loud even at a distance. The Audi pulled up harshly beside him and the rear door flew open.

"Get in," grunted Oliver.

"Nice car!" yelled Jon, as they tore down the narrow road heading out of town. "How long have you had…" Then he saw the spaghetti loops of coloured wires where the ignition switch had been. Roger drove badly, and at high speeds; Oliver didn't seem to care, but Jon felt nervous. The wipers skidded across the screen. Roger turned the music off.

"Laptops?" He enquired. The car sped round a sharp bend, scrabbling at the soft verge. A car coming the other way blasted its horn. Roger swore at him.

"Not yet." Jon was dry-mouthed. Roger pulled the car into a lay-by. He turned round, his tattooed arm on the passenger seat back. He was wearing a tracksuit top over his white karate suit. His recessed eyes scrutinized Jon's face. He didn't invite explanation or excuse. All he said was, "The Apostle's word is his bond, Heath."

They left him there to walk back alone. By the time he arrived home it was past midnight and the rain had soaked him to the skin. The next day on the way to school he passed the car burnt out on a patch of waste ground by the canal, its leather seats gutted and rust already eating into the scorched paintwork. He shivered and hurried past.

•

They were finishing off their evening meal when Jon arrived. "Want some?" the Prof enquired. "It's chicken something tikka something else, there's a bit going spare in the kitchen if you like. Oh, and when you're out there, shove some water in the kettle."

His easy familiarity was offset somewhat by Naomi. She spoke to him stiffly and as little as possible. *'Is she always like this?'* he wondered, as he filled the kettle and sniffed the rest of the lurid chicken concoction lurking in a foil dish. On the draining board, a stack of plates teetered precariously. Incongruously the sink itself was playing host to a large reddish stone, crusted with dry soil. Needing a clean plate Jon lifted it out, but then found there was nowhere to put it down. Every horizontal surface was stacked with clutter - magazines, electrical bits, bin bags full of who knew what - and the stone felt heavy. For a moment Jon debated dropping it back in the sink, but behind him a cold voice said, "Put that down, you idiot! Can't you just leave things alone?"

She was surveying him from the doorway. He bit back the first thing he would like to have said; instead he grunted irritably, "it's just a stone, I'm shoving it down here on the floor."

"Oh no you're not!" She sounded genuinely horrified. Rushing across the room she seized the stone from him, and in a surprising feat of strength swept a heap of papers from a work surface before tenderly placing it in their place. Jon was taken aback. Words failed him. She rounded on him, brushing the soil from her hands.

"Granddad spent three days in Haifa jail for that stone!" She snapped. "It cost him five grand in fines and bail money. You don't just shove it on the floor!"

Despite himself Jon was impressed. "Why? What was he nicked for?"

Naomi enjoying his awe continued; "All these stones are from in and around Israel. That's where the Bible events took place!" she added sarcastically, as if Jon would never have guessed. "Granddad was out there for four months collecting stones from many of the holy sites and sending them back. Then he took this one from Mount Carmel and some pilgrims got upset. The police arrested him for his own protection, that's why you don't just throw it where you like!"

It was the longest sentence she had spoken to him, Jon reflected as he ran some water over a plate to clean it off for his food. Things were looking up!

•

It was still very early in the morning in Judea. A grey light was beginning to suffuse the sky so there lacked sharp clarity in the images, just a soft pre-dawn neutral glow, softening the edges and muting the colours. Nearby a dove cooed a long cry that ululated like a lament for the dead. For a time it would fall into silence, then start up again, *'coo-ooo-wooo-hooh uh!'*

"Wish it would stop that!" Naomi muttered shivering. It was the only sound that stirred in the gloom.

"I'll try and speed things up a bit. " The Professor had pulled up a menu and was trying to alter a list of figures. For five minutes they watched as the sleeping figures twisted erratically in their sleep. "Aw!" he grumbled as a series of error codes rolled up the screen. "That's as fast as I can get it to run at the moment."

"Jon, could you have a go at this?" The Professor handed him a wireless keyboard, the one that he had played with earlier. He had brought the viewpoint right back so that a group of travellers were tiny dots in the distance. "I just want to reassign some processing functions so that we can fast forward this a bit."

Jon nodded, as if he knew what he was talking about. "What do you want me to do?"

He was showed the data retrieval rate controls. "Very careful adjustment," he was told. "Too much and it can't cope and we lose data." At high speed the party awoke, held a consultation involving much rapid arm-waving, then two of them broke loose; heading in their direction.

"Why don't you just leave it to me?" Naomi sounded petulant. "I know how to use it."

"Of course you do! Why not let Jon learn?"

Jon hoped fervently he wouldn't mess up. But he did. For a while for each dab of the keyboard the action speeded up: the clouds scudded by and the daylight grew stronger by the minute. The two figures scurried up and down the rolling hillsides, sometimes visible, sometimes hidden by the brow of the hill: two small ants growing into beetles then bigger still into two recognisable human figures. Then as Jon tried one more dab at the keyboard, the screen faltered and went black. Naomi sniffed and said nothing.

"No problem!" The Prof sensed the tension between them. "I'll just go and reset the processor." He disappeared from the room.

"I'll laugh if it doesn't turn out as he expects." Jon watched Naomi for a reaction.

"What d'ye mean?" She frowned.

Jon smirked. "Well supposing the Bible's all wrong."

She stared at him. "You just haven't got a clue, have you?" She said finally.

"Why? Whatcha mean? For all you know the people who wrote the Bible made it all up. I mean, who's just going to lie down and be carved up?"

Naomi gave him a withering look. "I can see Granddad's wasting his time on you. You wouldn't understand if it were handed to you on a plate."

At that moment the Professor returned. He glanced at Jon, then Naomi and guessed that they were bickering again. "Now then you two!" he admonished as he reloaded a file. "Let's try and get on shall we? We'll run at real-time now."

The sound and picture quality were amazing now they were so close to the source stone. From the dry crackling crash as the firewood hit the ground, to the soughing, sighing wind in the scrubby bushes, there was little to suggest that they were not peering out of a clear glass window on to a scene happening right outside the house. The only weakness lay in the language translation program, which occasionally faltered over an unfamiliar word or turn of phrase and invented something weird instead. Most of the time this made no difference, the true sense was easy to guess, but the digital recordings, which the Professor kept contained some very odd phrases. A few times earlier, even Naomi had laughed out loud as the translation suggested a word or a phrase that made no sense, or even something downright irreverent.

Nobody was laughing now. For Isaac had a question for his father.

Shielding his eyes against the glare of the sun he turned round to behold the huddled figure. Not for the first time there was concern in his eyes as he gazed upon the evident misery of his father. Finally he spoke.

"You've got the fire," he said, "and I," he stretched his back upright; "I've got the wood! But didn't you say the LORD had asked you to offer a whole burnt sacrifice?"

Abraham, his face again sunk into his hands, nodded dumbly.

"Where's the lamb, father?" His hand swept the empty hillsides with a single wave.

Abraham said nothing.

"Father," said Isaac, moving closer, "where's the lamb for a burnt offering?"

Abraham began to weep. His shoulders heaved.

"Tell him Abraham," murmured the Professor.

Finally Abraham looked up, a picture of despair. Tears coursed down his face and he made no effort to restrain them. He looked at the strapping lad in front of him, the son of his old age, his mother's cherished hope. Year by year they had given thanks with laughter in their hearts as their son had grown, strong in body and spirit, placid in temperament and wise beyond his years. His boyish peals of laughter had further renewed them both in their old age.

But now the laughter was gone, replaced by a knife that twisted with every step that he took towards that hilltop in Moriah, where the laughter would cease, and Isaac would be in the hands of God.

Suddenly Abraham stood up, and rushed towards Isaac. In one swift move he threw his arms around him, his words muffled by the embrace.

"My son, God will provide Himself a lamb for a burnt offering."

Isaac broke free from him and looked long and hard into his eyes. Then as he looked, the expression of mild confusion was replaced by horror. Standing back he caught sight of the knife in his father's hand and the full meaning became clear to him. His jaw dropped and he stared.

"Am I the lamb?" He whispered, stepping back.

There was no answer.

"Tell me!" he shouted. "Am I the lamb?"

Abraham just managed a nod, and then buried his face in his hands again. Isaac looked dumbfounded.

"Y...you said that I was provided by God as a son of your years," he said finally, his voice hard with astonishment. "You said I was to be the son of your name to all generations so that all people would bless themselves in your name through my descendants, didn't you father! How can this be if you do....this... to me here?"

He waited for an answer; none came, he went on.

"You said that God was not as the gods of the heathen, He does not require human life. Human sacrifice is disgusting to Him. Why has He changed His mind, father. Answer me!" Isaac was shaking with anger and fear. His fists were tightly clenched.

'He's never going to do this,' Jon thought. 'He's going to run for it!'

Abraham still said nothing, but he was evidently trying hard to compose himself. Great sobs still racked his body, and compared to the angry young man towering over him, he looked frail and confused. Finally with an effort he spoke.

"It is as you say," he said dully. "The LORD abhors human blood shed for any reason. But this I know," he looked straight into Isaac's eyes, "there has not failed one of the things which He has promised me. He is true, and whatever He has promised will come to pass." He thought for a moment then said, "There was a time when I thought that we made our own fulfilment of His words. That was when we had Ishmael. But now I know that we must wait His pleasure, and his words will be fulfilled. You must believe this Isaac."

Isaac listened to this speech. His fists had dropped, but he continued to stare at his father. He was breathing hard. Faintly the speakers relayed his voice, barely a whisper;

"This can't be. You're wrong. It can't be!" Over and over.

Then he walked away.

Slowly at first, then longer strides, ten, fifteen metres from his shattered father, huddled on the grass.

Twenty metres, Isaac was still going. Heading back the way they had come. The Professor looked unperturbed. 'Wonder how he's going to explain this!' Jon thought.

"He's...not...going...to...do...it!" He mouthed silently to Naomi. She looked away. "Told...you!"

The retreating figure was descending the slope towards the valley floor when abruptly he stopped. He gave a loud cry, as if in pain and fell to his knees and with his fists began tearing up clumps of the long grass. He was at the point of distraction. Twice more he stood up and it looked as if he was going to carry on heading back. Both times he stopped, indecisive as if an invisible cage prevented him from going further. Then suddenly he spun round and started running back up the slope.

"Why?" he demanded, towering over his father once more. Abraham looked up briefly.

"I don't know!" he moaned.

"But this is madness! How can I have children, and why do you say He keeps his promises when you have not a field or valley to call your own?"

"I don't know. But your mother and I used to ask these questions also. How can this be, seeing we are old and worn out! Then you were born and we saw that God can be trusted. He will raise you from the dead, just as He raised your mother from the dead. Don't ask me how, and don't ask me why, He is God and we his children."

Isaac turned as if to walk away from Abraham once more. He was silent for another minute, and then abruptly he swung round.

"But do you know for sure that He wants this?"

Abraham shuddered. Clearly it was a question that had worried him too. "He called me. He called me by my name

Abraham, the name He gave me when He when he promised me a nation of descendants. It was as if He was deliberately testing me. He has told me to destroy my only hope of real children through you and leave the rest to Him. I believe Him, now I'm asking you to believe Him also."

Isaac sank to the ground beside him. Gone was the easy-going youth, full of vigour, life and energy. Suddenly he was facing a critical decision, the choice that would once and for all prove his loyalty to his father and his God, but would deprive him of his life in the process, or the choice to back away from the awful command that had brought them to this point. The minutes ticked by. Abraham sat trembling near by.

What Isaac said next brought home the dreadful truth of his predicament.

"Father?"

"Yes my son?"

"Father, I'm frightened!"

Suddenly the man was a little child once more, lost, and scared. A moment of panic, fighting the urge to run; run anywhere, to get away from this place.

There was a gasp. Naomi was wiping her eyes on the back of her hand. She had gone as white as chalk. Jon stared. Was the steel girl really about to cry? The Professor leaned over and touched her arm.

"Na? You OK?"

She gulped. "I'm alright." She said faintly.

"I'll stop it if you want," said the Professor. "It's a lot to take in, after all."

"No!" she said. "There's no need."

Jon was conscious of the hairs at the back of his neck prickling. He was recalling the Professor's response to his mindless bravado of Sunday morning.

"Sometimes the toughest person is the one who is prepared to be hurt."

So this was true grit! The concept turned his world upside down. He didn't like to admit it, even to himself, but he too was feeling a little scared. Was this kid, just a few years older than himself really going to offer his life? Not in the heat of battle but in cold blood, in obedience to a God who required him to do so?

"How do they kill sacrifices?" His voice was unsteady. The Prof and Naomi turned to him. "I mean," he said, "do they stun them first?"

The Professor broke the silence. "No, they sever the throat."

Jon tried to say, 'oh!' but no sound came out. Now he was really scared. More scared than he had ever been watching horror movies. He tried to swallow, but there was a huge lump lodged just above his windpipe. He was conscious of the room being suffocatingly hot, it had built up from the heat of the Judean sun which was now full and blinding.

"Father." said Isaac suddenly, rising to his feet. "I believe. I don't understand but I do believe. Maybe He raised me especially for this time that we might obey Him even in this thing. I only wish you had told me sooner, so that I would have time to prepare."

"How could I tell you? Would you have come this far?"

"Yes I would," said Isaac with difficulty. "We could have talked together of why the LORD would want this to be. We could have prayed together for strength to carry out this dreadful thing. As it is, now I must think and pray for a while, then we must prepare the altar."

Abraham gazed with astonishment at his son. It was apparent that he had not expected such firmness and resolution from him. Isaac stood a little distance away, his head bowed in silent communion with God. But despite his firmness, a steady trickle of sweat ran down his face. Abraham, deprived of the initiative stood by, but he was looking stronger than before.

"Where is the place where we must do sacrifice?" Isaac asked at length.

Both faces looked directly at the screen. "There is the place the LORD told me of." Abraham was pointing the way, his other arm around Isaac's shoulders, but who was supporting whom was not obvious. Isaac picked up the firewood and Abraham lit the spare torch from the remnants of the first. Then, together they went on. Neither spoke. Nor did Jon or the

Professor, but Naomi was slumped against her grandfather, crying softly. Jon was dumb with shock, wishing he too could hold on to somebody, even Naomi, right then. After another agonising ten minutes the travellers had arrived at the final destination.

Isaac was walking towards his father. "Unhewn stones, to build an altar. That's what you told me He requires." His voice trembled and he bit his lip to cover his fear. "I will get them and build the altar; you must prepare the wood and the fire. This is the mountain top is it?"

Jon was transfixed. Isaac was easily able to invent a dozen excuses to escape this dreadful thing, but instead here he was organising his own pyre. Abraham had little power to enforce this sacrifice should Isaac choose differently, he could be no match for the strapping youth. The stones were heavy but Isaac with no difficulty rolled them to the place on the top of the hill. Abraham was drawing strength from him, resolutely untying the sticks from the bundle and laying them on top of the altar in such a way as to ensure that the whole kindled easily.

After twenty minutes the altar was finished. Simple, but effective, the stones laid so as to draw air from below to feed the flame and generate as much heat as possible. They looked at each other. Jon took a deep breath; the tension was palpable.

"Father." Isaac's eyes were wide; his whole body trembled as if he were feverish.

"Yes, my son."

"Bind me, father. So that I cannot struggle." He held his hands forward, wrists crossed. "I don't want to let you down."

It was badly done. Abraham's hands were shaking so terribly that he could hardly hold the rope. A child could have escaped the crude knots.

And so this lad, a late teenager, lay down on the altar, his tied hands at his waist. Even then there were human touches; a stick that was prodding him between the shoulder blades and had to be moved, as if this crumb of comfort would alleviate the horror of the act; Abraham not being able to find the knife despite it being in full view on a rock. Then he saw it and stretched out his hand. His fingers closed around the handle of the knife one more time. Isaac seemed unable to keep his eyes open, but this wasn't surprising- the sun hit him full in his face. He turned his head to look at his father. Abraham held his hand over his face to shade his eyes.

"Does mother know?" He asked.

Abraham shook his head. "How could I tell her?" he said his voice breaking, "how can I go to her and tell her I have slain our only son?"

Isaac swallowed two or three times. He started to say something, and then stopped. "Tell her I love her." he said finally with difficulty. He closed his eyes again. His breathing was slow and measured, in and out, in and out. He was trying to calm himself.

A minute passed, Abraham's hand tightened a couple of times on the knife as if to strike, but he was not ready yet. Then Isaac spoke again.

"Father." In and out he breathed, slower now with deeper breaths.

"Oh my son, my son," Abraham reached out to grip Isaac's arm which was laid across his chest.

He turned his head again and unscrewed his eyes. Just then a cloud dimmed the fierce sunlight and he was able to gaze comfortably at his father.

"We will meet again in God's good time then, yes? At His good pleasure." Then he closed his eyes and continued that deep rhythmic breathing... in... out... in...out...

All that could be said had been said. He was ready; it was time. The slaying.

Abraham tightened his grip on the knife, placed his hand, fingers outstretched over Isaac's face, pulling his son's eyelids shut, and drew himself up to his full height. The sun blazed across the scene. The knife swung up into the air and began plunging down faster, faster, faster towards Isaac's throat...

Naomi cried out, her face in her hands, the Professor was sitting bolt upright, not a muscle in his face moved. Jon felt his stomach twisting and dropping…

"Abraham!" The voice thundered out from the loudspeakers, unearthly, irresistible. "Abraham!" One moment the knife was travelling downwards with killing force, the next it dropped with a thud into the grass and Abraham stood there, poised, listening to the voice of the angel.

"Here am I," he said. "What is it LORD?"

"Don't harm the boy, do nothing to him," said the Voice.

And then the picture went. Completely. It was as though the "camera" had slipped and pointed up at the sun. Except that the sun was so bright as to hurt the eyes. Whiteness, brilliant sparkling whiteness filled the screen. But the sound continued for a few seconds more.

"Now I know that you fear God. You have given to me your son, your only son."

Then the screen was full of error codes.

Jon, Naomi and the Professor sat in silence watching the message "OVERLOAD ERROR" marching up the screen. For a minute, two minutes no one said a word. Jon's heart gradually slowed from its mad pounding. The stillness was broken by the Professor; as he got up and threw open a window to allow cool night air into the room.

"I wondered why Abraham had to lift up his eyes to behold the ram," he said, almost to himself. "He was blinded by the glory of the angel, just as we were then."

The Professor and his granddaughter were choked. The sheer catharsis of what they had witnessed together had been so overwhelming, so majestic in its setting and drama that all they wanted was time to reflect. They, however, had witnessed nothing they did not already expect. It was a verification of a faith they had held all their respective lives.

But Jon struggled with the magnitude of the encounter. The Professor had explained the end of the story- how that a ram, its horns trapped in the bushes had been provided instead of Isaac; the two of them would then return to the waiting servants, one strengthened in his faith, the other rejoicing in his resurrection.

"I'll take you home, just let me get the car keys."

"Oh… yeah, sure, great!" Jon stumbled his thanks. Naomi disappeared upstairs. "She OK?"

"I think so. D'you want to see more?"

"Absolutely!" Jon's brain whirled with conflicting priorities. Alien concepts of loyalty, consistency and self-denial had burst in on him unchecked. Raw faith had scorched his conscience. But powerful as this experience had been it could not suffocate the insistent, urgent craving to see this turned to his advantage.

4
Gideon

Dad met him in the hall. "Terrence Prentice!" He said shoving his fingers to the back of his throat and gagging softly. Jon made a face and slipped past him into the lounge.

"Hi Mum!" She was bent over her laptop. Prentice was sitting too close to her for Jon's liking. He moved away discretely as Jon entered.

"Ah the wanderer returns." Prentice's mocking voice answered before she could reply. "Mary was getting worried about you!" His light grey suit had been exquisitely tailored to conceal his hefty stomach and fat neck.

"Where have you been?" Mum's voice was sharp. "And what have you done to your mouth?" She had her scary power-look, her hair waved and her shoulder pads giving her added angularity. Jon blinked inanely.

"Out with friends!" he mumbled, which was half-true.

"Jon, so nice to see you again." Prentice purred standing up. He sensed Jon's antipathy towards him but cared little about it. "We must find time for a chat- you know, let me know how things are going."

Jon missed this pleasantry, not just because he loathed him, but because an idea was hammering at the inside of his skull, demanding to be let out.

"Well, Mary," Prentice held out his flabby hand with its delicate fingers. "If you send me your thoughts on what we've got through tonight, I'll put your proposals to my staff and draft a policy document for your perusal by the weekend. Although there might be delays- staff sickness you know." He snapped his briefcase shut. "I'll do it myself if all else fails-don't want to let you down now." He smiled his oily smile and stepped out into the hall.

Mary followed him to the front door. The door closed behind her and their voices became muted. Jon seized his chance. He hit the email icon on his mother's laptop and rapidly opened up the address book. "Prentice… Prentice…" he murmured, "Prentice Jack, no… Peter Prentice…"

The murmur of voices had ceased, the front door had closed and his mother's hand was on the living room door handle.

"Ah! Prentice T. "

In a flash he had the address with its *.gov* suffix. He closed the application and was half-way to the kitchen by the time she had entered the room.

"Jon?" She looked tired. The creases around her eyes had arrived in the last two years, like ruts carved by rainstorms in a path. She debated whether to interrogate him now, but on second thoughts…

"You all right? Everything OK?"

"Yeah," said Jon. "Just getting a drink. You want anything?"

"No love, I'm off to bed."

"Goodnight Mum."

•

Big Ben struck the hour as Terrence Prentice switched on his computer at his Westminster Office. Running his elegant finger round his collar, he languidly removed his tie, then fiddled with his top button to release the pressure from his neck. Sitting back in his chair he cracked his fingers waiting for the password screen. He gave a prodigious yawn as he waited. Three o'clock. The city streets were quiet, not even the rubbish carts were out at this time of night. Just the occasional rumble of a lorry on the bridge. He liked this time of the night.

There were twenty new messages. Six of them were from the ex-Mrs. Prentice. He deleted them without even reading them. She had all she was going to get from him!

There was one from Mary Heath, a short note thanking him for the meeting two days ago and an attachment of the policy document they had discussed.

Leaning back he cracked his knuckles again and thought of Mary Heath. What a woman! Not the best looking female in his wide experience, but gifted with intelligence, commitment and energy. She would go far especially if she could see which way her bread was buttered –only a shame about that loser of a husband of hers, and that worrying situation with her son. He smiled. Oh the blindness of a trusting mother! If she knew what information he held on the activities of her precious son!

His reflections were interrupted by a soft 'bong' from the computer. A new message, frowning he examined the header. Not a name he knew, and what an odd title: *'You don't know what I know!'*

For a moment a shiver ran down his well-encased spine. Surely the Basilisk wasn't contacting him on this link? Just a recollection of those humourless blue eyes made his blood run cold. But no, this wasn't Jackman's style or method. Whoever it was had access to what was a very, very private email address. He toyed with the mouse. Should he open it and see?

It read; *'I know how to find out about anything, anywhere, anytime. It won't be cheap, but I know you're interested.'*

It had no signature, no ident, nothing he could recognise. The address was *'anonymous@freeflow.co.uk'* Set up especially for this, obviously.

"Clever." He rumbled softly. "But we shall see how clever shall we?" Swiftly he edited the cryptic message, bundled it into a secure outbox and with a click it was gone.

"Let's see what Trace makes of that!" He licked his lips, he felt hungry. If his secretary was doing her job right there should be a ham sandwich and a can of his favourite draught beer in the office fridge. There was.

"To anonymity!" he chuckled, downing the drink in several huge gulps.

•

It had been Naomi's idea to set the computers busy searching for clues that would find recognisable Biblical accounts. Just as Internet search engines can readily find a sequence of words in a document, so, she reasoned, couldn't the considerable computing power of the Timescope, scan images as they were being read off the stones, and match them against search criteria?

It didn't work.

Not that it was a bad idea; it was simply that there was no sure-fire way of making the search requirements exact enough for the computers to recognise what they were after.

"Why don't we search on speech? You know, things we know they said."

Naomi glared at Jon. "What with all the millions of things said by all the people? It'll never work!"

"But you only have to look for something unusual said by somebody you know."

The Prof looked awkward. "Jon has a point." He was fed up with the tension between them. "There are plenty of quirky phrases we can try looking for."

Naomi, breathing hard subsided into sulks.

It took an hour to pinpoint as accurately as they could the geographic location of the action related to the story of Gideon and find a stone from amongst the considerable collection in the house that was near to the area. Jon watched fascinated as the stone, nestled in a steel tray disappeared like a CD into a cupboard-sized device with a soft rumble and a clunk. They were in a small back room, similar to a photographer's darkroom and lit by a single red light bulb. Was it really this simple?

The headsets were a marvel in themselves. Back in the viewing room the Professor explained their function to Jon.

"This is what you were wearing when I…"

"The very same! Although it has been much improved. You see this silver strip here?" His finger traced the fine dashed band visible on the edge of the rubber face piece. "That's an EEG detector."

"You mean brain waves?" Jon's brow furrowed.

"Exactly. The brain gives a recognisable output for each desired muscle movement, so this headset reads the request and translates it into a direction. In effect you think, *'what's that over there, I'll go and have a look,'* and the software steers in that direction. It's quite uncanny!"

Jon whistled. "Cool!"

He chortled. "It's even better than that! The same programmes were capable of full servo feedback. I rewrote software to interact with the brain to make it feel as if you had carried out the actual movement. Hence that!" He pointed to the ceiling where an aerial hung precariously from a hook.

"To communicate with the headset?" Jon guessed.

"Just so. This gives you freedom to move around without wires trailing everywhere. It relays all the signals to and from the Timescope allowing you to explore the virtual landscape as if you were actually walking around it."

"Can I try it?"

He glanced at his watch. "It's late. Look, there's no point going in right now, but as soon as we get a recognisable hit on Gideon, I'll let you know. Can I have your mobile number?"

•

That had been two days ago. Jon had chaffed at the delay. At night he lay in bed, but sleep eluded him. The whole immense concept of the Timescope intruded. Such possibilities! Still he had little idea what to do about it, but getting hold of Prentice's email address had been a breakthrough. Nothing had come back yet; he checked his inbox regularly for replies. Then again, he reflected, watching the blinking light on his bedside alarm clock winking endlessly in the darkness, what did he expect? A suitcase full of notes? That was the trouble; he was out of his depth.

•

The headsets were remarkably light. The rubber material was a little clammy at first, but very soft to touch. Without anything to view it soon became oppressive, but with the scenery on the screens it was difficult to remember the headset was there at all. The sensation of movement, freedom and space washed over them both as they put them on. Taking them off was a different matter. Jon recalled the disorientation he had felt many years ago, emerging from a cinema after watching a matinee performance of a space film. The summer daylight had felt all wrong; surely it should have been night, and cold!

Although he knew that in this phantom experience, he could come and go through the skin of the tent at will, he still found the entrance and slipped in through the flaps.

As he entered, two faces turned to look at him, and in that instant he felt a wave of apprehension, as though he had been discovered. Then someone came in behind him, walked through him and sat at the far end of the group, seated around a fire, where the remains of a meal were scattered. Jon blinked in confusion. Of course they were looking at the newcomer!

Although the tent was low, there was room to stand and see all that was going on. An argument seemed to be in progress.

"What say you, my lord Oreb?" Although the enquiry was civil enough, there was an unmistakable undertone of distrust and dislike in the speaker. Oreb, the one who had just entered, picked around at the remains by the fire, and found something to eat. As he gnawed at the flesh on the leg of some bird or other, he was clearly biding his time to reply. Finally with a dissatisfied grunt he threw the bone into the fire.

"What comradeship amongst those who leave no food for their comrades?" he scowled.

There was no answer. He went on.

"Have you asked the men?" He jerked his thumb over his shoulder. "What say they to war?"

There was an angry reaction from one of the other men, a short man with many scars on a grizzled face. "They, like us, are unhappy to share battle with Amalek scum!" he spat contemptuously. "Midian for Midian. We need no allies."

There was a chorus of responses to this, and the interpretation programs briefly crashed, unable to cope with all the input. After a few seconds order was restored, and so was translation.

Naomi entered the tent beside Jon. "This must be a council of war," she said. "Have you found anyone called Zebah here?" Her voice had lost its hard edge; she was trying hard to be polite to Jon. "Oh, and the other one, Zal... Zalumun I think."

"Zalmunna you mean," came her Grandfather's voice through the intercom. "Try down the other end of the tent."

Jon and Naomi shuffled past sacks of supplies and stacked weapons to the furthest end of the room.

A small, lean and wiry man, with a face that could only be described as forgettable, stole past them. He looked pensive and awkward.

"Zulmunna!" he declared embracing a thickset man.

"Ah, our Mannasite friend!" Zalmunna's greeting was warm.

"Jashur is, ah... working for us!" he announced. "He is free to come and go in the Jewish camp as well as ours. Some wine for our guest!" He clapped his hands and a clay cup was passed to the little man.

The spy was in no hurry to talk. He sipped from the cup and picked from a loaf of bread that was placed on the ground beside him. As he ate, almost like lightning his eyes darted round the company, and then returned to his meal. Then again, flash and dart, then down to the food. It was obviously his habit. His audience began to grow impatient.

"There is no army of Gideon." Surprisingly his voice was measured and dull, giving the impression of a slow-witted individual. This impression was reinforced by his whole way of moving, he appeared stupid. Only the eyes betrayed him.

Zalmunna and Oreb, and a number of others around the fire leaned forward. Their expressions of interest glittered in the poor light.

"No army? How can this be, Jashur? Has there been a desertion?"

"Yes, a desertion. Word went around yesterday that soldiers were leaving for their homes, first in twos or threes, then whole companies drifting away. They have seen your numbers, my lord, and fear is all around."

"And where is Gideon?" The speaker was someone who had not said anything before.

"Gone into the night, with a small company." Jashur's voice and face were expressionless. "Fled before they are slaughtered, they say."

"Do you have any numbers of those who remain?" This from Oreb.

"Yesterday Gideon had many tens of thousands; they camped beside the water wells of Harod. Then the desertion began and reports said he was left with twenty-two thousand."

Zalmunna looked troubled. "You call this is a small company?" he asked.

"No, my lord. The army moved to water beside the lake. Something happened, of which I know nothing, then there was only two, at the most three hundred left with Gideon. The rest deserted and have melted away."

"What do you counsel?" Somebody else said.

Jashur looked shifty. "My place is not to counsel the rulers of my country."

"No," said Zalmunna. "But your place is to faithfully report what your eyes have seen. You must have missed something; this is a trap to fool us into attacking them. Even Israel cannot be defended with so small a company. Is there another force?"

"There is no other force," said Jashur flatly. He resumed his eating.

"Then," said Zalmunna, "the houses and pastures of Israel are ours to possess. We will attack at dawn."

"Jon, Naomi!" The Professor's voice was loud in the headset, making Jon jump. "Move to the Southern fringe of the camp, quick as you can. I think I've found him. Gideon, I mean!"

Jon emerged from the tent, the vast encampment stretched in all directions. "Which way's…?"

The voice came through again, impatient. "Right, you need to move about seven or eight hundred metres to your right. The ground should start to rise. Please, hurry up!"

They ran. Past the sleeping forms or more often through them. The ground did indeed rise, steadily at first, then more steeply. In the gathering darkness, away from the encampment, they could see shadowy figures, flitting about on the rocks.

Gideon and his servant moved rapidly into cover of the darkness, where he was joined by first a few, and then many more men. There was something uncanny in the way in which the whole company moved noiselessly like ghosts through the scrubland. When they were a safe distance away, Gideon gathered his men around. He stood on a tall rock, preparing to speak to them.

At first inspection, Gideon seemed a disappointment. There was nothing remarkable in the man at all. He wasn't exactly weedy, actually he was quite wiry. But he wasn't tall either. He had chosen to stand on a rock to make himself seen and heard. He had coarse, black curly hair, which together with a bushy beard completely framed his face. There was a certainty about him that made his manner and speech very listenable.

"I praise my God." It was a deep voice that carried clearly in the still night air. "I praise Him for He has shown me mighty things this day. This very night, Phurah and I went into the camp of the Midianites. There we overheard a man telling of a dream. A dream of a loaf of barley bread tumbling into their camp and overturning their tents."

There was a murmur from the company.

"What mean these things, brothers?" He let the question hover for a few seconds. Then his voice rose. "It means this; for these seven years the Midianites, the Amalekites, and the Children of the East have hounded us, oppressed, us, driven us from our homes. They have killed our brothers, sons and fathers. They have taken our women from us to humiliate them in their vile homelands.

For these seven years the tribes of Israel have wandered like sheep through the hills and mountains, wet with the dew and rain. Our children have died in the cold of winter; in the summer there was no rest from the sun. We have hungered and lacked for everything, whilst they have burnt our crops and looted our food supplies. And now they have come to take what remains from us, our land, our liberty and our lives."

Tension was growing in the men. His speech was effective, hands tightened on swords, muscles stood out in their faces, taut with anger at his words.

"There is fear amongst the enemy. A fear that spreads and poisons man against man. What do they fear? Three hundred men? Three hundred against so many? Brothers, each one of you is set against four hundred of them. Yet they are so very afraid? Of what?"

He was a charismatic speaker. His words modulated like waves breaking on a shore; without yelling or straining his voice he built the drama, playing up to and drawing his audience with him in rapt attention. When Gideon drew his sword and raised it to heaven the whole company responded as one man, their swords whistled out of their belts and stabbed at the moonlit sky.

His voice rang out to the small company. "They fear the Living God of Israel!"

There was a roar from the men. He waited for it to subside. "They fear the sword of the LORD, and the sword of Gideon!" Another roar. As Jon listened he felt a great knot of excitement tighten in his belly- what a man! The sort of man who you would die for. Conviction and courage in awesome proportions.

"Men of Israel know this. We will overturn their tents and there will be a mighty slaughter of these uncircumcised. Your names will be recorded in songs and stories for generations to come. You will return to your families to be heralded as heroes. But men of Israel know this. Our God did not choose you for your valour, or the might of your arm. This victory will be the LORD's and you will give Him the glory for it. You will thank Him and praise him. Never let it be otherwise!"

He raised his face to heaven, and the moon glittered in his eyes. The company roared their approval.

As they separated into three groups, each man took up a huge earthenware jar that reached to his chest. The moon glimmered down upon them. They seemed invincible.

Into the jars went a large brushwood torch dipped in oil. Each man carried a ram's horn trumpet with him; even encumbered as they were, they moved easily over the ground, dividing into their respective companies. There were no sounds of complaint or dissent. They were whole-hearted in their loyalty to their leader.

Jon and Naomi together followed Gideon's company as they deployed along the eastern edge of the camp. As they spaced themselves out, the mighty encampment below them turned over in its sleep. At least that was how it seemed. The watch changed. Those guards who were on duty woke the next lookouts, and then settled down to slumber themselves. It became clear just how good Gideon's timing was going to be. The new watch would be still dulled with sleep, yet raw, edgy and nervous. The ruse would catch the new guards at their most vulnerable. Seeing Gideon, it was obvious this was how he planned it too. He stood, his great jar upright on the brow of the hill still keeping the flaring torch well inside it. Jon looked up. Everything was coming together for them. The moon, which up to now had blazed from the clear skies, was being masked by thickening cloud. The darkness contributed to a sense of gloom and foreboding. Time was running out for the army below them.

"Over to the right!" It was the Professor again.

"What?"

"There's a small rise, get to it, you should be able to see the whole camp from there."

Jon set off for the hillock. The Prof was right; it did afford an unparalleled view of the enemy camp. It stretched out in all directions, thousands of tents, camels, sleeping forms, twinkling fires, spears stuck in the fertile ground of the plain of Jezreel. But above the sky was darkening and all around the trap was being loaded, ready to be sprung at Gideon's command.

Around the plain, in three hundred jars, three hundred torches flared, held in left hands whilst the right hand held the trumpet ready to sound.

By now the knot in Jon's stomach had turned into a wasp's nest. He was nearly sick with anticipation. The tension built steadily with every minute that passed. From his vantage point he could barely make out the dark outlines of a few of the jars, each enclosing its burning lamp, ready to explode into fragments in the night air.

Silence, minutes ticked by. A camel harrumphed, making him jump. Then all was quiet again.

When it came, although he was expecting it, it terrified him. The discordant blast of the trumpet first, followed immediately by a shattering boom, as Gideon's sword smashed the heavy jar to fragments then the blazing torch lifted high in his hand. Seconds later behind him three more blasts and simultaneous crashes. To his left another twenty, then more and more, booms, crashes and blazing torches whirling round the night sky. Shout after shout, "the sword of the LORD, and of Gideon!"

More trumpet blasts, this time in front. Crash! Boom! More blazing torches flaring out of nowhere.

He wanted to close his ears, cover his face and cry out "Stop! Stop! Stop!" but still it went on. The awesome sound of the trumpets, "the sword of the LORD," with the reply thundering across the night, "and of Gideon!" On and on it went, spectacular, unworldly, terrifying. And Jon had been anticipating it! He looked to see what the effect on the unsuspecting camp was.

It was a ghastly spectacle. At the first commotion, guards started to their feet, grabbing their weapons, but were unable to decide on which direction the attack was coming from. Their sleeping compatriots awoke hastily, but in the dark fell over each other in their haste to get up. Blind panic ensued. Those who had swords or spears lashed out at anybody in their efforts to escape. Fighting spread; those who thought that Amalek had attacked them, those who thought the assault was from Gideon's men. Whatever they might have imagined, the scale of the uproar was completely disproportional to the small number of men making it.

Confusion slipped quickly into stampede; then it was every man for himself. The screams of the wounded and dying quickly rose to a crescendo to equal the roar of Gideon's men. Fires started to spread; tents flattened by struggling soldiers ignited in the fire embers and were soon blazing; camels snorted and stamped, then broke free, running for cover of darkness. A few commanders made an effort to halt the pandemonium, but they were soon lost in the heaving, shouting, screaming mass of humanity driven by raw terror looking for a way of escape. And still more earth-shattering crashes, and sky-rending trumpet blasts, mingled with the roared slogan. To the right, "the sword of the LORD!" To the left and behind –"and of Gideon!"

Gideon's men, shadows in the gloom, stood their ground. They beat the terrified soldiers back like animals, gradually funnelling the great host up the far end of the valley that opened out towards the river Jordan. As thousands and thousands of soldiers poured through, throwing aside weapons, baggage, clothes, anything, in fact that would have slowed them; the pass became choked with them. More died here than at any other point. They climbed across the bodies to escape, and were in their turn trampled. And yet, inexorably the trumpets, shouting and vengeful swords of Gideon's companies drove them on. "The sword of the LORD, and of Gideon!"

Jon stood open-mouthed, frozen in horror. He was used to seeing simulated battle scenes on the television screen; gunfire, smoke and chaos. But nothing did justice to this carnage. The relentless, implacable routing of the enemy by Gideon's troops as they repaid the suffering of the last seven years in full measure. There was no mercy shown; Gideon's men had closed ranks and any soldiers who tried to escape between them were swiftly dispatched. Twice he saw men with their clothes ablaze dashing crazily through the mayhem until a sword-blow ended their misery.

This was the true horror of war. The fertile plain of Jezreel was trampled to mud and awash with blood, littered with the dead and dying. On and on went the carnage. And still the trumpets, blasting as the remnant of the host of Midian disappeared into the distance. Jon made an effort to follow them, but his knees buckled and he almost sank to the ground, shaking uncontrollably and tasting bile in his mouth.

Naomi cowered on the blood-slippery grass, her face in her hands and her fingers stuffed tightly into her ears. But the screams of dying men were not to be deflected so easily, their terrible finality scorched her eardrums. Something warm had splashed over her face a few minutes earlier, and now she had retreated, foetus-like into this huddle.

"Na?" There was no answer; she too was trembling uncontrollably. A burning tent nearby collapsed and the flames flickered on the exposed side of her face. The bloom of light picked out blood spattered on her neck. He reached out and touched her gently on the shoulder.

"There's blood on your face, Na," he whispered, conscious of the absurdity of this, "are you OK?"

She felt his touch although the question did not penetrate the shell around her. Unthinkingly she leaned her head on his hand, then reached around with her other hand to seize his fingers. For five, six seconds she clutched him, feeling his breath in her hair.

He sensed that something inside of her had reached out to him, and in the midst of the mayhem all around them, her insecurity transmitted itself to him. The realisation sparked a cascade of new feelings towards her- the familiar hostility was now mixed with curiosity and an indefinable thrill. Slowly she uncoiled herself to look at him. Her face was grey; her eyes were glazing in shock.

"Get me out of here!" she pleaded.

The voice of the Professor came through the headset, also very subdued. "I'll bring you back!"

•

It was Jon's second exposure to the remarkable powers of the Timescope. His experience with Abraham and Isaac had unnerved him. It had also challenged him with a new meaning of courage and loyalty. This time he felt crushed, but strangely elated. Gideon had had doubts. Who wouldn't given the odds against him? But he had risen above them in an act of heroic faith and courage. Such an example could not fail to leave its mark.

Notwithstanding, it left him disturbed. Days later his stomach still tied itself in knots when he recalled the scenes of destruction. He could still see the fear in those wretched men's eyes; hear their desperate cries as they fled, only to be cut to the ground. Curiously he could taste the wood smoke in his mouth.

The Professor's concern was apparent. When Jon and Naomi removed their headsets, they were both traumatized; trembling, pale and almost incoherent. Naomi was screwing up her eyes and blinking in the light. "Just smoke," she muttered, avoiding Jon's eyes completely. The Professor looked from Jon to Naomi and back again. He said nothing as he showed Jon to the door.

Outside it was a normal Saturday. Traffic was tailing off as people returned from shopping trips to town. Jon walked home, said something inconsequential to Dad. Then he went to the bathroom to wash the smoke from his hair.

5

"Your usual sir." The waiter hovered near his elbow with a goblet almost the same shape as Prentice perched on a silver tray. Prentice wiped his mouth, like his fingers, small and surprisingly delicate in his large face.

"Not tonight. Doctor's orders, you know." He patted his belly.

"Of course sir." The waiter glided away.

Actually this wasn't true. Prentice had ignored Doctor's advice for years. It was the time for changes, 'economic adjustments' is what his department would call them. And the extra special fine brandy with which he customarily finished his meal was just such an adjustment. The thought of how much Mrs Prentice had taken him for made him want to cry. Anyway he needed a clear head tonight.

Source of message: Portable notebook/palmtop PC using standard operating platform and off-the shelf email package.

Nothing unusual there.

Connection to web via cellular phone acting as modem. Cellular phone identifier shows it was stolen in Rotherham in December last year. Pay as you go tariff with thirty pounds eighty pence credit outstanding at time of theft. Owner reported loss the same week. Phone dormant until current message.

"Cleverer." He murmured, sipping a glass of water. "I like it."

Trace took a while to answer the phone. "That you sir?" There was party music in the background.

"This email search you conducted, the one that originated from a mobile."

"Yes sir?" He sounded grumpy at being disturbed late in the evening. Not that Prentice cared. Trace was paid well enough to be called on at any time of day or night and needed reminding of that now and then.

"I need to know more."

"Of course Mr Prentice." Trace struggled to keep his voice respectful. "But I don't see…"

"I need to know when that phone goes active. Got that? The moment it squawks its presence to the network I want to know."

"But sir, I don't have the staff for that! We're up to our neck in the anti-terror surveillance."

"Well find them! That's what we pay you for! And start now!" Prentice cut the call.

Prentice eased himself into a generous armchair and reflected. Who or what could be the source of this intriguing message? On his slim fingers he ran through the options; Mrs Prentice? Maybe. She had shown a great deal more resourcefulness than he had given her credit for- hiring that private eye to follow him and get the material she needed for the divorce. No. The motive might be there, but the method was wrong.

He pondered the address book of his laptop computer. There were a number of his colleagues who would gladly put the knife into his ample body; the problem was where to start! But neither did this ring quite true.

'I know how to find out about anything, anywhere, anytime. It won't be cheap, but I know you're interested.'

Was it actually a threat? He had assumed it was. Anyone who knew the way he worked would certainly be tempted to blackmail him. But suppose it wasn't? Suddenly he saw the message in a different light. Somebody who knew the furtive nature of his work was offering him a resource to do it better. Now that was different! *'I know you're interested!'* For such a brief message it was telling him a lot more than he first thought. Somebody out there knows me, he thought, and has something with my name on. Now who knows me well enough to say that?

He went through the address book again, mentally striking out the least likely candidates. His finger rested on Mary Heath. For some reason he couldn't eliminate her from his dwindling pile of suspects. Smart, yes. Ambitious, undoubtedly. But corrupt? Hmmm!

It would take at least six hours for Trace to get his act together. Time to consider his response to the enigmatic communication that had arrived in his tray nearly a week ago now. Then when the reply was sent, at least they would have a location to go on.

He typed a few words, set the message to be sent at four o' clock the next morning and closed the lid of the machine. The waiter was still hovering waiting for the summons to bring the bill.

"Actually," he drawled, "I will have that brandy."

•

Faris had to actually shake Jon's shoulder to get his attention. "Jon, my man!" his voice had its customary, mocking lilt. "You are hard to find and Roger, he gets worried about you."

"Let him!" Jon growled, halting his progress down the street. He wished Roger far away right now. The last thing he wanted was to be dragged into another brush with the law.

"You haven't told me what happened at that house." Faris persisted.

Jon felt like saying, 'well you didn't wait around to find out- great friend you turned out to be!' Instead he shook Faris' hand free.

"Some other time, look I've got to be someplace this morning."

"Hokey Jon, see ya." Faris watched until Jon was out of sight.

•

A week! Was that all it was since he last came here? Well central to his plan was the full confidence and trust of Professor Avery. That meant Sunday morning at Living Word. Fine by him!

Jon glimpsed her across the room and thrust his way through the crowd to reach her. He was expecting her to be shy with him, even a little diffident after that passing moment on the battlefield.

"Hi Na…" he started.

She simply ignored him and walked out.

•

Naomi was washing mugs in the kitchen when her grandfather found her.

"Problems?" He enquired.

"No, I'm just fine!" Naomi specialised in withering sarcasm. A mug crashed down on the draining board, soap suds scattered like shrapnel. The handle came off the mug. The Professor picked it up and wrapped it in newspaper before dropping it in the bin.

He watched her for a minute, choosing his words carefully.

"There's more to you and Jon than you're telling me, isn't there?"

She stopped; her hair had found its way into her eyes. She tried to brush it away but the soapsuds on her glove transferred themselves to her fringe.

"Here, let me." He gently wiped them away with a tea towel.

She knew him better than to try to conceal the obvious. Her face crimson she regarded him.

"Leave this for now." He said, "I'll finish it after the service. Look, Na, I know I don't give you as much time as I should, but you can talk to me about him- if you want that is." He debated with himself- should he tell her that he had seen Jon's hand on her shoulder and her warm reaction. 'No,' he decided. Let it be their moment.

Naomi had seldom felt as wretched as she did now. What could she say to her Grandfather? He had guessed some of the truth.

Tearing the picture of Jon up had been easy. Tearing up the horrible, hard lump in her heart had been impossible. For the last week, since he had crashed back into her life she had been powerless against the feelings that had erupted in her. Several times she had nearly convinced herself it was the remains of an adolescent crush, no more. Then yesterday as she cowered, trying to blot out the appalling sight of the near-obliteration of the Midianite army, she had felt that touch on her shoulder. And in the midst of all the horror and mayhem, a light had exploded in her, feelings so strong she had almost suffocated on the intensity of them.

How much had Jon guessed? How could she dare to share this awful vulnerability knowing how he would exploit it to his advantage?

"I'll get over it," she said finally.

He shuffled, and studied the mug he was drying in confusion. Finally he sighed.

"I wish your mother was still alive. You need female company. It's not right you're being stuck here with me in our house. I've said it before; I can't give you that kind of understanding."

"Well she's not, and we can't bring her back. Or Dad and Jessica for that matter."

•

For Jon, it was a strange morning. The orderly service, followed by the study session contrasted sharply with the raw Timescope experience. And yet the words, black against the crisp whiteness of the paper of his borrowed Bible conveyed the dynamic energy of the actual events. 'Living Word' workshops had been aptly named. Shame about Naomi though! A small part of him was beginning to like her, yet with her coolness towards him the gulf between them had yawned wider than ever. *Naomi Snotty Avery!*

That night he hooked his own laptop to the stolen mobile phone to check his mail. The new address had so far yielded nothing. Jon couldn't tell whether he was relieved or disappointed. For a few seconds as he waited for his account to open, he pondered the rightness of what he was doing. Uncomfortable thoughts oppressed him. The Professor deserved better. Would Gideon betray a trust like this? Would Isaac conspire to…?

Then with a soft thrill Jon read the message;
Tell me more

•

Jon had only seen Prentice draw up on the drive once before, and that was the second time he had visited on ministerial business. Jon's sharp eyes had spotted the deliberate way in which Prentice had peeled away his soft leather driving gloves and eased off the wedding ring from the finger of his left hand. The ring had been stowed in its box in the glove compartment, then Prentice had heaved himself from the car. This curious procedure needed no explanation to Jon- it was absolutely in keeping with the man. By day the ring would proclaim the stability and dependability of the conscientious civil servant; but when necessary it would be removed to subtly advertise the availability of Terrence Prentice!

From his window, Jon reflected with mounting excitement how smoothly things were going. Whether Prentice left his laptop in the car or not at that particular time was irrelevant. What mattered was that the car window was smashed and the car alarm activated. If Roger, eager for laptops, took the opportunity as planned, this would happen during dinner. Nothing short of a nuclear attack would induce that fat slob to abandon his food completely. After much hand-wringing about the high levels of petty crime, Prentice, himself and Mum would return to the table. The police would take ages to come and in the meantime the coast would be clear for Jon at a convenient moment to retrieve the vital object nestling in a plush-lined case in the glove compartment. Easy! The bonus was, if Roger managed to snatch the laptop from its place under the passenger seat, it would appease his displeasure following Jon's failure to return any loot from the Prof's house. Two birds with one stone!

Prentice was his usual oily self. He flattered Mary with a subtle skill, manipulating the conversation to highlight some achievement of hers. Jon had listened intently, at the same time fascinated by the way Prentice ate. His delicate hands reduced to a blur as he docked the food in immense quantities into his deceptively little mouth. Yet he still managed a non-stop dialogue with his hostess.

"On a totally different subject, Mary," he paused for a few seconds to watch her eyes. "How do you feel about the Surveillance bill that the opposition are forcing a vote on?"

Jon pricked up his ears.

"OK," she said, "too much surveillance and nobody's comfortable, but just think what…"

As if on cue there was a crash, followed seconds later by the outraged howling of a car alarm. Jon heard the brief scuffle of running feet. He ran nimbly to the window and parted the net curtains. The evening light showed the stove-in passenger side window, the glass droplets on the drive.

"It's your car!" he shouted unnecessarily, "looks like it's been broken into!"

With a curse, the fat man dashed past him and out of the front door. Jon watched in delight as he wobbled and weaved around the vehicle, wringing his hands, mopping his brow and crunching the glass under his feet. He glanced into the nearby shrubbery, as if expecting to find it teeming with villains, but Roger, or whoever he had deputised for this job had long gone. Mary joined him, the shock evident on her face. For two or thee minutes they talked; Jon's heart sank as Prentice shovelled his frame into the car. Was he going? Then Mary opened the garage and the car was driven inside.

Jon suppressed a smirk. Even better! The garage opened out into the utility room. Wait until Prentice was back with his face in the trough then the ring was his!

"I think that's the answer to my question!" Prentice dialled the police whilst Mary washed her hands. "What we need is better surveillance, Mary," he was peering sideways at her as he spoke. "Some way of watching everybody, every minute of the day! Oh…hello, is that the police…?"

6
The Golden Image

"So you really are ready for another episode?" The front door closed behind Jon as he entered the hall. He turned and fell over a waste-bin right in the middle of the hallway. Oddly enough the bin was empty, although the surrounding floor was carpeted with junk. It was typical of the confusion and clutter that surrounded the Professor.

"I visited the remains of Ancient Babylon in Iraq," he said as he disappeared into the kitchen to make some tea. It's one of the most exciting archaeological sites in the world, just waiting to be properly investigated. Not that that's very likely, certainly not until the troubles die down and the economy picks up. Then Western researchers may feel safe enough to sink some money into proper scientific analysis of the material there."

He ushered Jon into a small sitting room lined with armchairs. It was the only room so far that looked remotely normal. Two of the chairs were clear of junk, the third, bizarrely was occupied by an ornamental fountain, still in its box.

"Jon, please, have a chair," he said, lifting the fountain clear of the chair and placing it on a sideboard. "I paid a pittance for several pieces of stone masonry that I knew were originally high up in the palace buildings. Perfect location as well, right up high with a view over the whole city. What was more; I got them cheap because Nebuchadnezzar hadn't signed them!"

Naomi appeared in the doorway. She glanced curtly at Jon then turned to the Prof. "He signed his city, stone by stone?"

"Not stones- bricks," he corrected, "as they were made from the local mud they were stamped with his name."

"What you have to appreciate," he continued, "is the ego of the man. There's no doubt he was a remarkable individual, in such a short time he achieved so much. But what he doesn't reflect on is the human suffering upon which the foundations of his empire were laid. The indiscriminate and brutal use of slave labour, the uprooting of peoples, the viciousness towards those they conquered."

The Professor disappeared into the kitchen and returned with a tray on which were three mugs of tea and, most surprising of all some chocolate biscuits.

"So that's where we are going, Nebuchadnezzar's city. A city of unimaginable wealth, power, luxury and influence, brainchild of a megalomaniac egocentric who took a long time to learn his lesson. Corrupter of the world and cruel master of nations." He waved the biscuit packet in front of Naomi but she shook her head with a wry smile. "I can't guarantee it's going to be nice there! But I know it will be interesting!"

Jon bit into a biscuit. Ugh! It was soft! "So when do we go?"

"After your biscuit."

•

Babylon was jaw-droppingly impressive. They found themselves, not on any open plain, as the Professor had predicted, but on one of the main streets of the city, possibly the main street. Naomi said later that her first impression was of Oxford Street in London. The crowds, confusion and magnificent frontages to the buildings. There were stores, markets, bathing houses, private houses with enclosed gardens, temples here, there and everywhere. As they stepped into the scene the confusion enveloped them, carrying them along in a random fashion.

But as they adjusted to the change in pace, gradually the chaos began to assume an order and a pattern. People were flowing in particular directions, and by joining them they were able to discover more about this fabulous city. They merged in with a group of well-dressed men, merchants, who were converging on an open square in front of a well-guarded building.

"It's slave market day." Jon heard the Prof murmur through the headset intercom.

Indeed it was. He could hear snatches of conversation all around, excited talk of a new shipment. "Cultured stock," "easier to train" and "these won't be cheap!"

There was definitely an order of precedence in the crowded streets. The wealthy lolled in ornate litters borne by two or four slaves. Before them went other slaves, bearing heavy sticks with which they cleared the road before the carriage. Less wealthy people stood aside, and other slaves were simply pushed aside or beaten back. Everywhere there were slaves. They were easy to spot because they were simply dressed. A few had robes with insignia of the household they served; the majority were dressed with little more than a loincloth. Slaves worked by the road, slaves lead children up and down the streets, slaves carried water or provisions. Slaves just did everything.

In the slave market the new arrivals were being lead around the showground so that potential buyers could get a sneak preview of the human baggage that would be shortly available for purchase. Many were in very poor condition. Worn down and ill-treated, they would end their lives a couple of streets away in the square where public executions took place. Those who caught the eye of the professional vendor of human flesh would be given a great deal better treatment; well fed and allowed time to recover before they were put on auction.

"Where're these lot from?" Jon was inspecting a segregated group of captives closely. This batch comprised predominately men but there were a few women and even fewer children, looking out at the great city with wide, haunted eyes. Some of the men glared at their captors with contempt and hatred. This contrasted with the slaves in the street who seemed to be totally lacking in any spirit to do anything else than the bidding of their master or mistress.

"Egypt, obviously!" The tone of Naomi's voice seemed to suggest that anyone who didn't know where these slaves were captured from really shouldn't be walking upright. Jon's hackles rose. Did she have to be like this?

"I wasn't asking you!" He muttered. But the Prof hadn't heard his question so there was no other answer to be had.

"Suit y'self," she sniffed and wandered across the arena.

Over here a rapid-fire auction was in progress. The slave in the centre of the ring was clearly a prize to be had, and several well-dressed men were bidding furiously for him. His nut-brown chest and arm muscles had been anointed with oil so that they rippled and shone in the sunlight. For a moment the man seemed to have forgotten his condition and was flexing his biceps to show off his incredible physique. At the auctioneer's command he grinned wolfishly at the audience displaying a magnificent set of teeth.

Looking up, Jon could see that the sky was darkening over with great heavy clouds. Minutes later one of the well-dressed merchants lead the slave away and before any more could be viewed for sale the rain began.

Such rain! Great drops thudded into the dusty streets turning them to soupy mud in moments. As it lashed down with the force of a bathroom shower, in moments both Jon and Naomi were soaked to the skin. They dashed for cover under the market stalls along with many others, ignoring the wheedling of the traders lucky enough to have covered stalls and watching the rivulets running down the ruts in the centre of the main street. A crash of thunder roared overhead and many of the people genuflected towards an ornate building close by, presumably a temple of some god or other.

"Look Jon!" Naomi tugged at his sleeve. Her hair was plastered over her face.

"Where?" He shouted over the noise of the rain, trying to adjust his position so that it didn't run down his neck.

"Just there!" She dragged him by the arm to another stall, about fifty metres away.

There they were. Little images. Standing upright, different sizes and different prices, but unmistakeably based on a single design. Images of gold!

"What are you doing?" The Professor's voice in their headsets made them both jump.

"Sheltering, that's what!" Jon shouted back, as the roar of water falling on the roof intensified. "It's chucking it down out here!"

There was a long pause. "I'm bringing you back!" he said; then the images faded to black.

"Why did you have to do that?" Naomi demanded. "We were on to something!"

The Prof looked unsettled. "You were sheltering? From the rain?"

"Yes that's right," She replied, her fringe falling over her eyes.

Jon said nothing, but shifted uneasily. Something wasn't making sense.

"Jon, Naomi, listen!" The Prof's voice was hard as nails. "You were getting wet out there- yes?"

Suddenly Jon saw what he meant.

"We shouldn't have felt that rain should we?"

The look on the Professor's face was all the answer he needed.

•

It was half-ten when they broke up, still confused. The discussion was revolving in ever-decreasing circles. The Prof felt that the experience was something akin to that felt by audiences of the first moving cinema images. The sensation of a train rushing towards them from the screen caused some of the more nervous folk to scramble out of their seats. Similarly here, he felt, was an incomplete set of stimuli; sounds and sights, for which their brains were filling in the details, in this case, the sensation of wetness of the rain. The Prof admitted that he had experienced a similar overpowering sense of reality on two other times when he had used the headsets for exploring Timescope scenery. On both occasions the realisation of the impossibility of it all had not hit him until much later.

Naomi was still tetchy with Jon. Jon felt irritated with her superior attitude and wanted to get home. She was sulking and the Professor was absorbed in some program related to the networking systems. Jon made his excuses and left.

•

The late spring night was unseasonably warm. To the west the sky ribboned with purplish-black clouds that fanned out from the reddish afterglow of sundown. He drew a deep breath. It was weird, fantastic, surreal. He had been in Babylon! Queen and Metropolis of the ancient world. He had walked her streets, jostled and been jostled by her inhabitants. They had watched her living slave-commerce in operation and even felt the rain on their skin. Those people were so long dead it was unlikely even fragments of their bones remained; yet he, Jon Heath had seen them living, shouting, moving…

"Hey Heath!" The voice was close by and unpleasantly familiar. Jon's pulse accelerated.

There were three of them. Roger, Oliver, and skulking behind, George Mere. Faris wasn't there. At least that was one thing. This was going to hurt, he knew. There had been no laptop under the seat, or anywhere else in the car that Roger could find.

Roger had had his head shaved. His eyes glowered from their cavernous sockets. A cigarette smouldered between his fingers. He rolled it around a few times then deliberately flicked it at Jon. It stung the back of Jon's hand then rolled away into the gutter. Jon could not suppress a gasp of pain. Roger grinned evilly, his breath stale.

"Time to talk, Heath." His voice rattled like a distant train. Jon didn't feel like talking. Close by, Oliver leered nastily.

Jon had seen this situation many times before. Only then he had been part of the wolf-pack, grinning in anticipation of a little excitement. So he knew what to expect next. Roger would weigh in heavily with his grievance, demand would follow demand. He, Jon might be allowed a moment to defend himself, but it was only a show-trial. Any excuses would be drowned in invective. Very soon Roger's tone would change to an aggressive outpouring of violent abuse. The flood-gates would open and a torrent of filthy language would wash over him. At the same time the shoving would start, the belligerent push followed next by Oliver, the Enforcer moving forcibly into his personal space. Then as he went down the kicking would start, probably two at a time with the third keeping watch up and down the street. He, Jon, would quite likely pass out, curled up in a ball, his face lacerated and bruised and vomiting with pain.

He turned to the Enforcer who was looming up on Roger's left.

"Roger's too scared to hit me himself, did you know that?"

There was silence. Somewhere in the distance a car horn sounded.

"Uh?" Oliver looked nonplussed. The well-rehearsed intimidation procedure faltered. He looked to Roger for support.

Roger, unsurprisingly spat. But he made no reply. Jon persisted, speaking rapidly, hoarding the precious seconds he had bought.

"Haven't you seen it? He always lets you go in first. He lets you take the risks then he takes the credit."

"Nah he doesn't..." but Oliver's protest tailed off. He stood there, recollecting his experiences. His face registered incomprehension mixed with doubt. Jon had hit a tender spot. It was Faris who had observed the way Roger lead the verbal attack but stepped aside to let Oliver the Enforcer do the punching. Jon had stored that information for just such an occasion as this. Now it poisoned the water beautifully! Oliver was starting to look aggrieved with his leader.

"There is fear amongst the enemy!" The deep voice came clearly from the darkness. Jon jumped. Gideon's voice was distinct, confident, assertive. Nobody else noticed it, Oliver continued to waver, George continued to shuffle, and Roger... Jon looked him in the eyes.

"There is fear amongst the enemy. A fear that spreads and poisons man against man."

Yes there was! Suddenly Jon realised just how true Gideon's words were. He'd never seen it before, but now it was clear. Roger's face was sinister and unpleasant, but his eyes showed plain evidence of uneasiness. Jon could feel a surge of conviction, Gideon's absolute certainty. For a few more seconds the situation teetered, but Jon had control. He was watching Roger's fists for the first sign of movement...

When the blow came it came incredibly fast. Jon had no time to duck, but his arm shot up to deflect the blow. All the same it caught him on the cheek, knocking him backwards and ringing in his ear. In that split second he looked into Roger's eyes again. Yes, there could be no doubt! Roger was afraid! For all his meanness and cruelty, he was scared. Now Jon was going to take advantage of that knowledge.

Roger was expecting Jon to duck and cower. But Jon recovered his footing and swung heavily. The blow caught Roger squarely on the tip of the nose. There was a muffled, crushing *'crack'* and he yelled like a child. His hands went up to his face, giving Jon chance to clout his unprotected stomach. Roger staggered back, colliding with a tree and doubled up, clutching his solar plexus.

Then Jon was on him. With his left hand he seized Roger's collar, with the right he landed blow after blow on his face. *Wham! Wham! Wham!* A furious, but calculated attack that reduced his nose to a mess, split his upper lip, blacked both of his eyes and was coming close to knocking him out completely. Jon's world reduced to a few feet in front of him, where Roger Lord, the feared leader of the Apostles gang was sliding down the tree trunk, blood spraying from his nose, his head jerking from side to side with each blow. Dimly he was aware of things happening around them. He saw Oliver give a contemptuous shrug and walk away; then George and someone female struggling to separate them- the girl yelled at him to stop as she clawed at his arm, but still he went on. Roger, now unable to defend himself, was losing consciousness.

Take that you Amalek scum, *Wham! Wham! Wham!* Each blow resonated in him with utter satisfaction and justice. That'll teach you to mess with Israel, *Wham! Wham! Wham!*

The attack stopped abruptly. Jon felt himself lifted bodily and carried, fists still flailing, a few yards. A door opened and he was flung inside the Professor's cluttered hallway. Then the door slammed behind him leaving him in darkness; panting, exhausted but exhilarated.

From where he lay in the hallway, he heard the babble of voices, brief cursive explanations and the Professor's car starting up. Then silence, broken only by the ticking of a clock, descended upon him.

Half an hour passed…forty-five minutes by the grandfather clock ticking away solemnly in the hallway. It bonged the hour making him jump, just as he had been dozing off.

Naomi banged the door behind her angrily. Two inches shorter than Jon, but terrible in a temper. Jon felt a twinge of fear himself.

"You moron! You absolute moron!" She switched on the light. She trembled with anger, her face scarlet, her hair dishevelled. "What sort of a place do you think this is? Brawling in our street!" Her eyes scanned his face with ill-concealed distaste. She went away into the small downstairs toilet and returned with a dripping sponge. "Stand up! And I don't care if this hurts!"

Nor did she. She rammed the cold sponge against Jon's swelling eye with little concern, but it felt good against the hot skin.

"He started it!" Jon protested.

"He started it, he started it!" she imitated in a whiny voice. "Just that you didn't have the sense to stop it. Here hold this yourself!" She thrust the sponge into his hand and stood back.

The injustice of it all washed over him. "Now listen Naomi…"

"No! You listen!" she yelled. "You know he's trouble, so you could have made a run for it- even come back in here. But oh no! You just couldn't back down."

Jon stood up. He felt dizzy and his head throbbed. Above all he felt bitterly angry with her. He threw the sponge past her. "Just listen for once will you?" He kicked aside a pile of magazines and advanced on her. "For once in your life stop shouting and start listening! Do you know what I've done? Do you, eh?" His heart swelled with triumph. "I've smashed Roger Lord! He's not coming back for more. He's finished!"

"Too right he is." She snapped back. "He's in hospital!"

A cold feeling, like a dip in a winter lake burst over Jon. "Hospital?"

"Granddad took him to A & E. His nose is broken, and he's having stitches to his eye. Add to that concussion and he's probably in for the night. You utter moron."

"Is the Prof here?"

Naomi picked up the sponge and ground it against Jon's face. "George brought me back." As she examined the swollen area around his eye some of her anger abated. She had witnessed most of the confrontation from her upstairs window.

What she had seen had amazed her. Jon, by no means a physical lad, and a head shorter than Roger had him pinned to a tree and was beating him in a frenzied and sustained assault. The sound of Jon's blows rang in her ears as she and George wrestled to separate them. Most disturbing of all was what he was shouting at Roger; his furious blows interspersed with a peculiar insult; *Amalek, Amalek, Amalek!"* She knew what it meant.

"How's that feeling now?"

Jon was startled by the change in her voice. One moment she was screaming mad with him, the next concerned for his welfare. "Did you see it happen?"

She nodded. Now the drama was past she was feeling shaky. "I was worried about you, so I came out to help." She bit her lip to hide the wobble in her voice.

Jon held the sponge against his face. He failed to understand her at the best of times, but this was bizarre! She clearly detested him, but she had put herself at considerable risk to come to his aid. "Thanks." He mumbled.

When the Prof finally arrived home, the sparkle had well and truly gone from his eyes. He looked tired and depressed, and not a little disturbed. He gazed narrowly at Jon, as if uncertain what to do with him. Jon braced himself for a lecture, but it was in silence that he led him to the car parked just outside the front door.

The Professor held open the back door. "Get in!" he said curtly.

•

"Somewhere in the South of England?" Prentice could feel his blood pressure spiralling upwards. He almost dropped the phone in his fury.

"Sorry sir." Trace didn't sound apologetic and it irked Prentice even more. "There was just one short transaction and the phone went dormant again. We barely had time to register the handshake signals before we lost him again."

"When was this?" Prentice breathed hard. "What time of day?"

There was a pause, then a rustle of paper. "Seven-thirty yesterday morning. Very brief message to the mobile. Did you send one sir?"

Prentice ignored the question. "I thought you said this phone was in Rotherham. What's it doing in the South of England?"

"I said it was stolen from Rotherham, sir. But it has travelled. You know that's why they're called mobile phones sir." The moment Trace said this he regretted it.

"Thank you. That's all." He said curtly and hung up. Prentice made a mental note to circulate a rumour of forthcoming redundancies in Trace's department. Not that he would anticipate there being any, but it would unsettle them and induce a little more respect for a while.

•

The Prof took off his glasses, rubbed the bridge of his nose and sighed.

"Ok Jon, let's hear your version of events."

He and Naomi were the only students in their Living Word class that Sunday. Jon was taken aback by the directness of the question.

The Prof fiddled with his glasses again. He seemed very fidgety.

"I mean the real reason." He said simply.

"Whatcha mean, the real reason?"

"Jon, I am not a fool; I flatter myself that I know you quite well by now. You are not a brawling thug like Roger Lord; you are intelligent, calculating and cautious. This tough-guy stuff just isn't you."

Jon listened intently. What was he coming out with?

"Now, faced with a confrontation, suddenly you let fly at him, not defensively, but with an attack reminiscent of a psychopath. Why? What has changed with you? Why are you swaggering around like the top dog? This isn't you Jon! What's going on?"

Jon swallowed. The Prof's penetrating gaze was on him over the top of his glasses. Where did he begin? So he related hearing Gideon's voice in that quiet street inciting him to stand up to Roger.

"Gideon knew what he was about, Prof!" he insisted. "If you let them, people will walk all over you. Now Roger will leave me alone."

"Yes, he'll leave you alone all right," he agreed unhappily. "What self-esteem he ever had is now in ruins. His Dad beat him when he found out that his son had lost the fight and his stepmother is back on medication. I saw them down at the surgery on Friday. Dad Lord wanted to know where you lived. Do you want me to tell them, O great warrior?"

Jon shivered but said nothing. "Is it likely he'll be round looking for trouble?" asked Naomi.

He shook his head. "I was there for over half an hour putting your case, treading a fine line between excusing your behaviour and giving Dad a reason for taking matters into his own hands."

"Anyway," he finished, clipping open the file he kept his notes in, "I think he's letting the matter rest there. At least that's what he led me to believe. And knowing his parole conditions I rather hope he will."

Jon couldn't decide whether he was glad or disappointed. On balance he felt relieved that the incident would finish there. The Prof sat back in his chair, stretched his long arms behind his head and yawned.

"I have a few things to do this week," he said. "But are you available Thursday for another look at Babylon?" Jon nodded; relieved at least that he was still happy for them to go back into the Timescope.

"That's good then, I used the golden images you saw as a marker for the search program. I reckon within weeks the great unveiling of the big Golden statue will take place. I imagine the guy selling them will be there, and that's where we want to be too."

"How do we know it's not already happened?" Jon asked.

Naomi gave him a withering look. "Do you really think Nebuchadnezzar's going to allow souvenirs to be sold afterwards?"

"Jon," the Professor got up to leave.

"Uh?"

"Stay out of trouble till then, yes?"

"Sure thing Prof!" Jon grinned.

•

The town centre was deserted as Jon wandered past, deep in thought. A light breeze flapped chip wrappers around, and a drinks can rattled indecisively in the gutter, first one way, then the other.

The Timescope was powerful stuff; it had weird side-effects. It was too real, not only in the way in which rain had soaked them both when it should, of course, have been just a visual thing, but in the way in which he felt the influence of these extraordinary events were altering his behaviour towards others, in particular Roger Lord and co.

He knew the Prof was right. He, Jon Heath was no coward, but neither was he normally capable of such reckless aggression. The motivation had come from the Timescope- or more accurately the extraordinary characters he had encountered in its simulated world.

But that wasn't all of it. "Gideon was there, just as clearly as you can see me!" he had told Naomi last Saturday night. Of that he was sure.

As he arrived home, the familiar Daimler was hogging the drive. It reminded Jon of the next phase of his plan. And this week, Naomi was off to her Aunt Judith for a few days. She only lived across town, but it meant Jon had the Professor to himself, at least from Tuesday onwards. With the matter of the Apostles sorted satisfactorily, it was time to ingratiate himself that little bit more with the old man, and no Naomi to question the purity of his motives.

Twice Jon nearly backed down from his plan. The scheme was, in essence simple, there was very little to go wrong. But his guts churned in shame as he stood poised on the doorstep a few metres from the tree where Roger had slumped last week. Finally with a deep breath he hammered on the door.

"Ah, Jon!" As always the Prof appeared delighted to see him. He looked tired - that was good. There were creases in the creases around his eyes. "Did we arrange to meet?"

"Sort of," Jon fudged. "You said I could talk about all this," he waved his hand down the hallway in the direction of the Timescope, "if I wanted to."

"Sure thing!" The Prof struggled with the front door, but a washing machine motor had jammed itself between the door and the floor. "Hold on," his voice tailed off as he retrieved it and parked it on a side table. His face wore a troubled expression. "Getting nightmares?"

"Oh…yes," Jon followed him down the passage. This time they sat down on the floor in the viewing room. On the giant screen was a view of Babylon, but the light was fading and it was difficult to make out anything but the dimmest outlines of people hurrying to and fro. He waited for the next question. It wasn't long in coming.

"Tea?"

"I'll make it," Jon was on his feet in a moment. "No, don't get up, I can manage."

From then on it was simple. Two of his mother's sleeping tablets were all it took. Crumbled up and stirred in well. Jon avoided the Prof's gaze as he brought the drinks back into the viewing room. He was feeling dreadful- this man trusted him-inasmuch as anyone who had broken into his house could be trusted.

"Oh, thanks Jon. Put it over by the speakers, I'm just going to make myself comfortable, then I'll be all ears."

Even now, Jon considered spilling the tea. He'd plenty to feel guilty about but this latest dishonesty troubled him deeply and in an unfamiliar way. The Prof rearranged a few cushions and propped himself against the wall, the tea at arm's length.

"Now, what's happening with you?"

There was no new ground, no fresh information- at least nothing Jon was going to divulge to his host. But in spite of that, it wasn't difficult to talk. He talked about the weird experience of Gideon inciting him to attack Roger. He wondered whether the Prof noticed that this was stale news, but within twenty minutes the old man's eyes were rolling in his head.

"You alright Prof?"

"Jus' tired." He yawned. "Few broken nights catching up on me, I guess...Oh!" he yawned prodigiously, "'scuse me, please! Now where were we?"

In five more minutes his head had sunk to his chest and he was breathing deeply. Jon watched, excited, but appalled with himself. Beating up Roger was easy compared to this!

The ring nestled in the soft-lined tray, it winked in the red room light, twinkling brimful with scandal, intrigue, corruption and manipulation. One click of a mouse was all it took to start it on its short journey to turning queen's evidence on its luckless owner. Whatever qualms Jon may have had so far, he had none regarding Terrence Prentice. The house was unusually quiet; the pervasive sighing roar of the computers in their den seemed muted tonight, and the clock in the hall bonged out the quarter of an hour. As before the gas hissed and the drawer frosted instantly. The Prof had made a minor modification; as the ring finished conditioning, a message bounced up:

"READY TO ROCK!"

"Ha ha!" he murmured and went out to check on the Professor.

The Professor slept on. Jon watched as the progress bar crawled across the screen that nestled amidst the hardware of what they had come to call the 'Reading Room'. In the bottom left was clock readout, running backwards. The program had demanded very little from him at the outset, but one question it had for him now made sense:

DO YOU WISH TO ADOPT THIS TIME AS
REFERENCE?

And below the computer clock marked the current time in seconds, minutes, hours, days, months and years.

The files were huge- too big to be of use. Much irrelevant data- hours of sleeping or catnaps in the Westminster office, long meetings during which further rumblings that sounded like snoring could be heard. Then there were extended periods when the ring was consigned to the glove box of the car. And so much of Prentice's life seemed to be centred around restaurants, bistros, wine bars and even greasy spoon motorway services. Jon skipped these, but threw more interesting episodes into a temporary file. This rapidly filled up and Jon labelled it and inserted a blank DVD into the adjacent drive.

Three months' data. Jon fitted a second DVD in the burner. Another grubby, wretched three months. He smiled to himself- the biter was going to be bit! From what he could make out, there were a lot of important meetings; the same faces appeared time and again. There were different meetings- meetings with few present that felt clandestine, surreptitious and urgent. These were saved for future inspection.

Early on as the life of Terrence Prentice unravelled before him, Jon saw Prentice and his mother together, the slimy and too-long handshake and the casual touch of her waist as he held the door open for her. Jon was gratified to see his Mum recoil slightly.

One more DVD should be enough. Jon peeled back the cellophane wrapper and flicked it into the burner.

'DO YOU WISH TO BACK UP FILES TO STORAGE?'

If there was a key marked 'ABSOLUTELY NOT!!' Jon would have hit it. So he contented himself with 'NO.'

He checked the room before he left. The Babylon stone was back in the tray, the readout was compiling an error log. Jon scrutinized the codes. As far as he could make out there was nothing incriminating there. Power brownout? Coolant failure? Nothing to suggest deliberate tampering.

•

"Naomi?"

"Yes, what is it?"

The voice on the other end was cold. The ice-maiden was back in permafrost mode. Jon grinned. "I'm at your granddad's house…"

"Why?"

"Just listen will you? He fell asleep right in front of me. Does he often do this?"

She was in the same room as her Aunt. Jon could hear muffled exchanges, then another voice came on the line. "Hello, is this Jon?"

"Yeah."

"It's Judith here, Naomi's Aunt. Did you say you are with Professor Avery now?" Her voice was cautious, but a great deal warmer than her niece's.

Jon explained. He had been talking to the Prof for a couple of hours, but he went to the toilet, then when he returned the old guy was fast asleep on cushions on the floor, and difficult to wake. He wasn't worried, but felt they should know. Would he stay until they arrived? Ten minutes? Yes, no problem.

Aunt Judith arrived with Naomi in tow. She inspected Jon with a keen eye, but seemed to have swallowed the story entirely. Between them they manhandled the Professor across the junk-strewn floor to bed. He woke up enough to stumble upstairs himself, but was soon fast asleep again.

"Is he alright, d'ye think?" Jon's tone of solicitous concern was masterful.

She clicked her tongue impatiently. Jon guessed she was a nurse or something. "He goes on for weeks; just a few hours' sleep a night, so it's not at all surprising he gets like this now and then. He's not getting any younger, despite what he likes to think!" As she was talking Jon glanced across the viewing room. On the speaker was the empty mug. What a fool he was! All this time at his disposal and he had left the most important bit of incriminating evidence.

It was as if Naomi had read his mind. She crossed the room and picked it up, then stooped down to retrieve his mug from the floor. Her face was expressionless. For a moment Jon considered saying, "no, let me!" but he knew this would be sure to arouse suspicion. He forced his eyes back to Aunt Judith, as Naomi disappeared into the kitchen.

"Jon, I want to thank you for taking care of him tonight- oh and staying to help," she was saying. Jon smiled unconvincingly. The DVD's were burning his skin through his coat pocket.

"Uh… oh yes! No worries." He said distractedly.

7

There were huge gardens and parkland, with wide grassy spaces, the grass like thick wire, very short and close to the ground. To their left they could see the city walls as they straddled the river then marched on into the distance. Interspersed along the top of the walls were guard towers, but even here was little sign of life.

They traversed a broad road that followed the river for much of its course through the city. The river banks were made up with huge bricks, sloping steeply to the water's edge. On the other side was the distinctive shape of the Ziggurat with balconies hanging with lush foliage: palm trees, date palms on the lower levels, creeping bougainvilleas and something like clematis further up. The whole display was incredible. No wonder Nebuchadnezzar was a proud man!

Jon and Naomi "walked" for some time, their speed limited by the ability of the Timescope to peel off layers of images from the stone selected by the Professor. Just now and then, as if to remind them of their virtuality, the landscape would shudder whilst the system responded to their continuing change of angles.

There were definite changes in the cityscape as they moved across the region, the Ziggurat was obviously the focus of the priests and government; here the buildings were palatial, and they thought they saw between two grand buildings the king's palace itself. Then as they moved further along the riverbank, they saw a tidy array of small buildings which turned out to be army barracks.

Finally after what seemed ages the far wall of the city came in sight. Here the river again ducked under the city wall and out of sight from the inside of the city. The great tunnel under the wall was a witness to the extraordinary thickness of the stone walls; massive blocks of masonry, cemented together by mud from the river basin. The rest of the architecture was burnt brick, sallow in the bright sunlight. To the right of the river culvert was a massive gateway, with its doors flung wide open.

"Jon." Naomi's voice was level and sweet. Jon relaxed further - since he had arrived, the Professor's manner had been pleasant and easy. He had thanked Jon for taking care of him, and commented that he had never had a better night's sleep in years. Naomi too had been civil; clearly she suspected nothing- in fact, from what Jon could see his evident concern for her relative had impressed her greatly.

"Yeah?"

"Is it me, or are you hot too?"

He was. Sweat was trickling down his neck and his armpits felt wet. "Shh!"

"I heard that!" came the Prof's voice in the headset. "You're forgetting I can see you in the viewing room. You're both looking sweaty."

Naomi glanced at Jon. She was acting magnificently. Beneath the cool exterior she wanted to scream at him; 'you swine! You rotten, filthy, scheming little swine!'

It was pure accident that she had seen the chalky dregs in the tea mug. Just a glance at the whitish residue before it was flushed away down the drain. She had rubbed them between her fingers- she had no idea what exactly they were, but she could guess. Her blood had run cold and her stomach went sick at the implication- he had drugged her granddad! Why? There were any number of reasons- but her immediate suspicions were unfounded. Covertly she took stock of the chaotic house, but there was no sign of theft- and anyway, if he had been intent on robbery why phone her afterwards?

Should she tell the Prof? He ought to know, but there was a problem. He was fast becoming indifferent to her complaints about Jon. "Don't write him off, Na," he would chide her.

Instead she bottled her feelings, deciding to play a long game. Her grandfather seemed unharmed, and whatever Jon was up to would come out in the wash. So she elected to play the grateful granddaughter to wrong foot him for a change. "Thanks, Jon." She had whispered when he arrived.

•

The Plain of Dura was on the same scale as the city of Babylon. A huge floodplain which in the cooler months would be thick with grass. Right now the grass was burnt away and the light, bare earth reflected the harsh sunlight back with a vengeance. They could hear the instruments playing from some distance away and shortly joined the tail end of a massive crowd pressing forward towards the music.

It was clear immediately that this was some considerable festival. The whole event had the appearance of a carnival, with many of the market stalls they had seen earlier in the city now migrated to this plain. From the look of the place the festival had been going some time; the earth was beaten and trampled and a clear well-trodden track going to and from the city, as well as other tracks setting off in the direction of the river.

The Prof had assured them that they would have no difficulty finding the image. Even at this distance it was huge! He reckoned twenty-seven metres high and nearly three metres wide. The sun, approaching midday scorched down on the assembly, making the golden image blaze like a mirror. It was too painful to look at directly but by screwing up their eyes almost to shutting point they could make out the outline of a regal figure, clothed in splendid robes, with a stylised rectangular beard that seemed in keeping with the artwork of Ancient Babylon. The image had no immediate beauty. Despite being gold, it was out of proportion, the hips being narrow and the chest massive by comparison. It stood on a huge plinth made of brickwork that in itself elevated it by some five metres above the crowd.

As if on cue the music changed. The dancers moved to one side to form a wide corridor. Jon moved right to the front for a ringside view, and could see that temporary earthworks had been thrown up to form a huge level platform alongside the image. The height of the platform could not have been more than two metres, sufficient to form a rostrum, allowing easy viewing for anybody within a kilometre. To both sides of this the dancers congregated; the rhythms were more urgent, the pulse of the music intensifying and the energy building to an obvious climax. The pace of the dancing picked up likewise, at times it reminded him of the 'Mexican Wave' that was typical in large crowds, a surge of coordinated movements that swept across the dancers in keeping with the beat.

There was a human touch too, one of the women dancers started to sway uncontrollably, then without warning her eyes rolled up in her head and she collapsed gracelessly to the ground. The rest carried on around her, the tempo still increasing as they weaved and gyrated.

Abruptly the music stopped with the exception of a drumbeat. The beat was produced by a skin stretched tightly over a frame, the diameter being at least two metres across. The air shook as a musician thumped this drum with a soft mallet,

Boom! Boom! Boom! Boom! Boom!

On and on it went. The crowd which up to now had been obviously enjoying the show fell silent and attentive, as a large tent behind the Image flew open and from its rich interior came an impressive parade of dignitaries, viziers, princes and noblemen. They filed on to the platform, each one dressed differently yet sumptuously. Rapidly the rostrum filled up, as more and more of them stood before the assembly, proud, arrogant and silent.

Boom! Boom! Boom!

Now another figure in rich robes emerged and strutted to the front of the stage. His eyes scanned the crowd, which, Jon, from his vantage point could see was by no means randomly assorted. The assembly was divided into national groups, sometimes distinguishable by differences in dress, others more obviously by skin colour or other physical features.

"Do you think that's him?" Naomi had come alongside.

"Got to be."

But it wasn't. The man was a master of ceremonies, an official tasked with whipping up the crowd into a fervour, which he immediately set about doing.

His eyes ranged over the crowd; haughtily he regarded them as they stood there in near silence. All the time the drum beat shook the hot air behind them.

"Captives of Egypt and the lands of the Great River!" The voice rang out over the assembly. About three hundred metres away other criers took up the message and relayed it onwards, where several more in turn bellowed it out, giving a curious echo effect.

"Bow to your king!" ("Bow to your king!" "Bow to your king!")

A ripple went through the assembly to the far right as about two or three thousand bowed deeply. Simultaneously the whole assembly roared back a reply

"Oh king, live for ever!"

"Captives of Carchemish, bow to your king!"

Again a section bowed, and the response was roared back, "Oh king live for ever!"

"Captives of Syria and the lands of Phoenicia...slaves of Nineveh...peoples of Tyre and Sidon...."

"Oh king, live for ever!"

"Of the exiles of Israel and Judah..." the list went on and on, each time a portion of the assembly bowed deeply.

"Of the noble and free peoples of Babylon, those who bask in the glory of Bel's chosen One..."

"Oh king, live for ever!"

"Of his warriors, foot soldiers, bowmen, slingers, charioteers, brave and valiant men in the service of the king..."

A huge formation of troops, stationed to the three sides of the assembly held their weapons in the air and bellowed their reply.

He swung round to face those standing with him on the stage.

"His governors, Wise Men, Seers, Necromancers, Judges, Magistrates, Advisers, Princes, Prefects, Treasurers, Deputies and to all them charged with rule and law in His city,"

The drum beat stopped. There stood Nebuchadnezzar. Magnificent kingly robes, holding a jewelled sceptre and attended by personal servants and bodyguards. He sat down upon the throne. Next to Jon, Naomi snorted.

"Whassup Na?"

"Nothing... well, it's just that he's wearing high heels!"

He was as well. From their vantage point it was easy to see through a gap in the folds of his robe that his sandals were set on a platform, giving him easily three inches extra height. Without them he would have been noticeably short. But they made his walk slow and difficult.

"Shh!" Came the Professor's voice, "pay attention!"

"When you hear the sound of the horn, flute, zither, lyre, harp and all kinds of music, shall you fall down upon your faces and do worship to the great king, the Favourite of Nebo, the Anointed of Marduk, the bright and Morning Star."

Behind him Jon heard the Professor draw breath sharply. "Now wait for it…" he muttered. There was a stirring in the orchestra as the musicians lifted their instruments ready to play.

With a loud blast the trumpets sounded, snarling and strident. After a few seconds the flutes and stringed instruments joined in. The whole assembly fell on their faces, with another roar of "Oh king, live for ever!" The princes and the rest of the governors on the stage who up till now had remained immobile likewise prostrated themselves to the ground.

It suddenly struck Naomi what this reminded her of. It was the Nuremberg rallies that caused the Allies to sit up and take notice of the lunacy of Adolf Hitler. It was all there, the hysteria, the manipulation of the crowds, the repetitive chanting and the impressive display of force. And at the front sat Nebuchadnezzar, impassive, his eyes fixed on middle distance, a king, a god.

Three others immediately on his right in their robes of office were standing upright amidst the sea of bended backs and gazing into middle distance, unmoved and unmoving, their eyes surveying the scene before them. They stuck out like a sore thumb.

The herald who so far had been doing a magnificent job faltered in his tracks, completely thrown. He glared at the three but they seemed unaffected by the situation. For a minute nothing happened, then the spell was broken. The music faltered and died away. A ripple went through the crowd, those

,no were crouched down with their faces cupped in their hands, sensing something amiss craned their necks to look up slightly. The atmosphere of ecstasy was starting to evaporate. Some of the crowd relaxed, others looked fearful. The majority looked on, curious. Nebuchadnezzar and his gods had been affronted!

As they watched two or three of the princes on the stage disentangled themselves from their positions of abjection and approached the king. They approached slowly, warily and even at several paces began to crouch down before him.

"It is as was reported, O great king." Said one. "These Jews, Shadrach, Meshach and Abednego pay no attention to your royal decrees, they do no worship to your royal person, nor do they acknowledge or honour your gods, O king."

Nebuchadnezzar said nothing. He continued.

"We have all enjoyed the privileges you have lavished upon us O king, in your wisdom and generosity. We all come to do you honour as you desire, to recognise your power and might.

Far be it for us to speak against those to whom you have also showed such kindness, O great king. Far be it for us to accuse others in your most majestic presence, knowing that you discern our hearts and minds, and have no need of our advice or counsel.

But we wish to further your glory and majesty, O king, and are zealous against those who would wish to do you hurt or dishonour." His voice rose as he pointed to the men; "Therefore we denounce before your royal throne, these three Jews who openly sow sedition and dishonour to your kingdom, your city and your name!"

It was a good speech, carefully calculated to provoke the king at his greatest personal weakness; his vanity and ego. As it was being given, Nebuchadnezzar betrayed little emotion, as he spoke, his voice was level and measured. He gestured to the three to stand before him. They approached slowly and with dignity, and looked him steadily in the face saying nothing.

"Is this true, Shadrach, Meshach and Abednego?" Shadrach the one on the left was slightly taller but with yellow robes, whereas the other two were dressed in light green. All three had dark hair and beards, but Meshach, the middle one had a noticeably paler complexion. It was not easy under all the beards and robes to guess their ages, but they were somewhere in their mid-thirties, and all clearly in good health.

Shadrach had a neckband, presumably of his office in government, inscribed with cuneiform letters, looking like little arrows pointing here and there. He stood slightly forward of the other two ready to reply.

"Is it true, Shadrach, Meshach and Abednego that you do not serve my gods or worship the image of gold that I have set up?" His tone was soft and conciliatory. He paused, but nobody spoke.

"Now when you hear the sound of the horn, flute, zither, lyre, harp, pipes and all kinds of music, if you are ready to fall down and worship the image I made, very good." The voice hardened, "But if you do not worship it, you will be thrown immediately into a blazing furnace. Then what god will be able to rescue you from my hand?"

There was another pause during which Shadrach swallowed two or three times and moistened his lips. Abednego was visibly shaking, but Meshach remained composed. Surreptitiously his hand reached out to grip Abednego's elbow and give it a gentle squeeze. Finally Shadrach spoke.

"O Nebuchadnezzar, we do not need to defend ourselves before you in this matter.

If we are thrown into the blazing furnace, the God we serve is able to save us from it, and he will rescue us from your hand, O king. But even if he does not, we want you to know, O king that we will not serve your gods or worship the image of gold you have set up."

That was all. They had prepared this little speech and Shadrach delivered it quietly without any hint of defiance or bluster.

Nebuchadnezzar was still playing the nice guy. Composed and still seated he looked steadily at the three before him. Only the tightly clenched knuckles gave him away. He rose slowly from his throne and began pacing to and fro in front of them. Finally he stopped so that his face was just inches from Abednego's.

"Abednego, treasurer to my royal household, keeper of the royal purse and faithful steward." Abednego remained still, but he was shaking. "It is in my heart to do you much good, yea; I desire your promotion over the affairs of Babylon, the city of my glory. For you are a faithful steward over those things I have entrusted to you."

There was no reply. He went on.

"Do not throw your life away, Abednego. Stand aside from these rebels who have seduced you to this grand gesture. For there is but one reward for those who defy the great king!"

Abednego remained silent, staring steadily into space. Jon moved closer so that he was almost besides Nebuchadnezzar. He could see that unlike the others Abednego was petrified. His eyes were glazed, his chest heaving and sweat pouring down his face and staining the collar of his robes. Nebuchadnezzar gestured to the other two to move back; Meshach released his surreptitious hold on his elbow and stood back two or three paces.

"Clever, clever man," muttered the Prof. "Divide and rule. If only one gives way it's a victory for him!"

The look on Nebuchadnezzar's face had changed to one of faint amusement. He sensed a weakening of his prey and was probing his defences. Shadrach and Meshach could only stand by helpless. Now Abednego's body was visibly trembling.

He needed support, but there was no one near to give it. He stood there as the assembly watched enthralled; alone, scared and vulnerable.

"This isn't your idea, is it, Abednego? To defy me so openly?" The king's voice was soft and smooth. "You who have served me so well, yea, and shall serve me well hereafter. You have no desire to question my decrees, and but for these," he indicated the two friends standing by; "you would bow to my image and my gods without question. Yes, I can see by your face that I speak the truth. You can conceal nothing from my gaze."

Abednego was swaying slightly, and incongruously, yawning. "He's close to fainting," the Prof said.

"Bow to me." Nebuchadnezzar's face was again inches from Abednego's. His voice remained soft and gentle. "All these things are yours, but you must bow. Then you can return to your God and ask His forgiveness. But now when you hear the sound of the horn, flute, zither, lyre, harp, pipes and all kinds of music, you shall indeed bow and acknowledge that my gods are gods indeed."

To the side, as if on cue, the musicians picked up their instruments.

There was a scream. A scream of anger, rage and contempt.

"Leave him, leave him you pig! Let him alone!"

"Naomi!" Jon jumped, startled. Suddenly she was on him, her fists pummelling his chest. Although the blows were hitting Jon, they were clearly intended for someone else; her eyes were focussed past him at Nebuchadnezzar as he began to pace slowly around Abednego, looking sideways, snakelike, at him to see the effect of his words. The sight of her affected like this made Jon's blood run cold. The scene froze.

Jon struggled with the headset which had stuck itself to his sweaty skin. It came away with a rush and he felt cool air on his face.

The scene faded. They were alone in the viewing room, no longer in gloom. The Prof had switched the lights on.

Over a cup of tea they argued it through. Naomi felt stupid about her outburst, but as Jon pointed out to her, now she could understand the way in which he had been spurred into beating the senses out of Roger Lord. It wasn't just a memory, prompting him to act; it was a real sense of involvement, of being part of the situation, being there with Gideon and his soldiers, needing to play his part. If there had been a sword in his hand he would have undoubtedly used it.

"I don't know why I did it." Naomi fiddled with the handle on the tea cup. "I just got so angry watching him, so pompous and arrogant, wearing down Abednego like that. I mean, what's the matter with him? He's got the whole of the country bowing to him, but he's got to have everybody, even these three poor Jews as well!"

"They weren't poor," cut in the Prof. "They were influential men, that's what makes the difference."

"No I didn't mean poor like that, I meant, well, he's going to burn them isn't he? Just because they won't bow to his sad golden statue! It just, sort of, overwhelmed me."

"What amazes me," mused the Prof, "is the way this whole viewing system has gone from being crude and bitty, to so absorbingly realistic in such a short time. You two are both the product of the visual age; you know and can distinguish easily between real life and moving images, and yet you are fooled into feeling rain drops, and now you tell me, hot sunshine, and more disturbingly, you are so utterly sucked into events as to ending up trying to be part of the action. Why?"

He glanced at his watch. They had an hour and a half left. Did they want to carry on?

Jon glanced at Naomi she looked tired and drawn. "I'll go back in and tell you about it," he said.

"On your bike!" She retorted, picking up the headset.

The images restarted smoothly, as if there had been no interruption. Ancient Babylon washed, like a tidal wave, over their consciousness. In contrast to the coolness of the viewing room, the heat was suffocating.

Only a few minutes had passed, Nebuchadnezzar had resumed his throne, sceptre in hand waiting for the wretched Abednego to approach to bow down to him. Shadrach and Meshach had been moved further away, they too looked worn down, heads bowed, resigned to the loss of their friend.

The cheerleader had got into his stride again. At his direction many of the crowd were chanting. "Long live the king! O Nebuchadnezzar, live for ever!" But the rest stood silent, watching and waiting as the contest of wills unfolded before them.

Abednego, his head bowed shuffled towards the king.

"This can't be!" muttered the Professor.

Yet there he was, standing before the mighty king, his chin sunk into his chest. A smile played around Nebuchadnezzar's face.

"You have come to bow?"

Abednego said nothing. He remained inert, deaf and blind to the roar of the crowd.

"Oh king, live for ever!"

"Then bow!" It was not a request, but an order, delivered in a voice lined with steel.

Abednego swayed, looking as though he would collapse.

"Bow to your king!"

"Oh king, I cannot!" His face lifted to look directly at the king, and they could see that although grey with shock, a new resolution had crept in. "I cannot bow to your image, or to you O king. I cannot serve your gods or your image. There is but One Living God, the God of Israel. To Him will I bow and Him alone. In all other respects, O king, I am your loyal subject." He stood back, his breath coming in short bursts.

"Well spoken!" breathed the Prof.

The quiet, firm speech caught Nebuchadnezzar just as if he had been struck a blow. The smile vanished, to be replaced with a blank look as realisation sunk in. Then his face blackened with fury. Kicking aside his platform sandals that gave him added height; he leapt at Abednego and delivered a resounding slap with his hand across Abednego's face that knocked him back into the surrounding courtiers. His voice rose to become high-pitched, and virtually inarticulate. Strangled words escaped him. Grabbing Abednego by the robes he pushed and shook him.

"Won't bow, will you? ...filthy Hebrew ...bow to me!" *Slap, shake, slap.* "You will die, you and your rebels!" He released his grip on the captive, whose nose was bleeding profusely. On cue several soldiers moved in and seized the three men. "Bind them!" Nebuchadnezzar walked agitatedly in circles. Anybody in his way he pushed or struck. "Get out of my way!" he screamed. He was verging on madness.

The soldiers pinned Shadrach, Meshach and Abednego roughly to the ground and tied their hands tightly behind their backs. In minutes their fingers turned blue and congested. Nebuchadnezzar harried them, occasionally striking the soldiers to urge them on, his demeanour contrasting sadly with the resigned dignity of the captives. At one point there was spit running from his mouth. All the time, his voice, shrill and disconnected cursed and vilified the three friends.

Firmly secured, they moved towards the river, where for the first time Jon and Naomi saw the furnaces. There were four here and more dotted along the banks of the river. Mud from the river plain was mixed with water and placed in moulds of various shapes and sizes and left in the sun to bake dry. Then they were turned out of the moulds and stacked in these kilns to fire them. Charcoal was burnt in the furnaces to give an even, prolonged heat, then, when cooled the bricks were removed for use in the city.

Of the four kilns nearby, one was alight. In shape it was like a small aircraft hangar, built itself of brick with a chimney on the top to let out the fumes. Around the bottom, vent holes with bricks stacked in front of them controlled the flow of air to the furnace. It was about a third full of bricks but not intensely hot. A dull red glow came from its interior. A captain tentatively approached the raving king to await instructions. "B...burn them!" he spluttered. "Burn all these rebels that will not acknowledge me!"

He turned to the crowd, most of whom were watching in silence the unfolding events. "Why are you standing? Will you rebel also? Will you all burn?" The crowd fell to their knees in waves.

"Make it hotter!" he screamed at the attendants by the furnace. "Burn their bones to powder!"

Frantic activity burst out around the furnace. Dried wood, ready to be burnt to charcoal was brought in piles and hurled into the hot interior, where it immediately crackled into flames. In a matter of minutes the furnace blazed out, and the heat beat on the faces of the attendants and soldiers.

"Hotter, hotter, seven times hotter!" he shrieked as the men stoking the furnace were beaten back by the heat. They ran to fetch more wood. Now the flames roared from the chimney and a pall of black smoke spiralled into the sky.

"Bring them closer," Nebuchadnezzar's was wearing his smile once more, only now it was cruel and sadistic. "Let them feel the heat of their folly."

The heat became ever more intense causing two of the attendants to collapse, which did not please the king much. Yet he urged them on, piling in the firewood until there was very little left. The soldiers holding the captives stood by looking distinctly apprehensive. It was not difficult to see why they were unhappy. The exercise of getting bricks into and out of a cool kiln was an easy one. Getting three captives into this inferno was going to be a great deal more difficult.

"Burn them, burn them now! What are you waiting for?"

There was nothing else for it. After a hasty consultation, six of the beefiest soldiers picked up the captives by their chest and feet and pointed them, like a battering ram, towards the furnace. The glare of the flames reflected in their faces, as they screwed up their eyes. At a signal they gave a rush towards the opening and hurled them in.

It was a shocking sight. Instantly the lead soldiers caught fire, their hair and beards erupting into a blaze of flame. Within seconds their tunics and leather armour, only a short while earlier, smart and polished for a parade of Babylonian armed strength, turned into a fireball. The soldiers shrieked piteously, but carried on by the momentum of their charge rolled on into the furnace. Within seconds their cries were extinguished.

The remaining three soldiers, torn between duty and common sense fared no better. Two, having delivered their burden as close to the door of the furnace as they could, similarly erupted into flames. One staggered off into the crowd which parted to let him pass, the other threw himself into the river, but by the time he reached the cool waters, his injuries were so extensive he was unable to swim. His body bobbed around on the current for a short while, then drifted away downstream. The last soldier continued to push the captive he had been carrying into the furnace, showing a surprising resilience to the flames that engulfed him. Finally he too was overcome and collapsed at the side of the furnace. A stench of burning flesh swept over the assembly. Jon gagged and Naomi clamped her hand over her face.

For a while the increased blaze of the furnace made visibility impossible. More smoke billowed from the chimney and entrance, obscuring the view. Jon turned to see Nebuchadnezzar, suddenly composed again just about to sit back on his throne.

The cheerleader seized the initiative, "To all peoples, all nations, men of every language and region of the earth…"

There was a gigantic roar from the crowd, as everyone; the princes, governors, Wise Men, Seers, Necromancers, Judges, Magistrates, Advisers, Princes, Prefects, Treasurers, Deputies, soldiers, sergeants, commanders, priests, acolytes, captives, slaves, free, young and old, all with one accord threw themselves face down on the ground. On cue the angle of the sun glittered off the image making it blaze out like a fireball. Behind it the smoke of the furnace curled into the sky.

"Oh king, live for ever!"

Order was restored. A triumphant sneer played around the king's lips as he surveyed the vast assembly prostrate before him. King of kings and lord of lords. King for ever. Ruler of mighty Babylon, queen of the nations….

But nobody was paying attention to him any more.

A flare of bright light emanated from the furnace behind the stage. Not a blinding light, but a Presence, that manifested itself in an unearthly illumination. Soft but immensely powerful. A bluish-green Light that dwarfed the flames and made them look, by comparison, as dull candlelight. A Light that made the orange heat of the walls of the furnace seem cool and harmless. The roar of the gases escaping from the heat within became muted to a gentle hiss. Against this awe-inspiring Light even the afternoon sun paled to a watery grey. The cheerleader stopped in mid-sentence, aware that no one was listening any more. A hush settled over the whole congregation.

"Oh no, not again…" a rustle and the sounds of hurried activity from the Professor behind them. "No, no, not now!"

Jon closed his eyes, but the radiance punched through his eyelids. The Light burned deep into his brain, flooding his senses, driving away all other thoughts. A peace came with it, a sense of Strength and completeness. The Light now so intense as to make the walls of the furnace translucent to the brightness within. Shadows cast from within the furnace danced in the sky, four shadows, moving slowly around, hands moving animatedly, as if they were in intense discussion. The shadows flickered in the heat-distorted air, immense and wraith-like. The great assembly had fallen quiet. Without any further prompting, most had crouched, with their faces in the dust, or had their eyes shielded by their hands. The silence was absolute.

"Hold… just a little longer. Please…."

"What's the matter?" Jon screwed his eyes tighter, but still the Light poured in.

"The visual processors are saturated. We're losing it again."

The images were starting to alter. A deep cast developed around the scene, as though the pictures were burning through the screens and could not be erased. Ghostlike shadows began following Nebuchadnezzar as he rose hastily from his throne and called a clutch of bewildered counsellors together.

After a short discussion with one counsellor who seemed to have recovered himself, Nebuchadnezzar made up his mind. Removing his ornate crown, he approached the furnace with his head bared. Although the flames had died down, still it was dangerously hot, yet seemingly unaffected he walked steadily towards the mouth of the furnace and gazed into its blazing interior. None of the figures inside could be clearly distinguished, the Light overwhelmed everything. But with a truly royal stance he stood, watching the four men inside. Finally he reached down; scooped up a handful of ashes from the ground and holding them over his head he let the fine dust trickle down onto his golden brown hair. Then he knelt before the furnace in obeisance.

"Shadrach, Meshach, and Abednego, you servants of the Most High God, come out, and come here."

It was a request, not a command. Moments later the three friends emerged, all three looking fresh and strong, walking easily and confidently. Then Abednego with a gesture of compassion reached out and took Nebuchadnezzar by the shoulders and gently made him to stand.

The images were becoming almost indistinguishable now. Each old picture refused to fade so that new pictures were superimposed. There were seconds left before the system collapsed. It gave them enough time to see Nebuchadnezzar make his way to the front of the stage, ashes still trickling from his hair. Shocked and awed as he was, his voice rang out to the assembly, and was taken up by the relay spokesmen so that every man, woman and child within a matter of minutes was made to know the will of the great king of Babylon.

"Blessed be the God of Shadrach, Meshach, and Abednego, who has sent his angel, and delivered his servants that trusted in him, and have changed the king's word, and yielded their bodies, that they might not serve nor worship any god, except their own God.

Therefore I make a decree, That every people, nation, and language, which speak any thing amiss against the God of Shadrach, Meshach, and Abednego, shall be cut in pieces, and their houses shall be made a dunghill: because there is no other God that can deliver after this sort."

With a grunt the Professor threw another circuit board into the bin to add to the small pile already discarded there. Processors had overheated, drivers had failed and there was no remedy but to sort and discard. "Modern electronic circuits just can't handle the Glory of the LORD!" he reflected. "Ouch!"

He had touched a hot component on the board he was holding. With a flick of his wrist the board went spinning into the bin to join the others.

With unusually good timing the doorbell rang. It was time to go home. Jon sat in the car.

"What have you been burning?" asked Mum, winding down the window an inch or two. "Your clothes stink!"

He closed his eyes. He could not answer.

8

In the end Jon decided that less was more. Even in spite of his frantic editing at the Prof's house, there was still a lot of fascinating information on Terrence Prentice's activities. The night wore on as he skimmed through the material on the DVDs. But one episode caught his eye, and he kept on returning to it.

Prentice was alone. He busied himself checking the room, peering under a lampshade, inspecting the plant in a pot by the window and running his delicate fingers under the table edges. Satisfied with the security he lowered himself into a leather chair and placed his fingertips together. The blinds were half-closed, but the sun shone weakly through them, and judging by the clock on the wall it was the middle of a winter afternoon. Through the window could be seen the tops of tall trees, leafless and skeletal, motionless against the watery sky.

The room itself had high ceilings with ornate plaster cornices and rich burgundy wallpaper; all the appearance of a room in an old country house, but exactly where in the country Jon could find no clues.

Two men arrived together. One who spoke little English, whose appearance was Eastern European. He had an interpreter with him who introduced them. Shortly after an Arabic man arrived with a bodyguard, who, having briefly inspected the room and parted the blinds to peer through the window, removed himself to the corridor

Finally a slightly built man with grey-white hair appeared. He seemed at home with the location and settled himself in the last chair. Throughout the meeting he was to say little-when he did it was to request a clarification of a point. The drawl of his speech gave away his American identity. He appeared to exert tremendous influence over them. Most unsettling were the man's eyes- they were pale blue, as if they were of glass and cold and pitiless. Jon struggled to follow the flow of dialogue-but it was clear that this was one of a series of meetings and no one present wasted time going over old ground. What was apparent to him was that it was something to do with weapons, and not merely guns and ammunition either.

The memory of the man with the blue eyes lingered long after he ejected the copy DVD and placed it gingerly in its case. He wiped all the surfaces clean of fingerprints and sealed up the package with equal care before printing off an address label. It would have to wait until next week; Mum had invited him to London for a day. He would post it then. Somehow the blue-eyed man chilled him to the bone. He hoped they would never meet!

•

The furnace gave off a gentle hiss, like a swarm of bees. As Jon watched, it collapsed in on itself, the brickwork unable to cope with the terrific heat it had endured earlier. The falling brickwork released a stream of sparks into the air, where they danced for a few seconds before dying away.

Someone in the crowd nudged him in the ribs and again, hard.

"Jon Heath, bow to the king!"

"I cannot bow!"

"Jon Heath, you must bow to your king!"

Had these people learnt nothing? What they had seen and heard that day, were they going to have to see it all again?

"I will not bow, O king!"

He felt himself propelled out of the room, down the corridor to the school office. Mrs Lacey, the receptionist was on the phone when they entered, she put her hand over the receiver and had a brief discussion with Mr Lewis (head of maths), then Jon was alone. He waited, confused and shivering for someone to collect him.

"Yes, I see. Yes, that's fine Mrs Heath, I will ask somebody to get his things together and be ready when you arrive. No, he's fine, I think he might be going down with something…. No? Yes, that's not a problem, he's fine here for the moment. I only know what Mr Lewis told me, would you like to speak to him yourself? Yes, I'll put him on."

"Jon!" Mum sounded worried. "What happened?" She sounded distant on the phone.

"Hi Mum." He tried to sound cheerful but he knew it sounded hollow. "Look, I'm fine, I just stood a bit close to the furnace, that's all."

"Jon?"

Sweat was running down from his armpits inside his shirt. Get a grip Jon; you're back at school now. Ancient Babylon is ancient history. "No forget that, Mum, I was sitting right in the sun, and I think I might have got a bit overheated."

"Have you had plenty to drink?"

"I didn't want to drink the water there, it might be contaminated… no... hang on Mum, Mrs Lacey wants to have a word."

Jon sat back in the comfortable chair, listening to snatches of their whispered conversation. "No, I don't know either. No I assure you he hasn't been in the school boiler room, that's strictly out of bounds. … you'll pick him up right away? That's good, thank you Mrs Heath. I'll keep an eye on him."

He was asleep when his mother came in; he woke up briefly but felt the desperate urge to go right back to sleep again.

"No, I'm fine Mum, stop fussing!" Actually, Jon wasn't lying. Friday off school had been an unexpected bonus, but Saturday was upon him and he didn't want to be closeted indoors for the whole day. Mary Heath was working from home for much of that week, but as long as he stayed out of her way there was no problem.

Jon knew he could try for Monday off school too, but that would have meant he couldn't go out to Living Word tomorrow. There were things he wanted to talk about. The whole Timescope thing was getting out of hand.

What had happened Thursday had been weird. The daydream had snuck up on him whilst he had pondered the next problem Mr Lewis had set the class. One minute there was this equation needing solving, the next he was back in Ancient Babylon with the sun through the window playing the part of the dying furnace. Then Mr Lewis, had called his name, but he had been so far out of it that he had not responded at all.

In fact, only the action of being physically removed from the classroom and into the School Office had broken the spell. Even then it took the rest of the evening to really chase away the ghosts of the long past.

Supposing he was going down with flu or some such Jon had been consigned to bed where he dozed the night away. Next day he had been asked me about why the water wasn't safe to drink, or what he had been doing in the school boiler-house, but he feigned ignorance. After all, what else could he say? That he was having seizures? Or that he was off with the Ancient Babylonians?

Naomi answered the door. "Granddad's out." She said briefly, then remembered that she was trying to be nice to him. Jon however didn't notice her snappy tone; his attention was arrested by her face.

"Na! Good grief, what's that?"

"What's what?"

"Around your eyes."

"It's eyeliner. Never heard of makeup before?"

"But it's everywhere!"

She dashed upstairs to her bedroom. Jon heard a yelp and then the sound of the bathroom door slamming. She was ten minutes in there with the water running. When she emerged she peered furtively over the banisters.

"Why did you do that?"

"I... I don't know." She choked, then seeing Jon's smirk; "it's not funny Jon!"

Around her eyes were wide, red circles where she had scrubbed her skin to clean it. The initial effect had been startling, frightening even. But Jon knew instantly where he had seen it. It was the dark heavily made-up eyes of the Babylonian girl about town.

"Naomi?" he asked, not expecting an answer. "What's going on?"

"I don't know," she sniffed miserably.

The Prof wouldn't be back till late, he was told. Jon shrugged. He really did need to talk this time. The hallucination in school had freaked him badly. Still there was Living Word tomorrow. That left a long afternoon with not a lot to do. Tentatively he suggested to Naomi, maybe they could go for a coffee, see a movie?

She shook her head, well into the art of concealing her true feelings by now. She smiled regretfully and made a few unconvincing excuses. She wanted to say; 'what, and end up with something nasty in my drink? Like you did to my Granddad, you swine!'

"A'right." Jon knew excuses when he heard them. He turned to go.

"Hey, Jon!" Jon swung round. George Mere blocked the doorway. He looked more shifty than usual. It was clear from his demeanour that he was here by appointment. Naomi too, looked uncomfortable.

"Hiyuh." Jon grunted. He moved to go past him. He wanted to get away. In a flash the situation had become apparent- George was here to see Naomi. Fine by him. George was a dork, nothing much going on between his ears. He would suit her- she would boss him around, yell at him, give him a hard time; and George, being George would come back for more.

"Let me pass George!" he said quietly.

"Yeah, sure!" He looked flustered. "Look can I have a word?" He grabbed Jon's sleeve.

"Yep, you can have two of mine- get lost!" Jon shook the hand off.

"Oh leave him, George," Naomi disappeared into the hallway and returned with a book in a protective cardboard case. "Jon, Granddad got this for you."

"What is it?"

She smiled benignly, "It's a Bible, Jon. Granddad felt that as you were attending Sunday School every week, you should have your own. It's a King James' version- he always likes to work from that one."

Jon felt the colour rising in his face as he dumbly took the handsome book from her. He was aware of George staring open-mouthed at him. He was also aware that Naomi had never called the Living Word services 'Sunday School' before. Confused he mumbled something and hurried away.

Jon went home, aimless and indefinably irritated. So George was going out with Naomi! Why was he bothered? He wasn't! A couple of times he and Naomi had been just a little more than civil to each other, but then she spoilt things by flying at him. She didn't seem to know her own mind.

Anyway things were looking up! Two girls from the school year above passed him. He couldn't avoid the admiring look the taller one gave him. He heard them giggle as he passed, and distinctly caught the phrase, *"broke his nose..."* There was no doubt about his fame! The Apostles were finished- Jon was glad; he knew it was a matter of time before he stepped too far over the line and was caught. Anyway, he had bigger fish to fry now. In particular a very large oily fish...

In the end he lay on his bed, looking at the Bible the Prof had given him. It was a beauty! It had soft leather covers, a rich smell of quality hide and paper. The pages were thin, but crisp and pure white. Inside the flyleaf was an inscription- the Prof's writing was terrible, but he could just make out the words;

"Create in me a clean heart, O God; and renew a right spirit within me."(Psalm 51:10)

And below the Prof's signature and a date. It was a long time since Jon had read a Bible for himself, in fact even when he attended Sunday School at the Cathedral where his mother used to worship there had never been an emphasis on personal study or reading. But now the Prof never missed an opportunity to urge the youngsters at Living Word to read and study for themselves.

Idly Jon flicked around, just enjoying the clean, new pages, in the same way that he enjoyed getting into a newly-made hotel bed with fresh, pressed linen. A name caught his eye and he stopped surfing; the chapter was in the first book of Kings.

"And Elijah the Tishbite, who was of the inhabitants of Gilead, said unto Ahab, As the LORD God of Israel lives,

before whom I stand, there shall not be dew nor rain these years, but according to my word."

The story was familiar in outline; Jon remembered something about famine and priests of Baal. He felt a thrill of re-discovery as he settled down to read.

"This came for you sir." The waiter turned to go.

"No wait!"

"Sir?"

"Who delivered it? Was it by courier?"

"No sir, I believe it came in the morning post." Catching Prentice's look, the waiter hastened to explain. "It was addressed to us, sir, so naturally we opened the package. This was inside with instructions to give to you in person, sir. Will that be all?"

"Do you have the envelope it came in?"

The waiter padded away, returning shortly with a padded envelope.

Whilst he waited for his laptop to boot up, Prentice examined the envelope. Whoever had sent it had been cautious- very cautious! He approved. London postmark, a collection of anonymous stamps, typewritten label stuck on the envelope. He would send it for fingerprints, saliva samples and any other forensic giveaways, but he wasn't holding his breath. Too many people had handled this baby!

The contents, in a separate plain white envelope were simple; a DVD and a short printed note. It read:

I know you're interested!

Delicately he lifted the note by the corner and put it gently in the padded envelope. Let Fingerprints have a go at that whilst they were about it. Equally gently he lifted the DVD by its edges and slipped it into his computer. With a whir it loaded. Prentice turned his chair about so that the screen faced the wall. Whoever had sent it here had prior notice of his movements; that was clear. Unless the House was sitting late, this restaurant was his abode for Thursday evenings. His table, by a pillar in the far corner, with a panoramic view over the whole dining area and a handy escape exit close by, was where he would spend the evening. Here he could observe, but not be noticed, and here with the willing and expensive cooperation of the restaurant owner he could go about his other business ventures in the privacy he craved.

Two waiters dashed across the room in genuine alarm. Mr Prentice was experiencing health difficulties! He was clutching his chest; his face was grey and sweating profusely. Strong exclamations were escaping his pallid lips. His face reflected the soft glow of his computer screen, and he looked far from serene.

"Is everything all right, sir?" Customers were few that night; one or two had stopped eating and were gazing with interest at the immense bulk of Prentice, scrabbling at the table edge for support. Prentice, with extraordinary presence of mind affected to stagger forward, managing at the same time to snap the lid of his laptop shut. It would need a password to reopen the program now.

"Oh, thank you!" He took a sip of water handed him by a waiter. In his jacket pocket were his tablets. He took two and for a few moments felt calmer.

"Shall I call a cab sir?"

"Oh, no! Thank you but I shall be better in a minute," he gasped, though he knew this was untrue. How could he be better ever again after this? Somebody knew. Somebody had countered all his elaborate security measures with disdainful ease. What this somebody knew could sink him and at least three top-ranking ministers; not to mention unmask a conspiracy that spanned the globe. Interested? He was terrified! Just thirty seconds of damning evidence had unravelled on his screen before he had felt his heart was about to fail. What else did this person know? And how did they know? Beside him the waiters hovered.

"Brandy!" He whispered, loosening his collar and sitting down. "Double!"

"Are you sure that's wise, sir?"

"Of course I am!" He snapped; in his rising panic he felt the need to scream at somebody, anybody. He wanted to yell at the couple watching him from over by the window- 'what are you staring at? Got nothing better to do?' Above all he wanted to dash across the restaurant, scattering tables and chairs and disappear into the night. He fought to control himself… this wouldn't do! Calm down…deep breaths. A warm friendly goblet was pressed into his open hand. Gratefully he gulped a mouthful. The fiery liquid caressed his throat, steadying his nerves. Finally, unwillingly he sat down and gazed at the shut laptop in front of him.

"That you?" he breathed. Stupid question really.
"Sure."
Just one word, but he shivered. Jackman could do that to him through a scrambled telephone line even a continent away. Those blue, blue eyes, innocent as a summer sky but as cold as glacial ice.
"We got problems."
"How big problems?"
"Big enough. We need to talk."
There was a long pause. Prentice could feel those chilly eyes freezing the blood between his eyes. A millipede danced up and down his spine. What hair he had left on his neck prickled. But there was no option. Meet with Jackman he must!

"You look like hell!"
"You won't feel too good when you've seen this!" Prentice pushed the open laptop across to the occupant of the front passenger seat. Overhead there was a roar that shook the car with its elemental force. The 737 climbed steeply into the sky. For a minute conversation was impossible. But so was surveillance.
"Somebody was dirty." He said finally. He had watched ten minutes' worth.
"I assure you they were not! Trace had the place disinfected. They found nothing. Nothing at all!"
"How clean is Trace?"

Prentice quivered. This was the same ground he had covered, night after night, pacing his Whitehall office. Of late a potent mixture of sedatives and alcohol was the only solution to the cold, horrible nightmares that had plagued him since that evening at the restaurant. His job could go hang! For that matter so could his career and reputation; no, these were very much more dangerous waters that he had dipped his small feet into. Hence the man sitting next to him in the car.

Another jet bellowed its ascent overhead; the triumph of brute force and physics over gravity. The car throbbed with its power. He waited until its sound was diminished before he replied.

"That's for you to find out!"

"Who else knows about this? "

"Only you, me and him…or her."

Jackman glanced up. "You've an idea?"

Prentice slid the laptop back on his knee. With an ease borne of hours of minute examination of the clip, he located a section. "See here, and here. And here's another bit. What's the matter with them?"

His companion frowned, "there's something wrong with the whole movie," he mused; "It's kinda localised."

There was a lot wrong with this movie, Prentice agreed to himself. Where to start? The individual frames were so detailed it defied logic. Several times he had digitally zoomed on a feature, only to find out that the detail kept coming. Out of a window was a tree, zoom in on the tree and there was a lone crow, zoom in on the crow and there was a glossy purplish sheen to its feathers; and so on, for each frame. Was the perpetrator just showing off?

But Jackman had hit on the main problem; the viewing perspective was wrong. It had taken him a few viewings to spot it, but now he was sure of it.

"It's the view from my finger," he admitted.

Now even Jackman looked startled. "Miniature camera? Can't be. You'd have noticed."

Prentice told him of his other suspicions. The email messages, the theft of the ring from the driveway. It seemed improbable, but what else was there? If Mary Heath was responsible, she was a cool customer!

If... His lower lip quivered at the prospect. Jackman wrote the name with an invisible stylus on the palm of his hand. *M-a-r-y H-e-a-t-h.* It was his way of committing things to memory.

"I'll do what it takes," he said, as he opened the car door.

Over a ploughman's lunch, Prentice wallowed in remorse. When things had been going well, his conscience had struggled to be heard. Wars needed soldiers, and soldiers needed weapons. Who cared what the war was about? That was the way things were. If he, Terrence Prentice was too hung up to supply the necessary, somebody else would. That was also the way things were. Many missile warheads had limited shelf-life anyway, and former Communist bloc countries and developing Chinese producers needed a ready market for their more elegant hardware. All it needed was an arranger. Someone to put a supplier in touch with a customer and ensure the transaction went smoothly. Somebody with clout in ministerial circles but with an under active conscience. Someone like Terrence Prentice.

Now his scruples were clamouring. Night after night they berated him for his stupidity and greed. His long and greasy past uncoiled itself like a giant serpent, hissing its condemnation at him. Several times he had been violently sick with worry. His food, normally his refuge and consolation had turned to ashes in his mouth. For the first time in years there was slack in his trouser waistband.

In a quiet corner of Hyde Park, the American fished a towel out of the boot of his car and rubbed his face vigorously. It had been a longer run than usual; fifteen kilometres around the park in summer heat. But it allowed him time to think. Time to unclutter his mind of all Prentice's drivel. The man was beside himself with fear; that was obvious from the way he was sweating more profusely than ever. And in his fear he was making mistakes, bad ones. Who in their right mind would open a dialogue to a person who went so far out of their way to conceal their identity? At least it had exposed the weakness in their security, but it left no doubt in his mind that when all this was finished, the quivering Prentice himself would need seeing to. Permanently.

9

Carmel

"Who are you?" The young woman held out her hands in a gesture of supplication. She stood swaying slightly like a delicate flower in a breeze.

"Jon! Jon Heath." Jon looked at her arms; they were painfully thin, the bones showing through at her wrists and elbows. She was clad in a simple robe made of some fine material but it was badly worn, frayed at the knees and collar and heavily stained.

"Who are you?" He asked.

The woman did not answer. The shopping mall was near to closing, the shop assistants leaving in droves to enjoy the warm evening sunshine; a workman in fluorescent overcoat was emptying the bins and a road sweeping machine was sniffing around in the gutter. Close by, the shutters were already down on a jewellery store.

Nobody paid either of them any attention. She turned to gaze at the bakery window; the depleted trays of sandwiches were being removed to be discarded. Jon moved closer.

What hair! It poured down her back like a waterfall, and flowed to her waist. It was this that had caught Jon's eye as he mooched glumly through the city centre. The hair, and the way the girl was staring at the food on display.

She swung round to look at him. As she had been hunched up, she had initially appeared quite small, but drawing herself up to her full height, she had over an inch on Jon. Her face was of a Mediterranean complexion; olive hued, her eyebrows dark, her eyes darker still. Her features were disfigured by some affliction- her skin was loose and had lost its tone, but much worse were numerous lesions and sores that radiated out from the corners of her mouth. In spite of these, Jon was struck forcibly by her loveliness. He couldn't help but to draw in a sharp breath. Next moment the woman had half-stumbled, half fallen forward into his arms.

"*Yon!*" she gasped, "*Yon*, help our people before we all die."

She was so light. He could have picked her up with one arm. But she was like no girl Jon had ever seen before. Her arms and legs were wasted, but her hands were rough as if she had worked as a farmer. She wore no perfume that Jon could detect, but a fresh, outdoor scent clung to her. Jon tried to piece the evidence together- could she be a migrant worker brought into the country to work on fruit farms or the like? If so had she been ill-treated or sick so that her employer had got rid of her?

"Where are you from?" he said in a low voice, as they stumbled towards some seats in the middle of the shopping centre.

She made no reply; her breathing was light and rapid. As Jon sat down she slumped against him. Jon reached for his mobile phone fumbling it from his pocket. It was active, the screen indicating he was receiving a call. As he put it to his ear a high pitched buzzing burst from it, causing him to yank it away.

"That's odd!" he murmured. Unwilling to be distracted from ailing girl he pushed the still buzzing phone back into his pocket. "Wait here", he instructed propping her up against the back of the seat. "I'm just going to call for an ambulance. There's a telephone on the corner."

Her face did not register that she understood him. "Ambulance!" He repeated. "Hospital, help you… yeah?"

As he turned to go she caught his hand. Although the skin on her palms was rough, he could feel her warmth in that touch. She drew him closer and Jon could smell something like acetone on her breath. "*Yon*," she whispered, her eyes closing.

"Yeah?"

"He will come." Her voice was barely a murmur.

"Who will come?"

She smiled. "Elijah, the prophet of the LORD. He will come to save his people."

Jon felt confusion and panic rising in him. "Just hang on, please," he said, breaking free and turning to go once more.

"Yon!" She was sitting forward, reaching for his hand. "The king has sent soldiers to kill Elijah. You must go to him and warn him."

Her appeal was so urgent that in spite of his fear for her, Jon stopped in his tracks. "Where is Elijah? Where can I find him?"

Her outburst had expended what final energy remained. "By the Kishon," she breathed. Then she fell back like a rag doll on the bench.

By the time Jon raced back from calling the ambulance she had vanished. The seat was warm where she had lain, but of the woman there was no trace.

Jon couldn't decide whether the Prof was amused or disbelieving. Whichever it was, his indulgent smile was wearing his patience thin.

"As clearly as I can see you standing there!" Jon started to raise his voice. "I tell you; whoever she was knew all about Elijah and said he'd save his people."

"Perhaps you were talking about the Timescope," suggested Naomi acidly. "Then she picked up on something you said…"

"No I didn't!" Jon ignored the look on the Prof's face. "I said nothing about the Timescope, as if I would! She came out with it on her own."

"And then disappeared into thin air?" Naomi was loving this. "Leaving the ambulance men hunting around for, let me see, a thin Jewish girl dressed in a robe somewhere in Carter Street."

Jon felt he would explode. But the Prof was looking curiously at him.

"Jon, did you say she had funny-smelling breath?"

"Oh go on, that's it, make a joke about that as well…"

"No, just tell me what you said."

"I said her breath smelt of those sweets, pear drops, you know. Why?"

"OK," he sighed, "just supposing she did exist, it's a curious detail. When somebody is starving, their body breaks down fat to survive at first then when those supplies are all used up it goes to work on muscle tissue. As it is digested it gives a smell of acetone on the breath. That's the pear drop smell."

"He already knew that," countered Naomi belligerently. "Just threw it in to make it seem more, er... plausible."

"Are you calling me a liar?"

For a moment Naomi contemplated confronting him about drugging her granddad. But she dismissed the idea. The evidence was too thin, and he would only lie his way out of it and make her look worse.

"No," she said steadily, "but I think you're losing it. Do you really believe that somebody from Elijah's time has arrived in the shopping precinct asking for your help? Maybe she's a manic time traveller who preys on little boys. "

The Professor ignored her venom towards Jon and said ponderously; "Whatever it is, it isn't time travel. That is simply not possible. If what you saw was real Jon then it has to be something more believable than time travel."

The Prof thought again and announced. "Let's just go in at Mount Carmel see if we can spot her shall we? We'll go in this evening," he promised. "If she's there we'll find her."

As he was leaving, Jon heard the door open behind him.

"Jon, what was the time this girl appeared? Do you remember?"

"Easy, five forty-five. The shops were closing."

"Mm! Interesting."

"Why?"

"That was when the Carmel stone started uploading the first images," he said deep in thought, then the door was closed.

With an affected air of stoic grief, Prentice watched the casket begin its final journey into the baked soil. The priest threw handfuls of soil down the hole as he incanted a final benediction. On a nearby tree, a bird, blissfully ignorant of the gravity of the event issued a full-throated warbling song.

Nearby Trace's wife sobbed in the arms of her eldest son. Trace's other two children, another boy and a younger sister stood still, numb with shock at their sudden loss. The eldest son's face was set staunchly; his eyes fixed on middle distance; with his father gone he was the new man of the household now.

"I'm so sorry. If there's anything I can do," Prentice held her gloved hand loosely. Why it was expected to say this sort of stuff at funerals mystified him. Who really meant it anyway?

She nodded but made no reply. Her eyes were myopic with tears. Tonight, tomorrow and for the next few nights she would have relatives around. Medication to take the savage edge off the heartache; visitors, friends and professionals to organise her through the crisis. But eventually the door would close on her loneliness, and a new, unexpected and totally unwelcome chapter of her life would begin.

The casket had been light, Prentice knew. When the plane had plummeted to ground halfway across the Australian outback, by the time the rescue services arrived, the remains of the Trace, the pilot and another passenger on board had been subject to the attentions of dingoes. Prentice had scrutinised the accident report thoroughly, 'Mechanical failure' was the summary, but he knew that anyway. Jackman and his sophisticated outfit covered their tracks too well. How they did what they did amazed him. There was seemingly no part of the globe they could not reach out to. And they had reached out to pluck this internal flight out of the Australian sky with casual indifference.

Back in his office, later that night he allowed himself the luxury of a twinge of sympathy for Trace. Too bad he hadn't known what he was getting into. But his indiscretion and greed had been a nagging tooth, in need of drawing. It couldn't be allowed to fester. And the golden opportunity of this supposed visit to sort out the estate of his deceased sister had been too good to miss.

Deep down, something else troubled Prentice. Trace had had a sister in Australia, and there was evidence she had died very recently. All of this was on file. So either he had used the facts as convenient cover for his underhand activities, or a mistake had been made...

No, he decided, Jackman might be ruthless, but he was thorough. If he had reason to believe Trace was on the make, then that was where the matter rested.

'Bong!'

The laptop softly alerted him to an incoming message. It roused him from his meditations. He sat forwards in the chair, feeling the old familiar feeling of a full stomach and a fine brandy. Then he froze.

'I know too much about you now.'

'This can't be right!' Jon thought. His Internet research on Carmel had yielded images of green fields, lush hillside slopes and vineyards stretching into the distance. Well-irrigated landscapes that gave Carmel its name, "Vineyard of God."

But their feet sank into deep, gritty dust that deadened each footfall. The dust hung in the air, settling like a cloak on their skin and clothes. Above them the sun pressed down on their shoulders, scorching their flesh with its savage intensity.

There was no greenery; no vineyards, olive trees, grasslands, fertile plains and wild flower strewn uplands. Not a bird moved in the air, nor animal crawled in the dirt. As far as they could see was greyish-brown dust and rock, the latter reflecting back the sun's heat with vengeful ferocity.

"I assure you Elijah's somewhere in the area; either that or he will be very soon." The Prof was getting impatient with their scepticism. "Don't forget, three and a half years of famine isn't going to leave much standing."

Despite his assurances, he, himself struggled to comprehend the change wrought by the famine in an area of Israel he knew well from numerous visits.

"I'm going to find her!" Jon felt light-headed with the heat and his throat was swiftly caking up with the cloying dust. "I guess that's the river down there?"

Just a thin ribbon of silver wound across the plain below.

Just as Jon was about to set off down the slope, Naomi called him back. "Look over there, somebody's up here anyway." Jon gazed in the direction of her outstretched finger.

"Where?"

"No over there... up in the sky!" A thin column of smoke curled upwards into the brassy sky. There was no breeze to disperse it. Jon shrugged and followed her.

Rounding the rocky outcrop they spied a small company; a man who was in the act of dismounting a scrawny horse, two soldiers sweating heavily, one was holding the bridle of the horse; and an older man kneeling in the dust. In the distance their faces were not clear. Then a fifth figure crouching by a small campfire straightened up. A rush of hair fell down her shoulders to her waist.

"That's her!" Jon almost shouted.

"Shhhh!" Naomi dragged him into the cover of the rocks. Then realising her mistake let go his arm.

All the same they approached cautiously, using the rocks as cover. The horseman they soon identified as King Ahab. He was handsome, a strong face and a lean frame of an outdoor, athletic man. The soldiers likewise looked fit and muscular, in stark contrast to the older man and the girl. They both showed signs of wasting and exhaustion. Over the campfire was a small vessel in which something was cooking, and from this the older man, clearly a servant was ladling some kind of thin stew onto plates and distributing them to the king and his guards.

The king scanned the area around them, his face creasing into a sulky scowl. Then turning to the older man he demanded,

"Is this the place of which he speaks?"

"My lord. You have spoken with the prophet? What does he com... What does he desire?"

"He commands me to call the priests and prophets of the gods, and all the people to this place."

"For what reason, my lord?"

"He did not say. I suppose it is some contest, his God against our gods."

"And who knows of this?"

The king growled. "By now most of Israel know. News travels fast even in these troubled times. Who is he to command me as a man commands his slave? He has troubled Israel; I should put him to death before all the people."

The servant paused, studying his hands, thinking carefully about what to say.

"My lord, he wishes you to summon the priests to this contest; would it not be wise to summon all the prophets of our lady Jezebel as well? The greater show of strength will be the greater glory when Baal speaks through them. The people will not forget easily that Baal is lord."

The king looked at his servant for a few moments. "That would be to leave the land blind and deaf. Is this what you want?"

"Of course not! My lord speaks with the wisdom of the gods," The servant turned to the girl; "Baalaomi, bring water for the king!" He was rattled and nervous.

She hoisted a jar and poured some water into the cup. The water was dirty, and the king's face showed more displeasure. However he drank it and stood to leave.

"Of course," said the king, as he turned to his retinue, "if Elijah does not get to this place, then that would be much better for us all. The people will know that he is a coward and a fraud, and the matter will rest."

"My lord," replied the servant, "what you say is true. When I spoke with him, we were in the plains to the south. He said that he would ascend this hill by night, so to be ready for the people when they arrive. If you have a guard ready to receive him there, then, as you say, he will trouble us no longer."

The eyes of the king shone. "Well said!" He exclaimed. "Are you sure of this?"

"As sure as I can be, O king."

"Then it shall be so. I will ride to my guard now and command an ambush for this old fool."

"Very good, my lord." The servant bowed. However the king had not finished with him yet.

"You have spoken with her?" He inclined his head towards the girl. "She will make ready for the marriage?"

The servant writhed. Beside him the girl hung her head. Finally he spoke.

"My lord, the mouthpiece of the gods does us such honour. We are unworthy of this status. We are not a family of esteem amongst the tribes of Israel. We cannot…"

"What is this babble Baalshalish? Your family have been held in honour amongst our nation for generations. Your service to the royal household is well-known. It is a fitting union for her and the High Priest!" The king's voice was harsh to add to his rudeness. "What says the damsel?"

Jon recognised her voice. She spoke clearly but with an effort. But her manner was demure, as if she had just been deeply flattered.

"My lord, the king; I too consider myself unworthy of this great honour you see fit to bestow upon your handmaiden. The great mouthpiece of Baal has many wives and mistresses, and many more of the daughters of the land would much more fittingly grace his household. I cannot allow the poor reputation of my family to become a disgrace to his honour and person."

The king brushed her aside. Swinging himself up into the saddle of the horse he glared down on the pair. "The High Priest has expressly desired to have you. It is the will of the holy gods. Your family is influential and greatly respected; your joining together will establish the true worship for once and for all." The tone of voice forestalled any further argument and with a flurry of dust the king and his guards were gone.

"They're a bunch of crooks!" exclaimed Naomi.

"Don't judge by appearances," replied the Prof. "I have more than a fair idea who he is for a start."

"Who then? He seems to be out to get Elijah."

"Obadiah, that's who. In the days of Ahab, the king's trusted Governor renders apparently loyal service to the king, whilst squirreling away the remaining faithful prophets of the LORD, right under Ahab's nose. He's living a double life, poor chap. It was to him that Elijah appeared at the end of the drought to call the people to Carmel. No, he's good and no mistake. Hang on... they're still talking."

The man and his daughter watched until the king and his company was out of sight. Then his daughter turned on him.

"Father!" Her eyes were flashing with anger, "Must you call me by the filthy idol's name? Command me as a slave, if you wish, but I can't stand bearing the name of his unclean idols!"

"Hannah." The man placed his arm around her thin shoulders and pulled her close to him. "You will always be God's Gift to me. But the king has commanded that all who make mention of YAHWEH, the God of our fathers, to be burnt. There are many who depend on me for their lives. Do not chide me because I have to follow his wishes."

The girl began to sob, her thin, wasted body shaking with fear and emotion. "How long will this continue, father?"

"Take heart, Hannah." He savoured the illicit name. "The messengers have set out to summon all Israel to this place. Then Elijah will show who the God in Israel is. In the meantime, you must go to your uncle in the village and instruct him to tell Elijah not to go by the way of the South. Instead he must cross the Kishon and ascend from the northern slopes. But first my child, you must eat. You are thin, and need nourishment. There is some food left, it is poor but will help."

"How can I eat when our people suffer hunger?" she objected. Nevertheless she took some of the stew, swallowing it with difficulty.

On impulse Jon set off after her. She stumbled down the rocky track, pausing to rest by a rocky outcrop.

"Hannah!" The dust choked his throat, she didn't hear him. He drew closer. As she saw him, her eyes grew wide with astonishment.

"Yon!" she gasped, rising to her feet and swaying slightly with the effort. *"Yon,* is this really my lord come to me? Do you stand before me?" As she spoke she reached out her hand, the fingertips extended tentatively to touch his face.

"No," she decided; "it is too long since anything so good has happened to me. I must be still dreaming."

Jon seized her hand and held it firmly, squeezing her long, roughened fingers.

"No, Hannah, you're not dreaming, I am here, I have come to find you. You disappeared last time; I went for help but you..."

A remote look crossed her face. "When I saw you before, my lord, I thought it was a dream. We were in a strange land. A land of plenty. A land of rock and towering buildings where the sun is gentle. You were kind to me then, *Yon,* you helped your servant when she could no longer stand."

"Yes, that's right! It was in Carter Street shopping centre. You were looking at the food in the shop window, then I took you to a seat, but..." The look on her face showed she wasn't following this.

"Is Carterstreet your land? It is a strange land, *Yon,* nobody spoke to me. Everyone was strangely dressed, they rushed around. I felt very alone there. I was weak and faint, then you came to me." A radiant smile broke through her confused expression; "How came you here, my lord?"

A dozen explanations ran through Jon's mind. What could he say? 'I'm here from three thousand years, or whatever it is in the future? An incredible machine called the Timescope has read all this information off a piece of rock and now I'm here talking to you?'

He shivered. This was getting weirder by the minute. He stared at her. She was so beautiful! He wanted to put his arms around her again. What must she have looked like before famine left its calling cards on her person? She grew aware of the intensity of his gaze and flushed slightly. Jon felt like saying, 'next time you're in my time, will you agree to stay there?' Instead he said;

"Elijah will be here tomorrow. Hannah, he will show, OK?"

"Oh-kay? What speech is this?" Nevertheless relief showed all over her face. "My lord does not speak as my people do. And how knows my lord these things? Are you a prophet?"

"Don't call me lord, Hannah." Jon felt uncomfortable with it. "Just call me Jon, OK?"

She gazed at him steadily. "Are you a worshipper of these abominations of the Zidonians?" Jon shook his head. "Then you serve the Living God. Therefore you are my lord. Oh...kay?" She stumbled over the strange expression, then started swaying again and coughed; "Oh!"

She leaned over and with a huge sob vomited the recent meal into the dust.

It was an event that stood out from all the other incredible things Jon had seen so far in the Timescope. More upsetting than the slaughter of the Midianites, more moving than the resolute faith of Daniel's friends- she was very ill; her body heaved and shuddered as her stomach rejected the unfamiliar food. Jon caught her and held her gently, as convulsions shook her slender frame. But there was an inherent dignity about her, even wasted as she was. Whatever her stated opinion about her family and background, she had the bearing of a princess.

No planes bearing Red Cross parcels or relief supplies would fly these skies for many tens of centuries yet. No television camera crews would focus on her desperate eyes, or show the mounting numbers of fresh graves appearing outside each village and town the length and breadth of the land. No international appeals would raise funds to help their desperate plight. Neither was flight an option, the surrounding countries cared little for refugees of any origin. Most likely they would be enslaved or slaughtered if they sought sanctuary. As for the king who was supposed to care for the people of Israel, his top priority was the welfare of his war-horses.

"Hannah!" Jon helped her to sit back down again. "Hannah, you must eat slowly. Drink plenty of water, but only small mouthfuls of food. Do you understand?"

She leant against him, her head turned slightly so that her face was towards him. Jon could have looked at that face for hours. She was impossibly pretty. No wonder the High Priest, whoever he was, wanted her.

"*Yon,* my lord," she smiled slightly as if amused. "My people die, family by family, day by day, year after year. We have forsaken the Living God, and He has forsaken us. Should I eat and live, and be united to the mouthpiece of Baal, or should I die and sleep amongst the tombs of the faithful?" She closed her eyes, and leaned her head on Jon's shoulder.

Jon put his arm around her thin shoulders and held her close. He tried to estimate her age, but the usual clues he was familiar with were absent; hair style, dress, friends and so on. He guessed from her height she was about eighteen or nineteen.

Sitting there, Jon felt a slight tug around his head and face and a whiff of cooler air in his scalp. The girl was almost asleep. He could see the soft downy hair along her arms contrasting with the blackness of her long tresses.

"Hannah!" Jon shook her gently. "Hannah, please wake up. I'll help you home." The thin form had relaxed further.

"Hannah, it's time to go. Come on!"

The sun above had lost its heat. Its light dwindled to a number of soft points around the wall. The dust hardened to wooden boards and the mountain landscape pixellated and dissolved.

"Jon, are you with us?" Naomi's face was out of focus, Jon's pupils; diminished to tiny points to cope with the glare of the sun struggled to dilate enough to see in the dimmed light of the viewing room. The cushion he had been holding slipped to the floor. Beside him the Prof was holding the headset, his face a study in bewilderment.

Two whole minutes after the Professor had removed the headset from him, Jon had continued to lovingly stroke the cushion, finally urging it to get up and meet him tomorrow. It would have been funny if it had not been for the terrible distance in his eyes, a displacement not only of location, but encompassing many tens of centuries in time.

"Remind me to set up an error retrieval log." Professor Avery murmured to Naomi when Jon had gone. "It's the only way to really find out what's going on."

Prentice was grey when they met. His normally-immaculate exterior was a thing of the past. His breathing came fast and heavy and his speech was slurred.

"Where're the files I asked for?" Jackman demanded. Listlessly Prentice pushed his laptop across the scratched and stained coffee table of the safe house. Then he sat or rather fell back on the imitation leather settee with something like a sob.

Several times he had contemplated staggering up to a policeman and begging to be arrested so that he could relieve himself of this immense burden of fear and guilt. Earlier that same day he had surveyed the oily-grey waters of the Thames wishing he had the courage to heave himself over the parapet and end it all in their comforting embrace.

From what the American could make out the job had backfired, they had wasted the wrong man. Tough on Trace, but that didn't concern him much. What worried him was the state Prentice was in. His hard blue eyes scanned the grainy pictures. *'Jon Heath, Jon Heath'* he muttered to himself over and again. Next picture, group of youths heading away from an incident, one highlighted with a light blue ring around his face, long hair, clear profile.

'Jon Heath!'

He lingered over the clip of a car windscreen being smashed. He zoomed in on the boy's face; caught full on by the street camera. *'Jon Heath!'*

"Some kinda street punk?"

How could a teenage yobbo have done this? How could Mary's loutish son have the resources to mount such a sophisticated surveillance coup as the one that had just happened to him? It was unthinkable!

Deep down, however, something was starting to click. Since Jackman's discoveries pieces were crawling into place. Unwillingly the puzzle was coming together. Why not Jon Heath? Well above average intelligence in both his parents.

Dad was a chancer with an eye for a quick profit too. His wedding ring, apparently the source of the damning video files; well that went missing at the Heath's family home. Or at least that was the last time he had seen it. Come to think of it, wasn't Jon there too? At the meal table, eating with them, behaving for all the world like a dutiful son! Now that wasn't the Jon he knew either.

He laughed weakly; it was starting to seem obvious. One unguarded moment and Jon could have copied his private email address from his mother's computer. His gang contacts were on hand to break into his car, diverting any suspicion away from Jon himself.

He sat up. The neat greyish head was bent over the computer. "You're right. It's him!" he said with certainty. "I don't know how, but I'm sure it's him!"

The impassive eyes drilled into him, boring through his skull. But this time he held Jackman's gaze.

"No sudden moves, OK? No…"

"Killing?" Jackman supplied for him.

"We need to know how he did this." The effects of the alcohol were receding from Prentice's brain. "We can't let this slip, do you hear?"

Jackman chuckled softly. "Oh I hear you. I hear you good and clear." He punched the off button on the laptop. "OK, I need to know as much as you. And I will find out what this little punk knows. And how he knows it."

His voice became so soft; Prentice had to lean forward to hear him at all.

"But when I've found out, I'll decide what to do with him – OK?"

10

Thousands of people streamed towards them from the plains below. From this distance they resembled ants pouring into an anthill. They arrived from every direction, thin, ragged and bewildered. Ahab, the king was there too, his lip curled in a childish pout. It would seem that no news of any unfortunate mishap overtaking Elijah had reached him yet. His household and guards assembled around him, and again the contrast between them and the gaunt, shabby people was striking. He glared at the assembly, searching the sea of faces for any sign of the turbulent prophet. Seeing none, he strode back to a flat rock further up the hillside and sat down. Jon and Naomi heard several barked orders at his bodyguard and staff, none of whom were having a good time today.

The spot for the confrontation was ideal. Behind them the highest point of this part of the Carmel range sweltered in the unrelenting heat. But on this shoulder between two peaks, the ground formed a natural, massive amphitheatre, with a flat central region as its focus. In the middle strewn about the ground a scattered pile of stones, and by these were tethered five bony bullocks, lowing occasionally and searching the thin soil in the hope of finding a blade of grass.

"Is that her?" Naomi with her back to Jon was watching even greater crowds flocking up from the valley below. Jon dashed over to her side.

"Yeah," there was no mistaking her, even amongst the multitudes. Her father was over with the king, but Hannah had a little lad by the hand. From the shape of his face it had to be her younger brother. He looked weary and not a little scared. Jon moved closer. The child had dark eyes, like his sister's; for a few seconds he fixed them on Jon, blinking curiously. Then he turned back to her.

"Shh!" she knelt down in the dust before the child. "Whatever happens you must stay with Micah, do you hear?" She cupped his little fist in her hands and kissed it gently. "Now then, be brave." Then she pressed her brother's hand into the hand of a tall lad standing close by.

With a thundering announcement of drums, a huge company of black-robed men poured down into the arena from the slopes above. They weaved as they came, their robes flapped and fluttered like ragged ravens.

Naomi laughed nervously. "They look like Goths!" she said.

They did too. Their robes were black, their faces had been whitened but the eyes had a black substance around them making them look like deep pits. The contrast of the eyes with the overall impression of shadow was sinister.

"Don't get ideas, Na," Jon murmured.

"Shut up!" she retorted.

Amongst the priests, there were two who stood out. The one Naomi had spotted was certainly the high priest of Baal. His robes were as black as coal, but he was adorned with amulets, jewels and bracelet charms. He was extraordinarily tall, at least six inches above the rest. His lean body was grasshopper-like in its aspect, but nevertheless lithe and active. Like the king, the priests looked distinctly better-fed than those they ministered to. The other was shielded by many of the other priests, she was a wizened little woman hunched over a bowl in which she was grinding some leaves to a paste. Now and then she would spit, sometimes in the bowl, and mutter horrible-sounding incantations, all the time her muscular arms flexed as she ground away at the contents of the vessel. After a while she called the high priest to her and placed a pinch of the substance in his mouth. He chewed and thought for a few moments. "Make it stronger!" He pronounced at length. "We have much to do this day."

As soon as the High Priest had led his entourage down the slope, he started scanning the crowds. Jon knew he was looking for her. The High Priest was selecting men and sending them out to comb through the throng. Hannah could not remain concealed long.

"Hannah!" he hissed, "over here!"

"My lord!" She was delighted to see him. Her face which had been pensive now broke into a radiant smile.

"Hannah, get away from here, at least get out of sight. The High priest is after you." Behind him Jon could hear raised voices, somebody called out; "she's over here!" Beside him the crowds surged.

"No my lord, it is not the time to flee. Too long have we cowered before these polluted ones. Too long have we worshipped Yahweh in secret. It is time to defy them openly."

"But he'll kill you!"

"Then I must die. It is all he can take from me."

Men were surrounding her, pulling her roughly into the open. Jon cried after her;

"At least wait for Elijah!"

"Shalom, *Yon!*"

The High Priest's displeasure showed itself in every gesture. He did not rebuke the rough treatment of the woman dragged before him. Jon threaded his way through the crowd to where she stood upright, with her chin lifted slightly.

"So Baalaomi, I have to draw my wife by force? Will you hide like a whipped dog?" He spoke quietly, standing close to her, invading her space.

She made no answer. He went on, a cruel smile spreading across his painted face. "Do not think I need your agreement; oh no, my rose of Carmel. The king has already agreed on your behalf."

"You cannot have what is not given gladly." She hissed back. "And my will is my own on this matter."

He laughed softly.

"Can I not? Then perhaps this will bend your will!" The Priest placed a finger to his lips and made an exaggerated gesture of sharing a secret. "Do you really think I am ignorant of what your father is doing? A prophet of the forbidden One turns up here one minute teaching the forbidden things, then 'Pff!' he is gone the next! And your respected father has no idea where he has gone!"

He chuckled. "What a fine dowry that would make, to force him to reveal where these prophets are and slay them on our wedding day."

Hannah lapsed back into defiant silence. But the news of his knowledge of her father's activities had shaken her. Her face had gone white and she bit her lip to control her nerves.

"Baalaomi," his voice changed abruptly. Now it was conciliatory, almost kind. "What could we do together for our nation? Your family commands respect, many look to you for a lead. We can win the waverers to Baal; Israel will be strong once more amongst the nations of the earth. With you beside me all this would be complete. What is more," he surveyed her wasted figure, pathetic in its slenderness, "at least in the temple you would be able to eat well. And of course," he finished, "I would be so much better disposed towards your father's treachery!"

"My name is Hannah! Hannah bath-Obadiah, the servant of Yahweh." Hannah raised her voice so that the prohibited names were clearly audible. "I will not submit to your demands," she cried, "neither will I teach the people to corrupt themselves yet further. I defy you and your abominations and your unclean food; the Prophet Elijah is coming to this place and he will show you that the LORD Almighty, he is the GOD in Israel."

Around her, heads were turning at the mention of the forbidden names. The High Priest's face became stony.

"Very well, Hannah bath-Obadiah. Of course, I should kill you for your insistence on your ancient name, as indeed you probably wish me to. But what a shame that would be to destroy you in a moment when I can destroy you slowly." Once again he bent close to her, his face within inches of her own.

"Can you see yourself years from now, the lone voice of your God, friendless, unloved, forced to bear my children who will grow up to worship the true gods. How will you weep as if you were a barren woman for your offspring who will swear by the name of the lady Ashtoreth and follow their father in his duties to the lord Baal. I see you will make an agreeable task for me. Breaking you will be difficult but I will take great pleasure in the months and years ahead."

"I will kill myself long before that," she was shaking either with fear or anger.

"I think not!" The arrogant smile showed he knew his quarry. "You are a fighter. You will live to fight me all of the way, if not for your own sake, then for the sake of your people. My conquest of you will be all the more rewarding."

He turned away. "Watch her," he said to his soldiers, "not that she's going far. Make sure she is set where she can witness the humiliation of the Prophet and the end of all her hopes."

"Yon!" She said in astonishment as Jon appeared beside her. "How did you get past the guards?" They had her penned in a natural enclosure formed by the rocky crags; two soldiers lazed by the entrance.

"I…I don't sort of belong here," Jon stumbled. "They don't see me properly."

The Timescope was playing still more strange tricks on them. During their previous encounters in Babylon, a certain amount of tactile sensory input was felt in the simulated landscape – the rain, smells, heat and so on. But they took it for granted that their existence was ethereal; they were ghosts in the machine, at liberty to drift around and through objects at will. This was no longer the case. No longer could Jon wander through people or things. The stones felt solid, the dust gritty between his toes. Moreover the crowds jostled him, as he worked his way through them. But although men might glance at him, it was if though they did not register his existence. Children, like Hannah's little brother were the most likely to fix their inquisitive gaze on him. But even they turned away unperturbed after a few seconds.

"You are here," she sighed. "I would it were in happier times, I would have taken you to my village to meet my family. They would approve of you, I know."

'No they wouldn't,' he thought. 'Not if they knew what I'm really like.' Her straightforwardness disarmed him. She liked him, and she took no pains to conceal it. She was without coyness or shyness with him.

"Elijah's here!" he heard Naomi's excited shout. A muted roar ran through the crowds.

"My lord! You must go. Come to me and tell me what he does." She caught his hand, her face shining with almost childish glee.

"Of course Hannah, but can you not see from here better?"

"Famine robs us all, *Yon*. It takes a father here, a brother there, a son or a daughter…"

"Yes, but…"

Her eyes were wide open, but he realised she had difficulty following his movements at any great distance.

"It took my eyes, *Yon!*"

The crowd parted to let Elijah pass through, and some people jostled him angrily. Others shouted abuse, but the most part watched him, their faces impassive; wide eyes and aching bellies as he went to meet his opponents. As he moved closer to the Prophet, Jon threw a backward glance at Hannah. She was sitting in the dust with her head between her knees. Was she feeling faint, or just crushed by the turn events had taken? He would return to her as just as soon as he could.

Elijah was awe-inspiring. Like the high priest of Baal, he was tall, but he was much broader, with a huge beard that shook when he spoke. In his hand he held a staff which he planted firmly before him with every stride he took. There was no refinement about him, his robe was of coarse camel hair, his hair straggly, his features gaunt, and he looked as if he were used to sleeping rough. As he advanced into the centre of the stage, Ahab moved forward to meet him, his face a mixture of apprehension and hate. Elijah glanced at him once then turned his back on him, facing round to the people. It probably wasn't a snub, but Ahab's face became livid. But before he could make any move, Elijah addressed the people.

"How long will you limp between two opinions? If the LORD be God follow him: but if Baal, then follow him."

It wasn't a speech, it was a roar. With his considerable lung-power and the natural acoustics of the place, his voice carried far and wide. There was a silence. A few people muttered amongst themselves, then fell quiet.

"How long will you limp between two opinions? If the LORD be God, follow him: but if Baal, then follow him." Same words, only heavier emphasis on the 'ifs.' Still there was a deafening silence. More people were arriving by the minute but their presence did not affect the uncanny silence.

Moments later there was a surge behind, and the whole retinue of the priests of Baal started pushing their way forward, with the high priest looming at the front. He was going to try to seize the initiative from Elijah, but clearly Elijah wasn't going to let him. He gave them barely a glance before turning once again to the people.

"Behold I," he roared, "even I only, remain a prophet of the LORD," his hand threw out a gesture that included all those behind him; "but Baal's prophets are four hundred and fifty men."

The High Priest drew level with the Prophet of the LORD. His voice likewise was considerable, but it lacked the sheer power of Elijah's foghorn. "Baal has been challenged!" his voice was heavy with disbelief. "Our lord Baal is greatly wrath with his people. He withholds the harvests, your children die, your women miscarry, the streams turn to dust. All these things come from Baal to show his burning anger. Why?" His hand shot out and pointed to Elijah. "Because we suffer this false prophet to live amongst us! We must destroy this impostor or the land will be destroyed because of him."

Whatever effect was intended, it failed. Nobody moved. A few soldiers surrounding the king started moving down the hill towards Elijah, but they too looked uneasy. Then from the behind came a shout,

"Baal must answer the challenge!"

Jon swung round. "Hannah!" he cried, "don't provoke him!" She took no notice. She had pulled herself upright and using the rock as support was yelling her taunts at the black-robed figures below. For a few seconds there was calm- had the priests been quick enough they could have started chanting; her lone voice was insufficient to be heard for long.

But before they could, someone in the crowd repeated the heckle.

"Baal must answer the challenge!" Then far to the right, "answer the challenge, answer the challenge, answer the challenge." It swelled fast into a mob- chant.

Elijah stepped forward again, and with his hands called for silence.

"It is well spoken," he cried. "I only, remain a prophet of the LORD, but Baal's prophets are four hundred and fifty men. They have brought sacrifice to do at this place, let them do sacrifice at this place."

He went on, "Let them therefore give us two bullocks; and let them choose one bullock for themselves, and cut it in pieces, and lay it on wood, and put no fire under: and I will dress the other bullock, and lay it on wood, and put no fire under:"

He paused to let this sink in. It was absolutely fair so far. Who could object?

"And call on the name of your gods, and I will call on the name of the LORD: and the God that answers by fire, let him be God."

The high priest looked uneasy, he glanced at the king, but no help came back from that quarter. He moved forward, "Who is this man to command Baal?" he began.

There was an uneasy stir in the crowd. From where Jon stood he could see ripples of indecision spreading across the assembly. Would they agree to the contest? Or would years of indoctrination in the worship of Baal wash back over them?

Hannah was on her feet again. Propping herself against the rocks and unconscious to the vitriolic glares from the High Priest, she gathered her strength and bawled out again;

"It is well spoken, let Baal plead!"

This time the crowd cottoned on quicker, in minutes there was a roar like a football crowd in full voice, "well said; let Baal plead!" There could be no doubt the suggestion had caught their imagination. Elijah stood there, aware of their dislike of him, and his low standing in popular opinion, but enjoying this rare moment of empathy with the massed ranks of Israelites gathered here. After a while he lifted his hands and the crowd fell silent, hanging on his every word. Deliberately now he turned to face the priests.

"Choose you one bullock for yourselves, and dress it first; for you are many; and call on the name of your gods," everyone present must have heard the roar of his voice as he threw down the final, deadly instruction; "but put no fire under."

The High Priest licked his lips nervously, but one glance at the crowd showed him that there was no escape. Baal was sacrificed to with offerings made by fire, the length and breadth of the land; the people were familiar with this procedure, as indeed those who could remember the true worship of YAHWEH would also know that He was worshipped by sacrifices offered by fire. It was a point of agreement, and neither god would be offended by such an offering.

He made no immediate reply to the turbulent prophet of the LORD. Instead they went into a huddle, debating furiously about Elijah's proposal. Jon edged closer, until he was able to overhear their discussion.

"Hannah!" Jon raced back up the dusty slope to where she was penned. "Hannah, they will accept the challenge!"

She raised her face from between her knees to look at him. Her voice was calm "My lord," she said, "they have no choice."

"But Hannah, they're going to cheat! They will bring fire to the sacrifice. They'll make out it was Baal's doing. Once the fire is lit they won't even let Elijah try."

She remained composed. "My lord," she murmured, holding out her arms.

Jon helped her to stand. She stumbled to the entrance of the enclosure. The guards moved to block her way.

"Call my father!" She demanded. The soldiers shook their heads. "High Priest's orders my lady," one apologised.

She moved right up to him. "There will be no High Priest by this time tomorrow. He and his filthy brood will be destroyed by the hand of the true Prophet of the Living God."

A look of genuine concern spread across their faces. "Orders are orders, my lady," said the other.

"These are my orders," she snapped back, "and I will hold you to account tomorrow if you do not obey them. You," she turned to the first guard, "you will summon my father here to me."

The guards glanced at each other, then the second guard gave his colleague a gentle push down towards the centre of the arena to where the king and his retinue were gathered. The guard set off at a run.

Jon helped Hannah back into the shade- the sun was fierce now and the heat building up relentlessly. His concern for her grew; each outburst was sapping her strength, even for the short time it took for the guard to return with Obadiah, she had seemed to drift off to sleep.

"Ba- Hannah. What is it my daughter? Are you unwell?"

"No, I am Oh-kay." She smiled at Jon. "My father, there are devices afoot to deceive our people."

Briefly she outlined what Jon had told her. It was possible, Obadiah agreed. He had witnessed worship of Baal where sacrifices had mysteriously exploded into flames. They were practised in the art of deception and illusion, and even here, in full view of the multitude, nothing could be taken for granted.

"It would be a disaster if they lit their sacrifice," he decided. "Leave it with me- there are many soldiers and influential men here with us who will ally themselves even now. Elijah has commanded me to gather a force and be ready to pounce upon these heathen when he gives the signal. I will inform them of this new strategy and station them so that it will be impossible for the fire to be put to the pyre."

Suddenly his composure broke; he threw his arms around the thin girl.

"Oh Hannah, Hannah, firstborn of my family," he choked. "They have told me of your defiance of the High Priest. There is no going back now, if Elijah does not bring the people back to the LORD then…"

"Then we are all dead." She finished. "But, father, were we not already dead, dead in this corrupt nation, dead to our God?" She smiled at him, her eyelashes wet with tears; "but we have not wavered, have we? No, not, you, me, or any of our family. The good LORD knows we have not." Jon felt shivers run down his spine. As her father hurried away, she settled back down in the shade. Soon she was asleep again.

"Urgh! That's disgusting!" Naomi cried. Jon followed her gaze.

The priests had built an altar around a flat stone. They had selected the best of the bullocks for their offering and the high priest had offered a weird prayer to Baal in dedication. Some of the things said were downright embarrassing; it was clear, if they didn't already know it, that Baal, and his mistress, Ashtoreth were fertility gods. The prayer was voiced by the high priest with responses by a number of the other worshippers.

Now as Naomi watched, they dragged the bullock across to the altar. It struggled, its eyes rolling in fear but they were well-used to dealing with sacrificial animals and in no time had haltered the beast. Naomi's exclamation came as the high priest, almost casually drew a knife across its throat. The bullock flailed for a moment, then dropped into the reddening dust. A team of priests descended on the animal and rapidly dismembered it; while this was going on others had fetched wood from the surrounding valleys where there were dead trees in abundance. In less than half an hour the altar was ready with its pile of bone-dry wood and the portions of the carcass cradled on top. Everything was ready; all that was needed was a flame. No problem for Baal, the Sun-god, the lord of the fire, surely?

The priests began a chant. It was like nothing any of them had heard before. Jon and Naomi strained to hear the words, but the language programs made no attempt to interpret, which was odd.

"Leh-ho, ishi, Leh-ho ishi, Baali ishi shekundai.
Fakura kundi, Ashtoreth-shikali
Fakura kundi, Baali inshwabe
Severy, severy leh- ho ishi."

"What are they saying?" Jon asked the Prof, but he made no answer. The priests had formed a loose chain around their altar, and their hips swayed and gyrated suggestively in time to the chant. The two words they could distinguish, "Baal" and "Ashtoreth" were shouted loudly, and many of the people joined in the cry of the names of the gods. The high priest danced alone, his angular body capable of extraordinary agility of movement. He would shout sentences in between the chanting, but again the language interpretation failed to attempt to translate.

"Kundi, kundi, kundi, sheehoni" the last word turned into a whistle that was piercing, as it was long.

"Leh-ho, ishi, Leh-ho ishi, Baali ishi shekundai."
The chant glided up and down the scales, it carried on the still air for miles, and with most of the priests giving it all they had got, the effect was mesmerising. They could see more and more people in the crowd swaying in time, and joining in the responses.

"Leh-ho, Leh-ho Hi-yi-yi-yi-yi-yi"
The dance gained momentum. For the first time Jon looked to see what Elijah was doing. He had taken Obadiah aside for a quiet word.

"Where are the four hundred prophets that sit at her table?" Elijah hissed to the nervous Obadiah.

"The king would not allow it!"

Elijah grunted in annoyance. "Did you not try to persuade him? At a stroke I would have cleansed the land of their filth."

Obadiah looked distressed, "My lord, I could not persuade him further without raising his suspicions."

"Then it is so." His voice softened, "You have done well, Obadiah, you have taken great risks, the LORD will reward you. Now when He answers, we will strike."

"It must be done quickly," they heard him say to Obadiah. "You will arrange for as many loyal soldiers as you think will be necessary. Your word must be heard before the king can overrule you. They must be seized, every last one of them. Let not one of them escape."

"How will I know, my lord?"

"I will give the word. But beware, they are numerous and have the hearts of many of the people. Delay would be fatal."

"And what shall I do once they are secured?" It seemed an unnecessary question.

"Take them to the river, and destroy every cursed one of them. They spared not the LORD's prophets, neither would they spare me. It is what they deserve."

"Very good, my lord." He slipped back through the crowd to Ahab. From some of the looks he got his chances were slight if things didn't work out as planned.

Allowing for the time it had taken to arrange the sacrifice, the priests had probably been dancing for about thirty-five minutes. Yet they showed no sign of slacking. The hypnotic chant reverberated through the hills, the ground vibrated with the synchronised thumping of their feet, and all the time,

"Leh-ho, ishi, Leh-ho ishi, Baali ishi shekundai.
Fakura kundi, Ashtoreth-shikali
Fakura kundi, Baali inshwabe
Severy, severy leh- ho ishi. "

"Prof, can't the computers translate this?"

"Ummm, well they could, but they're not going to."

"Why ever not?"

"Jon," His voice was brusque, "what they are chanting is obscene. It's best you don't know."

To one side of the hill, in a patch of rapidly diminishing shade were a number of barrels. Beside these were clay pots that the people would use to dip into the water inside them. A steady stream of men, women and children formed by this supply. Jon took a cup to Hannah.

She had been asleep. When she awoke she looked in astonishment at the water Jon held out to her. "My lord! It is not right that you should serve me! " As she spoke she attempted to stand. Gently, but firmly he pressed her back down.

"Drink, Hannah." He held the cup to her mouth. Shakily she took it and drank the water. He could hear it washing into her empty stomach. As he watched he became aware of a terrible sense of foreboding. She could barely stand! She probably had struggled to walk for some days now, but still she had hauled herself to this mountain plateau in confident assurance of vindication of her faith. Now she was starting to lose strength, dwindling before his eyes.

"Thank you, my lord." She whispered, then, "What's happening?"

Jon stood at the entrance; the soldiers' backs were toward him. They were avidly watching events unfolding, as were everybody else present.

"I think Elijah's winding them up." He reported, then noticing the puzzled look on her face; "I mean he's... um..." he struggled, then inspiration struck; "he's having them in derision!"

"Cry louder!" Waiting the moment of silence in the chanting before the high priest bawled his contribution, Elijah cut in with his sarcastic suggestions.

"Cry louder!" But the high priest was already crying his hardest. His eyes rolled up in his head in ecstasy as he intoned his incantation;

"Kundi, kundi, kundi, sheehoni"

Elijah was clearly enjoying baiting the priests, but they were so caught up in their devotions that it was not clear whether they heard or heeded him. Suddenly one of them rolled into the dust, shrieking with laughter and convulsing spasmodically. This was taken as a sign by some of the people, they knelt on the ground, murmuring "Oh lord Baal, hear us."

The wild, shrieking laughter continued for some time, senseless and maniacal. The dancers continued uninterrupted but eventually overcome with exhaustion the priest passed out altogether. Elijah regarded him with amusement.

"Cry aloud, for he is a god!"

"Oh Baal hear us!" This was in the language of the people; the high priest was showing the signs of the strain he was under. The sacred language of devotion to Baal was slipping in their desperation; although the rest of the priests continued their keening, hypnotic chant.

"Louder!" roared Elijah. "Perhaps he is talking and is not listening to you!"

Ashtoreth-shikali, yi-yi-yi-yi-yi-yi

"Is he at home?" bellowed Elijah. "What if he has gone away? He has important business in a far country!"

"Leh-ho, ishi, Leh-ho ishi, Baali ishi shekundai

"I know what the matter is, he is asleep! Cry louder and he will awake. He will answer his challenge."

"Or perhaps he has gone to the toilet!" Elijah bellowed.

Behind him, Jon could hear Hannah laughing softly. Before him the drums rumbled, the ground reverberated and the dust rose in clouds to mix with stench of sweat. The people watched, still in near silence at the awesome spectacle of so many black-clad priests weaving, chanting, cavorting and swooping around the altar and sacrifice they had prepared. Jon looked harder; Obadiah had done an effective job. All around the perimeter, looking like a police cordon, were a ring of soldiers, standing arm-in-arm and preventing entry to or exit from the arena. Now and then a priest would remonstrate with a soldier to go past him, there would be animated gesturing and raised voices; but the cordon remained firm and implacable. Whatever their allegiance, they were going to ensure that no covert flames were smuggled into the area.

"I don't think they could sneak a lighted match into there now," Jon crowed.

"Yon?"

"A match, it's a wooden stick for lighting…Oh never mind." Jon sat beside her and she nestled against him. Jon looked steadily at her. There was something other-worldly about her, but in spite of this she had her feet firmly planted on the ground. Her devotion unsettled him. There were no chinks he could see in her moral stand. Whatever the consequences, she remained absolute in her resolution.

It forced him even more drastically to review his own activities. Had he not betrayed the trust of the Professor? Had he not actively sought personal gain at his expense? Sat here, beside this incredible woman, a sense of self-loathing arose in him to choke him like the dust still being thrown up by the party below. Perhaps if he cut the links with Prentice, and made an honest attempt to reform his life, then perhaps he would not feel this burden of inadequacy in Hannah's presence.

"Hannah? Are you awake?"

"Mm…"

"Hannah," the words lodged in his throat, "I'm not all you think I am. Honestly I'm not."

"Mm…" She was drifting in and out of sleep.

"But I will be- that's a promise!"

The voices from below were thinner now, less resonant and not as confident.

Ashtoreth-shikali, yi-yi-yi-yi-yi-yi…

…..Fakura kundi, Baali inshwabe

"Jon, are you with us?" The Prof's voice cut through his reverie. "Take a look, you won't believe it now!"

The sun blazed on, and the mountain thrummed with the beat of hundreds of pairs of feet. Two more priests succumbed to hysteria and at least a dozen had collapsed, foam drying around their lips. At this, several of them launched themselves on to the altar, spreading themselves on their backs with their arms and legs wide apart and their faces to the sun. Clearly they were inviting their own destruction along with the fiery destruction of the sacrifice. There they lay, panting and spread-eagled, but the plot was wearing thin and the people were starting to lose patience. At the beginning of this performance there were a considerable number who had swayed and chanted the unholy chorus, but now this number had dwindled to a handful. The rest watched, impassive and unimpressed. The High Priest could see it was time for drastic measures.

Seizing one of the sacrificial knives, he straddled the altar, and squinting into the sun held his right arm high in a gesture of supplication. Then slowly, deliberately he drew the blade down his arm, a deep furrow from wrist to elbow that gushed blood over the prone priests and the dead bullock. There was a deep sigh from the priests and many in the crowd. "Ahhh!"

"Leh-ho ishi, Baali, with my life I worship you, giver of life, lord of new life."

This action seemed to spur on many of the priests to new heights of frenzy. Catching up knives they slashed themselves down the forearms in a similar manner, others drew the blades across their chests, or bit into their own flesh. As they danced they threw still more dust into the choking air; the blood spattered and gushed across the arena and their cries became ever more vehement. "O lord Baal hear us!" No longer was this fascinating or intriguing, no longer did Jon, Naomi or the Professor find any amusement whatsoever in their antics as they had done earlier. There was a disturbing intensity and ferocity in their worship; it was ugly, almost alien in its latent evil. Their gestures, actions and self-mutilation were gross and manifestly lewd.

Jon turned away, sickened, and sat back down next to the sleeping girl.

Obviously this could not go on. Exhausted by their earlier exertions in the fierce midday sun, now bleeding freely from multiple wounds, many more collapsed and lay still in the dust. The activities of the rest dwindled to a halt. Elijah became busy again.

"Hannah!" He shook her gently. Her eyes popped open, she was aware of the peace that had descended on the hillside.

"Has it happened?" She struggled to sit up. "Has the LORD answered..?"

"Shh!" He helped her sit up on a rock. "No, not yet, but it's Elijah's turn now."

She craned her head to squint at the sun. "The time of the evening offering approaches," she murmured.

Calling willing hands amongst the crowd, Elijah sent some to collect more firewood. Others he assembled into groups of three or four, and halting by the scattered pile of boulders they had seen when they first arrived, he directed the groups to roll them together into a rough altar, forming three lines of four stones side by side. The interest of the crowd moved from the priests of Baal to this lonely, rugged figure who now occupied centre stage. Before the wood was placed on the stones, he directed a handful of men to dig in the loose, crumbly soil around the hilltop. With their hands they scooped out the earth so as to form a trough all around the altar. The sense of puzzlement was evident in their faces as they dug. Still the crowd watched, impassive and absorbed.

He was the master of the scene, he ran an expert eye over the remaining bullocks, selected one and led it to the altar. "Ugh!" Naomi exclaimed for the second time as the dying creature threshed in the dust in grim imitation of the almost catatonic priests nearby.

"Come near to me, come on, come close." He called.

"My lord, go and see."

"Okay, Hannah."

The crowd moved closer; men, some women and a few children, peeping from between the legs of their parents. Jon and Naomi too approached the Prophet. At this distance they could see that his face was very lined, not just weather beaten, but careworn. There was a drawn look about his eyes; too many years being alone and hated by his own people. The voice with which he bade the people draw near had lost its stridence; it was the voice of a weary teacher who would have to repeat a difficult lesson once more to an unresponsive class.

For the next few minutes he worked with only his servant to help, piling the tinder dry wood upon the altar. Then selecting a sharp knife discarded by one of the priests, he set about dissecting the bullock- in itself this was no mean task, and tentatively two more men came forward to help him divide the carcase and lift the slabs of wet meat onto the bed of wood.

As Elijah worked, Jon edged closer to the High Priest. There was something furtive in his manner that made him uneasy. He had moved away slightly from the main body of Baal-worshippers and now and then glanced up to where Hannah was penned; then he scanned the guards who had previously thwarted any plan he had made to set fire to the sacrifice. They were standing down now; they still formed a loose ring around the priests, but their attention was riveted by the austere Prophet of the LORD centre stage.

Jon's blood ran cold. There was no way of knowing for sure, but he felt danger in his bones. The High Priest was going to murder her! In his hand he clutched the same long knife with which he had slashed his arms earlier. He stowed it away amongst his robes and stepped backwards, slowly but deliberately, now and then casting a quick look over his shoulder. There was about fifty metres between him and the semi-conscious girl.

Frantically Jon ran through the options; he could outrun the lanky figure with no difficulty; but would Hannah be able to do anything? Around him the multitudes watched absorbed as Elijah finished preparing the bullock.

"Pour water on it!"

A ripple of surprise went through the assembly.

"Four barrels of water; pour them over it!" Elijah's patience was wearing thin.

The High Priest still edged backwards, closing the gap between himself and the helpless girl, his hand concealed under his cloak. Not one person noticed him; soldiers, men, women children, priests, king and princes gazed captivated at the rugged man in the centre of the arena.

The crowd parted to allow the men who had helped with the carcase to collect water. There were still many full barrels left in the supply Jon had drawn from earlier, and these were carried to the altar and upended over the sacrifice. The water cascaded over the carcase and poured through the timber and ran out at the base of the rocks.

Jon spun round, strafing the crowd with his desperate search. Hannah's brother was there, somewhere with the tall lad, what was his name? Micah! Yes, - it was his only remaining chance!

"Do it again!"

More barrels were hoisted and tipped over the altar. This time the trench half-filled with muddy water, in stark contrast to the dryness of the surrounding ground.

Jon raced across to where the pair stood a short way from the front, the little boy's hand still clutched by the tall lad. He crashed to his knees before the child and seized his other hand.

"Listen!" *(please, please notice me!!)* In the child's eyes the reflection of Elijah danced against the blackness of his pupils. The eyes did not move, the child's attention was engrossed in Elijah's activities.

"Do it again," shouted Elijah.

Four more barrels, water running over the rocks and soaking into the parched soil. Now the altar was a bedraggled, squelchy mass of dripping wood, sodden flesh and wet stones. The assistants waited with the barrels expecting to be sent for more, but Elijah motioned them away.

"Listen, look at me won't you?" Jon was screaming, shaking the child by the shoulders. "No, not at him, look at me! Please, please look this way!" He spun round; the High Priest had slipped through the cordon of soldiers and like an erect cobra, poised to strike, was slithering towards Hannah. She was sitting up.

"Hannah's in danger!!" The child's eyes focussed with agonising slowness on him. Jon took his hand and pointed it for him, stretching out his finger at the dark figure, approaching the rocky enclosure. "Look!"

The boy's gaze fixed itself on the High Priest. His face registered concern for his sister, but he had no idea what to do next.

"Tell Micah!!" shrieked Jon. "Now. Go on!!" The child gazed for a few seconds more, then tugged at the older lad's hand, his finger still pointing. Micah shielding his eyes against the sun stared up the slope. The High Priest had drawn his knife. The sun flashed momentarily from the blade.

Horror rushed across his face. "Hannah!" he screamed. He let go the child's hand and charged forward, pushing folk aside as he pelted across the centre of the arena and hurled himself up the hill. Jon ran behind him, stumbling in the thick dust, oblivious to all that was happening elsewhere. The High Priest, knife concealed behind his back dismissed the guards; not that they were paying much attention to their charge and advanced upon Hannah. Micah, still yelling wildly, "Stop him, stop him!" dashed towards the cordon, pointing to where the black robed figure loomed over the girl. The two guards and the soldiers in the cordon dithered, then in a supreme effort Micah covered the last ten metres, dust flying, and burst into the enclosure.

The High Priest had been so intent on his prey that the disturbance had not registered on him. Hannah had her back to the rock whilst over her, like a giant bat the High Priest was gathering her hair in his fingers and tugging her to a standing position. Hannah gasped with the pain of being hauled upright by her hair; her eyes shut tight waiting for the sharp point of the knife.

"So Hannah bath-Obadiah," he hissed, bringing the blade round to her exposed throat; "this is a challenge I cannot now win. But you have shamed me, and now I will destroy you. There will be no gloating from you." Her head was forced against the rock, a thin gasping cry issuing from her lips.

With a bellow Micah threw himself against the High Priest, a teenage lad against a fully-grown athletic man. The Priest was hurled sideways then bounced off the rock-face; there was a crack like an egg being smashed and he rolled over and over in the dust. Hannah, released from his grip slid weakly back to the ground.

"Hannah!" Jon held her close to him, shaking with the sudden exertion and feeling her shivering in his embrace. "Hannah, are you alright. Please, speak to me."

"My lord, I am Oh-kay." Her breaths came in ragged bursts. Jon felt himself pushed aside by Micah who lifted her unsteadily to a standing position. Behind them the guards had secured the High Priest and were dragging him upright too.

Below his right eye was a ragged wound with the whiteness of the cheekbone showing where the collision with the rock had split his face. He looked more diabolical then ever. Blood had stained the sleeves of his robes, and now fresh blood was running down his throat. He was disorientated and concussed.

"Bring him to the entrance." Hannah's voice, though weak had lost none of its presence. "Let him stand with me and see the hand of our GOD."

Micah held the swaying girl, the guards pinned the High Priest's arms behind his back and they watched the end game. The disturbance had barely registered on the assembly, they were hypnotised.

Elijah turned to face the altar, lifted his hands to the blinding sky and his voice to God. His voice carried on the quiet air.

"LORD God of Abraham, Isaac, and of Israel, let it be known this day that you are God in Israel, and that I am your servant, and that I have done all these things at your word.

Hear me, O LORD, hear me, that this people may know that you are the LORD God, and that you have turned their heart back again."

There was a screaming roar of burning air as a gigantic column of fire at least three or four metres across struck the altar and engulfed it. The fire appeared solid, so clearly defined was it from the surroundings, and its heat struck them like a body blow out from the centre of the arena. The crowd scattered, stampeding in animal panic; screaming and clawing at each other to escape. Elijah stood stock-still with his arms uplifted, a look of sheer ecstasy on his face. Before him rose clouds of steam as the water surrounding the altar vapourised instantly. Of the sacrifice, nothing could be seen, just a blinding wall of flame. The wood and carcase never had time to burn; they were simply consumed in a flash. The heat struck the rocks around where Jon, Hannah, Micah and the High Priest stood, a terrible withering blast that rolled over them, sucking their faces and throats dry. For five seconds the conflagration continued then just as abruptly it ceased, with a shattering thunderclap that shook the mountain, as the air above the altar rushed back into place, followed by an eerie silence. Jon's knees buckled and he fell to the ground.

Through his scorched eyeballs he could see two people standing; his Hannah, clutching the rock for support but a look of absolute triumph stamped across her face, and Elijah, his rod still held above his head.

The rest; the king, the priests, the soldiers and the people, as one had fallen to their faces in terror. They crouched in the dust, trembling and stupefied. The silence continued.

Of the sacrifice and wood there was nothing; no charred wood, no ash, or bone fragments. The rocks that formed the altar were blasted clean and the surfaces had melted to a glassy finish. The trench around was dry and the soil baked to brick.

"The LORD, he is the God! The LORD, he is the God!" Hannah exulted, her chest heaving, tears streaming down her cheeks.

"The LORD, he is the God! The LORD, he is the God!" behind her Micah gave it full voice, and beside her, unheard but uncaring Jon bawled it. Across the crowd he could see Naomi, rapt, take up the chant.

It spread across the assembly, soon becoming a massive roar;

"The LORD, he is the God! The LORD, he is the God!"

The king with his face to the ground shouted it, the generals surrounding him, still trembling and visibly shaken added their voice. Children with their mothers piped up with the chant:

"The LORD, he is the God! The LORD, he is the God!"

On and on it went, like tidal waves breaking on the shore, a mob chant, many were now standing upright and waving their arms like a jubilant crowd at a football match. The chant had now changed slightly; they were shouting the prophet's name;

"Elijah! Elijah! Elijah! Elijah!"

Elijah's face lost its exultant look; he waved his hands to quell the noise, but no one paid attention. Then he gave a signal to Obadiah who moved to the front of the crowd.

"Do it now! Take the prophets of Baal; let not one of them escape!"

It was easily done. Most of the prophets were in no condition to resist. Some were unconscious, lying prone in puddles of their own blood; a few would not survive anyway. The men surrounding them closed in rapidly, pinning their arms behind their backs or simply picking up the comatose ones and flinging them over their shoulders. The high priest was picked up from the dust where he cowered and dragged down the slope to them.

"Take them to the brook Kishon," Elijah commanded.

"My lord," Hannah whispered in Jon's ear, "Come with us to see the end." She refused Micah's offer to carry her, instead he supported her as they stumbled down the rocky path behind the company of priests being herded like cattle. Jon supported her from the other side, she threw her arm over his shoulder and they followed. The sun was beginning its descent in the sky, its fierce heat abated; hurry was of the essence.

If Elijah had any concerns about Ahab intervening, they were unfounded. The king had lost all authority, he simply sat on a rock his eyes unfocussed and a terrified look stamped across his surly features. Perhaps he feared the next bolt of flame might get him if he moved from his place.

Elijah with his willing helpers herded the priests roughly down the track towards the plain below, but they did not have far to travel. At points the river had cut deep into the soft rocks of the mountain range, leaving steep, craggy outcrops over sixty metres high, and it was to these that the priests were unceremoniously bundled. At one point the track narrowed and the company was forced to go single file; here the faithful Obadiah stationed himself and counted the priests, with their lacerated bodies and torn black robes. When, by the look on his face he was satisfied with the tally, he nodded to Elijah.

Jon blanched. Elijah had produced a long, curving sword. Without a moment's hesitation he drove it under the ribs of the nearest semi-conscious priest, withdrew it and flung him over the edge. The priest made no sound as he died. Elijah never even troubled to watch the man's headlong flight. Without ceremony he grabbed another, this one conscious. He uttered a brief cry as the sword went home then he too was thrown from the ledge. The expression on Elijah's face was set in grim determination, this was a job he did not relish but one he could not delay. The soldiers holding the captives thrust another one forward.

"Hannah!" Jon cried, forcing his way through to where she stood, swaying. "Hannah! Make it stop!" Behind him the sword, its blade running with blood sank into another priest.

"My lord," Hannah's voice had an edge to it he had not heard before. "There have died many at the hands of these filthy ones. They have practised and taught abomination, and it is the judgement of our GOD."

"Hannah, it's murder. You can't let it go on!"

"*Yon*. Would that you could have witnessed the cruel destruction of the prophets of the LORD. These vermin hunted them and their families for their lives, they spilt their blood in the desert places and mountain caves. Their children cried for mercy but they were shown none. Their cruelty and disgrace was without limits. It is just, and it will finish here." Her voice softened. "My lord, turn away; it pains you to behold."

"Naomi!" She was beside him on the ledge. She threw her arms round his neck and forced his gaze away from the scene of carnage.

"Jon!" She insisted, aware of his horror; "this has to be done. Really it does!" More raw-throated screams rang out as two more priests were stabbed and thrown.

Another followed, then another and another. Some screamed curses at Elijah, others begged for mercy but there was to be none. Now many of the soldiers had joined him; efficiently despatching the priests and throwing them from the cliff top. Below the river ran deep red.

"Let him be last," Hannah said to the men holding the struggling, cursing High Priest. "Let him see the enemies of the LORD dashed in pieces like a potter's vessel."

The Priest turned to her and spat in her face. She regarded him, impassive.

Jon watched aghast. There remained about three hundred ragged men penned up like beasts on that narrow path. As their fate drew closer, those who were conscious screamed, wept, begged or scrabbled at the rocks to escape; but Elijah's grim determination to see the job through had communicated itself to his helpers. The soldiers who pinned them were stony-faced and deaf to their cries.

More screams, more distant sounds of human bodies hitting rocks or shallow water. Jon held Naomi tighter and tried to blot out the horror of it all.

After ten minutes the number of priests remaining had dwindled, there were less than a hundred, struggling, spitting or pleading. The river below was dark with their corpses, but still they were slaughtered. Jon had found the rout of Gideon's enemies upsetting enough, but at least they had died fighting to survive. All that was left to these miserable wretches was to wet themselves in helpless dread before they joined their companions. The ledge stank of their fear.

Obadiah checked them off as they went, and after another ten minutes there remained only one black-robed painted face on the ledge.

"Wait!" Hannah commanded, as the soldiers holding him pushed him towards Elijah. "Let him be thrown alive."

Jon broke away from Naomi and looked over the edge. He drew back, his heart pounding. It was a giddying height!

"Many mothers in Israel will rejoice this day," said Hannah softly. "For you have corrupted this people and brought us to the edge of catastrophe. Your sword has made many childless in our land. Your abominations have caused us to stink in the sight of the God of Israel. You have stolen the sweetness of my nation and given us instead this dust and desolation."

The High Priest glowered like an animal.

"Breaking you will be a good deal quicker!" She turned away.

Then with a rush the soldiers propelled him from the ledge. Flapping and howling he disappeared into the void.

"It is done!" grunted Elijah, as if he had just taken out the rubbish, which to his way of thinking he probably had. "So perish all who rise up against the God of Israel." He wiped his blood-spattered face with a blood-drenched sleeve. The dusty floor was slippery with it. The air was clammy with the stink of it. Jon fought back nausea.

Hannah began to collapse. This time she did not protest as Micah caught her and lifted her gently in his arms. "Take me home," she whispered.

Elijah turned and led the way back up to the plateau. The shadows were longer now as they emerged before the people once again, and the breeze which had ruffled his garments earlier had strengthened into a steady flow of air from the sea. Jon could smell the salt on its breath.

Ahab had still not moved. At the sight of Elijah's bloodstained form his face showed fresh fear, but Elijah had a kinder tone for him now.

"Get up, eat and drink; for there is a sound of abundance of rain."

He looked confused. He was expecting punishment, to be made an example of.

"Go on; get up for the rain will come quickly!"

Elijah's tone was gentle, deferential and carried no hint of censure. To the bemused servants he commanded, "Get food for your master, for we cannot linger here long!" With that he strode away, first to wash his face and arms, then upwards to the topmost peak of this part of the range. The people watched him go, the freshening wind picked at his robe, his beard fluttered like a pennant as he went. One man followed him; his servant, the rest looked on as the Prophet of the LORD went to supplicate his God on behalf of the nation.

Naomi looked at Jon. He was following alongside Hannah. "Are you coming? With him, I mean."

Jon shook his head numbly. "She's going home. I'll go with her."

"Is she alright?"

"I don't know." Jon's face was ashen. The presentiment of dread he had felt earlier had intensified. Hannah was having difficulty remaining conscious. The tremendous exertion of the day, on top of months, even years of poor nutrition had crumpled her. As they placed her tenderly on a stretcher, she seemed to have visibly shrunk; she lay beneath a blanket, her face towards the sky watching for something, though she didn't say what. Several servants, summoned by Micah picked her up and the party began to pick its way down the mountainside.

Her arm slipped down near Jon. He took her hand and squeezed it. With an obvious effort she turned her face to look at him

"Yon." She smiled. "Thank you for saving me."

"It's Micah who saved you," he pointed out.

"I know, but you warned him." She must have picked up the tone in his voice. "*Yon,* Micah is a dear friend, we grew up together."

"I can see that." Jon felt a sick feeling starting in his stomach.

"My lord, it is not as you think; Micah is betrothed to my cousin. They will marry in the New Moon."

A wave of relief swept over him. "Hannah, you need to rest. You are ill. Please try to sleep."

Then the rain began. Such rain! At first a few heavy drops, falling on the dust with hardly a sound, then more and more, a great curtain of rain, then a waterfall, soaking them all to the skin in seconds and turning the ground beneath their feet to porridge. The servants in the group cheered, and Micah and Obadiah threw another covering over Hannah. Her hair became lank as water pounded down on her face. Jon thought she opened her mouth slightly to sip the moisture, but he couldn't be sure. An hour passed as the party negotiated the slippery rock path to the plain, now shrouded in black clouds.

"Hannah!" He squeezed her fingers again, harder, "Hannah! Wake up, Hannah!"

Her face had relaxed. The shadows muted the sores around her mouth and filled in the hollows below her cheek bones. Micah shook her, gently at first, then with increasing desperation as realisation dawned. "Hannah, Hannah Bath-Obadiah."

He placed his cheek near her mouth feeling in vain for the slightest stirring of air. His voice broke. "Hannah, answer me!"

Beside him the servants shifted uneasily then lowered the girl to the muddy gravel. Obadiah turning round saw them stalled behind him. He hurried back, looking from his daughter to Micah and back again. Micah gave a slight shake of his head.

With a howl like a wounded animal, Obadiah threw himself on her, shaking her, willing her to live, breathe, open her eyes- anything. Shouting her name, "Hannah, Hannah, Hannah!" he shook her fiercely, as the tears poured down his face.

Grief drained his remaining energy; he collapsed beside her in the mud with his face against hers and sobbing uncontrollably. The thin, wasted figure lay, unheeding and lifeless. And the life-giving rain, withheld for the past three and a half years wept its eulogy for the fairest of the daughters of Carmel.

Jon felt the strength go from his knees. There was a massive ache in his chest and a cold, dry pain in his throat that threatened to suffocate him. He fell into the soupy mud, uncaring.

Something was lifted from his face, something that clawed at his skin and felt hot and clammy.

The Professor was beside him, his hair plastered down over his head, the torch light flickering over his angular face. Naomi was with him too.

"Come on Jon," he said, "it's time to leave."

"No, not yet," Jon pointed to the body. "Leave me alone."

His gaze followed Jon's pointing finger, but there was no comprehension. "Come on Jon, let's go."

They helped him stand. Around them the rain, the mud, the wild lightning tearing up the sky faded to the wall lights of the viewing room. Jon turned for one last look at her peaceful face; the servants milling around miserably, Micah gasping with grief and Obadiah still stretched out over his motionless daughter. Then it was gone.

"Here, Jon, drink this." At any other time Jon would have been amazed at the soft kindness in her tone. But right now he could hardly breathe, let alone drink the water Naomi held out to him. Nevertheless he took it, but as a fresh wave of sorrow convulsed him, he spilt most of it.

Naomi sat beside him, quietly supporting him. Jon leaned against her; she settled his head on her shoulder. On the other side of the room, the Professor regarded him with anxiety.

Finally, at a loss to suggest anything else, he said;

"Jon, do you want to go home?"

Outside the rain came in sheets driven by a still-rising wind. Lightning flashed and crackled across the sky, the thunder bellowed then he was out of the rain, nestled amongst the clutter of the front seat of the Prof's car. The wipers skidded furiously across the windscreen attempting to clear the water away and Jon wondered whether the river would burst its banks over the tiny village.

Tiredness and such extreme weariness, Jon was glad to climb into bed whilst the storm played out its wild symphony in the skies above.

•

The moment he returned from dropping Jon home, Naomi rounded on her Grandfather.

"OK," she fumed. "Just tell me for once what's really going on, will you?"

He stopped, hand on the door knob, shocked by the tone in her voice.

"What?"

"You," she cried. "You and your, 'suggestibility,' that's what! It's rubbish and you know it!" She pointed to the door; "Jon's fast becoming a basket-case, and all you can say is 'suggestibility!' Why don't you tell me the truth?"

That hurt him more than she intended. His hand flew to his mouth. She thought he was going to get angry, shout at her, and insist on apologising. Instead he went very quiet. Finally he said;

"Come over here, Na love."

The screen was a mass of data, and at first glance there was no pattern to it. Then as his finger traced the lines, she thought she could discern a sequence to the codes. Recognisable words rubbed shoulders with gobbledegook, but with them she began seeing names, "Jon Heath," "Obadiah," "Hannah" and then her own name amongst a dense cluster of codes.

"What's it doing?"

"Have you heard of backfilling?"

"No," she wondered where this was heading.

"It's a word my English teacher used to use," he reflected. "I think she made it up, but it's very apt. It's what you do if you're writing a novel, and you have a change of mind about a character or event. Say you want to bump somebody off, or show a different side to somebody's character."

Naomi watched his face; was this a more creative way of dodging the question? "So?"

"So you back fill. You go back through the text and insert hints here, pointers there. Nothing too obvious or the reader will cotton on. Just subtle changes to the text to sow the seed of the event or whatever it is you want to introduce."

Naomi was still baffled. He picked up some printouts.

"These are some reports the Timescope has made on various characters it has encountered; ones we've shown particular interest in, if you like. The Timescope throws everything it knows into a file, then it can draw on that as and when it sees fit. Jon's here, as am I, you and most Biblical characters we've come across."

"So in what way is the Timescope 'backfilling'?"

"These printouts were current about a week ago. Since then the Timescope has added more physical and psychological data. That's fine, quite normal. But it's not only that."

It was dark in the room Naomi couldn't make out his face. But she could tell he was nervous. "Go on," she said.

"It's difficult to say for certain. But the Timescope has altered previously established data. Things it knows about people, like you and me, it's...well... mucking about with things it shouldn't."

"Such as?" Naomi felt a cold finger tracing a track down her back.

"Time-slice references for one. You know, the way the system tracks data as it is read off the source stone. It labels each frame with its own absolute time reference. Helps navigation no end. When we go into the Timescope, it knows that we don't belong in the same historical time as the main data, so it generates an error file; two sets of data, present day and ancient, and ne'er the twain should meet."

"But they have!"

"Not exactly..." he faltered, "but they are starting to merge. Jon in particular is no longer being exclusively recognised as present-day material. It's getting a little blurred at the edges."

"What about me then?" The cold finger was playing with the nape of Naomi's neck.

"That's even stranger, much, much odder in fact. You're getting confused with this Hannah girl! It's starting to show in the outward appearance of Hannah, and in the way she behaves. She's copying you."

He let this sink in. Then he said. "And there's something else. I take it you didn't authorise the Cairo connection?"

"What Cairo connection?"

No, he mused, he didn't think she had. Somebody or something did though. The Timescope had requisitioned a mainframe at the University there and carried out a number of memory-hungry file processings. Angry emails had alerted him to the situation, but he had no idea how it had come to pass. His only dealings with Cairo University were years ago. The address was still on his files, but that was all.

"Could somebody have hacked in?" Naomi had more than an inkling who to blame.

"Possible, but not likely. It is my encryption after all!"

'Not that that's likely to stop him' she thought. Aloud she said; "Are you going to tell Jon? About this backfilling, I mean."

"Not until I know more, much more. I've structured the error-trapping system much better now; it will collect data and sort it into separate files. Then we should be able to see exactly what it's doing."

"Granddad," Naomi faltered, "is this safe? I mean, it's not only Jon is it? It's messing with me and you as well. Did Jon tell you what happened with me and the eyeliner?"

She told him, embarrassed to relate how she had plastered the stuff all over her face. He listened intently, his face lost in the shadows.

"The worst thing, Granddad, was that it seemed, well, just the most natural thing to be doing, making my eyes up like that. As though I'd been doing it all my life!"

When she turned the lights on she noticed his hands were shaking violently.

•

Mary Heath examined her reflection in the mirrors mounted along the wall, the entire length of the marble washbasins. The mirrors were discretely lit to flatter the clientele of the restaurant; but she was not in a mood for compliments. Terrence Prentice.

He had called this meeting on a pretext; that was clear. He had hardly mentioned the Absent Fathers' bill or associated legislation. Instead he was asking questions about her son of all things. Silly questions, little questions, questions that would have lead her to snap, 'mind your own business!' to anyone else to whom she owed no professional debt.

Terrence Prentice had watched her slim figure disappearing to the ladies washrooms. So far his attempts to solicit information were proving counterproductive, but her last remark had confirmed the connection he had become aware of in his rendezvous with the American earlier that day.

". . . he attends some church, something to do with a friend of his, a Professor Avery. "

"Pay dirt!" Jackman's blue eyes were looking almost, but not quite excited. Prentice was unfamiliar with this 'pay dirt' expression, but he assumed it was something gratifying.

"Rufus Avery. Professor Rufus Avery," he announced, his notebook in his hand. "Formerly joint head of 'Avery associates' a software team who designed programs intended for deeply-embedded applications- sort of stuff that never sees the light of day, but is crucial for processor operation. Lead a research team in applied computing at Kansas State University..."

"So he's American?" Prentice enquired.

"British. Studied at Kansas then ended up Professor of Computing Science in their faculty at Kansas back in the seventies. Pioneered some pretty groundbreaking stuff. Then his team patented some deeply implanted software used, until recently almost universally in mainframe and personal computing resources. Following a sharp disagreement he left; something to do with the Pentagon wanting to acquire their technology and use it for their own purposes. Apparently Professor Avery was strongly opposed to the military application of his ideas." He flicked through the notebook pages. "Of the team that produced these applications, most are millionaires, and Avery a multi millionaire."

Prentice, nervous as he was, was intrigued. "He has a yacht, mansion, usual stuff?"

"No," Jackman replied. "He lives in Keswick Avenue. Nice house in a nice area by your British standards, but nothing special. Overgrown garden, house needs attention, it's all in a trashy state."

"Are you sure you've got the right man?"

The blue-eyed American gave him a withering look. "You need proof? Just look at these!"

The reports were like utility bills, only they were from a company supplying specialist gigastream connections to the world wide web.

"A large utility like a brewery or hospital might use one such connection at the outside to cope with all their data traffic. A few American companies use four or five..."

"And how many does our man use?"

"Nine!" he said flatly. "Costing him sometimes upwards of nine hundred pounds a day in connection fees."

Prentice spluttered over his drink. "What's he doing with all this... this, resource? What's going in and out?"

"I don't know," Jackman admitted. "All data is in an absolutely secure encryption. Our team back at HQ have seen nothing like it. They're still working to try to crack it. But here's the best part," he leaned forward. Prentice shivered. "It's the way in which this data is sent to corporate mainframes, processed and returned. All the time, different mainframes, or networks, different times of the day or week; but twenty four seven it adds up to one giant global computer! Very, very clever."

"And what has this to do with Jon Heath?"

"They struck up together recently." As he spoke Jackman produced a sheaf of photographic prints and began dealing them like cards on the table. "Jon was a hoodlum, as your pictures show. Then something happened to change all that. Now he's around at this Professor Avery's shack every other day, and weekends too. Something happened to him to do with our Professor. Something which I guess is connected to our little lapse in security."

Prentice picked the top picture up. Jon had been snapped waiting, leaning up against the peeling paint of the Professor's front door. Then another of Jon and Naomi, emerging from the wooden building where the Living Word sessions took place.

"Who's the girl?"

"Naomi. Naomi Avery, his granddaughter. Very bright, top marks in High School, interest in computing- chip off the block as you would say." The photo had caught her in the act of flicking her fringe out of her eyes. "Nice girl," he drawled.

Prentice wasn't sure if this was a compliment or a threat.

11

For the third time Professor Avery looked nervously towards the door of the church outbuilding. Then he glanced across to his granddaughter, and met her gaze. "Where is Jon?" he mouthed.

"Don't know!" She shrugged back. Seconds later the question was answered.

"You're a liar!" Jon's voice was strained and contemptuous.

Every head swung round to see. Jon was flushed, shaking with emotion and wild-eyed. He stood, framed by the doorway for all the world like an avenging angel. He pointed at the Professor.

"You're a liar!" He yelled. "A filthy liar!"

The Professor said nothing; his eyes narrowed dangerously but he did not reply. Jon advanced down the centre aisle.

"God of love? That's a sick joke!" Jon turned to a few young boys sitting in a knot on the floor nearby, their mouths gaping. "That's what he'll tell you. 'God of love.'" He gave a short bitter laugh. "Well she believed that too. Didn't she? She served Him when nobody else did; and what did she get out of it? Anything at all?" His voice had risen still further in volume, but it had an odd cracked sound to it, as if he was about to cry.

"You ask him what Hannah got before she died! Nothing. Not even a mouthful to eat. And that's the God he'll tell you about. A God who rewards His followers: it's all lies, lies and more lies. And he'll tell…"

"Jon!!"

"No, I'm not listening. You listen for once! You think you've…"

"Jon, just shut up will you!!" the Professor thundered, now white with rage himself. In spite of the state he was in, the tone of his voice stopped Jon in his tracks.

There was deathly silence. Not many assembled there at Living Word had seen the familiar person of Professor Avery so incandescent with fury. A young child at the front began to snivel; Naomi led him to one side, her mouth tight-lipped.

"How dare you barge in here like this! What gives you the right to speak to us like that?"

"Just answer my question!" Jon was chewing his lip.

"First sit down, and stop behaving like you've got a monopoly on suffering and then perhaps I'll explain things to you. But I'm not yelling things out at the top of my voice. I think everybody here might like to know what you're shouting about."

Naomi froze. Surely he wasn't going to tell the full story? Jon, his outburst expended flung himself to the floor.

The Professor reached over to a tray, his hand shaking, and poured himself a glass of lemonade. For a few seconds he sipped it, thinking hard. Looking round, he smiled nervously at the audience.

"I'm sure Jon wouldn't mind if I tell you what has happened. Jon's friend Hannah lived in another country, where food was very scarce. She served God faithfully, but in spite of that died of starvation. Many thousands of people like her died in the same way. Because of the terrible behaviour of their rulers, the whole nation was afflicted and suffered together."

"You don't understand, she was different, she wanted nothing more than to serve God. And God couldn't even feed her!"

"Oh grow up, Jon!" The Prof snapped back. "Don't come to me with your twenty-first century ideas of fairness. I thought I knew you better than this. Do you think Obadiah, or Hannah, or Elijah served God for what they could get out of it? After all you've learned, is that all it comes down to? I'll scratch your back, God, and you scratch mine? You've got a lot to learn."

"So have you!" Jon, nettled, got up to go. "When did you last see someone die?"

"That's enough!" The Professor cried, his fists clenched as if to strike him. "Hannah died, as did many thousands of others because of Ahab's folly. Did she ever blame God for it? Did she? You've no right to take issue with God like this.

You're way out of your depth, Jon. You and your sense of armchair justice, just because you've seen a bit of real suffering you think that gives you the right to rant at God as if He doesn't know any better."

"Your generation hasn't seen any thing worse than the odd road accident, and now you think you're qualified to take it up with the Almighty!"

Jon stood at the door.

"I've had it with this!" he said surprisingly quietly, his rage choking his words. "I can't take it anymore. It's too stupid. It's too . . ." He didn't want to say it but it came out anyway. "...Painful!" he said and left.

●

Faris regarded his friend steadily. Although he was curious to discover what had actually happened that night at the Professor's house, he shrewdly refrained from asking questions. Instead he said.

"Sixth form party, Jon. How about it?"

Faris was a party animal. Some weekends he gate-crashed two or even three parties. He was definitely on the unofficial invite list for most festivities for a radius of ten miles around. He throve on the noise, the lights and the chaos. His very presence was proof that the party was a success. It was a difficult aspect of their friendship for Jon who found those very elements disorientating and tiresome. Jon had long given up trying to have yelled conversations with Faris's cast-off girlfriends, none of whom had much to say of interest anyway. Habitually he avoided Faris's invitations.

Tonight Jon had sought him out. Whilst he felt no desire to go to one of Faris's type of parties, he desperately needed distraction from the memories of Hannah. The blare and racket would dull the fresh wounds inflicted by the events at Carmel. Partially, too, he had to break away from the recent pattern of life.

●

"How long are you at Judith's?" The Prof slowed the car right down. He missed his granddaughter a great deal when she was away, even if it was just a few miles separation.

"Ten days." She replied distractedly. The events of that morning worried her; she knew it had worried her grandfather too. All day he had been tense, his face set in a glum frown.

"Is that it with him then?" he said, more to himself. "Gone back to the mire?"

Naomi was about to agree when she saw the look on his face. He had aged! It was heartbreaking to see him like this. "You really liked him, didn't you, Granddad?"

"I still do. Present tense." He was going to say 'from the moment he broke into the house,' but he was too tired to analyse the feeling he had about Jon. Right from the start, though, he had sensed potential. Now it had gone.

"Granddad," she said softly, "he wasn't to know about Gran, was he?"

He winced. "She was committed, really hard-working, you know. Didn't stop her getting ill and…" he paused, the memories as fresh as if they had happened yesterday. "I said the same as he did, then. Why? Why her? Why did she have to die like that?" He glanced covertly at Naomi, curled up in the front seat. Poor kid! She'd had her fill of tragedy to contend with but she had learnt to put up with it. He bitterly regretted his angry reaction to Jon, especially in front of the young people at Living Word.

Naomi thought hard. "Why do you think he flew at you like he did?"

"He's upset about this Hannah girl, I suppose."

"It's not just that." She cleared her throat "You're really putting him through it."

"Me putting him through it… that's rich!"

"No, just think about it, you've virtually challenged everything he believes in. Everything turned upside-down. He was going to lash out eventually. Hannah dying didn't help, I know."

The Professor stopped the car. He regarded her for a moment or two, then for the first time that day creased into a curious smile. "Come here Na," he said and folded her in his arms. "You're right, of course. He's kicking against the goads. I never saw it quite like that! You're like your grandmother; she could read people straight away."

Naomi, her head buried in his coat inhaled his smell; a tang of decades of experience, a wide-ranging knowledge of life suffused with a straight-talking kindness and generosity. She grinned; for once she had thought of something he hadn't.

"Are you seeing George this week?" he enquired.

Before she could stop herself she sighed, then to distract him asked. "Did you sort out the Cairo foul-up?"

He examined the backs of his hands minutely. "Um, yes. The Cairo network hijack. Interesting."

"Why?"

"Well after we spoke, I reconfigured the network connection so it couldn't happen again."

She felt him tense up. Once more the familiar cold finger began tracing her spinal vertebrae. "And?"

"It went elsewhere! Canada, Cape town, Buenos Aires, Norway, Vietnam; anywhere it could locate processing facilities. As fast as I closed one link it opened another."

"What went elsewhere?" How had Jon Heath managed to gain so much access to the Timescope? Was he hacking in from home?

"The Timescope. It's recruiting other networks and mainframes to use."

Naomi felt her skin crawling. Her face screwed up in disbelief. "How can it? I mean it can't take these decisions, can it?"

"Why not? It is programmed to requisition resources to carry out its functions. If you have a computer that's running slow, what do you do? You install more memory, more processing power, more network capability. Well that's all the Timescope's doing; making itself more efficient, only on a much larger scale."

"You call that all?" Naomi disentangled herself from him, wide-eyed in alarm. "The Timescope is making high-level decisions and you're going to let it?" She took in the look on his face. "You're telling me you can't stop it?"

"No, don't be silly;" he laughed with an unconvincing attempt at lightness. "Of course I can stop it; I just need to pull the network connectors out. But I need those error files filling up so we can see where it's going wrong first. Then if needs be, I'll isolate it from the Web. Time to go, Na." He pulled the handbrake on. "I'll just come in for a few minutes if Judith's got the kettle on."

"Granddad? Are you going back in?"

He didn't need to ask into what. "I thought I'd just try one more incident from Elijah's life. Why?"

"Oh, nothing." She swept the hair out of her eyes and opened the car door. "Just take care won't you?"

"Sure thing, love."

•

The venue for the party was along a rough track through fields at the end of a lane. As Jon and Faris picked their way along the broken surface of the track, the notion of this being a Sixth Form leaving bash seemed to evaporate. They usually held their party on the school premises. This party was in amongst farm buildings a long way from anywhere.

An indefinable unease filled Jon as they approached. Something felt wrong with this situation, and he felt dislocated, his presence an aberration. He shook himself; he was getting worked up about nothing. He had been to these sorts of things before! Why not now?

Inside the sound level was truly awesome. The music was of a very high energy beat type, the sound system composed of two stacks of gigantic loudspeakers at one end of the barn, and in the middle of the floor, intermittently lit by flashing chasing lights were a huddled mass of dancers. They weaved and shook moving with a rapidity that seemed quite unnatural. Immediately on entering the room an overpowering smell of sweat hit Jon, stronger even then the smell of straw; this was not surprising considering the manic speed of the beat the dancers shook their bodies to. Sweat poured off them, some of them seemed in a trance, and others frequently dropped out to get drinks of water. A few were drinking some stuff in a large tub nearby. Half-hidden by the darkness, a group of revellers were slumped against the straw, just the tips of their cigarettes marking their position.

"Bone's doing the drinks!" screamed Faris in his ear. "Should be classic stuff!"

Bone had long, black hair tied behind his head in a pigtail. Dressed entirely in black with more ear piercings than anybody Jon had ever seen in his life. Not one millimetre of his ears remained free for more jewellery. As people dipped their glasses in the concoction at the makeshift bar, he added more from an assortment of bottles on the table. He was like a pharmacist mixing a drug. He didn't even glance up as Jon and Faris took a glass each and dipped it into the pungent mixture.

Faris was in his element in the shrill noise and frantic atmosphere as much as Jon was out of his depth. For a moment he considered slipping away; then he saw to his relief that there was a second room through an open door, slightly better lit and containing food on bales of straw. Faris set off in the direction of the dance floor, Jon made a bee-line for this second room.

"Oi, watch out will you!" The boy who had elbowed him turned a belligerent face to look. He was considering his response to Jon's angry outburst. Jon bunched his fists.

"Don't go there!" Another youth whom Jon recognised from Lower Sixth yelled in his ear. "It's Jon Heath! You know, the one who trashed Roger Lord!" At once his face relaxed.

"Sorry mate!" he mouthed. Then another glass of Bone's concoction was shoved in Jon's hand. He finished the first off quickly and started on this one. He tried to have a conversation with a couple of people he recognised but with all the yelling his throat felt dry. More of the drink appeared in his hand. He started to feel good. Older kids were recognising him and coming up to bellow their greetings. Jon Heath had achieved notoriety at last. Faris had come into the room and was pointing him out to a couple of girls. It was clear from his gestures that he was relaying the Roger Lord bashing exploit. One of them had long, dark hair, and eyes that reminded him of Hannah.

She appeared in front of him; he took her hand and they danced together, the rhythms seemed to loosen his joints and bones. Soon he was sweating as well. But she didn't seem to care. She was at least two years older than him, dressed in a tight-fitting top that showed her stomach off. She smiled provocatively at him.

The combination of alcohol, high energy music and sense of fame was a heady mixture. The voice of doubt in the back of his head that had been nagging him all evening dwindled to a sullen mutter. A new voice had arisen in its place.

'I am Jon Heath; I am the one who put Roger Lord in hospital. I am respected, even feared. Now here I am in the middle of the action, feeling good, better than I have felt for a long time.'

His self-confidence surged, the girl was smiling radiantly at him, as she held his hands to dance. The subtle undertones of her perfume invaded Jon's senses as they spun round. He held her gaze, feeling himself drawn closer to her with every minute that went by.

As the music continued to whip the dancers up into an even greater frenzy, Jon found a detached part of himself comparing this experience with the calm of Living Word Workshops. Somehow the two events seemed so far apart as to be almost entirely different worlds; parallel existences. There the venerable, slightly crusty Professor listened quietly to their questions, and turning the pages of the Bible explained in measured tones how to go about sorting out the problem in hand; here the guest presenter called 'Trancedance', with a tight glittery jacket and trousers, long Afro-Caribbean dreadlocks and huge quantities of gaudy jewellery on his arms and fingers screamed and swore into a microphone in between endless dance tracks.

He felt a tug at his sleeve; Faris pulled him sharply to one side.

At first Jon couldn't make out what Faris wanted; he seemed pleased with himself and had been dancing with a taller blonde girl. Unable to make himself heard, he held out his hand, palm uppermost.

Two tiny tablets.

He should have known, of course. How did those dancers keep going the way they did? Not by natural means. This was no healthy workout. Instead it was a drug-fuelled rave. How many of the dancers were on this high-octane additive?

'Go on!' Faris's sign language was clear. Even though he was taken aback, Jon was tempted. People died from drug-taking, but not that many. Many more had exhilarating experiences, time and time again. Faris had been right so far, the night had been better than he could ever have imagined.

Jon hesitated, then took the tablets and put them in his pocket. 'Later, Jon', he told himself, 'later'. Then he could impress his girl with his extraordinary new energy. Right now, the room seemed roofless; the music pulsed through his arteries, bounced down his veins and spun him round and round. In the sporadic flashes of light, the dark-haired girl smiled at him. He had no plans for the rest of the night, events were sweeping him along. It felt wild, it felt good, so very good, and he sensed it was about to get better.

Then she draped her arms around his neck and pulled him closer.

She was thinner than he had anticipated. Confusion trickled into the back of his brain - her scent that had caught his attention earlier seemed to have evaporated. Her hair smelt of open fields, pollen, sun-baked dust and deeply-warmed afternoon air. The long tresses reached to her waist and shimmered as they moved. Her movements too, had changed. Moments earlier she had been gyrating frenetically; now she moved with serene, graceful steps, lithe yet tranquil.

"Yon!" Her mouth was close to his ear.

"Hannah!" Jon's heart punched into his diaphragm. "What are you doing here? I thought…that is…"

"My lord," he could feel her breath on his ear, "What are you doing here?"

Jon broke free of her arms and grasped her shoulders; in the sporadic flashes of light his eyes searched her face, looking for confirmation. Then, once more, her perfume broke over him like a tidal wave.

"Hannah?" But the girl's face was different. Deep red lip gloss and mascara-coated eyelashes.

She looked petulant; "Come 'ere," she slurred, putting her arms around his neck once more.

"Hannah...your perfume..."

"D'ye like it? ... 'Heathen;' ish my favourite." She pulled him closer so that she didn't have to scream above the pandemonium.

Jon writhed in shock. It had been Hannah! Absolutely sure! The smell, the figure, the movement; his heart, still pounding was settling down from its initial wild surge.

"My lord!" This time Jon was in no doubt. Shaking with excitement he pulled her closer.

"My lord, leave this place. Get out now."

"Hannah, I saw you ..."

"Die? Yes, my lord. I don't know, but there are many things with you I don't know. One day we will be told all things, but now, Yon, you must go, go quickly!"

"Hannah! I don't want to leave you. Let me stay."

Her voice came back, desperate. *"Yon! These people are evil. Listen to what they're saying!"*

Trancedance held the microphone in front of his mouth. The words carried above the flagellating dance beat, strident and heathen.

"Leh-ho, ishi, Leh-ho ishi, Baali ishi shekundai.
Fakura kundi, Ashtoreth-shikali
Fakura kundi, Baali inshwabe
Severy, severy leh- ho ishi."

The people in the crowded dance floor swayed in time, and joined in the responses.

"Leh-ho, Leh-ho Hi-yi-yi-yi-yi-yi"

Jon stopped dancing and stared stupidly around him. When did that happen? When did the words change? What was going on?

"Don' shtop." The girl yelled. Jon put his lips near her ear. *"Hannah! What's going on? Where did they come from?"*

"They were always here, Yon. They will always be here. You have to choose whom you serve. But Yon: your friend, the old man. You must go to him. He is in great danger."

"The Prof... why, what...?"

"Go to him, my lord. Go now."

"Leh-ho, Leh-ho Hi-yi-yi-yi-yi-yi"

Almost paralysed with indecision Jon stood for a few moments more in the maelstrom of noise and confusion. "We've got to get out!" He yelled to the girl.

She hadn't heard, he pulled her close and bawled, "Let's get out of here!"

She smiled provocatively which was unexpected but made no resistance as Jon dragged her to the barn door. On the way out they stumbled over a body. "Vvv off!" it slurred and rolled to the side.

The cool night air did little to clear his senses. The girl had her arm around him, but they were both having difficulty staying upright. By the low yard wall a barely-clad girl was being sick, sobbing as her friend supported her. Jon's sense of disgust intensified tenfold. He stumbled with her to another building some fifty metres away where it was possible to hold a conversation without yelling. Even so his ears were singing and his voice too loud. What was more he felt sick himself.

The girl reached her arms up and threw them round Jon's neck. He pushed her back. "Washmatter?" she blinked, nonplussed. "Don't cha like me?"

"We've got to get further away from here!" Actually this was what he wanted to say, but the words kept coming out the wrong way round. Nevertheless she understood. "I'll jush tell Sue that I don't wanna lif'"

Jon caught her arm. "Don't go back in there!"

Over the night air the party thundered on *"kundi, kundi, kundi, sheehoni"*

"Leh-ho, Leh-ho Hi-yi-yi-yi-yi-yi"

"Listen, Hannah," he gripped her shoulders, trying to communicate his urgency; "You said the Prof was in danger; what did you mean?"

In the floodlight her face was cold and expressionless. "Why're keep calling me Hannah?" She demanded. "I'm not Hannah, I'm Kay."

"Sorry Kay," he mumbled, "jush getting bit confused, thash all."

"Come 'ere." She slurred, putting her arms around his neck again and leaning against him. She went to kiss him, but Jon placed his mouth firmly near her ear once more.

"Hannah, are you there? Hannah, please talk to me. Tell me how I can reach you."

Then his world exploded; a blinding pain, and a thunderclap of sound.

"Are you winding me up?" Kay yelled, and then looked at him closely. "You're serious aren't you?" She hissed. "You're using me for Hannah- whoever she is. Well you're sick!"

"Sorry Han... Kay," Jon protested lamely, nursing his face where she had slapped him. "Honest, I do like…"

But he was addressing the back of her head. She stalked across the yard, and then the party swallowed her up.

"Fakura kundi, Baali inshwabe Severy, severy leh- ho ishi"

The cool night air did little to clear his head; the ground kept rising up in front of him, then receding to an alarming distance, like looking down the wrong end of a telescope. His face burned, from a mixture of pain and embarrassment. Within three metres he had trodden in the first of many cowpats.

Dimly, as he stumbled across the field, Jon recalled a cattle drinking-trough he had seen earlier. He weaved towards it then plunged his face gratefully into the chilly water. The droplets ran down his shirt front, prickling his belly, but it numbed the pain and took the sweatiness away.

His mobile, of course why not just ring? He pulled it from his pocket; put it to his ear and once again the rush of high pitched screeching assaulted his ears. Just like the last time in the shopping centre. What was going on? This was getting crazier by the minute. If only his head would clear! He had to get the Prof and quickly.

12
Horeb

He bashed on the front door again. The place was in darkness, and except for the Prof's car in front of the garage could have been deserted. Not once did Jon stop to consider that the old man might not be in. Gone was his bitter anger of the morning. Gone too was the confusion felt at the party. If only his head would clear! Jon wanted desperately to pour out his story to the Prof, to tell him, it was all right. He had spoken to Hannah. She was alive. He had almost forgotten that he had been sent here to stop the Prof doing something dangerous, so excited was he about his news.

In the end he let himself in through the back window. It wasn't difficult as the wooden frame still needed repair and the window lifted easily. As he dropped into the cluttered hallway, the constant roar of the computers wafted up the dark passage, as if to remind him of their first encounter. Only this time their sound had risen in intensity, as if mighty trees were being shaken by autumn gales.

"Prof? Are you there, Prof? What's that noise?"

His voice no longer seemed loud in the darkness. The rushing sound drowned his words. As he picked his way forward he realised that it was not coming from the computer room at all, but from the viewing room beyond.

As he opened the door, the blaze of light made him screw up his eyes.

"Hi Prof!"

He was huddled on the floor with his hands over the back of his head. One Virtual Reality headset was hanging on the door behind him, the other lying in the corner of the room. On the wall the giant video screen showed a mountain landscape; although dust and sand thickened the air so that it was impossible to see far. The roaring, rushing sound was the wind, howling around the mountain top. It was no ordinary storm.

Jon shook the Professor. But the prone figure remained in a tightly curled position. He had no injuries Jon could make out;

he seemed to be just protecting himself from the vicious tempest. Finally he picked up the discarded headset and gingerly put it on. Even sober he would have been awed by the sight that greeted him; in his delicate state it was terrifying.

The Prof was crawling up the last few metres of a rocky path that lead to a small cave, more like a cleft in between two jagged rocky peaks. The force of the wind hit Jon within seconds of putting the headset on, it pushed him over with contemptuous ease. Jon landed in the dust and started to crawl after the Prof.

It wasn't easy, the wind slammed him into the dirt; stones and grit carried on the gale bit into the exposed skin on the back of his neck and hands. His light coat developed a will of its own and began to flail at his back, alternately bellying out, then smacking painfully down on his flesh.

"Prof!" the old man couldn't hear. Jon's voice tired from all the earlier yelling couldn't carry over the screaming storm.

With an effort he dragged himself to his knees and half-crawled the remaining distance to the cleft. Just as he got there, the Prof turned and saw him. He reached out his hand and hauled Jon the rest of the way.

"What are you doing here?" he bawled.

Jon ignored the question. It was useless to try to explain the full story. "What's happening?"

"Elijah's going...!" the rest of the sentence was torn away.

"What?" Jon cupped his ear to the Prof's mouth.

"Elijah's going to meet GOD," he screamed back. He pointed ahead to where a familiar, robed figure stood at the far end of the cleft, his staff planted in the ground in front of him, and his other hand gripping the rock as the wind intensified its fury around him. For all the fear he showed, he could have been part of the mountain itself. Where Jon and the Professor huddled, they were relatively sheltered in the cleft, and even though the wind funnelled down between the rock faces and roared like an animal in pain, it was quieter here than out on the bare face of the mountain. He was standing with his back to them, but at that moment he half-turned and they glimpsed his face, wrapped in his robe apart from a slit for his eyes, gazing straight out across the desert plain before the mountain.

"Look!"

In spite of the cacophony, Jon could hear the panic in the old man's voice. He had lost his composure. He sounded and looked frightened. Jon turned to follow his finger.

A gigantic yellow wall of sand and dust billowing thousands of feet high was streaming across the desert toward the mountain on which they stood. It was unlike any natural catastrophe they had ever seen or could imagine. It was moving at the speed of a jet airplane with a deep, throaty roar that was loud even at this distance. Elijah remained motionless at the far entrance to their shelter as the unearthly phenomenon raced toward them. With a shock Jon realised that the wind that had punched him to the ground earlier was only the preview of what was heading for them now. Despite this he struggled to his feet, sheer awe at the spectacle drawing him to where Elijah stood. He was snatched back behind a boulder that half-blocked the cleft.

"Jon are you mad? Get down!" The Prof yelled, shielding his eyes from the supersonic particles of grit and dust. The screaming wind rose in relentless intensity.

When it hit, the sand, dust and rocks obliterated everything even a few centimetres away. Jon had a brief impression of the air turning a soupy yellow then the Professor's arm was over his shoulder, his weight pinning them down against a force that was capable of stripping both of them off the face of the earth. In seconds his unprotected mouth had filled with sand and dust, even his eyes screwed tightly shut were sealed with the stuff. The boulder afforded some protection but pebbles, grit and larger stones barrelled up the cleft like bullets and ricocheted off the walls with a sharp, piercing *twang!* Larger stones began arriving, some of them smashed into the boulder they huddled behind and shattered into deadly shrapnel; *twang, twang, twang!*

All the time the fury of the wind increased, sucking whatever breath he could draw out of his lungs and filling his mouth with yet more sand. The mountain beneath them vibrated, as if it too sought to shrug off the pair of them; at one point Jon felt a floating sensation and realised with awe that he was actually nearly airborne, pinned at the shoulders by the Prof's arm, but the rest of his body stuck out like a flag.

What would happen if he let go? Jon wondered. Would they bounce down the mountainside, pitching over the jagged rocks tumbling to their deaths; or would they just end up back in the viewing room? Right now with the fury of this elemental storm upon them he did what the Prof did, he just clung grimly to their handhold and waited for the end.

Minute after minute the storm intensified. Jon was conscious of sharp stings from fragments glancing off his back and legs, his skin rasped raw by the sand blast and then of blood trickling down his face, to be instantly mingled with dust and end up as a paste in his eye sockets.

His world had reduced to a tiny refuge from this killer storm. In his elemental terror, he cried like a petrified child, overcome by genuine fear that they would be unable to survive this for much longer. There was another colossal bang as a huge rock the size of a suitcase, splintered overhead, spraying them with more shrapnel. Jon felt a cruel whack on the side of his head, then numbness and silence.

"Are you all right Jon?"

The wind had ceased. In its place an eerie calm. Shakily Jon picked the crusts of dirt off his eyes and spat out more sand and dust. After a few moments he was able to see again. The only sound was the thundering of blood in his ears.

Miraculously Elijah had not moved. No human being could have withstood that power unaided and survived.

"We'd better get out of here." The Professor looked very scared. He ran his hand over his face, reaching for the edge of the rubber headset. Jon's heart sank; he knew what was coming next.

"Where's my headset?" the Professor reached up with both hands, at first disbelieving, then frantically running his gashed hands through his hair.

Jon shrugged; he was dimly aware in the midst of the chaos of his own headset being torn from his face. "It's happened before," he said.

"This is absurd!" The Professor snapped, looking accusingly at Jon as if it was his fault. "We can only see these events through the viewing screens inside the headsets. You haven't got yours on, neither I mine. How are we still seeing these things?"

"It's happened before," Jon insisted. "When Hannah died. Even though you took the headset off my head, the pictures kept coming."

"How long for?" Surreptitiously the Prof was pinching the back of his hand.

"Oh, several minutes, then they sort of got mixed up with things outside." Jon's head ached and the wound in his scalp was oozing into his hair. The Professor's white hair had turned a dirty grey. "The whole thing's just getting more and more real!" Jon said, waving his hand around the landscape.

"We need to get out of this place." The Professor dashed to the end of the cleft, as if expecting to see the viewing room out there. "This simply can't be happening."

Outside, Elijah shook his robes of dust and sneezed several times. Clearly he was expecting more.

Jon recalled Hannah's anxious warning. "Why, what else is going to happen?"

When the earthquake struck the Professor turned a shade greyer. As with the windstorm they could see the spectacle approaching from a great way off- the soil and rock of the plain that erupted like a giant tidal wave buckling the land, throwing trees, boulders and a great cloud of soil and dust into the air as it hurtled toward them. There was a deep note, like a ten mile string being plucked and the landscape shifted from side to side too, shaking like a wet dog drying itself.

"Get down!" bawled the Prof. They flung themselves to the earth again, praying that the rocks to each side of them wouldn't collapse and bury them alive. It was not unlike a water flume ride, only far worse- the entire mountain would rise up, then dive dizzily down, some three or four metres. The rocky hillside pitched and yawed, all the time the deep booming sound filled Jon's skull. Great cracks crazed out in all directions as if the mountain were a shop window hit by a sledgehammer. Next moment a huge trench opened in the rock beneath them.

This time it was Jon's turn to grab the Professor before he slipped into the chasm, he held his arm tightly as he swung himself back onto the ledge- then with a groan the rocks moved back together. They had no time to ponder the seriousness of their situation, the bucking continued unabated; rocks tumbled down the slopes and crashed down around them.

Elijah still occupied his position at the head of the cleft jumping nimbly from side to side, skipping around to maintain his foothold as the solid ground beneath shivered and shook.

Jon was the first to recover "What's next?" he asked.

"What?" There was blood running from a cut on the Professor's forehead, his face was clammy and sweating.

"I said, what's next? Or is that it?"

He nodded, the worried furrow on his brow deepened. "That!" he pointed.

Across the plain a wall of fire advanced. It stretched skywards as far as they could see, neither were its ends in sight. It emanated an ear-splitting roar as it swept towards the mountain. Around it the atmosphere boiled and lightning flashed continuously before it. If the sandstorm was fast, this was far faster. They had no time to take cover, one moment it was a full five kilometres away on level ground, the next its heat wave was igniting the dry fallen trees as it surged up the slopes just below where they stood. Jon had a brief recollection of a TV documentary of a nuclear detonation. It occurred to him as he watched the awesome spectacle that it was as though the component parts of an atomic explosion, the blast, the earth shock and the firestorm had been separated and presented in turn. Then it was upon them, a mighty endless curtain of fire capable of vapourising them both instantly. Jon closed his eyes, awaiting the blast of heat he had felt at Carmel to turn his skin to charcoal, aware that on this exposed mountain top there was nowhere to run, nowhere to hide. In a few seconds, in a searing pain it would end.

Just as before, the silence afterwards was oppressive. Not just a lack of sound, but a tangible deathly quiet. Moments before breasting the peak of the mountain, the wall of fire had split in two, pouring by on both sides of them. They had felt its heat and heard the unearthly roar as it rushed onwards, then it was gone. Briefly, just out of the corner of his eye Jon had thought he had seen a human-like figure outlined in the flames, but he couldn't be sure. In its wake the rocks distorted, many of them melted out of shape were cooling into new bizarre shapes on the mountainside. What vegetation the wind and earthquake had not destroyed was blackened and thrown over the hillside or tumbled into deep trenches opened by the quake.

The Prof's colour had gone ashen. He looked very ill and even more scared than he had at first. He was shaking uncontrollably; sweat running down his face and holding his head in his hands.

"Prof," Jon felt anxiety swelling into gut panic. He coughed to try to shift the grit from his throat. "Stop it, let's get out of here!" He could see the distress the Prof was in, but overwhelming everything was a need to escape. What horror would arrive next? He didn't want to find out. He reached and clutched the old man's sleeve.

"Stop the Timescope," he insisted, closing his eyes, trying to control his breathing. Moments later when he opened them, he caught sight of the look in his companion's eyes. "It's over isn't it?"

The Prof shook his head, disorientated. "No." He whispered to himself. "Now GOD speaks."

He was, like a child caught in a nightmare. In the silence Jon felt the old man's profound dread transmit itself to him. The voice of GOD. This was going to be very bad!

"Elijah!"

It was a still, small voice- no huge echo, no mighty overtones. Clearly audible but soft. It was… just so pure, so right, so …. GOD.

"What are you doing here?" The question was directed at Elijah, but they were in the way too.

The voice of soft, absolute Truth. It took Jon's breath away. His knees went weak then buckled. In an instant it was as if the top of his head had been sliced off and brilliant sunlight was pouring into his brain. He felt utterly naked, completely defenceless against this Presence. With a gasp he sank to his knees.

The wind, earthquake and fire had challenged their physical defences, their ability to survive the extreme conditions, but this Omniscience scoured their minds, revealing and challenging every decision, every motive, every thought and every action.

"What are you doing here?"

Images and recollections began to pour like a dam-burst into Jon's mind- some trivial misdemeanours, many inconsequential episodes; some recent, many more long-forgotten from years back; they flooded relentlessly through his memory.

"Jon, one last time, did you take that money?"

"No, mum, honest. I promise I know nothing about it!"

"Break his nose, Heath!"

"Jon, my friend, you distract him, I'll grab what I can…"

"OK, if no one's prepared to own up, the whole class will stay in…"

"Do you have a ticket?"

"She's only an old hag anyway!"

"No don't hit me!"

With each fresh image a sense of burning shame. Shame, shame, shame. Was nothing hidden? His whole life open to inspection and critique. More images, dancing before his eyes; his Mum's purse open on the dining room table. Faris, his eyes sparkling, holding up the collection of magazines snatched from under his brother's bed; the sound of the fire taking hold of the school gymnasium, the sleeping tablets dissolving in the

Professor's tea- there was no let up, no respite. Like layers of dead leaves in a gale, memories stirred, lifted and took flight. Little lies, big lies, minor cruelties, broken promises, crude insults; they whirled and eddied around his head.

"I'm sorry, I'm sorry, I'm sorry, I'm sorry, I'm sorry, I'm sorry." Jon mumbled over and over, the words running together. He wrapped his head in his arms, but the pressure of the Light could not be blotted out.

"What are you doing here?"

It was as if the pictures racing through his brain were supplying the answer to the question. What was Jon Heath doing here on Planet Earth? Anything constructive? Anything of consequence? Anything beyond pleasing his miserable little self? Crushed by the weight of this realisation Jon sobbed into the dust.

Now he understood, too, the Prof's fear. They weren't meant to be here. This wasn't just a voice; it was The Voice of GOD. Its softness concealed a Purpose of Steel, a consistency of granite and a quality of timelessness that was frightening. Even in its gentleness it was drawing his breath from his body. His heart was racing, his blood thundering through the arteries of his brain. A grey mist floated before his eyes.

Jon looked out at Elijah. His face was entirely shrouded in his robe. He was shaking too, his gaunt frame silhouetted against the bright daylight that had returned. He was leaning heavily on his staff to stay upright. Finally he spoke.

"I have been very jealous for the LORD God of hosts: because the children of Israel have forsaken your covenant, thrown down your altars, and slain your prophets with the sword; and I, even I only, am left; and they seek my life, to take it away." He buried his face in the collar of his robes.

The Voice spoke again; it felt as though Jon's brain was being pushed out of his skull. The Prof's hand was on his shoulder, holding onto him for support. He was exhausted too, and trying to say something in his ear. But before Jon could make out the words, the Voice was all around them again.

"Go, return on your way to the wilderness of Damascus: and when you get there, anoint Hazael to be king over Syria:

And Jehu the son of Nimshi anoint to be king over Israel: and Elisha the son of Shaphat of Abelmeholah anoint to be prophet in your place. And it shall come to pass, that him that escapes the sword of Hazael shall Jehu slay: and him that escapes from the sword of Jehu shall Elisha slay."

Elijah bowed deeper. His posture proclaimed his sense of failure. This, then, was his last commission from the God he had served faithfully- go and appoint your successors; your task is finished. The nation has turned against you despite your magnificent victory at Carmel, now they were destined for destruction.. So what was there left to live for? A wife and family? No, even simple home comforts were denied this austere man.

There were a few moments for Elijah to absorb these last instructions, in effect to put his house in order. Then the Voice spoke one last time. Its tone had completely changed. It was gentle, kindly, reassuring.

"Yet I have left me seven thousand in Israel, all the knees which have not bowed unto Baal, and every mouth which has not kissed him."

Elijah straightened up in astonishment. For a few moments he stared in wonder. He repeated softly to himself what he had just heard. *'Seven thousand?'* *'Seven thousand faithful in Israel?'*

His leathery face, so downcast just a few moments earlier lit up in a radiant smile. Seven thousand true believers, obstinate in the face of public and peer pressure. Hazarding their lives in their rugged determination to stand fast to the ways of the True God. Seven thousand of the staunchest companions he could ever ask for.

At his shoulder Jon felt the Prof's grip relax. He could hear his incoherent muttering.

"Prof?"

There was no answer. He had fallen on his face holding his head in his hands and moaning in pain. Elijah brushed past them both, joy lighting up his face like a beacon. Then he disappeared from view.

"Prof? What's the matter?"

"Get suh 'elp …. lease." He struggled to lift his face; the corner of his mouth had sagged. Actually the whole side of his face was unnaturally relaxed and motionless. His right eye was staring straight ahead, unfocussed.

"Call an an..lance.. lease… elp .."

He was covered in cuts and bruises but there was no obvious sign of serious injury. Jon suspected that the whole experience could have caused him to have a heart attack or something.

"Prof…? Please, say something." But the Prof was incoherent. Frantically Jon tried to remember the smattering of first aid he knew. *Loosen collar*; his hands trembled uncontrollably, the old man's collar was quite loose anyway. What was next? If only the Timescope would release them both.

"Prof!" He uttered a low moan. Jon felt new panic welling up in his chest, choking him.

"Help! Somebody help me!" he screamed. His words were swallowed by the silence of the bare hills around. Could he be heard? The Prof's house was huge, the viewing room well sound-proofed. And in this crazy machine was he actually crying out loud, or was the Timescope only giving his brain the impression of shouting? And why wouldn't it let him go? Was he stuck here, on this hill with a dying man? This last thought filled him with an even deeper sense of foreboding. The Professor reached out and clutched Jon's hand; it felt like a drowning man, hanging on for dear life.

Then inspiration struck. The phone! He could feel it in his pocket. This time the line was clear. His hands trembled so much he could hardly find her number.

Her phone rang for ages. 'Pick up!' he muttered. Finally she came on the line.

"Jon? What sort of time is this? It's three in the morning!"

"Na! Listen, the Prof's seriously ill. He's having a heart attack, I think. Can you come over?"

Jon could hear the sound of something being knocked over. Then her voice, alert and tense, lined with fear.

"Granddad? Where is he?"

"He's here with me, listen; is your Aunt able to come?"

"No, they're both out for the night," the note of panic increased. "Have you called the ambulance?"

"Listen Na, I can't! I'm on top of some mountain with him, I need you to come and get us back…"

"Jon, where are you?" then with a harder edge in her voice, "Why are you with my granddad? Have you been drinking?"

"Stop asking questions, will you? Just get down here fast!" Jon held the phone close to the semi-conscious old man.

"Nay..ee..?" It was all he could manage.

"Can you hear him?"

"I'm coming," she gulped.

It was a full ten minutes later that the phone rang. On top of this desert mountain, in ancient Israel, Jon's tiny pocket mobile phone rang, connecting him with the world outside. "Na, that you?"

"Can't you see me?"

"No."

"I'm here, standing in front of you. No here, right in front of your nose. The headsets are over by the door."

"I can't see you at all, honest! I'm not mucking about. The Prof's ill. Have you called the ambulance?"

"Yes they're on their way." She sounded at breaking point. "He's lying on the floor here. Jon, what happened to him?"

"I'll tell you later, please, you got to get us out of here!"

"How? Didn't you ask the Prof?"

"He didn't know earlier. Can't you just turn the Timescope off?"

"I'll try," she didn't sound sure.

Moments later she was standing next to him on the mountain. Jon's heart went cold. "Have you put a headset on? That's stupid! Now we might all be stuck up here!"

"I haven't touched a headset," she snapped, "I'm standing in the viewing room. I just gave the computers the three-fingered salute, that's all."

"The what?"

"Control, Alt, Delete! Always works eventually. Can you see me now?"

To his relief, the landscape began to break into pieces, pixellating and fragmenting. Rocks dissolved to cushions and wallpaper. In a minute or two they were back in the viewing room.

It took a moment for Jon's eyes to accustom themselves to the change in light. When the spots had stopped swimming in his field of vision he looked at Naomi. The look he got back alarmed him. She was cradling her grandfather's head in her lap, wiping the crusted blood and dirt away with her handkerchief. Her distress had given way to terrible anger.

"What have you done to him?"

"Wha-"

"What have you done to him this time? Oh don't give me that! I know about the tablets you put in his tea!"

The Prof was trying to speak but all he could do was mumble and drool from the corner of his mouth. His words were very slurred, and he didn't appear to recognise either of them much. By contrast Naomi's lips were set in a thin, tight line.

"I don't know why you did it, but I saw the dregs in that tea cup. I thought you were had nicked some stuff, but that wasn't it, was it? You used the Timescope, didn't you? And now you've drugged him with something else, haven't you?"

Jon felt as if he was about to have a seizure himself. His last vestiges of self-respect were blasted away. Never before had he believed he could feel so wretched.

"Just tell me before I tell the police!" she insisted, her voice hard with contempt. "What have you done to him?"

Jon slumped against the wall, his head in his hands and let her rage wash over him.

"I'm sorry, Naomi. Really I am so, so sorry."

"So you admit it?"

"Yes," he said tonelessly. "I did drug the Prof a while back. It was sleeping tablets. But not this time."

"You scum… you nasty, filthy little…"

"I know."

Her eyes were wide, incredulous; "but why, what's been going on?"

"Please Na; let me tell you before the ambulance arrives."

She held her grandfather protectively as if Jon would suddenly pounce on them both. She soon realised that she had only suspected a fraction of the truth. Jon told her of his plan to exploit the Timescope for money, then of getting in contact with Terrence Prentice, and sending him a file scanned from his ring. Her initial reflex was to challenge every aspect of his story- after all why should he suddenly change the habit of a lifetime and start telling the truth now? In her lap her grandfather continued to moan softly. "Hold on, Granddad," she whispered.

"We were on this mountain," Jon finished. "Hannah, well, she was at the party and told me to get here as fast as I could because he was in great danger. When I got in, he'd lost the headset, and was on this mountain with Elijah,"

"What mountain, Horeb? Earthquake, wind and fire?"

"Yeah, that's it. Only it was like nothing I've ever seen. They were bad enough, but then...He...He spoke."

Looking at him, Naomi shuddered. "God, you mean?"

"It was like being turned inside out, Na. Everything you've ever done, said, thought; all the real reasons for what you do all hitting you at once." His chest was heaving and he was having difficulty speaking. "It sort of ... makes you realise how... rubbish you really are."

"And Granddad couldn't cope with it?"

Jon shook his head. "Nobody could cope with that." He said slowly.

"You have to be pure in heart," she answered. "Okay Granddad, I can hear the ambulance coming."

He made no reply.

They travelled with him to the hospital. Seeing him pale and nearly unconscious in the ambulance brought on a shock reaction to them both. Naomi cried almost all the way, Jon tried to answer the ambulance man's questions.

"Did you find him like this?"

"Er... no- I mean yes."

The man looked from Jon's cut face and shoulder to the Prof's bruises. He was putting two and two together and making five. He leant over to flick a switch and Jon realised he was surreptitiously smelling his breath.

"'Ad a few Sonny?"

"Uh huh!"

Let him think what he liked. The journey in the ambulance was like a roller coaster ride and seemed interminable. The paramedic's face kept going out of focus. As they raced through the empty streets, he listened to the paramedics as they radioed ahead to the hospital. He caught the words *'Ischemic attack.'* Was that a stroke? Because his Gran had had a few strokes before she died. So the Prof was probably going to die then?

Jon rang home. It took ages for the phone to answer, but eventually his mother came on the line. She grasped the situation swiftly, and was mercifully sparing with her questions;

"Just give us chance to get dressed; we'll see you down A and E."

"Thanks Mum."

Jon and Naomi sat glumly in the waiting room, watching the clock hands as they crawled around the dial. Outside it was daylight, traffic was moving and the city sounds increasing. Voices shouting, trucks reversing, ambulances arriving and departing.

"Jon? Who is this Prentice guy?"

"Oh, nobody special. Just a civil servant who works for my Mum. I don't think we'll hear any more from him."

Once a younger Doctor came out and asked them a couple of questions. Then Mary Heath appeared, looking tired and worried. She didn't ask many questions, she just hugged them both and told Naomi not to worry, which started Naomi crying again. Then Mr Heath appeared having found a nearby parking space. In an effort to appear useful he fired questions at the nursing staff behind the reception desk.

"They think it was a stroke." He looked grave as he sat beside them. "Quite a major one too. They won't know for twelve hours or so what the outcome will be. I've left our number and they will contact us as soon as they know more."

So they left. It felt heartless, but there wasn't any other option apart from sitting around worrying. Naomi relaxed in the rear of the car as they threaded their way to her Aunt's house and gazed vacantly at Jon, sitting opposite, withdrawn and miserable. What was she to make of this latest turn of events? She had little room for doubting his story. He had told it with remorse, leaving nothing out, conscious of how cruel his betrayal of the Prof must seem. Something had flattened his spirit. That she could see for herself. He looked and sounded crushed.

"Jon," she said softly, her voice just audible over the purr of the car.

"Mmm?"

"Thanks. For going to help him, I mean."

13

"Hi Jon, Naomi!" They both liked Sister Marsha, seated at the ward desk. She was chatty when she wasn't busy. Her Caribbean accent took a little getting used to, but she was always ready with a smile. Neither did she treat them as if they were little children.

"No change, sorry loves. Let me have your phone numbers on the way out, I promise you you'll be the first to know if he comes round."

"Thanks Marsha. Can we go in?"

"Yeah, sure- Doctor's rounds in half an hour, but just stay out of their way and you'll be fine. They don't notice lesser mortals like us."

The Prof lay there quite still. He was breathing normally but unconscious. A tube disappeared down his nose, and a urine bag was hooked on the side of the bed. They sat, some time without speaking, watching the steady rise and fall of his chest. After a while the silence became oppressive.

"Aunt Judith had a call from the police yesterday."

"The police? Why?"

"Jon, think about it! An old man is brought into hospital covered in bruises and bleeding from a head wound. He can't tell his story, and you had been drinking, so what do you think they want? The ambulance crew probably passed on the details."

"What did your Aunt say?" Jon was dully aware that yet another problem was looming. But still feeling very flat after his recent experience he could hardly trouble to give it a thought. The last six days had been very difficult. At times he had hardly the energy to get out of bed. It had been a relief to come here and talk to the prone figure in the private room. Talk, talk and talk some more. To pour out the account of his treachery; hear his own voice spelling out in detail what he had done. The old man had said nothing; but Jon liked to think that if he were conscious he would have forgiven him by now.

That much he was certain of in his estimation of Professor Avery.

"She defended you!" Naomi watched closely to see what Jon's reaction would be. "She told the Police that it was very unlikely you would have harmed him."

"I'd like to see anyone try! He's strong!" Jon nodded to the Prof. "When he pulled me away from Roger- well he practically picked me up with one hand!" He looked and sounded relieved.

Naomi smiled. It was the first spirited thing he had said since Horeb. She had been astounded in the change in him. His swagger and bravado had been swept away. He seemed quieter, even humbler in her opinion. How long would it last?

Jon felt that the Prof would understand his jitteriness. He had heard that Voice too. He had felt the searchlight sweeping through the recesses of his mind, laying bare his soul with ease.

There he lay beneath the covers, breathing gently without any assistance, just occasionally twitching. Once he muttered something, but for the last six days he had been completely out of it. His face was still sagged down at one side, and this made him dribble now and then. He had had dozens of visitors, they had held his hands and talked to him fondly at length but he had made no response. Others had bent their heads in prayer around his bed, still others had cried openly at the sight of him. Their old friend was very close to quite a few people- young and old.

The door swung open. Naomi let go her Grandfather's hand and it flopped back on the covers. Three white-coated doctors came into the room. A fourth person loitered in the doorway. He was dressed entirely differently- a light grey suit to match his hair. Jon glanced at him, and then looked again. The face returned his gaze impassively. Then he was gone.

This then was the doctor's ward rounds. As Marsha had said, they gave them barely a glance but clustered at the side of the bed, examining the charts, notes and diagrams attached to a clipboard hung on the bedrail.

"Rufus Avery...." began the first doctor, the one in a white coat; his tone was deferential to the senior man. "It's unusual, in my experience," he said, holding up the file of notes "to see such external indications of cerebral lesions in a subject without any internal evidence on the CT scans. In fact I was so convinced of an error in the patient data that I asked for a rescan. That too," he produced another X-ray film from an envelope and held it up to the light, "shows absolutely no sign of bleeding or clotting anywhere."

The older man took the film without a word. Impatiently he took it to the window and held it up. For two or three minutes he remained silent, scanning the picture.

"There's been a mistake!" He snapped, breaking the silence.

"I assure you, there has not!" The doctor retorted.

"This is a perfectly normal scan!"

"I know."

"Then there must have been a mistake. Is there another 'R. Avery' on the system?"

"Do you think I haven't already checked?" The doctor sounded tense.

There was another long silence. The third man in the party looked at the rest of the notes in the file.

"Bloods... normal, urine... normal, sats, blood pressure... uh huh... Ummm..." his voice tailed off into a murmur.

The older man was now shining a flashlight into the Prof's eyes. Straightening up he addressed the other two.

"You're right this is unusual. He has completely shut down even though his health is normal. I'll trawl through my records for anything that resembles this, er... catatonic state."

The first doctor shuffled. "There's something else."

Jon and Naomi listened intently. It appeared from EEG scans that the stillness of the patient belied the facts. Although his body was almost immobile, his brain was in overdrive. So much so, the Doctor related, waving folded printouts in the air, that they had been obliged to double the nutritional supply to compensate for the extra calorie requirements. When he had finished there was an awkward silence, broken only by the older man jingling his keys in his pocket. Finally the first doctor spoke;

"What do you suggest in the meantime?"

"What can I suggest? Keep him fed, observed and wait. He'll come out of it when he's good and ready." He turned to go. "All the same, I'd be fascinated to know what caused this!"

Despite the warmth of the room, Jon shivered.

After they were gone, Naomi picked up her bag. "I've got to meet my Aunt at the Prof's house," she explained. "She's been waiting for an opportunity to get into his place and tidy up a bit. I'd better be there to make sure she doesn't do too much damage. Goodness knows what she might do left to herself! You staying here?"

Jon shook his head. "Nah! Do you want a hand?"

She was pleasantly surprised at his offer. After a moment's thought she said; "Yeah, but wait until my Aunt's away from the place- she's a bit nosey. I'll ring you."

She bent down and kissed her grandfather on the tip of his nose and they left the room.

"Jon, Naomi, would ya wait?"

A figure detached itself from the nook by the water cooler and moved expertly across their path. It was the Light Grey Suit. There was something practised in the way he intercepted them without appearing to block their way. Naomi stopped, but Jon started to go round him.

He was American. The accent was not pronounced, but it was there. More worryingly was the way he seemed to know them. Jon found his way unobtrusively barred; the man had piercing blue eyes which held his gaze, mesmerising him like a rabbit powerless before a snake. He knew this man, he was sure!

"Where'd you get our names?" Jon demanded.

He shrugged the question aside. "Can I have a little chat? I won't take too much of your time."

"We'd best be home." Naomi too was trying to escape past him.

"It's about Professor Avery."

They both stopped. "What about him?"

"As I said, can we talk? No, not here," he pushed open a door of a small waiting room. Somehow he manoeuvred them both inside before they had chance to think.

Naomi asked, "Are you the police?"

"Should I be?" He fixed his eyes on her, his face inscrutable.

"N...no, I just, I only thought..." Naomi stumbled to a halt.

"Sit down."

Jon glanced at Naomi. He was telling them what to do, but not giving anything in return.

"All right, stay standing," he shrugged. He sat down and opened a small attaché case. From it he produced a sheaf of papers. They looked like computer printouts.

"As you might guess I'm from America," he said, without glancing up. He was riffling through the papers. "Ah!"

"Yeah, well?" Jon said, more for something to say.

"May twelfth. Thirty-five seconds online, followed by a further one minute, twenty at eight pm USA time. May fifteenth, seven and a half minutes, May nineteenth, five and three-quarters." He glanced up at their mystified faces. "And so it goes on. These are only the most recent."

"What goes on?" Naomi said.

"Your brilliant grandfather is borrowing huge computer resources from American Universities." He tapped the sheaf of papers. "These are for Kansas State University. He accesses networks, locks up mainframes into processing his applications, then leaves without a word of explanation. Why?"

"How should we know? Anyway, why do you let him?"

"He has access rights, He's doing nothing wrong."

"Then why all the fuss?"

He looked at them for a few moments, his face wore a 'trust me. I'm your friend' look, but the light blue eyes were cold and hard. Jon shivered again.

"Jon, Professor Avery is one of the most brilliant men ever to come to the States from England. He pioneered a huge amount of research into computer languages and operating codes. You have no idea how clumsy things were before he got started, and how refined they were by the time he left to come back here."

Naomi glanced up at the small clock above the door. "We know all this," she said uneasily. "So what?"

"I thought you might. But you have been spending a lot of time with him lately haven't you?"

"Look!" began Naomi. "What's it to you if we have? Can't I spend time with my own Grandfather? " She was getting cross. "More to the point; how is it you know so much about us? Our names, what we do, what he does?"

He smiled, but the eyes didn't. "I'm sorry. I didn't mean to annoy ya, I just wanted your cooperation. That's all." He opened his jacket lapel and flashed an identity badge. "My name is Bradley Jackman. I'm from Kansas State University. I was an undergraduate at the time Professor Avery was over in the States. Look, please sit down, will ya?"

They sat down and listened to his story. He had, he said, been much influenced by the Prof in years past, both as an undergraduate and a scientist; and had followed avidly research findings submitted by the Prof since he returned to England. They had shown further and further promise in many aspects of computing, but after some later work was met with bitter scepticism and acrimonious debate; he went very quiet.

Jon interrupted. "What sort of work?"

He smiled, slightly embarrassed. "Oh, some research into the validity of Biblical records. It was far removed from his main field of applied computing. I don't think he meant it to be taken seriously."

Now it was Jon's turn to smile quietly to himself.

"But it was?" asked Naomi, cautiously.

"Yeah, I should say!" He laughed loudly, too loud in the small room. "Professor Avery is a very wealthy, very successful man. He can afford to be outspoken. And he often is." He fidgeted with the catch on his case. "He has a load of critics. They seized his more wacky work as evidence to discredit him. He was asking for trouble! But he wouldn't back down."

"So what do you want?" Naomi looked puzzled. Some of this was new to her, but why was this American so involved?

"Quite simply this," he said. "What is he doing with all this computing power? These are terabyte file sizes, and a lot of people are asking questions. And we're only the tip of the iceberg; computer networks are being hijacked in Australia, Denmark, Sweden, oh, all over the world. And now this:" he withdrew a document from his case. "He's grabbing mobile phone networks- oh not so's anyone would be inconvenienced, just a few seconds here or there. Somebody was bound to notice eventually. So they sent me over to find out!"

"Why don't you just open some of the files and find out?" said Naomi sweetly.

"Look, Missy," he said, "have you heard of encryption?"

Naomi shook her head. It went against the grain, but she opted to play dumb.

"It's a way of encoding transactions so that nobody else can see them. Most encryptions can be read eventually with the right software to crack them open. Not so Avery encryption! We've been trying for weeks to see what he's up to. There's just no way in."

Jon stood up. "Look, I don't understand this either. If I find anything out I'll let you know. We know he was into computers, but he's our Sunday School teacher, OK? That's all."

For once he looked nonplussed. "Sunday School?"

"Yes," Jon said

He rose too. "Look, here's my card, anything you might find out, I'd be sure glad to know."

Jon took the card. It could have come from any business card vending machine at any airport in the world.

"Director of software resources, Kansas State University" and underneath a series of email, telephone and website addresses.

And in bold print across the middle of the card:

"Dr BRADLEY JACKSON"

"We'll be in touch if we hear anything, Doctor Jackman." he said, watching his face closely.

"Sure thing!" The American held the door open for them.

"What are you smirking about? Demanded Naomi as they emerged into the bright sunshine.

Jon held up the card. "Doesn't even know who he is!"

She squinted at the name. "He just misheard you, surely?"

"No, I said it very clearly, I called him 'Doctor Jackman,' and he didn't bat an eyelid."

"Don't you think this is kinda scary? If he's not who he says he is, then who is he? "

"I don't know for sure," Jon said slowly, "but I need to check something when I get home."

"What's this about the Timescope using mobile phone networks?" They had come to a point where she was heading in a different direction. Jon, for once, was enjoying her company. Horeb had cleared the air between them and he was seeing a nicer side to her. "And while you're at it, is that why my mobile was making that terrible noise the other day?"

"What noise?"

"Sort of screeching sound. Wouldn't work at all."

Naomi hesitated, tongue-tied. Part of her wanted to stay and talk. Even to continue walking with him in the same direction. But to do so would be an admission that she liked his company. The idea at once tantalised and appalled her. She tried hunting for something to say that wasn't connected with their recent experiences, but her mind had emptied of small talk. Instead she felt her cheeks blushing furiously.

"No idea at all!" was all he got by way of reply as she dashed away.

It didn't take Jon long to find the file he needed on the DVD he had collated from Terrence Prentice's less-than salubrious life. As he fast-forwarded through the endless motorway service stops, ministerial meetings, late-night office slumbers and a host of other assignations; he was conscious of a knot developing in his guts. No, it wouldn't be one and the same man. It would be just his imagination working overtime. Once he had found the clandestine meeting that he had copied and sent on to Prentice, his fears would prove groundless. There were thousands of grey-haired Americans in England at any one time, it would be somebody completely diff...

'Oh no!' he breathed. 'Oh please, no...'

One frame of the video had caught the American full in the face. Even on his laptop screen the blue eyes froze his blood. They were pitiless, cold and dangerous. As the events unfolded Jon noticed again how the man exerted a chill over the proceedings- he spoke seldom, but when he did the other delegates listened slavishly. Nobody contradicted him. Nobody questioned his opinions. Most obvious was Terrence Prentice's anxiety; he would constantly lick his lips, crack his delicate knuckles and loosen the collar around his podgy neck. For once in his life, Jon felt some sympathy for him.

"On your own tonight?" Marsha called. "You'll have to wait a few minutes; he's having physiotherapy right now."

Jon's heart leapt. "Do you mean he's conscious?"

"No love, but even though he's still out of it, he's got to have regular massage and movement to stop muscle wastage. Sit down; do you want a cup of tea?"

"Is it out of that machine?" he asked.

She leant forward, conspiratorially. "I'll tell them you're a relative; they'll do us a real cuppa from the trolley."

With a plate of chocolate digestives in front of them, and a chipped mug of tea, Marsha sat back in her chair. The soft wall lighting threw her face into shadow.

"Tell me about Professor Avery," she said.

"What do you want to know?"

She sat back and dipped her biscuit in the tea. "I get the feeling he's a very kind, very popular sort of gentleman. You've no idea how many people have been in to see him. We've given up trying to enforce visiting hours- some of his friends have come halfway across the country to be with him." She selected another biscuit and held the plate out to Jon. "So what's the attraction?"

"They're mostly people from his church," he told her. "They kinda look after him there." She remained silent, so he went on hesitantly. "He's well, just the sort of person you would want for a Granddad. He's always ready to think the best of people, you know." As he stumbled on for a few minutes more, she seemed to lose patience.

Behind them the door of the Prof's room opened and a woman emerged with a trolley.

"Is it alright for this young man to go in now?" called Marsha. The woman nodded.

"You've got an hour, Jon," she said, looking at the computer screen. "We have to put our foot down somewhere about visiting hours!" She turned her back, and then as something occurred to her, spun round to face him once more. "Jon, I know he's unconscious, but try talking to him. Tell him what you've been doing; things that you know will interest him. Anything you like. You never know how much they are taking in even when they're unconscious. Oh, and give him my love."

"Will do!" Jon called back, rather uncertainly and went in.

The sheets were tucked in tidily around the still form. He was so, so still. Nothing had changed since the morning. The feeding tube still went down his nose, and the urine bag was still clipped in its usual place. Pale evening light streamed through the window, illuminating his features, making his thin nose look beakier than ever. The only change was that the sag in his face had noticeably improved.

"Hi Prof!" Jon called. "How are you?"

He didn't expect an answer, but talking to him was better than nothing. The silence of this evening seemed to want to swallow up the room and its occupant. Jon went on; talking to him became easier as the minutes passed.

"Mum and Dad say hi, and you know Marsha, no you probably don't, but she's usually here on duty, she sends her love too. Naomi's over your place right now; she's helping to tidy things up a bit. Actually, she's making sure Judith doesn't chuck out anything important."

It could have been imagination, but the muscles on the Prof's neck tightened. Jon looked again. "Is that OK?"

At that moment the door burst open behind him. Marsha bustled in wheeling a small trolley. "How is he?" she enquired, but didn't stop for an answer. She placed a cuff on the Prof's arm and inflated it, stethoscope under the cuff listening for his heartbeat. "One-twenty-nine over eighty-seven…" she muttered, scribbling on the clipboard of notes. "Nine o' seven pm…wish I was as healthy!" A small syringe of blood was drawn from his arm and placed in a bag, and his temperature taken. She fiddled around for a few moments more, then like a miniature tornado she was gone.

Jon sighed. It was time to dispense with the small talk. "I think I've messed up again," he admitted to his silent confessor. "When I sent those files to that Prentice bloke, I thought it had gone no further. Now this American guy is hanging around asking questions."

This time there was no doubt about it, the hands twitched and the deathly still face screwed up in a frown. Then it relaxed and all was quiet again. A gentle nasal sigh escaped past the feeding tube.

Encouraged by this Jon pressed on. He related the conversation with Jackman yesterday. What did he really want? Who really was he? He found himself wondering what the Prof would do in his situation. "Should I own up to Prentice?" he wondered aloud. Throw himself at his mercy? Something warned him that however well-intentioned this course of action might be, the consequences would be dire.

"Tell Naomi?" The old man's neck muscles relaxed. "OK, I'll go see her tomorrow. At least then she won't say anything to Jackman."

Jon glanced at his watch. It was getting late. He'd stay another five minutes then head home. The silence in the room was settling round him like a heavy fall of snow, blanketing and muting every other sound. It was just as he turned to leave that he saw that the figure under the sheets was unnaturally still.

"Help!" Jon crashed through the doors into the corridor. "He's stopped breathing!"

Marsha had her face close to something on the desk. She shot up cracking her head on the low shelf that went round the nurse's station. But in one swift movement she pushed her chair back and pulled a red alarm button. Along the corridor a hooter blared and an amber light flashed. In thirty seconds the area had filled up with medics.

"Resus, room eight!" She barked, "I'll be right in." Three men clutching cases and equipment burst through the doors. Jon tried to follow but was abruptly elbowed aside by Marsha. "Just stay out!" She snapped.

The sound of commands, the whining of some apparatus charging up and unpleasant thudding sounds dropped abruptly as the thick doors swung closed. Jon was left reeling down the passage.

Almost immediately he was aware that something else was amiss. At the nurse's station where Marsha had sat, the sounds from inside the room were louder. They were tinny, but clear. *"Stand clear: shock!"* It was a male voice. Then a creaking of bedsprings. Then further commands. It took a few seconds for Jon to comprehend what he was hearing. The intercom was on. Marsha had been listening in to his conversation!

The events of the day went round and round his mind. Prentice, the American, Jackman, Jackson whoever he was and now Marsha spying on them. And where was Naomi? Not at her Aunt's house, and not answering her mobile either. He tried again, but all he could get was the recorded message; *"we are not able to connect your call at this time."* He was starting to feel truly scared.

He didn't sleep much that night either.

"Jon?" His phone had been ringing for some time.

"Na, that you?" Jon peered blearily at the bedside clock. It was nine in the morning. He had slept after all. Then as the events of yesterday tumbled back into his mind; "Na, thank goodness! Did you get my message?"

"Jon?" She sounded upset. "Please say it wasn't you, Jon!"

"Wasn't me what?"

"Someone has been in the house and mucked around with the Timescope. It wasn't you, was it?" She was trying her hardest to keep the accusation out of her voice. She wanted to try to trust Jon, but this latest incident had set her resolution back somewhat.

She and her Aunt had cleared much of the rubbish from the downstairs floors yesterday evening, but under Naomi's supervision, the Timescope hardware had been left well alone. They left at just before nine o' clock to get something to eat. She had personally checked before the house had been locked up when they left. This morning, however, she had discovered that the Carmel stone was missing from the reader. It had completely vanished; and other items of equipment had been tampered with and examined.

"I was in the hospital most of the evening," Jon assured her. Then; "Did the ward call you last night?"

"No, my mobile battery's shot, they wouldn't have got through. Why?"

"Your Granddad stopped breathing last night."

"Oh, no, please no…" her voice began to stifle in tears. "Is he…"

"I rang your Aunt when I got home. She went there straight away, then rang me about half-eleven. They resuscitated him. Apparently he's stable. She tried to contact you on your phone, she said you were at a friend's house, but she didn't have their number. Is your phone charged up now?"

Not much, she gulped, it needed a new battery. She was going straight over to the hospital. "Jon, could you come too?"

"I was going to anyway. Na, we need to talk."

In contrast with the frenzied activity of last night, the hospital was quiet. They had moved the Prof to a more clinical-looking room; he was on a ventilator and his heart was being monitored. He was still immobile, but looking thinner. If it were not for the change of scene Jon could have imagined it all to have been a nasty dream.

"What was it you wanted to talk about?" Naomi's hair was mussed up, she looked tired and strained and her eyes were puffy.

"Not here!" Jon led her out of the room and into a small lounge nearby. In low tones he told her about Marsha's eavesdropping. Then he told her about Jackman. By the time he had finished, he could have told her that thousands of CIA hit men were scaling the hospital walls and she wouldn't have taken it in.

To Jon's amazement she threw her arms round his neck and buried her face in his shoulder. He had a fleeting thought; 'George won't like this! Then her body shook as she gave way to fresh waves of sobbing. Finally wiping her face with the back of her hand she said;

"Are you sure? About Marsha, and this Jackman guy, I mean."

"Marsha, maybe, maybe not. Jackman, definitely, I'm afraid. Do you want to see the files?" Jon was struck unexpectedly by the sight of her smeary tear-streaked face. She was definitely pretty. He either hadn't noticed or had avoided noticing this before.

She shook her head and sniffed. "Some other time. Question is; what does he want?"

Jon thought the question too obvious to need an answer. "Let's get out of here, he said."

The coffee shop only sold huge, extra-huge and bucket-size cups of coffee. All the toilets in the shopping area were 'pay-as-you-go'. Jon was sure this was a scam as he carried the colossal cups to where Naomi moped at a table by the window, overlooking the river. Outside a fine misty drizzle filled the summer sky.

"Thanks, Jon," she said. "How much do…"

"On me," he said firmly. Then looking around the coffee shop he sat down. "I don't think we'll be overheard here."

In difficult situations in her life, Naomi would count off on her fingers the problems that arose. Although this crazy situation defied comparison with anything that had gone before, it helped to catalogue her points. She had a habit of bending her fingers right back as she did so. Jon tried not to notice.

"One! This Jackman guy is something to do with Prentice." Her knuckles cracked. Jon winced.

"Two! Marsha is spying on you...us. Yes, come to think of it she was showing an unhealthy interest in me on Wednesday."

"I only said maybe." Jon interrupted.

"Three!" she went on; "somebody breaks into the Prof's house. I thought it was you,

"I wish it had been,"

"Probably this Jackman character. So he's aware of what you sent to Prentice and has come sniffing round. Whoever it was takes a stone out of the Timescope reader," She was calm, unnaturally so, Jon thought.

"And now to cap it all Granddad has a heart attack."

The thought struck Jon as she said it. Was the sudden downturn in the Prof's condition a coincidence?

Jon stirred his coffee. Guilty memories of their earlier hug haunted him. She had turned to him for support, yet he had found himself strangely drawn to her. Oh, it wouldn't continue. Tomorrow they would fall out, and normal permafrost would resume. Still it was nice while it lasted. "So what next?" he pondered.

Naomi fell silent. So Jon prompted; "What does the Timescope do when it's not, er... bored? I mean what was it doing before it was stopped last night?"

"Oh a variety of things. It reads the stones almost continually. Sometimes if it needs extra processing resources it goes hunting- we've allocated it time slots on different computers around the world where it can get its number-crunching done. Then when we go exploring, it really cranks up its operation. The files get gigantic."

"Something else doesn't make sense, though." Jon put in. "The Prof told us that we could feel things in the Timescope because of those artificial limb programs, you know the ones which give a sensation of touch and movement in the brain.

But how on earth do we get from that to being half-killed on that mountain? I mean it's quite a step."

Naomi sipped her coffee. "It's all beyond me," she admitted. "Granddad's systems are neural networks. They learn from themselves. What's more they never give up trying to improve. Those programs probably started out simple, but the neural nets have adapted them to produce much more realistic effects. It's a consequence of the way he designed the Timescope, I suppose."

"What way?"

"Well, the Timescope doesn't actually live anywhere," she said. "It's not like there's one huge program you can load into a computer; it's out there, on the internet, in mainframes, networked systems; oh anywhere where there's spare computing resources going free. That's what Jackman was showing us. At any one time a server in a hospital or a Government department might play host to Timescope files for a few milliseconds before they move on. It's got all it needs, virtually unlimited capacity and an ability to redesign itself."

Jon was taken aback. "I thought it was based mainly in his house. How does he control it?"

"It used to be, but it was much too slow, so he started negotiating with his old contacts around the world. Most were quite happy to share capacity, no questions asked. He's quite a household name in computing circles. As to controlling it, he has written the codes so that every single Timescope file ever generated has a common identifier. Like a DNA fingerprint. Anything Timescope can be tracked, located, controlled and reprogrammed or..." she paused, uncertain; then went on, "or if needs be destroyed."

Jon noticed the pause and guessed. "But only he knows the way to activate its destruction?"

Naomi didn't appear to have heard. She fell silent for some time, fiddling with the ends of her hair.

A Big Idea was forming in Jon's mind. He struggled for a minute or two to rationalise it. "Na, tell me if this makes sense."

"Fire away!"

"When you closed the programs down after Horeb, do you know whether they stopped completely?"

"No, they never do. They just get on with something else. Why?"

"Well that's it! Don't you see?"

At that moment her phone rang. She fished in her shoulder bag. "Aunt Judith, oh…"

She turned white. Jon could clearly hear the strident voice of her aunt. "Yes, right… I'll be right back." Her bottom lip trembled; she bit it to control herself.

"Granddad's had another heart attack. A big one. I've got to go back." In her haste to get up she spilt the rest of her coffee on the table. "Sorry, Jon…"

"Naomi," Jon had to almost run to keep up with her as she dashed across the street. "Wait, just listen for a second. I think I know what's causing this."

Distracted she swung round. "He's dying," she said flatly. "I've got to go to him."

Jon grabbed her arm, blocking her way. "Just listen. What time did the Timescope stop yesterday? Was it logged? Think!"

"About nine-twenty," she made to get past him. "Please Jon, let me go!"

"Nine-twenty! That's exactly when he had the first heart attack. Don't you see?"

"No I don't!" she gasped, threading her way through the crowded pavements.

"Think about it!" Jon panted, "Marsha said his heart was healthy- I heard her. The doctors say his brain's in meltdown; it all adds up. You forced the Timescope to close; it's did its own thing, and the Prof is in a sort of limbo. Now somebody removed the stone it was reading and suddenly he's a lot worse. It's too big a coincidence!"

"You're hurting my arm!" Naomi tore her arm free and raced up the street. Abruptly she stopped. "So you think the Timescope's causing this?"

"Positive! Where're you going?"

She shoved past him. "Back to Granddad's. If you're right we can't do anything for Granddad here but if we can put another stone in maybe we can save his life" she said.

Jon was having sudden doubts. If the old man died and Na wasn't with him...

"No, you go to the hospital; I'll sort the Timescope out." He said.

"No, you'll need entry codes; it's not that I don't trust you, I just want it sorted as quickly as we can."

Five minutes later Naomi, her hands encased in gloves was sliding a reddish piece of sandstone into the reader. It was as well she had gone; she explained. The stones took a while to condition, but those already conditioned had been stored in a separate deep freeze, ready for use. With a sigh of chilly air the stone slid silently into the machine.

"Is that it?"

"No, the Timescope needs some direction. Jon, what's the label on the wrapper say? Over there, by the door."

Jon picked it up. "Rameses," he read.

She punched the keyboard. "I've set it to find Joseph. He'll do."

The console screen flashed up a progress bar. SEARCHING.... They slammed the door behind them and ran the rest of the way to the hospital.

As they pounded up the stairs, they almost ran into her Aunt. She was ashen-faced.

"Na, love...I'm sorry, he's gone."

Her screams echoed down the stairwell.

Jon felt dizzy with all the running. A lump settled in his throat. It was more than he could bear to watch Naomi and her Aunt slumped in the chair, bawling for all they were worth. He felt useless, a spare body. More than that he felt as if he had cheated her. It was his stupid idea! If they had gone straight to the hospital then she could have spent his last moments together. Sickened, he drifted away, heading for the exit.

As he passed the room where the Prof was, Jon could not avoid a glance. The door was open; the still figure was tucked neatly under the sheets. A steady *beep, beep, beep!* emitted from the bedside monitor. He walked on glumly.

It took a few seconds more before Jon spun round and darted back to the room. Even then he could make no sense of the sight. The figure had its face covered, but its chest was rising and falling gently. The monitor showed a firm, even heartbeat. *Beep, beep, beep!* Quiet and reassuring.

For the second time in as many days Jon raised the alarm.

Aunt Judith was nosey. Of that there was no doubt. But she was paying for the meal, and her nosiness mainly concerned the amount of time her niece had been seen in Jon's company. Where was George? She had asked pointedly. Naomi coloured and said he was at his brother's in Southern Ireland. He would be back tomorrow.

Aunt Judith had been there when the resuscitation team had battled with the Professor's failing heart. Eventually she had calmly and professionally instructed them to desist from any further attempts to revive him. When she left the room, he was dead. Of that she was certain. Then Jon had burst from the room hared down the corridor yelling that he was still alive! Used as she was to medical anomalies, even she was astonished. "I tell you, there was no pulse." She said firmly. "Do you think I wouldn't be able to tell?"

His condition was still perplexing. It was as if a giant hand was holding his consciousness submerged. Would his heart fail again? He was under close observation. Despite the concerns Naomi beamed radiantly at Jon, giving her sharp-eyed Aunt further cause for curiosity.

They dropped him off at the end of the street. As he turned to go, Jon heard the car door open and the sound of rapid footsteps. As he turned sharply Naomi threw her arms round his neck and kissed him full on the lips.

"Thanks, Jon." She whispered and flitted back to the car. Aunt Judith could think what she liked!

Jon lingered the rest of the way home wondering at the unfairness of it all. His reintroduction to Naomi had been on the worst possible footing all those weeks ago. Since then the relations between them had varied from a polite tolerance to an open hostility. Until very recently. Then she had hugged him- that was unexpected enough, but he reasoned that she was probably a bit emotional at the time. But that kiss! The sensation of it still lingered delightfully on his lips. She felt wholesome. She did not reek of cheap perfume as Kay had done, neither was she dressed in any way that could be labelled as showy or provocative. But Naomi Avery had an understated femininity that exerted a curious attraction to him. She was clever- that much was apparent, and more than capable of expressing herself clearly. But the steel girl had shown vulnerability lately that drew him to her. He was sure she had feelings for him. He could discard the notion that she was trifling with him; she was too clear-cut for that.

He stopped abruptly. The Daimler was filling the drive. What did Prentice want now? Was this a showdown? Was the fat greaser relaying his suspicions about Jon to his parents? He hesitated, loitering in the shadow of the hedge and automatically began planning his defence; deny everything then counterattack him if necessary. His mother would blow the whistle when she heard of Prentice's skulduggery; that was certain. His heart hammering, Jon inched towards the door.

Before he got there, the door was thrown wide open. Both his parents stood in the lighted hallway and Prentice, car keys twisting in his fingers was about to leave. There was no hint of reckoning, quite the contrary- his father was actually shaking Prentice's hand and both Mum and Dad were smiling from ear to ear.

"I assure you the privileges committee are fully aware of this, Mary," he purred. "You know I wouldn't even mention it to you otherwise…"

"Liar!" thought Jon. *"What's he up to now?"*

"Jon!" Prentice seemed genuinely pleased to see him skulking in the light. "I'll leave your parents to break the news- good news," he added with a chuckle. "And I'll bid you all good night. Mary," his tone was solicitous, "I think it's a good offer- Parliament rises tomorrow, and in my experience opportunities like this are few and far between."

The Daimler sank on its suspension as he heaved himself in and drove away into the night.

"What offer?" Jon could smell wine on his Dad's breath. His Dad clasped him round the shoulders.

"Jon, my son," he chortled, "your mother's been a very clever girl!"

They giggled like newly weds. They were well on their way down the second bottle of fine red wine, provided, Dad informed him with glee, by Prentice. "Three cheers for junkets!" he chortled, pouring Jon a large glass.

"This is a serious lecture tour," she reprimanded him with a slight hiccup. "We mustn't forget that, but why me though? Out of all the possible experts they could ask for."

Dad squeezed her slender waist. "You're a very clever girl Mary. That's come to their notice. It couldn't remain hidden long. Your Mother has been selected to go to Thailand, to give some talks about her work," he explained to the bemused Jon.

"How many lectures will you have to do?" Jon wanted to know.

"Five hour-long seminars over two weeks. Spaced out over the peninshula." She giggled again. "Sorry I meant Penin-su-la." Jon couldn't help smiling- it was good to see them so relaxed at last. "Jon, we'll take you somewhere afterwards, I promise."

"Nah, don't worry!" Jon meant it, two weeks freedom to come and go at leisure. He went up to his room and lay on his bed absorbing the news. Neither Mum nor Dad were making much sense now; from downstairs came another round of raucous laughter. But what he had established was that a Professor someone-or-other had been booked to give a lecture tour in Thailand. He had dropped out through ill-health and his mother had been asked to step in for him. Dad was free to go with her if he wished- there were two club class airline tickets on offer.

They were leaving Jon a wad of cash- enough to eat out every night if he chose. He would have liked to roll up at Aunt Judith's house and grandly invite Naomi to eat at Dolce Vita with him. But that would embarrass her and hurt George, and he had had enough of hurting people right now. He'd eat cheap and keep the rest for something else. For once in a very long time Jon felt an almost tangible warmth towards Prentice. Mum and Dad needed a break, a bit of pampering, and Prentice had provided the perfect opportunity. Some of the tensions in their home would dissipate, Mum would get chance to unwind, and Dad would get the holiday of a lifetime.

14
The Plague of Darkness

"Just listen to the message yourself!" Her hands shaking, Naomi replayed the voice mail to Jon. Jon yawned, trying to get a grip on himself.

It was too early for him, much too early. Even if Living Word had been on this Sunday morning, he would still have an extra hour in bed. But her summons had been urgent. The dew was thick on the mown grass. In the distance a wood pigeon cooed in the huge lime trees that lined the park. They sat on a mostly dry wooden seat whilst Naomi tried to explain.

"It came about four o' clock in the night. I thought I heard the phone ringing, then it stopped. This message was on it when I woke up."

Jon struggled to catch the words; they were patchy, as if the speaker was confused. There was a great deal of repetition, some incoherent mumbling and one clear section. There was a palpable sense of fear in the speaker's voice.

"Dark, can't see…. Dark. Na, can you hear me? Darkness, all around. Can anyone hear me out there? Please come and get…"

"It might be his voice," Jon admitted.

"'Course it is!" she snapped. "Do you think I wouldn't know my own Granddad?"

"You've contacted the hospital?"

"Yes, first thing. No change. No movement during the night. Marsha checked the records."

"Marsha?" Jon exclaimed. "Is she ever off duty?"

"I don't know!" Naomi's agitation increased. "The point is; Granddad needs help. It's like you said, the Timescope's still running, and he's still locked into it. It all fits- his brain activity, even the heart attacks when the Timescope was halted. He's in there, Jon, I know. And he's in trouble."

Jon could see where this was heading: "Oh no! No, no, no. Never. Not again!"

She reddened. "Jon, please. I wouldn't ask but George is away…"

"You'd tell George Mere about the Timescope?"

"Why not? He's not stupid you know! Anyway what choice do I have if you won't help?" She stood up to go. Jon wrenched her wrist, forcing her to sit back down.

"Naomi, please understand this. I don't sleep much any more. When I sleep, I see killing, I hear men and women screaming, I feel the ground shaking, walls of fire scorching my face. I wake up yelling most mornings- Dad told me that yesterday. Worse than that I feel like somebody has… well… known me. D'ye know what I mean? Seen everything there is to me; left nothing untouched. My whole life has been inspected, put on display…"

"Yes, yes." She shook his hand free. "Sorry I asked. I get those sort of nightmares as well."

"Where are you going?"

"Sorry, Jon, I gotta do this. With or without you."

The pigeon had stopped cooing. It was seven o' clock. A mower started up, raucous in the distance. Sunday sounds, light traffic, an aircraft far above rumbling softly. Jon remained seated for many minutes. He could see her point- who wouldn't be concerned for Professor Avery if, as seemed likely, his mind was trapped somewhere in the ancient past whilst his body was withering in a hospital bed? Twice he got up to follow, but both times his legs gave way. He held his hands in front of his face and tried to stop them shaking.

He had watched her disappear into the distance. Hurrying strides, her hair a mess, heading purposefully towards Keswick Avenue. It took no effort to recall the catty remarks, snide comments, put-downs and general sense of contempt she seemed to bear towards him. But he sensed things were changing. Not only in her treatment of him, but in his feelings for her. He found himself daring to believe that she liked him. And he knew that Naomi Avery did not bestow her regard cheaply.

His guts churned, and despite the coolness of the summer morning, he was sweating freely. "For you Na," he breathed, finally struggling to his feet, "and for the Prof."

When Jon let himself in through the Professor's back door, he had found that Naomi had already loaded a file and was standing motionless in the viewing room, her head encased in the Virtual Reality headset. With a thundering heart, Jon picked up the other headset and felt his consciousness spiral down the centuries until it came to rest in a dirty, narrow city street.

The first things to hit him were the heat and the flies. Although it was dark, the heat was sultry and stifling. Every pore in his body erupted, sweat coursed down his back, his sides and down his arms and legs. Black flies descended in clouds upon him, settling on his face and even on his eyes. He brushed his hand over his face, almost dislodging the headset in the process. But the moment his hand had moved away, the flies swarmed back onto his skin.

The second thing happened moments later. Between sweeping the flies away, Jon had a glimpse of a small knot of men gathered in the light of a window. They were deep in discussion. The flies didn't seem to be bothering them as much; maybe they were fewer there. Jon, his arms swatting furiously, strode towards them. He was a few metres away and conscious that they were all ragged and stank of stale sweat when one of them said decisively:

"But we must take Joseph's bones with us!"

That was all Jon heard before mayhem erupted. A shout rang out behind him, and then he was shoved aside. The whole group whirled around as a squad of men raced toward them, yelling and cursing, brandishing short leather whips and stout poles. They wore uniform and it was obvious they were a police force of some sort. At the sight of them the group scattered, Jon was barged aside and thrown against a wall. One old man was hustled out of harm's way, three of the men lingered to block the charge. It was an incredibly brave thing to do; they were no match for the well-trained police. In minutes three of the ragged men were down in the dust and a savage beating was being meted out. As he ducked into the shelter of the nearest doorway Jon's ears were assailed by their cries. At nearby windows faces popped up momentarily, and then disappeared from view.

One of the men scrambled up, eluded the grasp of his captor and pelted away from the area, the remaining two were pinned down, their faces rammed into the ground. Round the corner came a fat dark-haired man, the squad leader, slapping his leg with a short heavy stick.

"Where is the man they call Moses? And his brother Aaron? Were they not here with you?" The heavy-set thug put his sandaled foot on the younger man's neck.

"I know of these men," he lifted his face with difficulty, his mouth full of dust. "Let me stand and I will tell you all I know."

He looked to the rest of his squad, grinning evilly. "And have the vermin run like a rat? What do you take us for? You will tell me where these men are and now." His foot pushed his face back into the dirt.

"May your guts fall from your fat belly!"

Naturally this was not the answer he had expected. But he showed little annoyance. A curt nod was the only signal his men needed. They stripped the wretches' thin clothes from their backs and flogged and kicked them mercilessly. The whips bit deep into the flesh, as they took it in turns to administer the beating. Between lashes they would spit curses, or kick more dust into the eyes of the victims. The victims, in turn responded with defiant insults, but as the blood flowed freely, they weakened and finally lost consciousness. Finally, with a few kicks to the stomach, their laughing captors drifted away into the night.

'This isn't a good place to be,' Jon thought, reaching out for his headset. But it was gone. It had been dislodged when he had been knocked flying. His heart sank. "Oh no, here we go again." Then a movement caught his eye.

"Naomi!" She dashed from a doorway across the street and knelt beside one of the injured men.

"Jon! You came. Oh, I'm glad!" She chewed her lip trying to stop it trembling. "Can you help me with him?"

The beaten man was young and handsome, but his nose was weeping blood that ran into his beard. Over his back, beneath the fresh lacerations, were the marks of older thrashings, criss-crossed into the muscles. Naomi eyes were wide with fear.

"Do we have any water?" She indicated the fresh open wounds.

A young woman ran from a nearby doorway carrying a clay jar, dipped a rag into it and wrung out water over the lacerated back. At the sting of the water, the man groaned and his eyes flickered open. "Deborah!" He croaked to the woman. "You are safe?"

"Shh!" said young woman. She turned to Naomi. "He is badly injured, go and get help to carry him, my child."

"Who, me?" Naomi looked at Jon, perplexed. Then they saw that the young woman had been speaking to a young child standing in the gloom behind them. He turned and ran to the door of one of the nearby houses, and let himself in. Moments later he returned with an older man and between them they carried the wounded man inside.

The other man was lying face down in the middle of the road. Jon and Naomi waited a few moments for the couple to return, but unexpectedly the door closed behind them, almost as if they had no interest in his plight.

"We'd better help him ourselves, then," Naomi glanced at Jon. The water vessel and rag were nearby, so she carried them across to the prone figure.

"Oh no!" she breathed.

"What's up? Na? What's the matter?"

Naomi had gently rolled the figure onto his back. His face was filthy, dirt and sweat combining to coat his skin. But the hood of his robes had slipped away revealing an immense shock of white hair. There was no question of his identity.

"Granddad!" she screamed. "Granddad, how has this happened?"

His head turned and he smiled, looking upwards through his eyes that were so puffy that they were almost shut tight. His breath was shallow and came in short bursts. He tried to sit up but sank back to the ground with a groan.

"Ahh! My God, they will pay in full measure."

"Granddad, it's me, Naomi! Your granddaughter. Can you hear me?"

"He's not looking good, Na." Jon had noticed his shallow breathing, and that he appeared to be in great pain.

The Professor, with great difficulty, prised his eyes open. He looked at the pair, but there was no recognition in his face. "Phurah?" he murmured, "Is that you, Phurah?"

"He doesn't know who we are," Jon said. A short distance away was the sound of renewed shouting, harsh voices of the aggressors. The sound was coming closer.

Heavy blows were being dealt out; whatever was causing it was moving towards them. From the corner of his eye Jon glimpsed one of the ragged slaves. He scanned the street as if looking for something, then spotting the injured man turned around. They thought he was going to melt into the darkness, but he cupped his hands and called softly. Three other men appeared and gathered around them, talking rapidly in low voices. Then with a grunt they picked up the Professor between them.

Jon expected the Professor to cry out with the pain of being lifted so quickly from the ground, but he was quiet. "I think he's unconscious again," he whispered, "We'd better follow."

The three men bore the injured Professor swiftly away from the street. They made carrying him look easy, but then they were used to bearing burdens. Down several dirty side-streets they hustled him, to where the darkness grew thicker. Then abruptly they stopped and hammered on a narrow door. It opened and the Professor and his attendants went inside.

"Quick, before they bolt the door!" Naomi panted.

The small room was crowded. With difficulty a space was cleared on the dirt floor. "Careful with him," Naomi implored.

"Isaac! Oh my husband! What have they done to you?" Naomi spun round. From the shadows a small, arthritic old woman stumbled out and knelt by his body. She took the Professor's gnarled hand in hers and rolled his fingers in agitation.

"He has had a bad beating," said one of the younger men. "I saw it happen. He was set upon by the Taskmasters. He is lucky to be alive."

The old woman turned on him angrily. "And you stood by and watched it happen? My Isaac, who sat you on his knee, who taught you the ways of the True God? You let them beat him?"

"Hush, Phurah," an old man they recognised emerged from the shadows; he had been hurried away from the earlier fracas. He had a thin face, and a beard that reached to his chest; mostly grey but flecked with dark hairs. The old woman jumped back, startled at the sight of him.

"My lord Aaron!" she gasped. "Is your brother here? What news of Pharaoh. Will he yield?"

Beside her the Professor stirred. Aaron regarded him sadly for a few moments. "Take care of Isaac" he sighed. He sounded exhausted. "He can remain here until the streets are safe."

The old woman, whose name they knew to be Phurah had made the Professor comfortable with a rolled up blanket for a pillow and another blanket to cover him. She murmured endearments to him alternately cursing the Taskmasters for their cruelty. He was breathing painfully in light gasps and shivering. At Aaron's words she turned away and the party departed to an inner room.

"What do we do now?" Naomi asked.

"I don't know." Naomi knelt by the old man. "Granddad!" she called softly, her hand on his forehead. "Please, speak to me."

In reply the Professor groaned. Then with an effort his eyes opened. "Phurah?"

"No, I'm not Phurah," she squeezed his hand. "I'm Naomi."

Now the Professor's eyes were wide open. Before he could think better of it he hauled himself to a sitting position, and then gave a yelp of pain. He grabbed her arm with his other hand. "Naomi!" His eyes flicked over her face, "I know you, but you are not of this captivity. Where are you from my child?"

"Granddad," Naomi spoke urgently. "Listen, I am your granddaughter. You are in the Timescope. Do you remember? You went into the Timescope then Jon," she beckoned Jon closer, "Jon Heath; do you remember him as well? Jon found you on Horeb."

"You were taken ill," Jon supplied.

The Professor's face contorted with the effort to recall. "Naomi...Jon... are you of another land?" Then he coughed and clutched his side. Jon noticed with a shiver that he was coughing flecks of fresh blood.

Naomi waited until the spasm was past. "Professor Avery," she insisted, staring him straight in the face. "England, twenty-first century. You must remember that!"

But his face took on a dreamy aspect. "Ah, my child," he smiled through the pain. Then he closed his eyes and sank back on the pillow.

Naomi turned to Jon. "What do we do now?"

"We wait?" It was all he could think of. In the next room was the subdued murmur of Aaron and his group. Outside were the sounds of further rioting in the gloomy streets. The old woman brought a little water to moisten the Professor's lips.

"How come he's got a wife?" Asked Jon in a low voice when she had gone. Naomi just shook her head, bewildered. "It just gets more and more bizarre. He's here, dressed like all the slaves, with a wife, and probably a family, and yet the rest of him is in a coma in Chessington ward."

There was an outraged growl from by their feet. "Chessington? That's a private ward! How much is that costing, Naomi?"

"Granddad!" she cried, kneeling down beside him. "Oh Granddad, I'm so glad you know who I am." Inadvertently she leant against his chest. He gave a choked gasp of pain.

"Two, maybe three ribs broken?" he opened his robe and explored the area around his chest tentatively. The slightest pressure caused waves of pain to cross his face and sweat to start afresh. Then he stopped and collected himself.

"Jon, Naomi, please listen closely. I don't know how much time I've got."

"But Grand…"

"Shh!" He motioned her to be quiet. "I must say this now; I might not get a second chance."

Jon and Naomi listened as he wheezed through his account. He clearly remembered Horeb (with a mixture of awe and dread,) but after that nothing but a peculiar twilight experience which he could only describe as 'existence.' He was aware of himself, but not in any sensory way. He could not see, hear, taste, smell or feel anything. He hung suspended somewhere 'out there,' just barely conscious.

He was drifting towards oblivion. The blankness had welled up and sucked him down, like an all-encompassing curtain of Nothing. The next thing he knew he was in Egypt, surrounded by chaos, noise, heat, flies, animals, slaves and a thousand and one other stimuli.

"Granddad," Naomi interrupted; "right now you're in hospital; in a coma, but you've had two heart attacks since. They happened when the Timescope was stopped and the second one killed you but we put the stone back in the Timescope and you…er… restarted, if you know what I mean…"

She explained what had happened. Despite his pain he listened intently. Then he sat forward as best he could and said;

"You have to understand what the Timescope is doing to me here. As I said, I don't have much time. Then perhaps you'll be able to sort it out."

It was merging the information relating to the real Professor Avery with a Hebrew slave called Isaac. For the past few days he had alternated between being 'out there' as he called it; an onlooker, a spectator; to suddenly and disconcertingly finding himself in the body of man called Isaac, at the receiving end of a taskmaster's whip and labouring in the blinding heat at one of the numerous building sites that surrounded the city of Rameses. But the day before yesterday a great clinging blackness descended on the Egyptian streets, and work had abruptly ceased and there had been a marked rise in violence on both sides.

"You should see the place," he commented. "It's pretty well in ruins. Buildings scorched, dead animals everywhere, stink, filth, oh it's a battle-field. All we worked so hard to build ruined in a few months. "

Jon sensed he was starting to drift. "Why is time running out?"

"The Isaac episodes are getting longer, I'm losing track of myself. The Timescope is winning. It's absorbing me."

Jon listened closely as the Prof, trying to blot out the pain from his chest, leant forward.

"Error files," he said with difficulty. "The answer lies in there somewhere. Can you find out? Find out where the data is being merged and why? Don't give up, Na. Stick with it; I know you can sort it out."

"And if that doesn't work...?" Jon wondered.

A spasm of coughing interrupted him. It was several minutes before he was sufficiently comfortable to speak once more. He reached out for Naomi's hand and gingerly pulled her close to him in an awkward hug. His tone was grave;

"If all else fails, use the codes. Finish it. It's getting too dangerous to be left to carry on. The taskmasters are getting stronger. Do you understand?" She made no reply but hung on to his neck. His voice hardened; "Phurah, answer me, do you understand?"

"Granddad!" There was a note of panic in her voice. "You haven't given me the codes. Tell me them now."

A crafty grin twisted his face. "And have you tell the magicians, the princes and the astrologers? Are you mad?" He removed Naomi's arms from his neck. "Phurah, you are a good woman, but these things do not concern you. Oh!"

His eyes rolled up in their sockets and he lost consciousness once more.

"Are those the codes you said about...?"

"Yes, the termination codes. Enter these codes and the Timescope formats every Timescope file in existence. Then it formats itself and just becomes a mass of empty data. In effect it ceases to exist." Anticipating his next question she went on; "Granddad was going to let me have the codes; but..."

"He never got round to it!" Jon finished for her. "Na, whatever else happens, next time he's making sense, get those codes off him."

She shook her head. "But that'll kill him! Look what happened when the Timescope was stopped, Granddad almost died then."

Aaron and the rest of the group came into the room. His thin face was lined with fresh anxiety. The old woman, Phurah was in tears, wringing her hands and holding on to the cavernous sleeves of his robe. The rest of the men unbolted the door and peered furtively out. Acrid burning smells flooded into the room. They slammed it shut again.

"He cannot stay here!" Aaron declared. "The Taskmasters are burning houses. There are safer places for the both of you."

"My lord Aaron," the youngest man of the group stood with his back to the door. "The streets are more dangerous still! And if they recognise you they will kill you. Is this wise?"

Aaron shuffled, pondering his options. Finally he made up his mind. "We will take him to Yahmose. He has healing arts, and his house is in the city."

"That half-caste!" Somebody spat. "The Egyptian who dares to take the Name of our GOD? We have no dealings with his sort."

Phurah rounded on him. "Hold your tongue!" she hissed. "If it were your father or wife lying there, perhaps you would think differently."

Aaron intervened, standing between them. "Yahmose is not as the rest of his race." He said hastily. "He is sympathetic, and has vowed to go with us. We must not despise his kind. Now let us go."

Once more the Professor was picked up. Jon could only imagine the pain he must be in, as they jolted him through the door. Outside, in the street, there was a lull in the commotion, but the flies swooped on them once more, as they scuttled across the street and further into the dingy blackness that marked the border between the slave quarter and the limits of the city. Jon dashed after, keeping closely in their wake. He turned round and saw to his surprise that Naomi was lagging behind, her face barely visible in the gathering gloom, but wearing a rigid, fixed expression.

"Na, keep up!" he called, as loudly as her dared. "We can't afford to lose them!"

"No, Jon, try to make them bring him this way." The edge was back in her voice.

"But that's where those thugs are. They'd be heading back into another fight." Jon reached for her arm and steered her quickly in the direction the rest of the party had gone. She hung back. Behind her there was the sound of more clashes and running feet.

"Come on! Na, it's better than waiting here!" She reluctantly allowed herself to be led further into the blackness. "Na, is there something you're not telling me?"

She did not reply to his question. Instead she started muttering to herself.

"Na, what's the matter?"

"Granddad!" she almost spat. "He couldn't stop this could he? He had to see it through!"

It was the first time Jon had ever heard Naomi be scathing about the Prof. "Stop what?" he demanded, hauling her down yet another maze of side streets, following the ragged figures.

"Self-replicating programs. That's viruses to you and me!" She laughed bitterly. "The worst sort of code. You can't control it properly, it protects itself, and the sort of stuff Granddad produces mutates almost by the minute. Each file changes other files, alters or improves them. Great! We get a clearer picture, better sound, and more sensation: but it's still going on, Jon. It's still changing. We started off feeling rain on our skin, now we can be beaten half to death! Do you know what else it's been doing lately?"

They had arrived at a junction in the narrow streets. For a moment Jon was paralysed with indecision. Then a movement showed Aaron and his group down a right-hand fork. The stench in this part of the city was appalling. Naomi ranted on.

"It's requisitioning networks for itself, Jon! It hijacked Cairo University without either Granddad or me knowing. Just because it wanted to."

"You make it sound as if it's alive…over here, down this way…" Jon tugged her arm. It was darker here, and cooler. The flies fewer now, in spite of the stink.

"Why now?" she cried. "Of all times to arrive here, why now in the middle of the plague of Darkness?"

"The plague of Darkness?" Jon didn't feel too bad about that. Then he realised why she was talking so fast. She was trying to hide her fear. "You're scared of the dark, aren't you?"

There was no denial. Instead the hand on his arm tightened its grip until it started to hurt. When she next spoke, there was no concealing the high-pitched note of impending hysteria.

"And now Granddad tells us the Timescope's rewriting our memories. It should ignore us as artefacts; we don't belong to this…this place. The Timescope knows that but it's trying to make us fit in. Why's it doing that Jon?"

"Na, ease up a bit," he tried to prise her loose, but she clung to him like a drowning child.

"I…I…it's no good," she was gasping for breath, starting to hyperventilate in her panic. "I've got to get out, Jon!" Jon could sense she was struggling to remove the headset. His heart sank. Any moment now… There was a sound of flapping rubber as the headset came away from her face.

She gave a thin, dry scream and tore free of him; and her hands shot out catching him across the face. In the dark Jon flailed his arms, trying to reach her.

"Na! Over here! Don't move, I'll come and get you!"

"Jo...o...o...on;" the thin scream continued. She was beside herself in panic. "Make it stop. Stop it, stop it now!"

He seized her in his outstretched arms; trying to hold her was like restraining a strong animal. She writhed under his grasp, sobbing and fighting. Finally after what seemed like ten rounds, she subsided against his chest, her shoulders heaving.

"Listen Naomi," Jon said softly. "I'll get you out, I don't know how, but I'll find a way out. Please believe me. Nod if you can hear me."

Slowly she inclined her head.

"Good, just stay close, don't let go d'ye hear?" it was unnecessary advice, but all he could think of. All the time he was hauling her after the group of men, stumbling, treading on each other's toes, running up against objects along the way. The darkness was palpable here. It settled on their faces like wet cling film, clammy and suffocating. Sounds had begun to recede too; it was remote and detached like listening down a long tube. Jon felt a formless dread welling inside him too, but he stifled it. It was bad enough that Naomi was incoherent with fear; he had to hold on for both their sakes.

On they shuffled, picking their way along the deserted streets, hands outstretched. "Naomi?" Jon called softly; he caught the scent of the hair on the crown of her head. It smelt of open spaces, fresh with the dew of the morning. Their meeting in the park seemed a lifetime away now. "Are you OK, Na? Just keep talking to me."

She whimpered like a toddler, burying her face in his shirt. The darkness was thicker still now, unrelieved in any direction. With it came another overpowering sensation, the feeling of doom. A sad, sad despondency, as if all that was hopeless and pointless had congealed in the air. It felt like the lifeless air of a mausoleum, tinged with decay. Every breath they inhaled drew this evil miasma into their lungs, suffocating in its misery. It was as though somebody had collected all the tears ever cried, all the anguish, apprehension, raw terror and depression in human experience; as though they had devised a way of refining it and bottling it and now had released its poisonous atmosphere in this doomed city.

What was the point? Jon began to wonder. Why struggle to breathe when every breath was an effort? To move, to think, when all around was just sadness and blackness? Just stop, he thought. Stop, sink to the ground and give up. The effort of moving in this condensed misery weighed on his arms and legs. Naomi's grip tightened. "Are you OK?" he asked again.

She was weeping, softly, her body shaking uncontrollably. "Just carry on walking!" she gasped. "We can't lose them."

"I think we have lost them," Jon moaned. He swung his head round, ears tuned to the slightest scuffle or cry. The coffin lid silence had noiselessly closed on them both.

The awesome blackness was total; it was a horror of great darkness. It took over, saturating everything with its depressive force. And Jon wasn't normally afraid of the dark. He felt another wave of sympathy for her, and a heartfelt relief that she wasn't stuck in here on her own. "Hold tight, Na!"

Jon tried to retrace their steps. Minute after minute, feeling their way along rough walls, sometimes stumbling, sometimes falling over objects in the way. Apart from the swishing of their clothes and their muted footsteps, everywhere was total silence.

"Na, come on, talk to me- tell me about anything you like... about...I know, Aunt Judith. She seems okay. What's she like Na?" He could feel the tendons on her arms rigid with fright.

"I can't go on." He could hardly hear her voice. Her fingers dug into his arms, her nails tearing his skin then she let go and collapsed to the ground with her hands over her face, shutting out as much as she could. She did not respond to a shake, nor could Jon prise her hands away.

"Na." he whispered, "please get up. Come on, we've got to keep going."

"I w-w-w-w-w..." She convulsed with fear, each spasm froze her words.

"W-w-w-want.... t-t-t-t-to..."

"I'll get you home." he finished for her. "Have you got your phone?"

Despite her near-paralysis, she managed to hand him her phone. *'Battery empty-recharge now.'*

"Naomi!!" he yelled. She did not move.

Jon ran through her address book. Her Aunt, no way! Prof-if only! School friends? It had to be someone close at hand, and hopefully at home. There was only one suitable candidate on the list who fitted; a cutesy little heart against his name. Jon reckoned on about one call before the battery expired.

"George?"

"Jon?" He sounded startled. "Whassup Jon? You OK?"

"George, listen." Jon spoke as firmly as he could. In his ear the phone was bleating its battery warning. "You've got to help us!"

"Is Naomi with you?"

"Yes. The battery is almost dead on this phone. Please George listen to what I say, I probably won't be able to say it again. Where are you?"

"At home." George sensed the anxiety in Jon's voice. "Is Naomi OK? What's happened?"

"Naomi's alright," Jon fudged, "but she needs your help." *Bleep, bleep, bleep.*

Get as quickly as possible to the Prof's house, he urged him. The back door was unlocked and he was to go inside and ring back. George's voice changed.

"Is this a wind-up? I was about to go out."

"No, please do as I say. Naomi's with me and she's freaked right out. I can't help her myself!" Jon was shaking; fear and exhaustion making a potent mixture. "George, just do as I ask, and I'll explain everything when you get here. I'm going to hang up now to save the battery, ring me when you're in the house."

"Alright," he said, "I'll be with you in ten."

It felt like ten hours. In that silent, hellish darkness imagination took centre stage. Naomi continued to whimper like a terrified toddler, the awesome blackness pressed down on Jon, as he sat next to her, his arm over her shoulders. His imagination kicked into overdrive. Out of the gloom, soft fingers ran over his face, like cobwebs in an attic. Something near them was breathing, he felt sure, the rancid air flowing in and out over his face. Ancient Egypt felt and smelt like a tomb. For a few minutes he struggled to think clearly about their predicament, but sank back against the wall, closed his eyes and wished it was over. Somewhere deep in his memory, Jon Heath used to go to school, watch DVD's, eat meals, play computer games, and do all the things commonplace in the twenty-first century. But it felt like another life; a million miles away and a thousand years ago. Was it true what Naomi said about the Timescope rewriting his memories? Would the modern Jon and Naomi dwindle like the fading light of Goshen, all their individual experiences and sophisticated lifestyle sucked away to be replaced by a half-life in the ghastly place? That was what had apparently happened to the Prof.

Here was nothing but death. Acres of dead, mummified corpses in tombs up and down the Nile valley. Their internal organs pickled, their brains discarded, their bodies packed with spices and daily the mighty army of the lifeless increased. The knowledge weighed on his mind. It was so infinitely sad. In the utter darkness Jon felt tears trickling down his face.

There was a glimmer of light! His eyes focussed on a small green light that winked up out of the gloom at him. It made a bonging sound that somehow seemed familiar. For several seconds Jon stared stupidly at the mobile phone before he realised that it was ringing.

"George?"

"Who'dye think? I'm in the back room. It's a real mess here."

"Yeah, I know. Listen George…"*Bleep, bleep, bleep, bleep*…"Are you still there? Look, I want you to come into the hall and go through the second door on the left. Wait!"

"What?" George sounded really brassed off.

"Just do what I say, yeah? When you come in, Na and me'll probably be in a corner of the room…"*Bleep, bleeeeep*… "Don't touch either of us!"

231

"Right!" From the dubious way in which he said it, it was evident that George was deciding whether it was safe to come in- was Jon raving mad? "So what do I do?"

"There's a black keyboard in a small alcove, the black one mind. Press Control, Alt Delete and close down all the programs running..." *bleep...bleep.. blip!* The line went dead and the display dark. Jon's heart sank through the floor. Had he heard?

"Jon?" Naomi muttered weakly.

"OK Na" He could feel her still trembling violently. "Any moment now."

The sun appeared over Egypt dimly at first, so that the atmosphere was only just tinged with yellow. Then a central lightness began to form, growing brighter by the minute. Around them the buildings loomed, huge columns that climbed to dizzying heights, a wide, paved street, deserted apart from a mangy dog.

The sun was brighter now, and curiously the buildings began to dissolve under its light. Egypt shimmered like a morning mirage; the yellow walls became a regular pattern of flowers against a light blue background. The pathetic dog yelped at them before dwindling into nothing.

"OK, so what's going on?" asked George, turning away from the keyboard; then he saw Naomi. "Naomi! Naomi! It's me, George!!"

She threw herself against him, paralysed by fear, unable to speak and clung to him. The look in her eyes was chilling. Jon had never seen any one in such a state of raw, animal fear. George turned accusing eyes on Jon.

"What have you done to her?" his voice was cold and deadly. "Tell me, what have you done to Naomi?"

"I haven't done anything!" Jon spat back, angry at the accusation in his voice.

Naomi slowly uncurled herself, her eyes tightly shut. "Jon, are we out, I mean really out of there? Back in our own time?"

"Yes," he assured her. "You can look now."

George looked at Jon, then Naomi, then back to Jon.

"Pardon?" He said faintly.

"Tell him," Naomi slumped against the wall.

"Let's get this straight," said George, again. "You can put those headsets on and travel back in time?"

They were sitting in the reader room, the chilly air a pleasant contrast to the suffocating heat they had just left.

"No!" Jon said grumpily. "No one can do that. But the Prof's Timescope can show you things that happened in the past. That's what we were doing when we called you; we were following Aaron around Egypt."

"What was it like?"

"I don't know it was dark. But the darkness was horrible."

"You should have seen yourselves when I came in," said George. "Jon, you were looking right at me, but you couldn't see me at all. Even when I turned the light on, you took ages to see me. Na, you were curled up in a ball, absolutely out of it."

Naomi wasn't listening. "What's the time?" she asked George.

"Half-one." He said. Jon was startled. Six hours in Egypt had flown by. "Where're you going Na?"

"Hospital." She said shortly, peering through the window. Outside the sun blazed in a cloudless sky. "I want to see how Granddad is."

Jon felt an indescribable anxiety tugging at his guts. The three of them pelted through the hot streets to the all-too-familiar low buildings of the city hospital. As they raced up the stairs to the second floor Chessington ward, they caught up with Aunt Judith.

"Aunt," Naomi said, "He's not breathing very well is he?"

"Where have you been? I've been trying to find you!" She snapped, looking at each of them in turn. "Oh, never mind, you're here anyway. I think you'd better come and say goodbye- again!" she added. "He's on a ventilator now."

"We'd better go, Jon." George muttered. Jon turned to leave.

"Jon," Naomi caught his arm and hauled him into the room. "Stay with me, please."

Jon caught just a glimpse of the confused, hurt look on George's face; then the door swung closed.

Aunt Judith bent across the bed and arranged the covers around the still form, now partially hidden by a mess of tubes and wires. Nearby a ventilator huffed and hissed adding its wind ensemble to the *beep, beep* of the heart monitor and the gentle whirr of the feeding pump. Naomi cried out in alarm.

"Mind his ribs! No, the other side!"

Her Aunt looked sideways at her. "Ribs? What do you mean? There's nothing wrong with his ribs."

There was, she insisted. He had injured ribs down the left side. She nearly added, 'from the beating,' but stopped herself in time. Aunt Judith shook her head, then as an afterthought ran her fingers down the Prof's rib cage. As she prodded, the figure under the sheets gasped, almost dislodging the ventilator mask. She tentatively explored the area. Then without a word of explanation she stalked out of the room.

15

"Punctured lung?" Jon and Naomi echoed. Aunt Judith had lost her brisk professionalism. She sat down with a lurch. "More accurately pneumothorax- the space between the lungs and the ribs has air and blood collecting in it, exerting pressure on the lungs and making breathing difficult." She sniffed, then fished a handkerchief from her pocket and blew her nose. "I'm furious with them! It probably happened when they tried to resuscitate him. That's not totally unexpected. What is appalling is that nobody bothered to check!" She smiled grimly. "When I worked here that would never have got past Matron! Now, I want to know how you knew about it. It's almost as if you were expecting him to have broken ribs."

Jon and Naomi exchanged glances. "Oh, it was something somebody said, I can't remember who. Jon, were you there? Can you remember who said it?"

"Search me," Jon fudged.

Naomi was fidgeting. "How long is he going to be in theatre? Only I want to get back to tidying up his place."

Aunt Judith seemed philosophical that her niece wasn't going to stay around. "I suppose we've said goodbye once, and it's only a matter of time from now on. All the same are you sure you don't want to stay? OK don't go far and keep your mobile on, won't you?"

"Are you still going to Philip's tonight? Or have you cancelled?"

Aunt Judith and her husband had been due to visit friends. As they were only ten miles from here, she saw no reason to cancel. "I'll stay around until he's back in this room and settled, then go straight on from here. Unless of course he deteriorates this afternoon." She was phlegmatic about life and death; for her it had been a part of her vocation in nursing. Stay in touch, she advised, and the indefatigable Marsha would be certain to keep them up to date. She gestured in the direction of the operating theatres towards which the gasping Professor had been rushed; "he wouldn't thank us for making a fuss about him!"

This time it was Naomi who was doing the hustling. Jon could barely keep up as they flew down the stairs. "What are you going to do?" Jon puffed, rubbing his shoulder where a door she had burst through had swung back on it. She made no reply, but dashed across the lawns in front of the hospital. The late afternoon heat hit them; after the air-conditioned hospital corridors it was unpleasant. Half-way down the grassy slope Naomi stumbled, then half-turned; "Jon," she began, her face pale, her hair almost shielding her eyes. She looked as if she was about to faint.

Jon just managed to catch her. She allowed herself to be lead back inside, sat down unsteadily and began to cry.

It was quiet in the cafeteria. Those who had meals were eating outside in the shade of the trees. Jon was glad of this for her sake as she sobbed and sobbed into his shoulder. He bought her a diet coke, but every time she went to pick it up she broke out into fresh waves of grief.

"Shall I call George?" Jon had no idea where he had gone.

She shook her head mutely. "He's going to die, isn't he Jon? I mean what can we do about it?"

Jon looked down at the thick mass of her hair. Poor girl! She was exhausted, upset, confused and pulled in several directions at once, not to mention more than a little scared at the turn these latest events had taken. It had been embarrassing when she had insisted on him, instead of George accompanying her into the Prof's hospital room earlier, but taken as an isolated incident, quite natural in the circumstances. In Egypt, she had been so freaked out; she would have clutched anybody for support. It was totally natural for her to turn to him now with things piling up on her. As he felt her soft warmth nestling against him, Jon reflected, there were a lot of "quite natural" moments happening lately!

"Jon," she said finally, blowing her nose which was becoming quite red; "I'd better go."

"Where?"

"To Granddad's house. I've got to look at those error files."

"Do you know what you're looking for?"

She fiddled with the ends of her hair. "No," she admitted. "I've only looked at them a couple of times." She stood up. "What do you think's happening?"

Jon debated how to tell her. In the end he said; "This guy, Isaac, he's in a bad way, isn't he? Unless this Egyptian healer knows his stuff, he isn't going to last long; Isaac, that is. According to the Prof, the Timescope is merging him and Isaac together. If Isaac dies, well... Do you want help with these error files?"

"Can you come with me now?

"No, I've got to go home right now," Jon had completely forgotten his news. "Mum and Dad are going to Thailand. I'm seeing them off at half-three."

"Okay!" she conceded.

"Keep in touch," he said. "I'll keep my mobile on."

"Will do."

"Na...hang on a moment."

Something in his voice made her swing round.

"I..." the cafeteria had gone silent. The serving lady was only pretending to read her magazine. Outside the traffic stopped, the breeze that had been playing in the ornamental cherry trees in front of the hospital held its breath. In fact the whole world had stopped what it was doing.

"Yes?" she said. He was flushed and swallowing hard.

He wanted to say; 'Naomi, I want you. I want to hold you in my arms and never let you go. I'm desperately attracted to you! I think I'm in love with you. He wanted to say this and a thousand other things. But something stopped him. He daren't take the risk. A punctured lung would be nothing compared to the hurt she could inflict on him. Instead he said;

"It'll be alright, I promise."

With a wan smile she was gone.

Naomi stretched her arms above her head. She glanced out of the window at the soft light of early evening. She would have desperately liked to get up and stretch for a while. Her eyes ached with the strain of focussing on the monitor screen.

But the last phone call from her Aunt had provided the spur to drive her on.

"He's not good, love." She was still at the hospital, uncertain whether or not to change her plans. "Breathing very shallow, running a temperature, in a lot of pain they tell me. What's that? No, they've no idea. Anyway, I'll know if it's safe to leave him shortly. I'll let you know love."

So much data on the screen before her, so little time. She felt better after a good cry, though. It helped clear her mind and focus on the task in hand. Firstly she had located Isaac using the monitor screen. (There was no way she was putting the headset on!) She had managed to place a marker on him from the last moment they saw him in the house with Aaron and the others. That had been at eleven o' clock that morning twenty-first century time. The darkness lifted after five hours, and she was able to see him lying on a rush mattress in a modest Egyptian house. A slave girl mopped his face as he thrashed weakly from side to side, coughing considerable amounts of blood. A few people, mostly Hebrews came and went, and a small, angular Egyptian who was probably Yahmose who directed operations. For another nineteen hours by the clock on the monitor screen, the tormented breathing and high fever continued, then after a final agonised spasm his eyes closed for the last time. With a muttered prayer, Yahmose covered his face and the still body was carried away.

Twenty-four hours! Of which by her reckoning seven were already gone. Then what would happen? Would, as Jon had almost suggested, the Prof die? Or would he be consigned to nothingness until the Timescope found another shell to merge his character with? Somehow, from the awful tightening in her stomach she felt she knew the answer already.

Then Jon had rung. He had seen his parents off. "How's it going? Do you still want me to help?" She would have dearly liked to say yes, but having him near would not help her concentration. And right now she needed to get some answers fast. She told him the grim news about Isaac.

"Nineteen hours! Are you sure? That makes it…um…"

"Eleven o' clock tomorrow morning." Naomi fought to suppress a sense of rising panic. 'Keep a clear head,' she reminded herself. This whole situation was unreal, a day dream gone mad. But it showed no signs of ending, and the latest information from her Aunt seemed to confirm the desperate, crazy diagnosis; *"oh, and now a rash across his back."* She had reported, *"They think it's an allergic reaction, looks like he's been, well it sounds strange, but...almost like he's been whipped."*

"Is there anything I can do?" Jon asked.

"Another hug?" The words were out before she could stop them. On the other end of the phone line there was a silence. Naomi's cheeks burned. What a stupid thing to say! "Sorry, Jon, only joking," she tried to make her voice sound light.

"Yeah...Ok Na. Look, I'm in all evening, just let me know. See ya." He hung up.

"Goodnight...love." She said softly to the silent earpiece. Trembling she put the mobile back in its charging holster.

The Professor had downloaded the error files a fortnight ago onto a separate database. They were up to date then, and he had separated the main protagonists into sub-files. They were mainly lines of computer code, but frequently referenced by active links to incidents in the scenes they had visited during their time together. Where the Timescope was uncertain about information it had processed, it threw the data into the error file with the link, making it easy to see where and when the anomaly had occurred. The links pointed to either further lines of codes, sound files or still or moving images.

After another precious hour of exploring links, Naomi let out an exasperated sigh. There were few clues obvious to her why the Timescope had decided a particular incident was anomalous. Such clues as were provided meant nothing to her. The phone rang again; it was her Aunt.

"He's stable, love. Marsha insists on me going to Philip's and I think she's right. They've given him antibiotics for the fever, and he's comfortable. She'll let both of us know if there's a change."

'Fine,' thought Naomi. 'You've got until eleven tomorrow morning.' "Ok," she said. "Say hi to them for me."

The interruption did serve a useful purpose. It stopped her going round in circles. After her Aunt rang off, Naomi sat back and reviewed her options. The error files were huge, too big to get to grips with in the short time at her disposal. Every minute wasted brought her Granddad closer to death. Peering in minute detail at the error files was too time-consuming. There must be a quick way; a short cut, something to reverse the effect of the last few weeks. She drummed her fingers nervously on the table, fighting the urge to scream.

Then it hit her! The files she was poring over were not current. They were the ones her Granddad had downloaded, now nearly two weeks old. In those two weeks, changes had taken place, changes to Jon, the Professor and herself. If she could restore the old error files and force the Timescope to use them instead of the latest ones, maybe instead of this amalgamated character that was part-Isaac, part Professor Avery, it would see two different persons and let go of the modern part. The more she thought about it, the more sense it made. It was like the function of reloading the last good configuration she sometimes used when her laptop crashed. Well, these old error files weren't awfully good, but they weren't that bad either!

Five more precious minutes elapsed before she had burned the latest error files onto a disc. She dashed back to the console screen and deftly loaded the latest files side-by side.

On an impulse she decided to try a dry run on her idea. Her Grandfather had intimated that Hannah, the enigmatic, dark-haired Carmelite was being merged in a similar way with herself. Well, here was a chance to see this for real. Half-way down page sixty of the latest data was an error heading which ran:

"CHRONERROR- CONDITION 5." That, she knew from her research meant that the Timescope was seriously unhappy with the anomaly, and it was a chronological type of fault.

Beneath that, it said in smaller print:

"Chronerror subject: HANNAH.

Chronerror type: IMAGE NONCONFORMITY."

The last two words were underlined as an active link. She clicked on the link.

She gave a sharp intake of breath. Hannah gazed from the screen. The dark-haired Carmelite woman, whose forthright and outspoken example had captivated Jon, and whose death had so broken him; she was slumped, trapped in her makeshift prison on Carmel. Behind her the sun-baked rock, before her the unearthly wailing and trampling of the heathen priests, themselves just a few short hours from destruction. Hannah Bath-Obadiah. Only the features had altered. The hair was long, but mouse-brown and wavy, the face oval still, but much more rounded. The face was very nearly hers!

She stood up, her heart pounding. What was going on? The Timescope was backfilling- yes that was the word her Granddad had used. Going back over previous data and altering it to make sense of something. But why? What drove it to tinker around with centuries-old information it had retrieved from ancient rocks? Did this mean she was in danger of wasting away just as Hannah languished before she died? No, that didn't seem likely.

Only when she brought up the related file from the older data did she see that actually the Hannah in the clip was in fact a blend. Hannah had lost height and gained weight. She had gained a mole on her neck like hers, just below her right ear but she had lost some of her Mediterranean complexion. The disfiguring sores and flaccid skin tone had also faded.

Why? She cried out loud to the empty house, suffused with the incessant roar of the computers. Was this just a massive computer joke with no punch line? Or was there a subtle logic to what was happening? She almost thought she saw method in the madness. The Timescope did what it saw fit to achieve its ends. Only her brain could not grapple with the immensity of the issues.

Just before she sat down at the console again, something else popped up in her mind. The moment she thought about it, she knew she was right. The Timescope was requisitioning mobile phone networks. That was what she had been told. She had assumed that it was greedy for memory and processing resources, and had left it at that. But supposing, in its deep and inscrutable logic, it had commandeered the mobile networks for a different purpose? Suppose it needed to communicate with its subjects even when they were not wearing the headsets? Suppose the Timescope had, for reasons best known to itself, wanted Hannah to meet Jon in the city centre. Jon had been miles from the Viewing Room, but linking them through the air was a vast network of microwave links, set on masts, just waiting to be adapted for its purpose.

The idea rocked her. It was bold, beautiful, but just typical of everything that the Timescope was doing right now. It had been given crude bio-sensory programs to allow the wanderers in its virtual landscapes to experience a physical sense of belonging to the surroundings; to enable them to touch and feel the scenery. But it had adapted and enhanced these programs so that a terrifying realism overwhelmed the unwary visitor. So why shouldn't the same apply for the communication system? Naomi glanced up at the antenna hung from the ceiling of the Viewing Room. It had eliminated the need for clumsy wires to the headsets; but there was no way it could transmit much beyond the end of the street. But mobile networks would free the Timescope to transmit and receive its information well beyond any such limits- in fact anywhere where mobile phone signals could be picked up. Quite possibly this accounted for the way in which the experience of being in the Timescope continued after the headset was removed- the mobile phone networks were invasive enough to allow direct and constant access to the nerve centres in the brain stimulated by the bio sensory feedback software. She shivered at the recollection of her horrible experience in the Stygian darkness of Egypt.

Did this mean that the Timescope could interface with its users just when and where it liked without the need for headsets at all? The thought sent more shivers down her spine. She reached out for her phone, Jon should know about this! Then it rang.

"Naomi, is that you?" She had been expecting Jon's voice. Disorientated she said;

"Who is it?"

"It's Marsha, love; at the hospital." The voice had a professional sadness about it, the voice that heralded bad news. Naomi's heart sank.

"I rather think you'd better come quickly. Your Grandfather, I think this is it this time."

Naomi cast a look around the Viewing Room. All around were the physical reminders of a beloved Grandfather. Muddle, clutter- despite her Aunt's best endeavours, nothing could displace this incontrovertible evidence of his occupation of this house for many years. On the wall the screen, the huge speakers, the headsets- the user interface to a magnificent creation that had proved his undoing. Not that he would have cared about the ill-effects- his final weeks, months and years of life had been absorbed in this project that had ironically, in the end absorbed him. He lived for this sort of experience. In that brief glance around the room she remembered the silly times they had shared together as he tried to fill the gaping void left by her parents and sister. The arguments Aunt Judith had with him as she took issue with aspects his unorthodox lifestyle- oh so many years to recall, but now it was slipping away towards an end. Suddenly the room felt very ordinary as if somebody had drawn back the curtains and normality, like sunlight, had flooded the room.

"Are you there Naomi?"

"Yes, er... sure. Does my Aunt know?"

"I rang her just now, she's on her way. She asked me to ring you."

"Thanks Marsha. Oh, what about Jon, Jon Heath?"

"On his way too. Hurry love. Oh, can you come to the small car park round the side? Security will mess you around this time of night; I'll look out for you and let you in."

Naomi glanced at her wristwatch as the door closed behind her. Half-past eleven. She was wrong, wrong by just under twelve hours. Compared to the centuries they had surfed with consummate ease, twelve hours was a pin-point in time. But it was everything to her, and now it was being snatched away.

There were few cars in the park when Jon cycled up. He locked his bike and scanned the side of the building for signs of life. Then a door opened and a light came on. Marsha stood at the foot of a stairwell.

"Here love." She spoke quietly, so that Jon had difficulty hearing her. She held the door open for him, and then followed him up the flight of stairs.

"Not this floor," she murmured, "next one Jon."

They emerged into the now-familiar corridor. It widened out to the nurse's station and a number of rooms led off it, all in darkness except the Prof's room which was emitting a soft yellow light. Marsha stretched to open the door for him, then shuffled in behind him blocking the exit. As before a soft *beep, beep, beep* came from the bedside monitor.

"Jon!" Naomi's voice was tense and her eyes wide. She was staring at something behind Jon. Beside her the Prof was lying exactly as he was when Jon had last seen him- prone and motionless apart from the steady rise and fall of his chest.

"Jon. Wouldya just sit down please?"

The door snapped shut behind him. Jon turned slowly round to follow Naomi's gaze.

Sitting easily in a soft chair to the left of the door was the Blue-eyed American.

Jon gazed at him, frozen where he stood. There was a huge bubble of fear welling up in him. He turned to Marsha.

"I don't understand... I thought you said the Prof was dying... what is this?"

"He is," said Naomi coldly, "He hasn't got much time left." She turned a furious expression on Marsha; "so you use that to get us here, you cow! How much did he pay you to spy on us?" Marsha paid absolutely no attention to her outburst. Jon asked;

"What do you want us here for?"

"My friend would like another chat with you." She said. She turned to go. Blue Eyes beckoned her to him. He spoke in a low murmur, but they caught his words clearly:

"An hour, then call for agency cover. Your mother is dying; you need to be away pronto. Let me get them away from here."

"So you've finished with me then?"

"Banker's draft." An envelope was put in her hand. She slit the envelope and looked at the contents. Her face broke into a broad smile.

"Thank you sir!" She laughed quietly, "That's it for me in this horrible, wet country. I'm back to Jamaica for good!"

"An hour then."

The door closed behind her. Neither Jon nor Naomi moved. Jon glanced around, through the windows he could see the car park, lit by sodium lamps. It was two storeys down. "What do you want?" he asked his throat dry.

"Sit down, that's right, on the bed." He sat; there was a little room on the bed between them and the Professor. Naomi's reached out and took his hand.

"No, no holding hands. Just sit where I can see you."

He regarded them intently, his face half in shadow. Even in the half-light Jon could see his eyes, hard and cold. Then he noticed the object in his hand. He was holding a gun!

So often watching action movies with the rest of the Apostles, Jon had rehearsed this scenario. Time and again the hero, confronted with an armed man would react with a lightning-swift karate kick, one blow sending the weapon spinning across the floor, the next kick crippling the assailant- so easy, so obvious. Strangely, here was the grim reality of being faced with a firearm being pointed at him; nothing he could recall from the movies seemed in the remotest bit relevant. He felt giddy with the cold horror of the realisation. But he did what they all usually did- raising his hands above his head. Blue eyes laughed softly.

"No need to reach for the sky," he drawled, imitating a Western gunslinger. "I doubt if either of you is armed." Jon lowered his arms slowly. "That's good. Just keep your hands where they can be seen, and no sudden movements, OK?"

"Who are you?" Naomi's voice was steady. Jon glanced at her. She had calmed down, good! His heart was racing, but his head was clear.

"I'll tell you that presently. First things first. Where I come from we are used to these," he lifted the gun from his lap slightly. "Please, no heroics, no stuff like in the films- it rarely works and I would have to... er... kill you both once I started. Do you comprehend?"

Jon's throat was even drier, but he managed a limp, "OK."

"Secondly, what I am about to tell you means that I won't need this gun anyway. So listen real good and then we can relax a little." Beside him Jon felt Naomi shiver. The Blue Eyes fixed themselves on him.

"Your parents, Mary and Alan Heath, are half-way to Koh Lanta, in Thailand." He said this conversationally. Jon felt his heart skip a beat. Naomi drew in a sharp breath.

"I understand that your mother had reservations about the tour; not so your father, Jon." There was a lifeless smile about his mouth. "But the wine helped her see things differently."

"Who are you?" Jon rose from the bed. The gun rose in response, mirroring his movements. Naomi snatched his hand and drew him back. She did not let go his hand but gripped it so tightly it hurt.

"That's better. Sudden movements can cause these things to go off. Just stay where you are and I'll tell you all you need to know. Got that?"

They both nodded. He went on.

"Quite an easy schedule, your mother has out there. Five lectures, actually only three now, two have already been cancelled, but they'll find that out next week. The rest of their time spent scuba diving, beach, swimming pool, sightseeing, do you know I'm quite envious! I've never been there, but I'm told it's lovely this time of year."

Jon, his head still spinning said miserably; "what are you going to do with them?"

He chuckled. "Oh, such a concerned lad! Quite a change from the hoodlum we've come to know."

"Are they hostages? Have you kidnapped them?" Naomi's voice was expressionless.

"Oh, that sounds a bit harsh! But I guess that's the sum of it. Yes, they are in my hands. One phone call is all it would take. Then a sudden diving accident, or a car wreck, helicopter mishap- oh the possibilities are endless. You see the Thai police aren't quite as thorough as we would expect from our cops. They will draw the obvious conclusions and you will get the remains of your parents in two wooden boxes on a charter flight. Very sad end to a super holiday!"

Jon felt sick. Naomi was silent for a few moments, then she said aggressively,

"My parents know I'm here."

"Is that so? And your older sister, Jessica too?" His tone was mocking concern. She slumped back on the bed, deflated.

"I didn't know you had an older sister, Na." Jon murmured.

"I don't, she was killed along with my parents in a motorway pile up when I was three. But he knows that too, I guess."

"Just assume I know everything unless I ask," he replied suavely. "Yes, I know about Ralph and Susan Avery and the tragic end to their lives. And your older sister- such a waste! Poor little orphan girl!" His tone was still conversational, but with a hard edge of mockery to it. "It's hard being an only child, as I know full well. But I digress; as you see, it is in your best interests to do exactly what I tell you, then I won't need this" – the gun disappeared under his light grey jacket.

In the pause that followed, Jon toyed with the crazy idea of simply getting up and walking out of the room. This wasn't happening! Armed men just didn't hold him at gunpoint in a hospital ward late at night. Then Blue Eyes spoke again.

"You asked who I am. Well," he turned to Naomi, "I am not, nor ever have been Bradley Jackman of Kansas State University. My name is irrelevant to you. Let me tell you what I do, then you'll be much better able to tell me what I need to know."

"I'm a fixer, an arranger. I find out things, make things happen. When people need to discuss important things, they need privacy, lots of it. I arrange that too." He paused, then lowering his voice said,

"Imagine our discomfort when it transpires that things are not as private as they would seem! Somebody spies on us, in minute detail. Hmmm, now that was very upsetting. Caused my obese colleague a lot of worry; that did." He leant back in the chair.

"Sorry Na." Jon's mouth was dry. She squeezed his hand.

"Your little trick not only ruffled a few feathers, it opened a whole can of worms. Once we worked out where the files had come from, we started watching you, and in particular him," he nodded towards the prone figure on the bed, "then it just got more and more interesting. We found there were huge computer files leapfrogging across the planet, so cunningly encrypted that no one could break them open. Whole networks requisitioned for a few seconds, then it all moved on somewhere else. Once we started asking questions, we just couldn't stop. What was in these files? Why the sudden bursts of activity? Oh, all so intriguing. So I asked you, you will remember."

"We told you what we knew." It was a barefaced lie, but Naomi was feeling desperate.

"Oh, I think not," he sneered. "You told me next to nothing. I had to do a little more digging to find out what you really know. But you youngsters nowadays make it so easy for me! The slightest thing and you immediately get out your mobiles and tell your friends all about it." He flicked open a pocket book and read;

"*'Someone has been in the house and mucked around with the Timescope.'* Wasn't that what you said?"

"So it was you!" Naomi was taut; Jon's hand was getting numb where she was gripping it. She looked as if she was going to say more, but thought better of it.

"None other," he acknowledged. "I expected to find some data storage device in that refrigerated cabinet. All I got was a highly-polished stone. And that's when you gave me a name for this system; *Timescope*."

Jon and Naomi sat motionless, numb with shock. He went on.

"Marsha gave me the best stuff. Or at least you did," he glanced at Jon. "In the quiet of Professor Avery's room, you told him all about how you were meeting people from history. Somehow, I understand, that's how our friend here got injured. Now I go from being interested to excited. I hear fragments here and there that suggest to me that the Timescope is a device that can look into the past." He snapped the book shut. "Is this so?"

"If you know so much, why'd you ask?" said Jon sulkily.

In a flash the man had crossed the room. He buried his fingers expertly in Jon's shoulder, digging under his collarbone. Pain blossomed out from his shoulder, up his face and down his arm. The other hand grabbed his mouth to stifle the yell.

"Don't play games with me, Jon. D'ye hear?" he hissed. "You will tell me all you know. You will conceal nothing. If I get the slightest inkling you are trying anything on I will not hesitate to destroy your parents. And you," he fixed his gaze on Naomi, then looked significantly at the Professor; "don't think for one moment I wouldn't harm him. Now talk to me."

Naomi looked down at the unconscious form in the bed. She felt sickened at the cruelty of the deceit that had lured them here. Her Grandfather stirred slightly and then coughed. A few drops of blood spattered the coverlet; his hair was slick with sweat and in the few moments of silence she could hear his ragged, laboured breathing. In less than half a day he would be beyond hurt.

"Okay it's true," her voice was toneless. "The Timescope can look into the past. It reads the pictures off stones. That's why there was a stone in the reader when you opened it."

For one horrible moment it looked as if he wouldn't believe them. Jon's shoulder ached from where Blue Eyes had gripped it. He eyed them narrowly, then said to Jon;

"So how did you get the files you sent Prentice?"

"From his ring. I stole it from his car."

"Aaaah!" He breathed. "Yes, that fits. So this ring had a stone too, that you were able to read? Then you copied the files and sent them to him. Clever lad!"

Jon wasn't feeling very clever at that moment. His shoulder hurt when he moved. That wasn't so bad in itself; what was worrying him was the full realisation of seriousness of the situation. Past midnight, in a quiet part of the hospital, with a man who handled weapons with casual expertise. A man who had arranged, or so he claimed, a trap for his parents that could be sprung at any moment, and who moved in lofty circles playing games with high stakes- now Jon had looked into those eyes at close quarters and he saw that they were utterly ruthless. His knees began to tremble. Outside an ambulance raced away from the hospital. The wailing siren seemed ominous. Beside him Naomi cast anxious glances at the Prof- what was it she said? Eleven o' clock tomorrow morning. Would they be able to tell Blue Eyes enough to satisfy him and still have time to save her Granddad? The Professor twisted painfully on the bed.

Jackman fired questions at them, which Jon answered as best he could. Where had they been in the Timescope? What was it like? How did it work? Jon answered with as little detail as possible, relating just the barest bones of the information. He sensed the American's patience was wearing thin, when suddenly Naomi, who all this time had been quiet and calm, burst out:

"We might as well show him," she announced. "I think it's time the world found out about it -it's too big to keep to ourselves, and Granddad's in no position to argue." She turned wide appealing eyes on the American; "please, if we show you let us go- Granddad's dying, and I want to be with him when…when he goes."

Jon turned to look at her. It was like when she was in the darkness of Egypt- she was talking to cover her fear. Who could blame her? She still held his hand tightly, but she was twitching, her fingers wrapped around his were squeezing gently but rapidly.

"Naomi…?" Jon began to protest, but there was something in the way she was squeezing his fingers, something that was saying, *"Leave him to me, I know what I'm doing."*

"Now we're talking!" Blue Eyes murmured. He stood up. "Take me to the Timescope."

With a sense of doomed helplessness Jon followed them from the room. Outside, Marsha was clearing her desk, putting things in a cardboard box. She nodded as they went past. "Goodbye loves," she chuckled softly.

"Traitor!" Jon hissed.

"Get on!" Blue Eyes prodded him towards the stairs.

The small car was parked under the sodium light next to Jon's bike. Dismally Jon wondered whether he would see his bike again. Or would it be the starting point for a double murder enquiry? Naomi, who had relapsed back into silence, was pushed into the back seat and Jon into the front. In the few seconds before Blue Eyes strode round to the driver's door, she whispered urgently:

"Jon, do exactly what I say! Do you understand? Don't argue or ask qu…" The door opened and he got in.

"Now do you have the keys to Professor Avery's house?" he enquired.

Naomi held them up. "Here!" she replied.

In less than five minutes they were back at the house. Naomi, her face expressionless was cooperating, explaining the Timescope to Jackman; not volunteering information, but clearly steering him towards the Viewing Room. Jon decided the safest option would be to stand back and let her get on with whatever she had in mind. Perhaps she just felt the safest thing would be to tell him what he needed to know and trust that he was telling the truth about his Mum and Dad. That and hoping to buy time to help the Professor, Jon wasn't confident, but what other ideas did he have?

"Conditioning the stones takes a few hours," She was saying, showing him the freezers full of rocks. "I can put one in if you want?"

"There's already a stone, er… conditioned?" She nodded. "Yeah, just fine, so what happens?"

They moved to the viewing room. Almost immediately Naomi was at the keyboard; to all appearances she was running scenes past them, speeding them up then stopping to show him something of interest. Then the scenes would fly past again, clouds racing through the sky, the sun and moon darting up and down in the heavens. All at once she slowed it right down to normal time.

"This is a good time to take a closer look," she said peering closely at the screen. "What we have set up at the moment shows what the system can do," On the large screen night had fallen but the streets were still busy.

"Ok," he said, "So what time are we going back to?"

"We don't actually go back in time…"

"I know, I know!" He was impatient "But we put these headset things on and can see inside ancient Egypt?" There was a note of awe in his voice, but he also sounded sceptical.

Naomi was studying the monitor screen. "There's only two headsets. I'll go in as guide. Jon, you stay here and watch from the monitor screen."

Half a minute ticked by and he thought about it. Then he shook his head. He turned to Jon.

"You say that you can see each other with the headsets on? Right, you put the other headset on; I want you where I can find you." Then to Naomi whose face registered dismay; "Come here!"

From his pocket he produced a small bundle of plastic cable ties. Selecting two he swiftly pinned her arms together and wrapped one tie around her wrists. It was then Jon knew for certain the danger they were in. The tie wrap cut into her wrists, making her cry out in pain, but he took no notice. Then the second tie wrap was looped through the first and fed through the handle of one of the heavy loudspeakers. She sat down awkwardly on the floor, biting her lip. Jon caught her eye for a fleeting second-*"hold on,"* he mouthed.

"There!" he said, "just remember that when I take that headset off, I want to see you haven't moved." She nodded, writhing from the discomfort of the manacles.

"That's great!" Jon burst out. "Why do those things up so tight? She's hardly going to want to escape even if she could."

He gave an unpleasant laugh. "Then show me what this baby can do and we'll soon be out again and you can both go. But just let me remind you, this is real life, OK? If I have to kill either one of you, I will kill both. I will also kill your grandfather," he took down the headset from the hook, "and your Mom and Dad don't get back. Is that clear!"

"You'll never get away with it!" Jon felt his head spinning again.

His face wore a faint sneer. "I have already- many times. I work alone, and can disappear just like that if I need to." He clicked his fingers in front of Jon's face making him shiver. "So can you! So do as I ask and everything'll be OK."

Now Jon definitely didn't believe him. The notion that co-operating with this man would secure their release was beginning to look like an increasingly forlorn hope.

16
The Last Plague

The night air was like the breath of a furnace and it crackled with tension. In their previous visit there had been a palpable sense of impending disaster, now that feeling was multiplied. All around were groups of Egyptians; well-dressed and wealthy, drifting in uncertain confusion. It wasn't difficult to see why; there was not a slave in sight. Sedan chairs that had borne prosperous individuals through the streets were abandoned unceremoniously by the side of the road. Children once cared for by slaves now turned to their parents for attention. Some sat in the dust, others screamed or whined. It reminded Jon of the time when the server crashed in the school computer suite. The class sat gazing listlessly at the blank monitors in front of them until the teacher had located some chalk and carried on the lesson with the blackboard. Bereft of computing facilities they had simply no idea what to do.

This was clearly the case here. Centuries of total dependence on human slave labour had produced a nation of couch potatoes. Unused to even the most commonplace tasks, they milled around aimlessly. Jon could hear one or two raised voices, complaining, others calling for the taskmasters to account for themselves.

His reflections were interrupted by Blue Eyes. He had put on the other headset and now appeared in the street. He was having difficulty coming to terms with what met his gaze. Shock, awe, disbelief, and incomprehension- he was going through them all at once. He swore fluently, moving from building to building, touching the still warm stones, inhaling the smells of a fish stall, feeling the wet fish. Lacking slave labour the fishmonger had failed to close his shop- either that or he normally stayed open after dark.

"It's a con, right?" He demanded. "Some sorta clever gizmo to make me think all this is happening?"

"It isn't a con," Jon assured him. "We've checked it out and it really is...kosher. We've seen right back past the Iron Age,"

"Where are we? Can we see the Pyramids?" His tone was one of utter incredulity.

"We'd have to know where to look." Actually Jon had no idea when the Pyramids were built. "We're in Rameses, a treasure city." There, he thought. That's about all I know!

"Who are these people? Why aren't they doing anything?"

"These people," Jon indicated the dazed Egyptians "are the Egyptians. They used to have slaves to do everything for them, now they're left to sort things out for themselves."

"Some kinda rebellion, huh? Right. Well tell me this, how come I can feel and touch things? And why is it so hot here? And…"

At that moment the sky burst with a stupendous bluish-purple flash, followed within two or three seconds by a titanic clap of thunder. The shock of it left them both reeling. Blue Eyes let off another volley of lurid expletives.

"How d'ye do that?" He demanded when he had recovered. "All this sound?"

"I don't know," Jon confessed. "We noticed it quite early on, but the Timescope learns as it goes along, so everything gets better. That's why you can understand what they're saying."

"Can you?" He yelled. He ran to the nearest group and stood by listening. One man was responding to the hostile anger of about ten men and two or three women.

"What will the King do?" screamed one of the women. She was immensely fat with flabby cheeks and a coarse, mottled face. Her hair fell long and straight to her shoulders- the picture of a rich individual, used to luxury but going to seed. "My house is in confusion, all of my servants have departed to their own places." Beside her a younger woman was weeping. She pushed her forward. "Aken is beside herself, she has guests arriving, food to prepare and no one to assist."

Two of the men elbowed her aside. "The king is slipping from his throne." Said one. "He has a well-trained army; he has chariots and the finest horses." There was a clamour from the group, he raised his voice, "let them show these upstarts who rules in Egypt!"

"Moses should die for this," declared another man, and the roared agreement. "Why does the king tolerate his presence? Why does he allow this Hebrew to teach our slaves rebellion?"

Another enormous clap of thunder drowned the rest of what he had to say. The king's spokesman waited until the company had settled before he replied;

"My lord, the king hears your complaints. He grieves for your plight and counsels patience from you all. Your slaves will return, they will resume their duties…"

"Lies!" somebody cut in angrily. "The slaves are leaving Egypt!"

"Be careful who you call a liar!" the spokesman threw him a warning look. "There are spies amongst the Hebrews who report every move to the king. The taskmasters follow their movements. Tomorrow the people leave to do sacrifice, three days they journey to offer their impure oblations. The gods are offended; they offer sheep and lambs to their God." A ripple of disgust went around the group. He continued;

"After three days their supplies, food and water will be finished. When they return we will punish them severely. Their men will die under the whip and we will hang their bodies by the city gates as a warning. We will throw their infants into the river to feed the crocodiles as we did in time past. We will make their lives so bitter that they will turn on Moses and tear him to pieces. Then we will have their loyalty once more."

"But what about my daughter?" The woman who had protested earlier spoke once more.

The official held up his hands in a placatory gesture. "It will be hard for us all. All the Hebrews have gone to their slums tonight to eat their detestable meats. Until they return we must fend for ourselves. No one has servants, not even Pharaoh!"

"Pretty upset, huh!" Said Blue Eyes. "Say, did he say those slaves are Jews?"

"Yeah," Jon noticed a look of satisfaction cross his face.

"So these kikes are going to get a good thrashing when they come back." He turned away, and headed up the street. Jon heard him chuckle, "best thing for them!"

At that moment his mobile rang. Jon glanced at the number. It was Naomi.

"Hello?" he said quietly.

"Jon!" Her voice was distant but very urgent. "Pretend it's your Mum! Whatever you do, don't let him know it's me!"

"Who's that?" Blues Eyes was coming back. Jon held the phone with his thumb shielding the display. Putting his other finger in his ear to block out the seething noise of the mob, which had now grown in numbers he shouted down the phone,

"Hi Mum! Where are you?"

"Jon...him!"

"Mum!" he yelled back. "I'm in a busy street, speak up!" From the corner of his eye he could see Blue Eyes making gestures- *'get rid of her!'*

"Jon! Can you hear me? Listen....must.... lose him..."

"Mum! Can I call you back later? My battery's low! When will you be in Thailand?"

The distant voice was barely audible. "Terrible danger, get away from him!"

Jon hung up. "What's she want?" his captor demanded.

"Just wanted to tell me they're nearly there. Stopped off at Singapore, I think."

"Loving parents, eh?" he sneered. "Must do all we can to get them back safely!"

"Whatever it takes!" Jon said under his breath.

"Now turn that thing off! And show me some more!"

Above them the thunderstorm rumbled on, distant now and fading. Jon took him through where the crowds were thickest. 'Lose him,' Naomi had urged, but how? Blue Eyes was in his element, threading his way through crowded streets. At no time was he any more than an arm's length away. Naomi had sounded absolutely emphatic about getting away from him- Jon began to wonder how on earth this could be done. They stopped at the stop of a stone jetty, some two metres above the water. Blue Eyes knelt by the edge and threw a small stone into the river.

"Incredible!" he breathed as the stone hit the water with a soft plop. "So real, so complete."

"I know people who will kill for this! A few selected samples and a brochure and watch the scramble begin. China and America can start the bidding, then when one of them thinks they have exclusive rights we'll sell the technology on to Russia, Africa, Europe... any government would pay anything for this level of surveillance."

"There's something you should know," Jon said, watching his reaction closely. "There's a huge problem with it."

"There always is!" He gave a mocking sigh. "Ok Jon, what's the snag?"

"The Timescope has a nasty habit of locking you in."

He didn't understand. Jon said again, "Once you're in for any time, you can't get out."

"Whatd'ye mean can't get out?"

"Go on!" Jon goaded him. "Try taking the headset off."

He fumbled the headset over his head then gazed stupidly at his surroundings. Holding the eyepiece up again he peered inside at the miniature images, then back at the Egyptian cityscape. Realisation percolated through, he rubbed his eyes. When he turned round Jon saw the look of a bully who had been unmasked. Now he was the one starting to feel real fear!

"Whatcha done?" He demanded. "How come it's still going on?"

"It's happened before," Jon said lightly, "and what's more the only way out is for someone else to halt the programs."

He glared. "You're lying! You've fixed this to trap me!"

"You wanted to see it!" Jon was watching his hand carefully in case he went for his gun. "And what's more Naomi can't help 'cos you trussed her up."

"Stop the Timescope now!" He demanded, standing up and moving along the jetty, his hand reaching inside his jacket. "You can't afford to play games with me, ok?"

In the dark Jon could sense his fear. He could see he was disorientated, uncertain and afraid. "Your rules don't apply here!" He shouted at him. "This isn't New York. You can't shoot your way out." All the time he was measuring the distance between them. 'One more step' he prayed, just a little closer...

Blue Eyes closed the distance between them in a rush. But Jon was ready for him. Ducking under his outstretched arm he threw his weight at him shoving him sideways. For a moment he teetered on the edge of the jetty then with a yell fell into the river. Jon turned and ran.

"Naomi?" He had left the river long behind and now in the shelter of the entrance to a temple adorned with hieroglyphics, he rang her number.

"Jon? Jon, is that you?" Her voice was still very distant. She sounded panicky.

"I've managed to lose him. Why do you sound like you're miles away?"

"I can't hold the phone, it's on my lap." Jon could hear the pain in her voice. "These tie-wraps are digging right in. My hands have gone numb." She gave a little yelp. "Jon, where are you?"

"Somewhere in the city. I threw Blue Eyes in the river. I hope the crocodiles get him..." He could share her sense of urgency- somewhere in this troubled city the old Professor's life was ebbing away. Before midday tomorrow they had to find him, untie the bonds that had merged him with Isaac and get him out. Oh and avoid Blue Eyes. Easy!

"Jon, get out of the city!" Even at a distance there was no mistaking the terror in her voice. "Get into Goshen now!"

"Why?"

"Do you know what's happening?"

"The slaves have all gone back to their homes. The Egyptians are hopping mad!"

"Jon, it's Passover!"

"Yeah, what happens at Passover?" Jon was mystified, but the alarm in her voice unnerved him. Vaguely he tried to recall what he had learned about Passover in Religious Studies. Something to do with a family meal...

"The angel of death goes through Egypt! Jon, are you running yet?"

"I am now!" Jon broke into a trot. "But what's the big deal?"

"At midnight all the first-born in Egypt will die!"

Still Jon could not grasp the significance of what she was saying. She sounded hoarse from shrieking at the phone, but there was no mistaking her terror;

"Jon, you're first-born. And you're in Egypt!"

If Jon had found previous situations in the Timescope frightening, they were nothing compared to the gut terror he felt now. Since he had arrived in Rameses on this evening, he had been conscious of a nameless dread hanging over its streets and buildings. Now forgotten details of the account of the approaching horror came back into his mind; tonight an Angel would skim low over Egypt, and by morning the first-born child of every household, not to mention animals would be discovered cold and dead; millions of them throughout the length and breadth of the land. A catastrophe. It was unthinkable that he, an outsider from several millennia later could be one of them, but by the recent record of the Timescope was he prepared to take the risk? He began running in earnest, dashing down the moonlit streets of the city.

In one street a huddled form lay lifeless in a doorway; the light breeze ruffled his hair and robes. He had no beard, which marked him out as an Egyptian. Jon didn't stop to investigate. The peril of the situation was becoming clearer by the minute. *'At midnight all the first-born in Egypt will die.'* Exactly when was midnight, and what time was it in Egypt now? Perhaps more importantly, where was the slave quarter from which the Hebrews made their daily pilgrimage to Rameses to wait hand and foot on their overlords? Surely not far, but far enough if he was lost!

"Na? Can you hear me?" Jon could hardly speak; his breath rattled and gasped in his chest.

"Just about." She gave another cry, Jon gritted his teeth. Why had that pig done those tie-wraps up so tight?

"Can you stop the program?"

"No, I can't move much at all. Are you still in the city?"

"Yeah, but I don't know where!"

She sounded frantic. "You're in terrible danger, Jon. Have you any idea of the time in there?"

Jon looked at his watch. Two and a half hours had elapsed since they had entered. It was mid-evening then, now it felt late. He had to think this out. He couldn't afford to waste time running around in circles any longer. "Can't be far off midnight!"

"Jon!" she too was so panic-stricken she could hardly speak. "Please keep going, get out of there!"

Despite his tiredness, Jon began running again; his throat choked and the blood thundered in his ears. All the time he was aware of the risk that he might be running away from the slave quarter and further into Rameses. Then his phone rang again:

"Na…" he gasped, but there was no answer. He looked at the display. It was not a number he recognised. He stopped for a few moments more to collect his breath in the entrance to a huge building that fronted onto a spacious plaza.

It rang again a few minutes later. Jon stopped and returned the call. The thunderstorm was gone and the city without traffic noise, radios, police sirens or any of the usual background roar familiar to him was deathly quiet. Faintly he heard another mobile ring for a few seconds before it was switched off. Blue Eyes was tracking him.

It made perfect conditions to locate anyone. He glimpsed the grey-haired figure once, emerging from a building behind at the far end of the square, but before he could be spotted. Jon dodged out of sight and turned the phone off.

By now he was tiring fast. His school's insistence on cross-country running had given him some fitness, but he had spent too much time in front of computers lately. His throat was raw, his legs racked with agonising pains and he felt sick. From that crushing grip on his shoulder, Jon guessed that Blue Eyes was in a great deal better condition than himself. Yet if he tried to dodge him he would lose precious time. The only hope lay in straightforward flight.

Trying to ignore the soreness in his muscles, Jon bolted from cover running away from the wide square and down a narrow street. Behind him he heard a cry from his pursuer, but down here the darkness provided better cover. He was encouraged to see that the city had changed considerably. Gone were the mighty houses, or even modest homes. Now the streets were flanked by small shops which even in the moonlight looked grubby and wretched. Between these were temporary stalls, and derelict buildings. Several were smoking, probably set on fire by angry Egyptians to intimidate the slaves, but there were few signs of life. A child peeped through a window, his face silhouetted against the dim light inside but that was all. Undoubtedly he was in a poverty-stricken area. He felt he was heading the right way for the Jewish zone, and sanctuary. But the searing pain each breath demanded was sapping his will to go on.

The narrow streets were filthy with piles of rubbish. Rotting trash gave off an appalling smell and made progress difficult. There were pot-holes in the road, some of which were deep and filled with muddy water. He emerged into a little open square. A skeleton of a small animal, a goat or a sheep lay by a well. It was surrounded by mangy dogs, gnawing at the ribs. Jon stopped to try to breathe, staring into the gloom to see whether Blue Eyes was still on his tail. There was no sign of him. He collapsed against a wall, closing his eyes and listening to the sound of his breath sobbing through his choked-up throat. His heart pounded in his ears- *thu-dump, thu-dump, thu-dump,* rapid and anguished in his spinning head. Then he froze, holding his breath.

Blue Eyes was picking his way across the square. He was still dripping wet and leaving sodden footmarks in the dirt. His gun was not visible. At twenty metres he stopped. He had his mobile phone to his ear.

"Get back here from wherever you are." He could not conceal the excitement in his voice. "Charter a private jet, do it now. I'll wait here. This is the biggest thing in history, this is history. We can't afford to let anyone else in on this until we're ready to name our price."

The person on the end of the line spoke briefly, then Blue Eyes continued;

"The punk gave me the slip, but he's leaving a trail as wide as a Greyhound. He can't be far away. I'll deal with both the kids, but I need you to deal with the parents... yes, Alan and Mary Heath. ...What's that? Yes of course that's what will happen! Pull yourself together man! And lay off the liquor!"

Over the stillness of the square, Jon could hear a familiar voice replying to him; the words were indistinct but the quivering tone left him in no doubt. His contempt for Prentice rose several notches.

"You won't regret it; this is the stuff billionaires are made of, I promise you. When can you..."

His voice tailed off. Jon could hear a familiar high pitched whining from the mobile; Blue Eyes rapped it sharply against the edge of the well then held it to his ear again. But the conversation was at an end. Jon could hold his breath no longer- he tried letting it out quietly, but his tortured lungs demanded a huge gulp of air. Blue Eyes turned at the sound. His hard eyes pinned him to the wall.

"Ah, Jon, we meet at last." He advanced towards him. "You obviously didn't believe me when I said 'no monkey business.'" He withdrew the gun from inside his jacket and in a smooth motion removed the safety catch. "All the same, I thank you for introducing me to this;" he twitched the muzzle around the square; "but I've seen all I need and it's time to tighten up security."

"Don't hurt Naomi," Jon was surprised at the steadiness of his voice. His knees were shaking. Overhead the moon was full and bright, bathing the square in milky whiteness. Blue Eyes raised the gun.

"You knew the deal- you tried to give me the slip and I told you what would happen."

"You were going to kill us anyway." Jon looked into his eyes and saw confirmation. So he was going to die here. This was it. The end. He screwed up his eyes and waited; and odd sense of detachment coming over him.

The sudden sharp pain in his chest caused him to gasp and fold up like a penknife. 'So this is what it's like being shot!' he thought dully; but when he opened his eyes he saw that the American had not moved. He too had frozen into rigidity and was wearing a puzzled look. Then Jon saw it behind him.

"Look!" he croaked.

Behind Blue Eyes there was something like a heat-haze on a hot road permeating the air. It had no substance that Jon could see; neither did it have any definition. The buildings, shops, dirty run-down stalls and filthy streets shimmered in the moonlight, the outlines buckling and bending; the most distant houses first, some fifty metres away, then the strange distortion moved across the square. The dogs by the well gave voice to a horrible howling and lay flat on the ground, their ears pinned back as the apparition rolled over them. Then one dog fell over on its side, jerking and thrashing its legs in the air. Seconds later it was still and the Thing moved towards them.

"Run!" Jon screamed, "It's the Angel!" But he couldn't run himself. The sharp pain in his chest was spreading up to his jaw and down his arms. It felt like a hand had reached up under his ribs and was squeezing his heart to a standstill. The *thu-dump* of his heart earlier was now a laboured *thu-thu-thu...* and the pain increased relentlessly. With it came a deep, primal sense of horror.

Like surf racing across a beach, the Thing poured towards them. Blue Eyes had half-turned, clutching his left arm. Jon could see he was really frightened now. The muscles on his neck stood out like wires and he had gone deathly white.

"Wha...what is it?" Then he gave a yell of pain and went down on one knee, his chin rammed into his chest.

The hand was squeezing harder now, *thu...*pause...*thu...*pause...*dump!* Jon felt strength draining from his limbs and a fog settling round his eyes. Every breath he took was a struggle, but his chest was too constricted by the agony to draw in enough air. He felt consciousness washing out on the tide.

Blue Eyes had hauled himself upright and was shouting at It. The shimmering haze engulfed him, he had his pistol in both hands. There was a series of immense explosions as he fired wildly at the Thing, then dropping his weapon he staggered erratically across the square like a wounded dog.

"Yon!" He could not open his eyes to see her, but he could smell the vineyards of Carmel on her clothes. Her arrival caused him no surprise; perhaps in their dying moments many people saw their loved ones- and in the stretched out moments of time, Jon was aware only of a sense of infinite gratitude at the sound of her voice.

"Hannah, oh…"

"Take my arm, my lord!" She seized him, and with a strength he would not have suspected her capable of possessing dragged him upright. He felt the rustle of her hair across his face; then she was half-carrying, half-pulling him away from the haze that was closing in on them both.

"Let me go Hannah," he sobbed, "please, leave me here, I can't…"

"Do it!" She said harshly, "Stand up, I can't carry you far. Quickly!"

The imperative roused him. Despite the cruel pain blossoming through his body, Jon straightened up and allowed himself to be drawn down a tiny side street. Hannah continued to yank him further down the street. The Angel of Death followed the pair, the speed of its progress closing the gap implacably. Five metres, four metres, three…

"No further…" Jon croaked. "Can't…go…" but she had stopped. Jon fell against a door. Even semi-conscious he realised the wood had a peculiar slipperiness which smeared his face as he slid down the rough timber. Hannah was pounding on the door, screaming to be let in, her voice was a long way away, he didn't care any more.

Just want to close eyes… blot out the pain… shimmering haziness all around… moon looking like a reflection on rippling water…fireworks going off inside skull… *thu…thu…thu…DUMP!* Falling forward onto cold hard floor.

There was the sound of a murmur of voices, then everything faded to black.

It was sometime later that he stirred. Outside the streets were silent. There was no way of knowing how long he had been unconscious. He was so tired that even breathing was a physical struggle. His head ached, his ribs were sore and his back hurt from being huddled on the cold floor. He sat up wincing at the pain and looked around the room. Small oil lamps clustered on the window ledges and along a table gave a steady light. It was crowded. All ages, apart from the very old were here. It could have been one large family; but judging by the faces Jon guessed at least two whole families were present. They were assembled around the table, some sitting on benches, others on the floor. Close by him a mother was feeding her baby, occasionally stroking the tiny chin to remind him to suckle. Apart from the noises the baby made, all else was quiet. On the table were the remains of a lamb. The ribs picked clean of meat, the legs missing but the rest of the carcase, complete with the head easily recognisable.

"My lord!" Hannah was squatted on the floor beside him. She had been gazing around the room, the yellow light from the oil lamps picked out her small, determined chin. As he struggled to sit up, Hannah crouched down and supported his shoulders. He looked at her closely.

"You've changed, Hannah, you've done something to your hair."

Almost as he said it, he was conscious of the idiocy of this statement. This girl died on the homeward journey from Carmel; now here she was in ancient Egypt, and he was more concerned with her hairstyle! But there was a notable difference in her hair, whereas it had been straight and waist length, now it had waves and reached only half-way down her back. She flicked it out of her eyes, and smiled gently at him.

"My lord, I am glad you are recovered. Will you eat?"

The smell of roasted meat was still strong in the room. Jon hadn't eaten much that day or yesterday, come to that. He tried to rise, but felt too weak. Hannah helped him sit back down.

"*Yon*, I will fetch you food," she murmured, "it is the LORD's Passover. I know not how we come to share it like this, but it is good for us to be here."

For the most part, as before on Carmel, the majority of people ignored him. They stepped around him, or over him, but no one commented on his presence. Everybody in the room had eaten; but the remains of the lamb yielded a plateful of meat. Beside it were some flat pancakes of bread and a dish containing a selection of green leaves. Hannah returned with a little of everything.

"It is my turn, my lord to care for you," she said softly. "Here we will be safe until first light, then everybody will leave together. The Egyptians will not trouble us further."

"You eat some too," Jon said, taking a piece of the flesh and chewing it. It tasted really good, slightly smoky from the wood fire it had been roasted on, but moist and tender. She demurred, but Jon insisted, and together they ate the first Passover, amongst the apprehensive slaves of Egypt, about to leave *en masse* the land of their cruel captivity.

The bread was hard work, heavy and stodgy, but the green leaves by comparison made the bread appetizing. Hannah watched Jon closely as, thinking they were a type of lettuce; he popped a leaf in his mouth.

"Urrgh! What on earth is that?" He spat it out in disgust.

She laughed, the first time Jon could remember her laughing. "My lord, it is hyssop. It is bitter, is it not?"

"It's revolting, why do you eat it?"

"It is to remind us of our time in this place;" she said. "Lest we forget the bitter and cruel bondage in this forsaken land, and amongst this corrupt people. A bitter taste to recall a bitter time."

Driven by curiosity, Jon, swaying slightly struggled to his feet, and looked around the room. The baby, still clamped to his mother's breast, was asleep. There were other children in the group; two older girls and a boy, and a smaller boy who was also asleep. They had been grouped together and an old man, the patriarch of the assembly was speaking to them. Jon took another mouthful of bread and listened:

"The LORD YAHWEH has commanded us to keep this feast."

The speaker had a soft voice, but the room was quiet so there was no difficulty in hearing him. He struggled with the Name as if it were new to him.

"We will remember this night for all ages to come. It is the first night of the year to us. You will tell these things to your children and your children's children- you will not forget this night." Jon shivered.

"This is the night that the angel of the LORD has passed over the dwellings of His people. The first-born of Israel are safe, as are you, my children; the first-born of your mother, and the first-born of your father who died under the whip two years ago. But the first-born of our captors this night have died as they slept."

Jon looked around. In the soft light he could see that every person in the room was wearing fantastic items of jewellery- necklaces, bangles, earrings, headbands, bracelets and fine brooches. Against the dowdy slave clothes they wore, the ornaments looked doubly impressive. Rubies sparkled in the yellow flames of the oil lamps, gold glimmered softly, buttercup yellow contrasting with the white items of silver. Even the very youngest child had a graceful necklace around her dirty neck that probably once adorned the throat of a fine nobleman's wife.

As the man talked, Jon walked around the crowded room. It ached to move but he felt less uneasy away from the door. The elder went on to instruct them how they were not even to let the names of the Egyptian gods come to their lips ever again, and talked further about the recent wonders they had witnessed. Most of the young children fell asleep after another hour, but the older ones listened intently to the recounting of the events of the last few months. Eventually, even they too began to look weary. Finally Jon sat down next to Hannah. Her eyes danced in the flickering light and Jon leaned against her, aching but feeling at peace. She nestled against him and took his hand in hers. A deep sense of calm and belonging stole over him as the minutes slipped past.

A scream outside broke the spell. Nervousness rippled through the group. For a minute they sat unmoving, and then shuffled in agitation as there was another scream, and another. Finally the speaker rose from the table and moved to the window. He peered out from between the small gap left by the shutters, cautiously assessing what he could see. Others left the table to look; the window shutters were opened a little more, and then thrown wide.

"Rise, it is time. Let us go!" He said.

The night was nearly over. It was somewhere between four or five in the morning. In the east there was just the hint of greyness in the cool air. Behind Jon the families streamed out of the house, various cooking utensils that had been stacked by the door were gathered up by the women and bound into their garments. The baby, swathed expertly at its mother's back slept on; its head back and its pear-shaped mouth open a little.

As they emerged into the street, houses around them were emptying as well. More slaves were pouring out, more dozy children rubbing their eyes, complaining freely to unheeding parents. There was urgency now, an objective. Jon saw the remains of the carcase he had spotted earlier, close by the well. The dead dog lay nearby, its limbs stiff, but there was no sign of Blue Eyes. It was strange how completely Jon had forgotten him.

Nearby two men carried an older man. By a larger house they were placing the corpses in a row on the side of the road amongst the piles of rubbish. It was terribly like the news footage following an earthquake or terrorist incident. Every minute more Egyptians brought out their dead and added their voices to the lamentation. Such misery, street after street yielding up their dead. Egypt wept.

In a large main street, the bodies stretched away, side by side into the gathering dawn. So did the numbers of slaves shuffling out into the light. The trickles of dowdily-dressed Jews, most wearing the same fabulous jewellery Jon had seen earlier, converged to streams, then rivers of human beings, choking the streets and flowing like a spring tide out of the city limits. For the most part they ignored the Egyptians, some made contemptuous remarks but Jon did see one older slave woman holding her former mistress in her arms and weeping freely with her before she was pushed away to join the exodus.

Now Egypt had a voice. The voice of utter desolation and terrible sadness. It keened like an air-raid siren from house to house, echoing from the stone walls. As the crowds of slaves multiplied, so their former captors brought out their dead in ever increasing numbers. Some of the Egyptians cursed the Jews, but no one made any threatening move against them. For the most part they shouted a single word at them;

"Go!"

Others rushed from their houses clutching yet more valuable items that they pressed into the hands of the slaves. It was still chilly and if the gift was clothing the recipient promptly put it on so that they stood out amongst their drably-clad neighbours. The Egyptians then fell to their knees beside their dead. As they walked on others called from their kneeling positions:

"Go! Just go!"

The sun rose. Bright, cheerful beams that tinted the grey dawn red and peach. A beautiful day to come. In its light Jon turned to view the city they were leaving. He gasped!

They were on higher land. Before them they could see in the clear light huge areas of the city of Rameses, and in the distance the river Nile stretching like a dark ribbon across the landscape. In the darkness Jon had visualised parks, gardens, trees, green fields and orchards. Nothing could be further from the truth. Egypt looked like a First World War battlefield.

Not a blade of green grass was visible anywhere. Neither was there a tree with leaves to be seen. There were trees, but they were smashed hulks, branches torn away, all foliage stripped. The fields, even right against the river's edge were brown and dismal. The buildings were no better. Many houses had collapsed; even great mansions were roofless and ruined. Most roofs had dark holes in them as if they had been bombed from above. The hailstones must have been like footballs to do this damage!

The saddest sight of all was the bodies of animals all around. The fields were littered with their brown carcases where they had been struck down. Some had been half-eaten, others were bloated and rotting. Egypt stank! It stank of decay, defeat and above all fear.

"Go!" They called heartbroken. "Go and bless us also!"

For now the tide had clear direction.

"Look," Hannah tugged his sleeve and pointed.

Far in the distance was the head of a titanic column of humanity, streaming away in front, heading south; and behind them the slums of Goshen were emptying fast. Every street was awash with people, caught up in an orderly but urgent haste to escape. As children, tired from the disrupted night whined, they were picked up by the men and carried shoulder-high. One or two complained of hunger and mothers fished out pieces of bread for them to chew on. But the faces of most were expressionless.

Far ahead following Hannah's outstretched finger, Jon could see another shadow, vast, stretching away into the west. It was the shadow cast by a massive column of cloud that was way, way in the distance. A pillar of clouds billowing in on themselves, as if a mighty bonfire burned beneath. It did not spread out as it rose, but was tightly defined, reaching as far as the eye could see into the morning sky.

Confronted with the obvious majesty of God, his mouth fell open in awe. Beside him Hannah smiled quietly to herself, a tired but satisfied smile. Around them some Jews paused to stare as they marched, but were rapidly shoved onwards.

In a trance they joined the throng, walking alongside those whose lives had changed overnight. They walked mostly in silence, watching the great pillar of smoke as it drifted slowly ahead. Captivated as he was by the awe-inspiring sight, Jon could not resist looking at the figure walking serenely beside him

"Hannah, you've changed." In the full light it was apparent. Apart from her hair that he had noticed earlier, there were a number of differences about her. Her skin was fresher, softer and had lost some of its tan and the marks of exhaustion and famine had receded greatly. Her face was rounder, and her eyes had lightened. She turned to face him, and Jon's heart almost stopped beating again. Could it be possible she was lovelier than ever?

"Shalom, my lord." There was jubilation in her voice. "My people are free! They are leaving the land of their captivity."

Around them the column of ragged humanity streamed by. She stopped and faced him, a half-smile on her lips.

She reached out her arms and gracefully placed them around his neck. Jon felt as if his heart was going back into failure. He held her close, listening to her breathing by his ear.

"Hannah," he had noticed another difference. "You've gained weight." Her figure was still slender, but no longer wasted. "You're a lot fatter now!"

"Gee, thanks, Jon," said Naomi, wearily.

Egypt vanished utterly at once. A shaft of daylight was lighting the room up from the window. Hannah was gone, the refugees, the cloud, the city, the stench. All gone as at the flick of a switch. Naomi was in his arms, her face twisted with pain and the black keyboard lodged between her fingers. "Jon, help me," she pleaded.

Jon gazed stupidly at her. The transformation from Egypt to Keswick Avenue had been instantaneous. Her fingers were blue and her wrists swollen. "Jon…please get these off," she opened her hands and the keyboard clattered to the floor. The tie wrap manacles had cut into her flesh.

He dashed into the kitchen and rifled through the overflowing drawers, then spotted the scissors on the draining board. As the tie wraps were cut she screamed with the pain of restored circulation. Jon helped her to the living room and sat her in a chair, massaging her numb hands.

"Jon…" he thought she was about to faint, but she rallied herself and herself and stood up. "Please, there's no time, you've got to help."

She led him to the console screen where the error files were still pasted, side by side. As she touched the keyboard, the two faces of Hannah sprang out of the screen.

"Whoa!" Jon cried. She has changed, she's more like..."

"Me! Yes I know." Naomi flushed. "Jon, I'll explain later, but please, Granddad will die at just past eleven," she looked at the wall clock; "forty-five minutes is all we've got!"

Jon was surprised how late it was. Only a few minutes ago, it seemed he had been watching sunrise over the wreck and ruins of Ancient Rameses, city of the great Pharaohs of Egypt. "What do you want me to do?"

She fought to remain calm. Her fingers were still too numb to use a keyboard, but she pointed to great chunks of data in the older error files; "Cut and paste, that...and that... oh, there's a bit more." She chewed her lip. "Hurry, Jon, please!"

"But there's pages of it!" Jon objected.

"I know!" she cried, "I would have done this last night but he, you know, Blue Eyes..."

"Ok," Jon could see she was losing her self-control, "What else shall I transfer?"

Minute after minute of frantic activity ticked by; "What are you trying to do?" Jon asked during a pause, still trying to haul his mind back from Egypt and that perfect moment with Hannah.

"No, not that...nor that...there, transfer that section," she commanded. "I'm trying to restore things as they were two weeks ago. No, I don't know if it'll work, but what else can I do? Take that section across as well."

Jon could hardly keep up as she directed page after page of modifications to the error files. Her agitation was rubbing off on him- sweat was starting down his back. Suddenly he said;

"Where's Blue Eyes? What happened to him?"

"Dead!" She said flatly. "No, don't stop, please Jon! Yes, I'll have that section too. He was in the streets of Egypt when the Angel of Death passed through. You know what happened to you; well he didn't make it to safety so work it out for yourself. No, leave that bit. He just about made it out of the house."

Something clicked in Jon's brain. It was a notion so outrageous that he could hardly grapple with the enormity of it. But it all fitted. He stopped and spun round to face her.

"You knew that would happen!" he accused. "You...you set it up! That's why you sent him into Egypt when you did. Naomi, you knew all along, didn't you?"

"Jon, don't stop, please, Granddad's going to die in five minutes."

Jon did not resume work.

"Please Jon, don't let him die!"

"Tell me!" She pushed him aside and seized the mouse. But it skittered away from her numb fingers. "Tell me!" He repeated.

It was true. She had set the whole thing up. From her knowledge of the Biblical events she had correctly guessed the time when the Angel would reap its grim harvest in Rameses. Jon, still transferring data listened awestruck.

"But how did you know he was a firstborn too?"

"He told us. You probably didn't notice. *'It's hard being an only child, as I know full well,'* – that's what he said. So I only had to try and get the right time. I wanted to lead him through Egypt myself- I had an older sister, yes, transfer that bit, so I would have been safe, but he took you instead." She battled with tears.

"You killed him!"

"He would have killed us both! That'll have to do. Please can you click along that top menu... there! There should be a menu that says, 'restore default files...'"

"You killed him!" Jon repeated.

"I had to Jon. I had to save Granddad, we had no time left."

Jon was too overwhelmed to argue. The modified data swept across the screen; a progress bar crawled lazily across the screen.

"Come on...." She muttered, "hurry up." In the hall the grandfather clock started to strike the hour. She was shaking like a leaf. "Hurry up, move, will you!"

"THIS DATA HAS BEEN MODIFIED. BACKDATED FILES MAY BE OVERWRITTEN. CONTINUE? YES/NO"

Her injured fingers crashed down on the Enter key. Jon caught her as she fell forward.

"Jon." For several minutes he had supported her, trembling like a leaf as she sobbed. Shock was setting in. The pain and seriousness of the recent events began to sink into her mind.

"I thought you were dead." She whispered. "You fell through that door with the blood all over it, then lay still for two hours. You went really blue. Oh Jon, I'm sorry, I tried to go instead."

"Na, are you sure Blue Eyes is dead?"

"I heard an ambulance stop outside at about seven fifteen."

"What happened to him, then? I mean I thought he'd shot me; there was this horrible pain, then he started firing."

"He let off three shots in the viewing room; two bullets are high up in the walls, one narrowly missed my head. Then he ran out shouting and swearing. He's dead, Jon." She sniffed and blew her nose. "It took me ages just to chafe through the tie wrap which held me to the speaker; and another fifteen minutes more to work the keyboard properly to stop the Timescope." She smiled wanly, "then you told me I was getting fat!"

"Sorry Na, I thought you were Hannah," Jon shuffled.

"Well, I'm going to phone the hospital." She said turning away. "Aunt Judith should be there. I'm surprised she hasn't rang yet."

Jon was still reeling with the enormity of her admission. She was right. He knew that Blue Eyes had no intention of letting them live, even if he hadn't been double-crossed, but he felt a mixture of horror and a savage pride that a ruthless killer had been destroyed by her. It was just what Hannah would have done; he recalled her suave rejoinder to the High Priest of Baal before he was thrown over the precipice: - *'breaking you will be a good deal quicker!'*

She came back, a puzzled look on her face. "Phone line's down." She said.

"What about the mobile?"

"Same again." She held it up. Jon could hear a high-pitched buzzing sound.

"Blue Eyes had that too... oh no!" He had forgotten that the assassin had made a last phone call before his final encounter.

There was a movement behind them. The door opened and a figure filled the entrance.

"Forgive me, Jon, Naomi." He smirked. "I didn't knock, but I thought it best to come straight in."

Naomi stared at Prentice, then back to Jon. Jon looked at them both, helpless.

17

Prentice slicked his hair back and moved further into the room. "Do you know," he purred, "Whilst you've been snuggled up together in here, rather important things have been happening outside?"

"What have you done to my Mum and Dad?" Jon demanded, advancing towards him. He could smell alcohol on his breath.

He raised his hands in mock defence. "Oh, nothing-yet! No, by important I mean much more earth-shattering than that." He nodded towards the phone Naomi was holding. It was still emitting a high-pitched buzz. "Strange isn't it? Not only that phone network, but landlines, microwave links, radar communications, internet, in fact any utility that relies on networked systems; gas, water and electricity, is experiencing the same interference as you have there. Not only here in Britain, but throughout wide areas of the developed world."

Both Jon and Naomi went very suddenly cold.

"My plane had to make a very bumpy landing this morning. No control tower, no radar, only emergency landing lights. I was lucky, most aeroplanes are grounded. The only things in the air right now are fighter jets."

Jon reached out and took Naomi's hand. It was ice cold.

"We're potentially at war, that's what the Prime Minister told the population before the television networks collapsed. Our computer networks have been rendered useless- all that is apart from safeguarded military links. Everything has stopped. I struggled through gridlocked traffic to get here, Jon, Naomi. The army have been deployed to keep order and stop looting. The cabinet are meeting on a war footing in their bomb-proofed bunker. Nobody knows what is causing this interference. Some say it's global terrorism, others are looking to the skies for aliens about to invade. Everybody's seeking for the enemy who's responsible; who's done this to us." There was a deafening roar of jet aircraft overhead.

He chuckled. "But I think we know, don't we."

Jon felt as if he was trapped in a nightmare. When would this end? He stared aghast at the civil servant; standing in the room with a greasy grin on his face. He glanced at Naomi. She too was ashen, but he could see she was weighing up what he had just said.

"What do you want?" She said faintly.

He looked around the room. He was nervous; peering closely at the computer hardware, licking his lips as he did so. Naomi repeated the question.

"Do you know, my dear, I'm not at all sure – yet. I received a call from a friend of mine whom I believe you've both met. I came fully expecting to find him here."

"He had to go," Jon ventured. Prentice looked startled. This was not what he had anticipated.

"Hmmm, strange, he said he would wait. Did he give a reason?"

Jon muttered something, finally Naomi said; "He just told us to stay here until he got back. Perhaps he realised you might need his help to get here."

"Sad," he said after a moment's thought. He turned to Jon. "Sad for you that is; you see, as my friend explained, as a result of your giving him the slip your dear parents are now living on a knife-edge…"

Jon's anger erupted. "If you've harmed them, you fat scum? If I find…"

"Jon!" Prentice's voice had a sharp edge to it. "I counsel you not to cross me as you did my friend. One of the last things I did before I flew here was to set in progress a chain of events that will result in one thing. Your parents will, unless I cancel the order, meet with a nasty accident that will result in both of their unseemly deaths." Jon noticed he was shaking, his fat neck quivering rapidly. "Call it a little insurance policy if you will. I think you know what I need. Now my American friend has a reputation for being, shall we say unemotional."

"So when I receive a call from him, and he is sounding, how shall I put it, *excited*? I tell myself that something quite out of the ordinary has happened to him. Furthermore," he wiped his forehead, "furthermore he relates an extraordinary account of how he has been walking around a city in ancient Egypt. This has been made possible by something he calls the Timescope. Now I have a choice; either I dismiss this as the ravings of an unhinged mind, or believe the incredible."

"Knowing Mr Jackman..." he went on;

"That's not his real name!" Naomi interjected.

"Call him what you will, anyway, my friend is not disposed to exaggeration or excitability, far less mental instability. So I boarded the first plane I could charter to get back here. As I return, below me, all over the country the lights are going out. This too ties in with what my American friend has told me- in its eagerness to carry out its operations the Timescope seizes network resources in ever increasing amounts, thus squeezing out legitimate traffic in the process. You've never seen the money markets in such a mess!"

"The whole of Europe wakes up to what America has already experienced for many hours- namely a comprehensive shutdown in every facility that relies on networked communications. The balloon goes up, the governments of the world assume the worst and hey presto! We're on a war footing!"

There was another sustained thunder of jets swooping low overhead.

"What do you want us to do?" Naomi cried.

"Well, I would have thought that it was obvious, don't you? We, that is Jackman and myself would like this," he waved his hand around the room, "the Timescope. We have many better uses than your Grandfather for it."

"What about my Mum and Dad?" Jon asked hotly. "Are they safe?"

"Oh, quite safe, dear boy. Quite safe. That is until tomorrow afternoon when they go scuba diving around the wreck of an old battleship. Your father is very much looking forward to it! Three o'clock Thai time." He rolled his immaculate jacket sleeve up and looked at his Rolex. "That's nine tomorrow morning. After then, I'm afraid the die is cast. No amount of phoning will bring them back safely from their expedition. So please, Jon, nothing silly, I want above all, particularly for Mary's sake to countermand that last order, and I will in due course. But I insist on your total cooperation, in whatever I ask. Do you understand?"

Jon's flesh crawled. He wasn't sure which was worse, Blue Eyes' implied and real violence or the greasy serpentine charm of Prentice. "Okay," he growled.

"Tremendous!" He rubbed his slim fingers together. "And you, my dear, I take it I can count on your assistance as well?"

"I need to call the hospital." She said. "I'm not doing anything until I know how my Granddad is."

"Ah! The great Professor Avery. Yes of course. It would be handy to know how he's bearing up." He reached into his pocket and produced a phone.

"Use my phone." He offered silkily. He held it out; it was minute, a combination personal diary, Internet connection and mobile phone. "One of the perks of the job, they allow us secure networks with which to do our job." He pressed a few buttons. They could hear the dialling tone clearly. "Oh and no covert messages, secret calls for help, there's a good girl!"

Naomi grabbed the handset and dialled.

"Aunt, is that you? Oh you're with him, thank goodness… yes, I've been trying to get through… no, I can't talk right now, but please Aunt, just tell me how he is."

There was a brief conversation; then Prentice started making impatient gestures. "I'll be round just as soon as it's safe to move outdoors," she finished, and then hung up.

"Well?" Prentice enquired, pocketing the phone. "How is the great Inventor?"

"Stable," she said shakily. "It was touch and go earlier," she glanced significantly at Jon, "but he's settled down again."

"Excellent!" Prentice seemed to have lost much of his nervousness. "Then we wait, and when Jackman arrives we take a tour. After that I make a phone call to Thailand and we see about freeing up the mess this has made of the communications networks. Does your Grandfather have brandy in the house?"

Naomi moistened her lips. She was thinking hard. Then she said; "Jon, do you know how long Jackman said he would be?"

"Search me!" Jon shrugged, "why?"

"It's just that the Timescope is running on standby power; there's a bank of batteries in the basement. Granddad reckoned on a few hours if they were fully charged. If we wait, unless the electricity comes back on, well it might not be working when we go in."

For the first time Jon realised that the wall lights were off. The sun shone brightly through the window, a cloudless Summer Monday morning. Where the sun did not reach, the room was in shadow. Then he saw that she was holding her fingers up to him; five…ten… fifteen. He understood, fifteen hours standby power until…well, once the batteries went flat, the Timescope would halt, then the gaunt body in the hospital bed would also stop living. Only this time there would be no reprieve, no second chances, and no borrowed time.

Prentice seemed apprehensive about this. He asked them again where Jackman had gone, but Jon pointed out that Blue Eyes was not the sort of man who would be likely to tell them anything. Finally, with a hollow attempt at geniality he said;

"Okay, we will go without him. Naomi, I think you should be my guide. Jon, let me once again…"

"Alright!" Jon said irritably. "Just see what you need then make sure my Mum and Dad are safe!"

"Very good. We understand each other perfectly."

The headset needed a good deal of adjusting to get the straps round Prentice's fat neck. He stood wobbling in the shaft of sunlight, then abruptly froze as the Timescope reached into the recesses of his head and overrode all the sensory centres of his brain. It was not a pleasant sight. Naomi, however, quickly ripped off her headset.

"Jon, what's the plan?"

Jon's gaped. "What plan? I don't have one!"

She winced. "I'm going looking for Granddad. I was hoping you might have an idea, something to get rid of him. "

"What happens next, after Passover I mean?"

A curious look crossed her face. Then she said; "Can you fast forward five days?"

"Why?" Jon didn't like the sound of this.

"Just do it! Five days, then stop it sometime in the evening." She started to put on the headset again.

"Naomi, please just tell me what you are trying to do…"

Her voice came back, just before she froze into immobility. "Please, *Yon*; if you love me, my lord." Then she was still. Jon's blood went cold.

"Na, what did you say?" he demanded. But she did not respond.

He could feel the hairs on his head and neck standing up. For a moment he entertained the notion that her last remark had been an attempt at light heartedness; Naomi did have her lighter moments. But the way in which she had said it, together with the effortless imitation of Hannah's vocal inflexions quickly squashed that idea. It left only one possibility- she had said that last sentence unconsciously: Hannah had been speaking through her.

Feeling wobbly Jon sat down on the floor. He looked Naomi up and down, her face encased in the headset, her hair cascading around the sides of her head and down her shoulders. Then like a thunderbolt the truth hit him.

She was Hannah! Or Hannah was Naomi! The likeness of the images drawn from the error files confirmed this. The Timescope was merging them together.

That helped explain some things. He had been fascinated with Hannah for the same reason- she was exactly like Naomi Avery! Not to look at initially; true. But in character, resolve and even innate ruthlessness, all the features that had attracted, even awed him so completely, she had them all.

Jon looked steadily at her. She was outstanding! She did not possess the heart-stopping looks of Hannah, but she was everything he had admired without knowing it. Her impossibly high standards that had led her, at first, to reject him out of hand had cloaked a vulnerability that warmed his heart. His Naomi! His lovely, lovely girl.

On impulse Jon stood up and gently removed her headset. Even though he had seen it before, the distant look in her eyes made him shiver. There she stood, breathing softly, blinking only now and then. Jon drew the hair out of her eyes, then without any self-consciousness kissed her on the lips.

"I promise I'll be there for you, Na," he murmured; "when you get back. I won't play any more games, I promise." He swallowed. "I love you, Na."

She blinked, and a tear ran down her face. Suddenly behind him Jon heard a footstep. He swung round. His fear that it was Blue Eyes returning to the house changed to embarrassment.

"George!" he exclaimed, flushing, "how long... how, did you get in here?"

George was red too. He couldn't have missed that kiss and those last words. He writhed on the spot. Then he said,

"I tried ringing the bell, but it doesn't work, but the door was unlocked so I let myself in." He sounded frightened, "Jon, it's gone mad out there! Everything's gone down- phones, water, electricity, I came to tell you. To see if Na's..."

"Yeah, we're both fine. Listen; does anyone know what's causing it? This network thing?"

No, nobody knew. Huge computer files with an encryption no one could crack were multiplying through the Internet and infecting every network. A state of martial law had been declared throughout most of Europe. The local radio stations were broadcasting emergency messages, George said. 'Stay at home unless absolutely vital.' They were reading lists of key workers who were to report to work- actually, the army were escorting them to their places of employment. George's Dad was an engineer in a power station and he had been taken to work in a jeep. Essential services were out, workers were being ferried in, but without the communication and control networks they were being instructed to power down generating facilities to avoid overloads. The same was happening in all the major utilities. Jon interrupted him.

"George, I know what's causing it."

His eyes widened, "You do? Then why don't... oh!" His face registered incomprehension, then disbelief and fear. "It's the Timescope, isn't it?"

"Yeah. It's doing its thing, and we can't stop it."

"Can't? Why don't you just turn it off? Like I did last time?"

Briefly Jon explained. Firstly the Professor's life depended on them not turning the Timescope off, until at least he had been released from its clutches, and secondly there was some kind of Trojan Horse virus which only the Professor knew the access codes to which was the only sure-fire way of cleaning it out of the computer networks of the world.

"So do you have to wait until he's conscious?"

No, it was worse than that, Jon tried to explain. They had to find the Prof's consciousness somewhere, hope it was still lucid and find out the destruction codes from him before backup battery power failed completely.

George, looking stunned nodded towards Naomi and Prentice.

"Who's he, and what are they doing?"

Jon told him as quickly as he could, then asked;

"There was this American as well, an assassin. Do you know if there's any report of a dead man being picked up around here?" He didn't think in all that mayhem outside it was reasonable to suppose that he would know, but surprisingly George did.

"I went to the hospital first; you can get to it without going on the main streets. Na's Aunt was there, the bossy one..."

"Judith?"

"Yeah, she was there trying to find Na. I said I'd come here and look. Anyway, just as I was leaving the porters were wheeling this stiff down the corridor, I heard them saying he'd been picked up in Keswick Avenue, this morning."

"Did you see him?" Jon's stomach lurched.

"Nah, he was in a body bag. Could be the same one though. Why is an American assassin mixed up in this?" George was past further incredulity. Or at least he thought he was until Jon told him how Jackman had met his untimely end.

Then he sat down heavily on the floor, running his fingers through his hair.

"I'm dreaming this…" Jon heard him murmur. "The Angel of Death, right…"

"Anyway," Jon felt useless sitting here discussing. "Now I know that Jackman's not coming back, I think my best bet is to go and help Naomi." He picked up her headset.

"I'm coming with you."

Jon started to protest. Then he shrugged. Why not? At some point system power would close the business end of the Timescope down, so they would both be released then. In the meantime, he might need help in finding Naomi, she might appreciate help from them both finding her Granddad, wherever and whatever he might be; and they all might need an extra pair of eyes watching out for Prentice.

The headset slid easily off Prentice's sweating face. He stood glassy-eyed and motionless, but damp patches were spreading out around his collar and under his armpits. George eyed the moist headset distastefully. "I just put it on for a few minutes, and then I don't need it after that. Is that it?"

"Yes but wait!"

Jon ran his fingers through Prentice's jacket. It was like picking the pockets of a corpse, but he soon found the phone. His fingers trembled with excitement as he flipped the cover. But the moment he touched a key the screen flashed scarlet:

"PASSWORD!!"

He felt like throwing it at the wall. Instead he shoved it in his jeans pocket.

Just as he was about to don the other headset, Jon recalled Naomi's instruction. He picked up the keyboard and set the programs running much faster. The last time he had done this was the first time he had really used the Timescope. Then it had crashed, and Naomi had gloated. Now, smoothly and without effort the hours flashed past on the wall screen. George watched bemused until five days had elapsed.

"So what's she up to?" He grunted. Jon shrugged. Something told him not to question her motives, particularly not with Prentice in the mix.

18
The Crossing of the Red Sea

The refugees were practically walking in their sleep. The column had shape now- rather than the straggle of dazed men, women and children who had streamed out of Egypt five days before, this was now a semi-ordered march. The column was over eighty wide, the younger members concentrated towards the centre. Those who could walk hurried. The adult men carried young children on their shoulders. There were very few who couldn't move themselves, the people streamed past them with rapidity, very little noise, even less chatter. There was a palpable sense of urgency. Now and then a glance would be cast back in the direction from which they had come. The ground throbbed with the tramp of their feet; the dry air scorched by the sun sucked the moisture from their throats. And still they pressed on.

Where Jon and George joined them, the column had thinned out, and behind them a company of fit, young men formed a rearguard. They had all walked from Egypt, day and night without a break, driven on by the power of the God who had delivered them and the fear of their erstwhile captors. Way, way ahead, boiling into the blinding sky was the pillar of cloud leading the exodus. It was just as impressive for Jon the second time round, stretching from earth to space- there was no top in sight, it just went up and up like Jack's Beanstalk, dwarfing a range of hills in the near distance. Jon heard George mutter with disbelief close by.

There came an unexpected breeze. Gentle, but in the superheated air a breath of balm. Only a few seconds afterwards the sultry heat re-blanketed them, but in that cool breath Jon smelt the salt. George noticed it too.

"Are we near the sea then?"

"Must be." More memories were flooding back to Jon from Sunday School lessons years ago. "Red Sea, I think."

They kept up with the tail end of the column. It was not easy, the pace was punishing. Children as young as nine or ten were trotting in the midst; from behind the occasional terse shout to hurry up. Mothers fished in their baggage and handed out yet more flat bread or water to whoever cried loudest. And all the while the ceaseless trampling of the arid dust underfoot.

"Look!" The cry came from one of the young men behind them. In front the column hesitated, but urged on from the rest of the rearguard picked up its pace again. Jon and George turned around to see what the alarm was about.

Far in the distance was a second cloud. Unlike the guiding pillar of cloud it was long and hugged the horizon. One of the men dropped, and placed his ear, Red Indian style to the ground. For a few seconds he listened, sorting between the sounds of his own company as they tramped away, and the new sound that was breaking the silence of the wilderness. Finally he stood up, his face ashen.

"Chariots!" He said, keeping his voice low.

"How many?"

"Too many to tell." He placed his hand over his eyes and scanned the widening dust cloud. "How many would the king need to bring his captives back? Five hundred? A thousand? They are moving fast, though!"

"How long?"

He squinted at the sun which was lowering in the sky and clicked his tongue; "We will hold our distance until sundown. After that they cannot travel."

To their left a brief flash of sunlight reflecting off something. As though a car windscreen had momentarily caught the sunlight. Then again, and again. The scout noticed it too.

"They have seen our people from the fortress at Pihahiroth," he said, the worried look on his face intensifying. "They are sending signals."

"Can you read them?" asked an older man. The scout squinted and slowly read out

'*Flash, flash, flash*-"they are halted," '*flash, flash,*' "they have reached the coast, they are hemmed in."

Followed by a series of flashes came from the dust cloud behind them.

'Flash, flash, flash' "They are trapped in the land, the wilderness has shut them in."

Now the rearguard was yelling at the exhausted people. The whole tail end of the river of humanity surged forward like frightened cattle. Men were cursing, women searching for their children and gathering them close, holding their hands tightly in the accelerating pace. Some children too tired to walk at the new rate lagged behind; they saw a mother, her face filthy with tears and dust dragging her daughter behind her.

"This is bad." George was close by. He looked and sounded subdued, sensing the distress around them. "Will the Egyptians massacre them?"

"They've just lost their first-born." Jon tried not to think of the outcome. "They aren't very happy," They increased their pace to keep up with the Hebrews. Some of the things the men were saying were disturbing- young men yelled bitter words at older men, who threw their hands in the air in gestures of despair.

"We will die here!" The speaker was a thick-set man, his ragged clothes barely hanging together. Beside him his thin-faced wife held a tiny child whom she was attempting to feed a little bread. But the child spat the dry bread back, and cried, a thin wail that seemed appropriate to their desolate surroundings.

"We will all die! This is a fool's errand," cried an older man nearby. "Why did we trust to Moses and his nurse's tales of freedom and plenty?"

"We should have died in Egypt!" Another voice joined in, "We had no graves, no honoured burial in family sepulchres, but at least we would have died in peace."

"Hold your tongue El-Nathan!" This was from a young man who had pushed in from the back of the group, probably one of the rearguards. He addressed himself to the older man. "Who appointed you a prince over the LORD's people? Who gave you the authority to speak on His behalf?" He paused, shaking with anger and breathing hard. "You should be a shepherd to the LORD's people, instead you whine like a brat! If you have nothing…"

"So *Caleb*," the older man sneered, "you are the mouthpiece of the LORD now, are you?" All the time the relentless flow of people poured onwards. "Did we not say in Egypt that we were better left alone? At least there we had rest, we had food and we could die in our homes. Now when they catch up with us," his hand swept back to take in the ominous line of dust now filling the northern horizon, "their vengeance will be terrible." He raised his voice deliberately so that those around could hear.

"First their chariots will sweep through our midst, cutting us down and crushing us under their wheels like ripe corn. Their horses are trained to bite and trample. Then their footmen will follow behind, opening a path through our ranks, spilling our blood in the sand. The last things your eyes will see will be your sons being slain and your daughters dragged away to satisfy their lust. Then you will know…"

He stopped, his voice choked off by a grip on his throat. Caleb's hands encircled his neck and his face was inches away.

"You seem to know much about Egyptian warfare, my friend." His tone was far from friendly. "Have they rewarded you for spreading dismay amongst us?" He let go his grip and El-Nathan stepped back, rubbing his throat and glowering.

"Or is this the way in which you show yourself a fit prince over the LORD's people? You who were chosen from the nobles of Israel, is this how you should encourage the fainthearted? Has the LORD failed us thus far? Has He brought us from captivity to destroy us now? Have you no trust?"

"Dog!" He spat back. "Gentile Dog! You are well-named! You are a stray hound following the sheep for what you can devour of the carcase. You and Moses, and Joshua. Between you, you have fed us your lies, led us to this place of death and incited our masters to destroy us here." He turned to the refugees, still tramping onwards, eyes downcast, walking as if in a dream. "Surrender! We must surrender whilst we still can!"

Caleb looked about to strike him down. His fists were clenched, his neck muscles tight with fury. But they were interrupted by a shout.

"The sea, the sea!"

A full breeze, spiced with salt, hit the column of refugees as they breasted a rise that formed a shallow pass through the hills. Before them the ground fell gently away towards the coast, a huge swathe of land opening out from the pass through which they had come. They could see the whole immense spread of the nation of Israel camped on this broad strip of land. The cloud had stopped by the shore, and the sun, low in the sky was tingeing it with deep reds, pinks, greys and shadows. Before it those who had arrived many hours earlier were already camped, the smoke from their fires rose into the air, to be caught by the onshore air current and wafted inland. They could smell it even at this distance. Caleb dropped his fists and returned to the very back of the column, some five hundred metres behind to chivvy the rearguard.

Best of all to Jon was that dark ribbon of water in the distance. Almost black in the evening light it nevertheless smelled and looked cool and held the promise of life.

"Wow! That's just unbelievable!" George breathed. Such a mighty assembly of people, clustered before the column of cloud. As he spoke there was a blaze of brightness and the cloud ignited; one second it was cloud, the next the whole thing had erupted into flames casting a soft firelight over the encampment. Many seconds later a faint roar of fire reached them. The pillar of cloud had become a pillar of fire. George fell silent, awestruck at the sight.

Only one thing spoiled the moment. Caleb had disappeared, but El-Nathan's voice, petulant and complaining reached their ears.

"Where do we go now? We're trapped here!"

"I had no idea just how fantastic this would be." The size of the encampment reminded Jon of the Midianite camp overthrown by Gideon, only by comparison that now seemed tiny. Night had fallen and hundreds of thousands of camp fires flickered in the dark, stretching away into the far distance like a galaxy of twinkling red stars. Despite the awesome scale of the scene, it wasn't difficult to pick up the fear and distrust in the camp. Everywhere voices were raised in complaint at their predicament. Men sat huddled in small groups, discontent written all over their faces. The whole camp stank of fear and despair. They were trapped, hemmed in by Pharaoh's host and the desert on one side and the sea on the other. The sea was flat calm, there was very little breeze to raise the waves. Nothing was happening. Nothing at all.

"Where do you think Na and that other guy is, what's his name?"

"Prentice!" Jon was wondering that himself. It wouldn't be difficult to spot his immense bulk, even in the semi-darkness. They had been in the Timescope for over an hour, and it was essential they at least located Naomi. What to do then? Still Jon had no ideas. He felt the need to be doing something, but the overwhelming scale of this mass of humanity ruled out just poking around looking for them. For a few minutes they wandered fitfully, and then events took a turn for the stranger.

They had just stumbled past one of the outlying camp fires, absorbing the sense of anxiety that pervaded the people. Voices raised, quarrelling, sarcastic comments; it began to get Jon down. He felt like yelling at them; "just shut up moaning will you?" But experience had taught him that as visitors to this ancient scene, their opinions remained unheard, let alone unanswered. Briefly he could hear the man Caleb had tussled with, El-Nathan the whining Hebrew and glimpsed his face in the firelight before they moved on.

"And where are you going, stranger?"

Jon froze. Beside him George stopped too. Out of the corner of his eye Jon could see a ragged figure standing behind George, and the dim light reflecting off a knife blade.

"Just stop still, George," he hissed, now he could feel the point of a knife blade at the nape of his neck, cold and intrusive. "Don't move suddenly, he's got a knife."

"Who are you?" It was El-Nathan's voice. "Where are you from?"

The point of the knife jabbed him in the neck, and he was propelled away from the edge of the camp.

"I thought they couldn't see us here?" George said through clenched teeth.

"So did I!" Whispered Jon. But what did he expect? The Timescope was creating the best reconstruction it could; everything was perfect, the heat, light, images, sounds- why not the total experience, full interaction? "Sorry, George, I didn't think this would happen."

They were some distance from the camp now. Their captor moved in front of them to inspect them. The red glow of the pillar of fire showed in his eyes and teeth, the rest of his body was in darkness. Two other men were with him. They looked to El-Nathan for a lead.

"Who are you?" he asked again.

"Jon. Jon Heath. We're travellers." His face showed not a glimmer of comprehension. He asked further questions, all of which Jon and George answered, but they could make him understand nothing. The men went into a huddle, muttering.

"George," Jon whispered. "I don't think the Timescope interprets what we're saying back to them."

"Uh huh!" he said unhappily.

"There are reports of other strange visitors in the Egyptian camp," one of the other men was saying.

El-Nathan nodded, a greedy look came into his eyes. "They will reward us well for delivering these two to them."

The other two men looked distinctly unhappy with the prospect of going anywhere near the Egyptians, but El-Nathan seemed confident. With the knives prickling their necks, Jon and George were directed across the stretch of sand between the two camps. As they drew near to the fire-lit border of Pharaoh's army, there was a sudden scuffling rush and El-Nathan's companions bolted back the way they had come.

At the sound a number of guards stirred, two or three stood peering after them. Before he could decide on what to do next, Jon felt himself roughly pushed into the middle of a group of men, lolling around the campfire.

"I bring a gift for my lord Pharaoh!" El-Nathan's voice sounded tremulous. "I bring strangers from the Hebrew camp."

The men around the fire rose lazily to their feet. There was no sense of alarm or fear. Jon could see who they were.

"They're taskmasters," he whispered to George.

"Is that bad?"

"Very bad, sorry. They're sort of Nazis."

Jon and George were seized and their arms pinned firmly behind their backs, but the main attention was on El-Nathan. One of the taskmasters ducked inside a nearby tent, and a few moments later appeared with the commander of their group.

"What is this you bring to our lord Pharaoh? Does he need more children?" The commander wiping his face advanced threateningly on the quivering man. "Will you win favour by such gestures, you filthy Jew!" His sandaled foot kicked out at the wretched figure before him.

"My lord!" He squealed, gasping from the blow. "These are no ordinary children, I swear it. Rumours have reached us of other strangely-dressed ones who have been taken to Pharaoh…"

"Hold your tongue, you stinking herder of sheep!" Several of the other taskmasters chuckled at the insult. "You came here to spy out our camp; you will carry back accounts of our weaknesses to Moshesh." He turned away. "We will reward you as we reward all runaway slaves."

El-Nathan looked round wildly; Jon caught the look of desperation in his eyes.

What happened next shocked both George and even Jon, used as he was to the extremes of this society. It was so casual and unnecessary. The commander gave the merest nod to another thug close by. It looked as though the other man then gave El-Nathan a friendly clap on the back. It was so swift Jon had barely time to register what had taken place. The shivering figure gave a short cry of surprise and fell face down in the sand. Only when Jon saw the second man re-sheathing a long knife did he register what had happened. He had been stabbed between the shoulder blades! Beside him George drew breath sharply.

"That's for my brother," the commander gave an ugly grin, made all the uglier by the firelight casting flickering shadows over the scene. "The jackals will eat well tonight!" Two men picked up the body and carried it into the dark.

"Oh...." George's face was in shadow but the strain showed in his voice. "Jon, we'd better get out of here!"

"Shut up!" bawled the guard, shoving George's arm upwards. He bit his lip, but went quiet. Even in the red glow he had gone white. Jon felt terrified himself. This latest turn of events had potentially grave consequences. These Egyptians were in an ugly mood. How far would the Timescope faithfully reproduce what might happen to him and George in their hands?

The commander surveyed them with unconcealed astonishment.

Finally he spoke. "Who are you?" He addressed the question to George.

"Shall I loosen his tongue?" The guard who had stabbed El-Nathan was itching for more bloodshed. He held the knife up, running his finger along the blade. George started sweating freely.

"George, George Mere. We're travellers."

The Taskmaster obviously failed to understand a word. He shifted from side to side in confusion. Then he repeated the question, still gazing unblinkingly into George's face.

"We're travellers. From another country."

"We're from Ethiopia." Jon's head was jerked up to face the Taskmaster. His breath smelt of garlic. He very nearly choked. In his eyes there was not the faintest trace of comprehension. He tried again.

"From Ethiopia. Another country. Visiting." Jon racked his brain for something that might be meaningful to him. But it was no good; he could not get them to understand anything they were saying. He dug his thumbs into Jon's biceps, the powerful grip making him wince.

"They're no slaves!" He said finally, contempt in his voice. "Never seen work. Not Jews either." He paused, looking from Jon, then to George. He stabbed out his finger.

"Kill them both." He said, and disappeared inside.

In that moment Jon realised that perilous as their situation was, they did have an advantage- they could understand them. They didn't know that so they didn't guess that they had understood the last remark. It was a slim advantage but there was no time to let it expire.

"Go!" Jon screamed at George, driving his elbows back and at the same time using the guard's body as a block from which to catapult himself forward. George had reached the same conclusion; simultaneously he burst forward, knocking his captor back into the fire. A scream of pain and rage reached them and the camp erupted into shouting and cursing. They both bolted in the same direction, running desperately, heading for the cloak of darkness that was the desert between the camps.

Vaulting over chariot poles, Jon was dimly aware of George stumbling in slow-motion, then scrabbling up again; a look of incomprehension and fear etched into his face.

George changed direction suddenly, slewing to the left, running along the perimeter of the camp. Ahead out of the gloom two more guards had materialised, blocking the way. Jon followed, more cries and yelling erupting, heedless of anything underfoot, anything just to escape.

"Jon! Help, J…" George's voice stopped abruptly. Dimly Jon could see he was being dragged down to the ground. What could he do to help? So many people, guards and Taskmasters swarming in from all directions; a straight dash and he would be past the final tent, head down, run, run…come on, ten metres to go, eight, five …

The camp did a cartwheel as his legs were swept from under him and he crashed to the ground. When he opened his eyes; a few inches from his head were a pair of sandaled feet.

"What is this commotion?" demanded an imperious voice.

The guards who took them deeper into the Egyptian camp were a great deal more refined. They held them firmly, but with no show of unnecessary force. Their rescuer growled angrily as he inspected Jon and George.

"I want to see Amahté tomorrow!" He declared, running his hand over Jon's forearm. "No marks, no amulets, no sacred symbols, just this strange band." He looped an elegant finger under George's steel watch strap and tugged gently. "Who are you?"

His face was thin; he wore a headdress that was surprisingly similar to the pictures usually associated with Ancient Egypt. In fact, if he stood sideways on he would be a figure from a tomb painting come to life. His name, they established straight away was Nebibi. People bowed and scraped to him. The moment he had seen them running from the knife-wielding psychopath, he had intervened, directing the guards to arrest them. Seconds later and they would both have been sliced up.

Clearly angry with the treatment meted out by the Taskmaster, he had ranted at the pursuers until he had uncovered the sequence of events. Heads would roll; Jon hoped Amahté's garlic-smelling head amongst them. But for now Nebibi was deeply interested in his charges. They were being taken to Pharaoh.

"George" He looked in a dream, Jon thought.

"What? Any more bright ideas?"

"George, don't let on that you understand them! Got it? Not a flicker!"

They arrived at a huge tent. It was almost a marquee. Guards surrounded it and oil-soaked torches burned brightly around the outside. Nebibi halted and addressed himself to the sentry at the entrance.

"Is my father awake?"

"The king awaits you, my lord." He stepped respectfully aside and we were ushered in.

"Oh heck!" Jon breathed. "He's Pharaoh's son!"

Inside the well-lit tent was divided into two main compartments, a bedchamber and a large room. The large room was like a council chamber with a number of rush mats on the floor laid out in a semi-circle. Some fruit in bowls was placed in the circle, and the Pharaoh was just handing a bowl with the well-picked remains of some kind of fish in it to a servant. Jon and George waited in silence as he washed his fingers delicately in a small bowl of water. Wiping his hands on a cloth he called to Nebibi,

"You have brought them with you, my son?" There could be no mistaking the authority in that voice. Nebibi bowed, and motioned them both forward. George dug his elbow into his ribs.

"Bow, you idiot!"

Jon dropped a deep bow. What he had seen of Pharaoh had been fascinating. A thin face, like his son crowned with an ornate headdress. His hair was long but where it showed over his ears it was peppered with grey and white. Stress and worry had etched deep lines around his eyes, and his noble posture as he sat on a wickerwork chair seemed to sag. He eyed them both for a few moments then turned back to Nebibi.

"What do you know of them?"

"My lord, they are of no country I know. Their skin is too pale even for the Northern peoples. Their tongue is strange, their dress stranger still. Amahté would have had them killed but I forbad him."

"He is a fool," said the king wearily, "a good soldier but a brute. He was not to know that they are children of the gods. Do not take hasty action against him until we have avenged your brother on these Hebrews."

George gasped. "Did you hear that?"

"No, I missed what he said," Jon had been distracted by a movement in the curtains behind the king. Hannah's face had peered out briefly, then disappeared.

"He said we were children of the gods! Does this mean we're in for better treatment?"

"Don't get your hopes up," Jon countered; "I think I've just seen their god!"

The rich curtains of the bedchamber parted, slid aside by two slave girls and Terrence Prentice waddled out.

There were a few people in the large tent with Pharaoh. But as he appeared, a small knot of onlookers gathered about the door. A buzz of subdued murmuring swelled into excited chatter and, as if by reflex, several taskmasters moved to form a cordon, their hands fingering whips at their belts.

Jon stared, his jaw slack. Prentice had on a rich robe, but through it showed his shirt and tie. He moved slowly, with affected disdain, his small chin and heavy cheek jowls held at an angle, his robes rustling. The slave girls rushed from behind him, two dragging a heavy chair, others clutching dishes of food, similar to that which Pharaoh had been eating when they arrived, but in predictably larger quantities. Also Jon noticed a flagon close by into which a delicate cup was dipped and held out to Prentice. After he had sipped a little of the liquid, a red stain appeared around his mouth. Jon guessed it was red wine. His mind went back over his mother recounting her experience of Prentice- he was, she said in an unguarded moment obsequious when sober becoming ever so slightly reckless and completely obnoxious after a drink or two.

"Ah, Jon!" Prentice's voice was slurred, slightly. "And another friend. What a pleasant surprise. We meet in the most privileged of circumstances, do we not?"

The tone of his voice concerned Jon. He knew Prentice was a bully, but what would he do given the mandate of a deity? He was not long in finding out. All around him, the onlookers had sunk to their knees with their faces to the sand.

"I advise you to bow also! The gods have come to earth, Jon, and demand honour due to their persons. I do not wish to make an example of you as I have had to Naomi."

"What?" Jon remained standing, a cold anger sending shivers down his spine. "What have you done to her, you vicious…?"

At a nod from Prentice, one of the Taskmasters had thrust her through the curtains. "My lord!" She cried as she saw him. A large bruise discoloured her right cheek. Nevertheless her face broke into a smile of genuine happiness. She was an even stronger amalgam of Naomi and Hannah now; dark, long, wavy hair that had fallen over her face, a slightly more rounded face but with high cheekbones and deep eyes. She would have run to him, but the guard had seized her wrist. Prentice turned to her.

"Are you ready to kneel before me yet, my dear?" he enquired. "Or will you carry on playing this ridiculous game with me? Come on Naomi Avery, you know who you are, and you know who I am."

Hannah turned a look of contempt on him that would have withered many a lesser mortal. "I am Hannah, bath Obadiah. I bow to none but the God of my fathers. I will not bow to you."

"So you say, Naomi," he sneered. "I tire of this charade, just as you must too." The taskmaster holding her put his weight on her shoulders, forcing her to kneel. It was a pointless exercise, however. Anyone could see at a glance that although her body had been crushed into a crouching posture, her spirit was proud and defiant.

"She's not Naomi any more." Jon spoke out, angry at what he had witnessed. "She's Hannah, a Jewish girl from Carmel. The Timescope is mixing them together. She'll never bow to you either way."

Prentice waved the objection away. "So you seek to fool with me as well? And with your parents in my power too! What a mistake! Still, no matter who she thinks she is, she has served me well. What an impact she helped me make on these people, claiming to be a Jewish princess of some sort or other, and yet so obviously in my power." He chuckled. "They think it's a sign against their enemies!"

He flicked his fingers and another dish was presented to him. "They couldn't believe their eyes; 'the gods are come to us!' they cried as they hastened me to meet their king. Naturally I complied with their story. And now here I am in the lap of luxury. Try some fish? It's excellent, I assure you!"

"What have you done to Naomi?" Jon spoke through gritted teeth.

"Oh nothing at all. That would be too much effort. No, I only have to give the word and these, my friends," he swept his arm out to take in the solidly built taskmasters standing nearby, "these fine fellows will do it all for me." Seeing the look on his face, he added hastily, "oh be assured I have shown great consideration to her. She interprets for me, you know."

"I didn't know she could speak Egyptian," George muttered.

"She can't," Jon replied. "At least when she was Naomi, she couldn't. I guess that Hannah could speak the local lingoes... Oh, I'll tell you about it later."

Whilst this had been going on, Pharaoh was watching them, his eyes narrowed to slits. Whatever the people thought of Prentice's pretensions to divinity, he was not quite so ecstatic. Finally he spoke.

"Oh great one," he began, his trained voice carrying far and wide. "Oh nascent light of the land of the Great river, oh wellspring of the power and majesty of Ra..."

Terrence preened himself, and demolished another cup of red wine. Then he settled himself to receive probably the most glowing salutation of his career. He waited for it to finish then said;

"What do you desire of me, overlord of the lands of the living, appointed sceptre of Osiris?" Despite himself, Jon was impressed. He had slipped so effortlessly into the role of minor deity. Hannah with a sulkiness that sat uneasily on her launched into a translation of his words, her voice kept deliberately monotonous. Perversely the Timescope translated her message with ease.

"What your servant desires, oh illustrious one..."

And so it went on. After many minutes of the same, George whispered to Jon; "I think he's asking whether they should attack the slaves."

"Yeah, I got that too."

Prentice mused over this request. Jon could see he was torn between a desire to ingratiate himself with the Egyptians and their obvious thirst for revenge upon the slaves, and his innate cowardice. Finally he spoke.

"The will of the holy gods is fixed upon this issue. We will withdraw and watch them. They cannot escape. We have them hemmed in. When they are beset by thirst, and their food supplies are gone, then we will take them captive and punish the ringleaders."

He looked to Hannah for translation. Without a blink of an eyelid she translated. However, this time the monotony had gone from her voice; she raised it excitedly, her arms gesturing with sword-thrusts and slashes.

"The will of the holy gods is fixed upon this issue. They decree that we shall follow these impious Jews and cut them down without delay. We shall herd them like cattle; between the sea and the shore we shall fall upon them and retrieve the plunder they took from us when they stripped the bodies of our fallen sons and gloated upon our downfall. We shall pursue them, if needs be to the very depths of hell. The gods have set us a sore trial this day of our faith and loyalty..."

Prentice rose from his chair, scattering food and dishes in all directions and grabbed her by the hair.

"That's enough you scheming cow," he hissed. "Why have you told them that?" He pulled her hair roughly so that her head shook.

But the damage had been done. On hearing her words, Pharaoh rose from his chair, seized a spear and waved it in the air. "It is truly spoken," he exulted. "We will attack this night; we will wreak vengeance upon them!" Outside the tent the cry was taken up by, the now sizeable, assembly and it roared across the Egyptian camp. "We attack! We attack!" Clearly it was what they wanted to hear.

It was also a signal. Within minutes the camp began to mobilize for war. Prentice stood watching helplessly, then lumbered back into the tent as the taskmasters hurried away to their platoons and began rousing their troops; chariots began wheeling in the sand, horses snorting, their nostrils flaring. In the intervening confusion, Jon ducked out of sight and dashed over to the inner tent where Prentice had taken refuge.

He came fully ready to tackle Prentice, expecting to find the fat bully taking his fury out on Hannah. But by the time he slipped into the tent, of Prentice there was no sign.

"My lord!" Hannah emerged from the shadows. There was a fresh bruise on the other cheek. Jon's heart leapt into his throat as without hesitation she threw her arms round his neck. It was a minute or two before he could speak. When he did he ran his finger lightly across the new bruise on her face:

"Did he do this to you?"

She nodded. But her face wore the look of ecstasy as when she had presided over the destruction of the Priests of Baal. "It is no matter *Yon*. He will follow them into the sea. But you, my lord…"

"Into the sea? Hannah, what do you mean? Surely they will drown?"

She shook her head. "Yes, my lord, these ungodly cruel masters will drown. But Israel will be delivered. And now, my lord, please go, get away from this camp, go to the camp of Israel, lest you perish with these cursed Egyptians."

"Hannah, I can't leave you. Come with us." But she pushed him away. "Hurry, leave now whilst the guards are preparing. There is still time…"

A new wave of commotion erupted around the camp. Hannah and Jon dashed to the entrance of the tent. An unforgettable sight greeted them.

The titanic column of fire had moved into the gap between the hills which led to the Jewish encampment, plugging it completely. The brilliant red blush flickered and flashed over the Egyptian camp. Hannah raised her face to look up, high into the sky and the light glimmered off her skin casting burgundy highlights in her hair.

"Be still and know that I am God," she breathed. She seemed in a trance. Jon could have died happy looking at her face. Then she spoke again. Her voice changed, it was faint, distant.

"Jon, please, get away from here. Please, before the Jews are all gone."

"Naomi, is that you?" Jon was confused with the sudden change. "Naomi, what happened? How did you get here?" Hannah came out of her reverie.

"My lord, that is a pleasant name," She replied dreamily, "it reminds me of something, long ago when I was a little girl."

"Naomi! Can you hear me? What happens next, why do I have to go to the camp of Israel?"

But there was no time to reply. With a rumble, Pharaoh's chariot pulled up sharply. Standing in the chariot, looking slightly seasick was Terrence Prentice.

"There you are!" he shouted angrily at Hannah, then glancing up at the mighty pillar of fire, he yelled, "What means this? Is this a trick?"

"Leave her alone!" Jon yelled back pulling her aside. He feared more brutality from Prentice, but it was not to be. Pharaoh himself was driving the chariot: lean, angular and athletic; a marked contrast to his podgy passenger who was clinging grimly to the sides. More chariots were wheeling round and pulling in formation behind them. From one of them George yelled;

"Jon, Naomi, back here!" He was in a lighter chariot with Nebibi.

"Come with me!" Nebibi called out of the gloom, he was in full armour.

"What's happening?" George asked as Jon led Hannah towards them. Nebibi pointed to the cloud.

"The slaves have a God who fights on their behalf." His hand pointed to the billowing mass, blocking their way. "Their God is mighty; He does great and terrible things. He brings destruction in so many ways by the hand of Moshesh. Moshesh only has to raise his staff and the skies rain lice, hail, flies and death."

He was gazing fixedly at the cloud, anger and sorrow playing across his thin face.

"My father will exact a terrible revenge upon them. He will slaughter them on the shores and stampede them into the sea. Then when they are subdued he will take the lives of the first-born and also the youngest of each family. Thus they will pay double for their rebellion. Then they will return to their slums and serve us until they die in their poverty."

He fell silent, for a full minute he continued to behold the cloud.

"My strange young friends." He said, looking at Jon and George. "If only he would show mercy. If only now he would turn back and leave them to die in peace." George looked bemused; "You know not what I speak. But come to me," he beckoned to them. "You will ride with me in the chariot and perhaps we can persuade my father to soften his wrath against these miserable people. And you, my daughter, there is room beside my lieutenant."

Jon, George and Hannah reached his chariot, larger than most and ornately gilded. Jon helped Hannah up into the nearby chariot, then joined George in Nebibi's chariot. A superb white horse, twitching with energy shook its mane at the sight of Nebibi.

The Egyptian camp was on the move. It was a demonstration of their outstanding discipline. A few minutes at first of chaos and shouting, feet running, fires being stamped out, then rapidly order emerged. Trumpets sounded, squadrons assembled and horses were tethered to the chariots. Soldiers leapt up onto the chariots, spears poised rock steady as the chariots wheeled and turned. The horses pranced and whinnied, eager to go. Ten minutes from the first shouted orders the whole convoy was plunging across the desert, a line of blazing torches marking their passage towards the huge cloud that barred their way.

George was hardly able to contain his excitement at the experience of racing across the desert. Better still for Jon, though was the sight of Prentice to the right, looking queasy and gripping the rail.

Ahead the cloud had moved. It no longer plugged the gap between the hills leading to the beach. It had set off down the slope, its blaze reflecting off the rocky outcrops to the north and south of the bay. The gap was wide, about half a kilometre, and the chariots poured through unhindered. Then at the top of the slope where Jon and George had sat earlier viewing the gigantic mass of humanity that was the Jewish camp the Egyptian army came to an abrupt, awestruck halt.

"Now wouldya look at that!" George could hardly get the words out.

The bay was empty, or very nearly so. Just as though a huge sink had been unplugged, and they had drained away. All they could see was a mass of dancing, twinkling torches, tiny pinpoints of light they appeared at this distance deep down in a yawning chasm ahead- a wide path that stretched through the water to the other side. The path was at least a kilometre wide. With the grey light they could see that it was saturated with refugees. A black seething mass of people, their blazing torches bobbing above them; young and old, babies, children and even Egyptians who had thrown their lot in with them- with their cattle and sheep, lowing and bleating they surged forward across the sandy bed of the sea and down into the blackness beyond.

The Egyptian soldiers watched in total silence. Behind them the rest of the army ranged out in a broad line, jostling to get a glimpse of this phenomenon. By the time the last of them had drawn up their war-chariots, the final stragglers had melted away into the gaping void left by the sea. Apart from the odd snorting horse, the complete company stood silent and still.

"Re be praised!" Said Nebibi softly, his hand on the rim of the chariot showing white knuckles. "They are beyond our reach at last. The time of the slave is over."

George was wide-eyed and breathing heavily, "Jon,…this is incredible. Just out of this world!"

To both sides of them, Egyptians had climbed down from their chariots and were walking around in a daze. The pillar of fire and cloud was drifting serenely after the tail end of the column, the blaze twinkling off the surface of the sea, reflecting like glass mingled with fire. Several Egyptians prostrated themselves to the ground and broke into wavering chants, devotional hymns to their gods. Nebibi stood stock-still and gazed on. Then he stepped down and walked across to another ornate chariot some metres away to speak with his father.

Hannah had dismounted from her chariot too. Her eyes were closed, her hands held high above her head, tears gushing down her cheeks. She smiled, a weary but triumphant smile as her lips moved in inaudible prayer. Slumped in the chariot, his flabby face grey with shock, Prentice could only blubber incoherent sentences.

"Naomi…Hannah?"

"Oh my lord! That I should see this day, is not our God mighty? Are not the works of his fingers past finding out?"

Jon put his arm around her waist. He could feel her excited breathing. "Hannah, what happens next?"

"They follow, *Yon!* Into the depths of the sea, they follow." She nestled up to him, shivering with emotion. Then Jon felt the mobile phone in his pocket. Realisation rushed in upon him. What was the time outside the Timescope? Was it morning yet? On the other side of the world, at the other end of history, his Mum and Dad were even now getting their swimming stuff together, maybe throwing some fishing tackle into a small motor launch. A crate of cold beer for his Dad, a chilled white wine for his Mum, helped by two or three paid thugs who had hardly to lift a finger to snuff out their lives. Dragging the phone from his pocket he advanced on Prentice.

"Ring them!" Prentice jumped at the sight of his mobile phone.

"Jon, give that back!" He swiped at him, almost falling from the chariot. Jon dodged nimbly.

"Oh, no! You give me the password to unlock it!"

"Listen boy!" A sweat was starting across his pallid forehead, "I will ring them when I'm ready, got that? Play games with me and they die."

"Listen yourself, oh great god, will you? Do you know what they're going to do? Do you?" Jon grabbed Prentice by the edges of his robe. Prentice glanced around for his muscle men, but they were paying careful attention to their king. "They're going to follow those slaves. They're going to follow them right down into there. You're going to die, Prentice. You, me, George, Naomi, everyone." He could feel the fat man shaking from head to toe as he gazed with fear-rimmed eyes at that terrible path down into the abyss. "So give me that password, unlock this phone, got that?"

"They wouldn't be so stupid," he whispered.

""Well just listen to what Pharaoh's saying," George cut in. "He's whipping them up to go after them."

"Do not I command the Sun? Does it not descend to the Underworld at my command?" Pharaoh's voice carried clearly across the silent shore. "Does it rise on its chariot without my will? I am Pharaoh, I rule the night and the day…"

"He's crazy!" Prentice gibbered. Pharaoh was standing tall in the chariot, thumping the butt of his spear against the floor of the chariot. The soldiers, hesitantly at first, but with increasing gusto copied him, beating their spear-butts onto the decks of the chariots. THUMP…THUMP…THUMP…

"Re has commanded that the waters part, not to free them, but to make a path for us to follow!" He swung round and pointed to the ashen-faced Prentice standing beside him. "The gods smile upon us; they command us to pursue them even to the deep." Jon glimpsed Nebibi, he was shaking his head in total incredulity, but he did not protest.

"Nebibi," Jon cried, over the racket. He turned; at least he recognised his name!

"My father has spoken. The will of the great gods has been made known. I will lead the charge. It is so." He regarded them, sadness in his eyes. "You do not understand the way of my people. They will follow my father to the Underworld if he commands it thus. But I cannot leave you here- it is a desert place, the nearest city is six days' journey and my people might not have mercy upon you as I have. You would certainly die here if you did not come with me." He flicked the whip and the chariot rumbled forward. The drumming of the spears had stopped. The huge line of horses, chariots, soldiers, Taskmasters and generals stood in silence.

Prentice had shed his robe and was furtively trying to stumble towards the rocks that lined the low slopes of the hills. A taskmaster trotted after him, there was a brief exchange of angry words, then with a curt "You can take your hands off me!" Prentice retraced his steps to the king's chariot. He was holding his mouth as if he was about to be sick. Meanwhile, Hannah, still in a dream climbed aboard her chariot. Jon looked wildly around, the useless phone held in his hand, and then Nebibi reached out and with a whisk of his powerful arm Jon was lifted on board. The chariot burst forward and the charge began.

There was a breeze, steady and strong on their backs, an easterly wind that blew the raised dust and threw it into the morning air. Nebibi yelled like a man possessed, shouting to his horse, flicking his whip now and then; although Kepi, his gorgeous white horse, needed no encouragement. The shoreline was two hundred metres and closing fast, now they were on level, firm sand and the pace increased. Ahead, like a hall of mirrors the channel through the sea- with the elemental sound of roaring waters, angry at the restraint, clawing to get back into their place. Then they passed the tide line, a fringe of seaweed and were into the steeply sloping downward channel. All around them were dead fish and sea creatures, motionless on the sand floor. Behind them the charge: maniacal and yet so beautiful in its raw courage. Before them the abyss: gloomy apart from where the dawn sunlight percolated through the coastline. The daylight turned dark green; the air became heavy with salt and moisture.

The charge became a formation, four deep, in a tidy 'v' shape, with their chariot in the lead, and Pharaoh's in the middle. As the formation tightened, Jon saw a mad chance- Pharaoh's chariot was less than a metre away; Prentice now huddled on the floor, gagging with fear. Jon jumped, caught the side of the chariot scorching his arm on the revolving wheel, but managing to swing himself onto the footplate. The chariot lurched, throwing him sideways, but his fall was cushioned by Prentice. The king was too involved in the split-second business of driving the vehicle over the uneven sand to even glance round. Jon could see he would have to be quick; Terrence Prentice was almost out of his mind with terror.

"Unlock it!" he screamed, grabbing the miserable man by the shirt-collar. It was like holding a wounded frog; his skin was clammy and moist. Jon shoved the phone in front of his eyes. "Unlock it and I'll get you out, ok?" The noise of wheels, the smell of sweating horses and polished leather mingled with the damp air. Jon yelled again. "Unlock it now!"

His hands were wobbling; Jon held the phone for him as he punched a code. There was a blip from the phone: - *"Password incorrect, 2 attempts remaining."*

"You fat pig!!" Jon screamed in frustration, tightening his grip. "I'm going to count to five, then I'm going to start hurting you real bad! Now do it. One…two…"

This time the phone was active. Jon almost shouted with relief. He could hear a high pitched dialling tone. He glanced at Prentice who, looking as little like a god as it was possible to get, was losing the contents of his stomach over the side of the chariot. No good getting him to call off the hit men, at least not in his condition! It would have to be a direct appeal.

"Jon! Oh, how nice to hear from you! Alan, it's Jon. No leave those beers in the fridge, love…"

"Mum! Where are you?" Jon thought he could hear an engine running.

"Are you alright dear? You're shouting. How come you're able to call? We've no communications at all here."

"Never mind, Mum, Dad, are you going diving?" (Oh, please Mum; just for once answer the question…)

She must have detected the frantic tone in his voice; "Shh! Alan, Jon's in trouble. Jon, yes they do diving visits to a wrecked warship; we're just about to leave. Why?"

"Don't go!!" Jon fought off hysteria; his throat was hoarse trying to yell above the noise. "Please get out of there! Do something else. Whatever you do, don't go out to sea!" The roar of the water to each side had increased in level.

"Whatever is that noise, Jon? It sounds like you're in a wind-tunnel."

"Please Mum, Dad, get away from there!" He could hear his Mum talking to Dad. Dad was protesting crossly. The light around them now was deep green, the bellowing waters overwhelming the sound of the horses and chariots.

"Tell her!!" Prentice was sobbing over the side of the chariot. Jon grabbed his slicked-back hair by the neck and forced his head up to the phone. "Tell them not to go diving!!"

Prentice yelped; Jon was inflicting a great deal of pain on him. "Tell them to stay on land or we both die here. Got that?" His only reply was a miserable gargle. Jon tightened his grip.

"M...Mary? Is that you?" Jon's grip was choking him; the paleness of his face had given way to a suffocated red complexion. "Mary, it's Terrence here. Please, Mary, do as he says, don't go out to sea..." then there was a violent lurch, accompanied by a tearing, snapping sound and they were rolling over and over in the sand.

The sea-bottom had levelled out, the firm sand providing a perfect surface both for the horses and chariots alike. From here on the route lead steadily upwards, the sand trampled flat. Ahead, about a kilometre away was the far bank, now swathed in sunlight, and the refugees pouring out like ants over the brow of the shore. The tail of the column swarmed up the incline pressing forward in panic to escape the oncoming Egyptian forces. Around them the men in the chariots had forgotten the weight of water that teetered unsteadily on each side. They spurred their horses on, yelling war cries and shouting to each other. The gap was closing. The cloud hung over the path ahead like a sentinel; boiling upwards out of sight, still blazing on its far side. Up till that moment the convoy had kept perfect formation, sweeping like a whirlwind down on their prey. Then something happened to break the flow.

Jon, dazed came to rest face down on the sand. Only now the sand was far from firm. As he struggled to stand, his hand and knees sank into the stuff. It sucked and quivered around him. In that fleeting moment he caught a glimpse of Pharaoh's horse, whinnying and struggling in the traces that bound it to the chariot. The chariot was on its side, one wheel missing, and both poles snapped clean off. The hurtling chariots had hit quicksand, overturned and spilt the occupants onto the sea bed.

Another chariot thundered past, narrowly missing them both, then sank rapidly. Ahead, as he fought free of the stuff, Jon could see Nebibi and his lieutenant, chariots still upright trying to negotiate a way round the swamp.

Then chaos broke out. The mad, headlong charge had too much momentum to stop in an orderly fashion; chariots pitched forward over the wrecked remains of the leaders, the cries of the drivers and soldiers were even audible above the awesome thunder of the waters.

The deep sand was more than just a patch. The sea bed was starting to saturate and the chariots wheels were simply too narrow. They pitched to one side or the other, then the strain became too much for the axles and their wheels snapped cleanly off. The horses struggled in the boggy conditions and the chariot shafts snapped as the beasts struggled to escape.

"Go Kepi, go whirlwind!" Nebibi lashed at the horse's sweating flanks. But the advance had collapsed. Some horses were bolting back the way they had come, their drivers shouting and cursing after them.

The roar of the mountains of water either side overwhelmed everything. Jon hunted around. The mobile had flown from his grasp when they tumbled; had it sank into the sand? Then he saw Prentice was hunched up, shrieking into the phone.

"Jackman, are you there? Jackman, help me..."

Jon snatched the phone from him. Prentice had wet sand over one side of his face. His arm was at an odd angle. He looked at Jon, his eyes bloodshot, with a look of dumb appeal. His hand reached out and caught Jon's foot.

"Please, Jon, make it stop."

"I can't!" Jon yelled, grinning with fiendish delight at his wretched condition. "And Jackman's dead! Do you hear? The Angel of Death got him. You'll have to run for your life!"

"My lord!" Jon spun round. Hannah wrenched his arm, pulling him away from Prentice and further down the channel. "See, Moses will not hold the waters much longer."

Against the lightening sky was a silhouette. He stood with his arms lifted high, in the right hand a staff. To either side of him figures jostled in a stream, young men were reaching out to pull them away from the water line. Cattle and sheep, bellowing in fear barged each other to get past him to the beach, then as far away from the shore as they could. Impassive, the figure stood as if carved from the very rocks that projected through the sand.

Nebibi cupped his hands and shouted to his father; "This is the work of their GOD! He fights for them against the Egyptians!"

Pharaoh was black with rage. "Moshesh the Hebrew is upon the bank. He shall see my face and die!" He was lashing at his horse like a man possessed.

Cursing, Nebibi turned away. Then he saw Jon, George and Naomi, wading around in the sucking sand. "Go, my friends, go!" he ordered. "May the gods smile upon you." He pointed to the shore, and turned away. They heard him yelling orders to the sorry remainder of the charge, some men mounted on horses, others on foot, very few had brought their chariots through this far. Again Egyptian discipline asserted itself. The companies had reformed, spears were hoisted and the army were preparing to dash for the shore.

With Hannah/Naomi between them and ignoring the whimpering cries from Prentice, George and Jon stepped forward. After a few metres their hearts sank with their feet. It was a fine shifting morass, George sank up to his knees at once and reached out to grab Jon's arm. They struggled frantically for several metres, the sand sucking each time they lifted their feet out. The effort was exhausting! By the time they had covered another hundred metres none of them were capable of moving a step further.

"Moses!" they screamed. The silhouetted figure stood erect, stock-still, arms still raised. He could have been carved out of stone. Could he hear them? Not a chance. They yelled because there was nothing else left to do.

"Moses. Wait!"

The roar of water drowned their words. Another few, painful steps, *suck! suck!* But the sand was running with water that sloshed around their ankles now. The translucent green

312

mountains were rocking and rumbling, spray was lashing down, salt water running into their eyes. Jon fixed his eyes on the outline figure, arms raised; now standing alone upon the shore.

The hands swept down. Then he turned and walked away.

Jon had a brief glimpse of the ghastly faces of the Egyptians, abandoning their weapons, chariots and horses, and struggling in the remaining seconds to pull off the heavier pieces of armour. Then the roar of tumbling water became the only sound, drowning their cries, and the piercing whinnying of the horses. He held tightly on to Hannah, George's grip on his arm became fierce, and they turned to face the colossal wall of green and white that bellowed, boiled and churned like a cloudbank towards them.

Any notion of taking a deep breath and riding out the inundation was hopeless. Once the sea closed over them, the pressure flattened them down, tore them apart and drove the air from their lungs. Jon had a brief, last glimpse of sky before the depth of water blotted out the light, and a last sense of unimaginable din before the water suffocated the sound. Then they were thrown over and over, pushed, pulled, battered and torn; over and over and over and over…a horse drifted by, its chariot still attached, then two soldiers, their arms flailing to pull themselves upwards against the crushing downward force. More debris, more tumbling and turning, a pain in his lungs, silt-laden water forcing itself up his nose and between his lips;

Don't try to breathe.

Sharp, searing, agonising sensation underneath his diaphragm.

Don't try to breathe

Did Mum and Dad get on the boat? Spinning over and over and over and over…

Don't try to breathe. Over and over and over…

Wonder where Naomi is?

Don't try to breathe.

Naomi, I love you… of all the things I wanted to say, now it's too late, it's over, finished.

Don't try to breathe.

Pain now clawing at the inside of his rib cage like a tiger trying to escape...goodbye Naomi... dimly he could see George; oddly enough he was swimming downwards, George was a county champion swimmer, he should know better than to swim downwards; was he swimming downwards, or was everything upside down? Then he disappeared into the green gloom.

Calmness, coupled with a sense of release enveloped him.

Don't try...to...

19

A sharp smell of seaweed was the first thing he knew. The pungent stuff was wrapped around his head, slimy and moist. But he didn't have the strength to pull it off. He felt something rising through his chest, forcing itself up his burning throat. The next thing he tasted salt as his stomach threw up the quantity of seawater he had swallowed. The retching hurt his chest but he felt better once he had got rid of it. Dimly he could hear voices.

"Is he alive?"

"He's moving," a hand was placed on his shoulder and he was turned onto his back. The seaweed was picked off his face, sunlight blazed through making him screw his eyes shut. Firmly but gently he was lifted into a sitting position.

"Here, drink this. The voice was familiar, but he was too exhausted to make any connections. A sharp-tasting fluid was poured into his mouth. He thought at first he was going to vomit again, but it settled in his stomach with an uneasy rumble.

"Is he of Pharaoh's host?" asked somebody else.

"I think not. Neither is he Syrian."

With an effort Jon opened his eyes. They were sore from the water, his eyelids crusted with salt. Everything was hazy, blurred figures standing around, a wide expanse of water flickering and spangling beyond. After the noise of the water, everything felt unnaturally quiet. He blinked and tried to recall events. Something was fluttering around inside his head. Something urgent, something he had to do.

"Naomi…" he mumbled, "she okay?"

"Here, have some more wine, that's good. Who are you my son?" The man supporting him pulled more bits of seaweed away.

"Jon, Jon Heath!" he said with difficulty. The man jumped, startled.

"What is it Caleb?" Another man loomed into view. Caleb gripped Jon firmly, turning his face to look him in the eyes.

"Say your name again, stranger!"

"Jon Heath." Jon had a twisting sensation in his gut. "Why?"

"Jonneath..." he repeated then turned to the man at his shoulder, "strange, but one of our number keeps saying that name, that and another name; 'Naomi'. He is weak and very sick, but he cries these names out."

Jon's head was hurting from the brightness of the light. "His name?" He tried to sit up. "Is his name Isaac?" Caleb looked at him in incomprehension. Jon had forgotten that the Timescope would not translate for him. He struggled to his feet. "She must be here," recollection was rushing back; the awful sound of the waters returning, the helpless sensation of being swept up and thrown around. Events further back were shouting for attention. Where was Naomi?

Trying to ignore the pain from his chest and head, Jon looked around at the shore. The sea was still now, the cloudy water thick with bodies rolling in the swell. There were another thirty or forty still forms on the sand, a gentle breeze playing over them. The waves washed around pieces of chariot and several dead horses, and garments drifted lazily on the tide.

"Naomi!" Jon's voice was almost a croak after all the shouting in the sea. Frenziedly he limped from one body to the next, here a Taskmaster, there a young soldier, all alike in one respect- they were lifeless, their faces blue or pale white.

It was almost the last one he saw; there were many more bodies drifting on the sea, but there were two a little further up the beach, huddled closely together. His heart beating wildly Jon approached, Caleb following behind. "Naomi?"

George was motionless. His face the same colour as all the rest, but Naomi, clutched in his arms was noticeably less pale. She was breathing but so terribly still.

"Naomi!" Jon disentangled her from George. When he rolled her away from him she coughed weakly, her breath coming in great gasps. "Please, Naomi, don't give up!" He rubbed her face between his hands, "Please live." His voice cracked.

Caleb was crouching beside him, staring keenly at her face. At once he stood up, beckoning to men standing nearby. "Kindle a fire," he commanded. "Quickly, she needs warmth. And call Deborah to me, she will know what to do." He crouched down again.

"She is Naomi?" Caleb was staring at her intensely. "Like you she is strangely attired!" Jon nodded miserably. He pulled her to him, cradling her in his arms. Her head lolled back, her blue lips fell slightly open.

Gently Naomi was prised from his grasp, and laid on the dry sand beside the fire. A woman, short, very old and wizened took charge of the situation. Immediately she made it clear that they were not needed.

"We must leave her," Caleb said, retreating rapidly. "She will be well attended to."

Jon shook his head. "No, I can't leave her."

Caleb turned to Deborah. "I understand not his speech;" he began, "but the little maid is of his people, and he must stay with her…"

Whatever authority Caleb had with the people, clearly he had none with this woman. With a screech she turned on him, and pushed him away. Jon had a brief glimpse of Naomi, still chalk white and limp, being helped out of her wet clothes before he was hustled away.

"Come with me," Caleb murmured. "I will take you to Isaac."

The main body of the refugees were gathered a few hundred metres from the shore. From all sides of the huge assembly, music and dancing were breaking out. A party was gathering momentum, women and children forgetting their tiredness, and clapping their hands or beating tambourines and singing a refrain:

"Sing to the LORD, for he has triumphed gloriously; the horse and his rider has he thrown into the sea."

The jubilation was spontaneous. It erupted from every quarter. The dazed, exhausted older men and women watched as the younger men threw their arms around girls, snatching them up and whirling them around, and children skipped and jumped in the dust with their friends. The clamour of excitement contrasting oddly with the rancid atmosphere of fear and dread of last night, or, for that matter the beach nearby where still more bodies were washing up on the sand. Caleb threaded his way through the seething melee, occasionally stepping aside good-naturedly to allow a dancing mob to pass. Jon hardly heard or saw much; his mind was occupied with that deathly-white figure on the sea shore. The wizened old woman certainly seemed in charge, but this was stone-age medicine. Could she deal with someone half-drowned?

"Yahmose!" Jon recognised the name. Yahmose was the Egyptian; all around him, his adopted nation was rejoicing at the destruction of his own race. "The people overflow with triumph at this time." Caleb looked uncomfortable.

The little man held up his hands in a gesture of resignation. He was struggling to hide his feelings. "We have oppressed your people for too long," he said finally. "It is…just."

"How is Isaac?" Caleb said to divert him. "Only there is someone with me who should meet him."

The anguished expression on Yahmose's face was replaced by a look of concern. "Ah, the old one is not well. He cries out in a strange tongue. He has a high fever, and this heat is burning him up. Come, you shall see him." He led the way to a makeshift shelter.

The Professor was lying in the shade of the canopy, a young woman dabbing his forehead with water from a clay jar. But the celebrations were distracting her, and her attention was on a group of young men nearby who were making signs to her to join with them. As they approached, she resumed her task, but Yahmose dismissed her curtly.

"As you can see, he is very sick," he whispered to Caleb. "I thought he was about to die five nights ago, but he rallied. He has survived in spite of the wilderness, in spite of the cold nights. Truly he has a will to live!"

Isaac had changed physically. His hair had whitened noticeably. But his obvious illness masked the differences since they had last seen him in Egypt. His face was gaunt and his eyes bright with fever, and a crust had formed around his lips. As he thrashed around on the sand, he kept up an almost unbroken murmur, "Jon, Naomi, Jon, Naomi, Jon…"

Jon's heart sank. There wasn't going to be any intelligent conversation with him! He was delirious. Sweat rolled off him as he twitched and turned. Nevertheless, Jon felt he had to try.

"Prof!" he called, speaking in a low but clear voice. "Prof, can you understand me?"

"Jon,Naomi,Jon,Naomi,Jon,Naomi…" the muttering quickened, the words running together.

"Prof, you've got to listen!" Beside him, Caleb knelt in the sand, peering quizzically, first at Jon, then at the Prof. "Prof, please, it's Jon. We need your help. Naomi needs our help."

"Jon,Naomi,Jon,Naomi,Jon,Naomi…"

Suddenly the tension was too much for Jon. He grabbed the old man by the collar;

"Prof! Just shut up and listen will you? We need your help!"

"Jon,Naomi,Jon,Naomi,Jon,Naomi…" In frustration, Jon let go, and the Professor sank back onto the sand. He turned away, bitterly disappointed.

"You're shouting at me again!"

"Wha…" Jon spun round. He was struggling to sit, one hand holding his injured ribs. "Pass us that water will you Jon?"

"How long… have you…?" The sentence tailed off. Impulsively Jon threw his arms round him. The Professor gasped;

"Mind my ribs will you, there's a good chap!"

"Sorry, Prof! It's just so good to hear from you again." Jon felt like crying with joy as he reached for the water and held it to the Prof's lips. He drank deeply. The transformation in his voice was total. Where there had been an incoherent mumbling, he now spoke, albeit weakly, with his usual slightly impatient but kindly tone.

"Where's Naomi?"

Jon told him. Naomi was half-drowned, but he thought she was in good hands. Her boyfriend George Mere was dead.

Ignoring the look of distress on the Prof's face he went on. He told what had happened. For a few minutes the Prof was attentive, listening keenly. Then suddenly the muttering started again. Only this time it broke off after a few seconds.

"Why's that happening?" asked Jon.

Using Caleb as a support, he pulled himself to a sitting position, wincing as he did so. "I'll tell you my story," he said.

"The fault is entirely mine," he began. "All the ingredients were there for a disaster, but I was too stupid to spot them." He gazed around at the scenes of jubilation and uproar all around and a distant look came into his eyes. "I built a system with the ability to replicate and improve itself. Mistake number one, I built in very few checks or balances. Mistake two, I gave it the power to interact with the human mind, but I gave it no limits."

A group of dancers cavorted a few metres away, crying the same refrain Jon had heard earlier:

"The horse and his rider has he thrown into the sea."

"Mistake three," he went on. "I gave a greedy program all it needed to spread and mutate. I let it loose on the Internet. I must have been mad!"

"Why what's happening?"

"It's becoming aware of itself, Jon."

Jon gave a nervous laugh, then stopped, seeing the look on the old man's face. This was the stuff of cliché, sad little science fiction stories he had read as a kid, absurd really. But now, here, all around them was evidence that the unthinkable was actually happening.

"Prof!" He said, "Let's just get this thing finished, shall we? Let me have those codes, the destruct…"

"No!" The Professor clamped his hand over Jon's mouth. "No, don't say it Jon!"

The exclamation triggered off another fit of coughing, pain spread across his face. When it had subsided, he said, keeping his voice low and even;

"Just assume it can hear you, Jon, ok? Keep your voice down and don't mention…that again!"

"Ok, anything you say. But what is it? The Timescope, I mean. Is it alive?"

The Prof lay back on the sand. Beside them Caleb watched spellbound, astonished at the transformation in Isaac.

No, the Timescope was not alive. Not in the usual sense anyway. But it had rampaged out of control, seizing computing resources in its quest to improve. As it ruthlessly infected networks, it caused power cuts. Power cuts caused networks to fail, so it had to keep moving on. Its aggressive surge had so far paralysed two-thirds of global data traffic flow, and it was showing no signs of tiring.

Jon interrupted; "Yeah, it's put the world on a war footing!"

"I thought it might." Jon couldn't tell whether he was bothered about this or not. Many times in the short time he had known him the Prof had railed against the sophistication of military systems and the ease with which huge forces of destruction could be unleashed.

"But what does the Timescope want?"

"To do what it was designed to do. To do this!" he waved his hand at the pandemonium around them. "To recreate historical images as fully as it can. It soon found out there was more than just sight and sound on those stones; it found history in every sense of the word. Pain, joy, love, hate, oppression, cruelty, freedom, slavery- oh, you name it and the Timescope found it leached like the centuries of rain and sunlight into the rocks. So it requisitioned the computing resources to faithfully and fully recreate the original experience. *Voila!*"

"So why can't we mention the... you know what's?"

The Professor looked anxiously around. "Something happened, something difficult to explain. Does the name Jackman mean anything to you?"

"Oh no!" Jon felt suddenly very cold, colder than he had when he had been soaked by the sea.

"I see it does!" The Professor pulled himself up again. "Would you mind telling me what you know?"

When he had finished, Jon helped him drink some more water. He looked seriously troubled. Suddenly he closed his eyes and began the muttering again; "Jon,Naomi,Jon,Naomi,Jon,Naomi…"

Again abruptly he stopped. Alarmed, Jon asked, "Why're you doing that?"

"The Timescope is trying to suppress me, Jon. As long as I resist, it will fight me. It wants me to be Isaac, inside and out. As long as there is any Avery in me, it will continue to try to rewrite me."

"Just like it's doing to Naomi?"

"Exactly! I've seen the coding, it all fits- it cannot understand our presence in a historical setting. Once it would have been content to treat us as aberrations, now it is throwing its weight around, trying to redesign our minds so that they fit. Do you know how many children I've got, Jon?"

"Two or three?"

"Eleven! My first wife died in childbirth with Samuel. He survived, he was number five. Now with Phurah I have another six. We have more grandchildren than I have time to mention. I know their names, their ages, I have years of memories of my life together with Phurah, as a slave, as a father- the Timescope has given me history, Jon. History I don't possess. That's why when it bears down on me, washing my brain of everything I once was, all the modern stuff it can't make to fit, that's why I keep saying your names. It helps focus on what's left of me, Jon."

"Hang on," Jon said. "You didn't tell me what you know about Jackman? We thought he was dead."

"He could very well be dead out there. In here he's very much alive!"

"What's he doing?"

"Looking for you."

"Oh!" said Jon unhappily.

"And learning the Timescope as well."

The chilly feeling he had felt earlier spread over him as the Professor explained what he had found out about the Timescope from the inside. "All this;" he picked up a handful of sand and let it trickle through his long fingers, "all this is data. Pure data. I'm data. The real me is lying unconscious in that ruinously expensive private hospital ward. Every hour here I lose sight of that reality and become Isaac, a Hebrew slave who came off the worst of a beating. Eventually I too will be pure data. Until then I am in a unique position of viewing this data from within, seeing programs being executed, files manipulated, fresh data generated."

"The Timescope is modelled on a virus- Naomi was right when she said that. Each program file is self-contained, able to spawn fresh programs at will and like a virus able to invade a host- in this case our brains, and rewrite our neural networks."

Jon shivered.

"Then I found out it was a matter of resisting the Timescope until the programs faltered, then learning how to terminate them. Then I could see the program code."

"You saw the program code? Where?" This was surreal!

"In my brain. Yes, there was billions of lines of it and it was going fast, but don't forget I wrote it. I could recognise the patterns and trends, what each chunk of data was trying to do. Once I had caused the program to arrest, I was able to search around to see exactly what it was up to." He paused, looking at Jon as if uncertain whether to continue.

"What?"

"You and Naomi have given the Timescope a lot of material!"

Jon felt he knew what was coming next, nevertheless he said cautiously, "what sort of material?"

A ghost of a grin crossed his face, making a welcome relief from the painful grimace. "The Timescope wants the complete experience. Complete in every detail. It's not content to just show heroism, or skulduggery; it wants to feel these sensations for itself, Jon. When it encounters examples of loyalty, generosity, or for that matter betrayal or meanness, it is desperate to know more. It is fascinated with our human emotions, especially love. Particularly the sort of love that's been going on between you and Naomi!"

Jon flushed. "You've seen…I mean you know what's…"

"Oh come off it Jon, I guessed almost from the moment you first introduced yourself. Naomi reacted so violently to you, I realised immediately you were both smitten with each other. Why else do you think I was so open about the Timescope to you? Then you go and spend weeks circling each other like cats about to fight. Talk about sustained denial!"

"Well Naomi's impossible!" Jon cried. "One moment she's…"

He cut him short. "Never mind that, that's your own business! As I said, the Timescope did every thing in its power to square that particular circle. That's why it created Hannah. It's thrown everything it had at you two. That's why when it tries to break into my mind; I chant your names,"

"To distract it!"

He nodded, but the smile faded. "Jackman!"

"What about him?"

"The Timescope wants to feel humanity, Jon. The stronger the emotions, the more it pays attention. Until recently you and Naomi gave it all it needed. Now it has found something stronger."

"Hate! Not the reckless hate of rage nor the hot anger of conflict; no, Jon, he's something different. He's the product of intelligence without compassion, he is greed without conscience. He kills without compunction; neither does he spend a moment retracing his steps to see if he could have done things differently. He's dangerous enough in real life, but now the Timescope has absorbed him into its way of thinking; I can't stress how serious the situation is."

Jon didn't reply. He was thinking of those cold, cold eyes. Finally he said;

"But what can he do, how can he harm me…us?"

"I wondered that. He's a virtual entity, a ghost in the machine. But he's learning. The Timescope's learning. The Timescope learnt how a psychopath thinks from Jackman; and somewhere along the way it acquired a cunning combined with an ability to manipulate…"

I know where it got that from! Jon thought.

"And now it is trying to kill me. It has tried several times here, but Caleb takes good care of me. But did you know that a powerful muscle relaxant was prescribed for me as I lay in Chessington ward? Prescribed in such quantities as to cause breathing paralysis? I know things up at the hospital are chaotic right now, but fortunately the nurse about to administer the dose had the sense to ask questions. It transpired that the computer system had inadvertently inserted the prescription. Oh no! It's coming back." He put his face in his hands.

"Prof! What's the matter?" The Prof had begun chanting again. The words were drowned by the exuberant partying all around; "Jon,Naomi,Jon,Naomi,...it's trying to get in...Jon,Naomi..."

This time it was many minutes before he stopped. Caleb was talking excitedly to Yahmose. Jon overheard snatches of the talk, phrases like, 'evil spirit', and saw Yahmose gesticulating wildly.

"It wants the codes, Jon. It knows."

"Knows what?"

"It knows I want to finish it. But it won't have them!" he said fiercely. "It's my responsibility; it's the least I can do to hang on and resist it. If it gets those codes, it will know where they point to in the system code and it will find the Trojan horse. Once it does that it will be invulnerable."

"Ok, Prof, what do you want me to do?" Jon's thoughts flitted anxiously back to Naomi, on the beach. If only she were with him, at least she would be better equipped to deal with this!

The old man grabbed his hand. He gestured for more water, then pulled Jon close to him.

"There's eleven minutes until the batteries fail, then you're free of this. Get to the hospital. When you are there you must... get him back!!"

Jon had a blurred sense of Yahmose's face close by; but the worried frown had been replaced by a greedy look. He was listening, hanging on every word. Without thinking, Jon spun round and pushed Yahmose savagely away. Caleb who had been talking to a group of young men dashed across. Jon pointed at him;

"Hold him, he's a spy!" he yelled. Caleb looked confused, but planted a brawny arm on the little Egyptian's shoulder. He bent down to the Professor.

"What have I got to do? Prof, tell me!"

"Jon,Naomi,Jon,Naomi,Jon,Naomi…"

"Tell me. Stop that and just tell me what to do!"

The mental battle was plain; his veins stood out on his forehead and the sweat poured off him.

"Jon,Naomi,Jon,Naomi,Jon,Naomi …hospital…Jon,Naomi, …I'll be ready there for you…Jon,Naomi,Jon,Naomi,Jon,Naomi…open website '*R-AVERY*'…Password… Jon,Naomi,Jon…I'll tell you when you're there… Jon,Naomi,Jon,Naomi,Jon,Naomi…"

For another forty seconds the babbling continued. Endless, without a pause even for breath. Jon looked around. Yahmose had shaken himself free of Caleb and was gliding across the desert sand towards him. He hated to leave the Prof here, but the danger had multiplied in the last few minutes. He stood up, then the Professor uttered one last coherent sentence:

"Jon. The Timescope will use anything and anybody… Trust nobody!"

Yahmose closed the last few yards in a rush. His apologetic look had vanished; in its place his yellow teeth were bared in an avaricious grin. Behind him Caleb was dithering, uncertain. Jon still ached terribly from the battering in the sea, he could not move fast and Yahmose was small and quick. The little Egyptian hissed through his teeth and as Jon stepped back he glimpsed a knife!

Jon retreated, keeping his eyes fastened on Yahmose. It was clear he was no assassin; he should have pressed his advantage immediately. Jon felt his way barred by the poles that held the corners of the crude shelter; thick wooden posts stuck into the sand. The wood must have been bone dry, for as he stumbled back on it, one snapped with a sharp crack. Jon seized it before it even had time to fall, and tugged it from the canopy. As Yahmose closed in, Jon brought the post down on his head. It was a hasty blow, it didn't knock him out but it glanced off the side of his face and sent him staggering sideways over the Professor. Jon ran.

From where he was the sea was visible as a bright ribbon, twinkling in the sunlight. Whatever shouting and chaos he left behind him was soon lost in the universal party that had gripped the Hebrews. A direct path was out of the question; heaving groups of dancers erupted from all sides; but that at least made as big an obstacle to Yahmose, should he try to follow.

He emerged on the beach some way down from where he had left Naomi. He could see the old woman sitting by the fire, the smoke rising into the still air. All around the corpses of the Egyptians cluttered the smooth sand. "Naomi!" He yelled, although nobody would have heard him at that distance. "Naomi!" He began running up the beach, the soft sand shifting beneath his feet; "Naomi, I'm coming!"

He ran hard, the will to get back to her overriding the pain in his torn muscles. Had she heard him? He couldn't tell. Even if she had, was she too sick to stand up? Still calling her name he ran, but the sand shifted and twisted beneath his feet. And the figures on the sand drew no closer.

He looked down; the sand was rushing backwards, pouring away at the same speed as he ran. He tried running faster; straining every muscle to close the gap, but around his feet the sand, like liquid slithered and squirmed. And now it was over his ankles, reaching to pull him down, quivering and shivering.

Soon progress was impossible in any direction except downwards. The pressure of sand gripped his calves and upper legs and held him tight. Dimly, as he threw his arms out to try to slow the descent into the stuff, Jon was aware of a tall figure walking serenely across the beach towards him.

"Hannah!" Sand was running into his mouth, he was being crushed by its weight all over his body; "Hannah, keep back!" He spat it out but more took its place.

"My lord." She gazed gravely down at him, as if puzzled by his predicament.

"Keep back!" Jon gagged as it began to fill his mouth up. In a few moments more it would be over his eyes, then he had only minutes to live. Black spots swam before his eyes. The thought crossed his mind that she could stand so easily on the stuff whereas he was sinking. He was aware she was giving him a pitying smile, and then it was in his ears. He couldn't hear what she was saying, but something was happening to her, her face was starting to lose definition.

With his remaining open eye, Jon watched her beautiful face and figure crumble into first a crudely defined image, then become more block-like, until finally only a weird pile of rectangles remained. The beach too, what Jon could see of it, now looked like an impressionist painting. It was a moment or two before Jon fully understood what had happened- the batteries had failed! The Timescope was, at least here, powerless. There pressure on his body released and he fell onto the floor of the Professor's house.

20
Shibboleth

The beam of daylight had shifted across the floor. It now fell directly on a huge bulk. Prentice's body lay with its feet towards him; the still face mottled and purple. Close by, George lay face down with his arms rigid; embracing somebody - somebody who wasn't there any more.

She was standing behind him. As she moved the slightest rustle of her clothes betrayed her presence.

"Na! Oh you're alive, oh thank goodness! I thought... that is I'd imagined..."

"My...oh," she stumbled. "I'm sorry, did I startle you...?"

She was calm, unnaturally so. Her lower lip trembled, and she was white as a sheet. She moved towards him as if to throw herself into his arms, but stopped in indecision, staring at George and Terrence Prentice.

"Na," Jon wanted to divert her away from the morbid sight. "Come here; let's go in the other room, away from...them."

"Oh, yes m..." she broke off and stood swaying slightly. 'She's going to faint,' Jon thought, and he caught her arm and led her into the small sitting room. She stumbled and sat down in the shade.

"We've got to get to the hospital," Jon parted the curtains and peered out. Outside, the streets glared and sweltered in the continuing heat wave. But they were quiet.

So was Naomi. She said little, and her voice was strained and odd, as if she were choosing every word carefully. Finally Jon said;

"Are you okay? Shall we go?"

Naomi glanced up. "Why should I be okay, as you put it? The man I love has died, saving me from the Red Sea. The old man, my Grandfather has died also, and I am ...upset."

The way she spoke chilled Jon. She was icy calm, speaking in this analytical way about herself. No wonder, she was probably deep in shock. But what did she mean?

"The Prof's not dead; I was speaking to him fifteen minutes ago."

"He died early this morning; I rang the hospital."

"But how? The phone lines are down!"

She held out Prentice's phone. "Sorry, Na, I forgot." Jon's brain squirmed in confusion. Why all this stuff about George being 'the man I love'? Strangely melodramatic for Naomi! And the cold, flat mechanical way she was speaking. If only she would break down and cry or something!

"Well let's go to the hospital, it looks safe enough."

"No, let us stay here. There will be time enough later on. Please, it is what I want!"

At that moment, with a hum and sound of dozens of circuits warming up, the power came back on. It went off, came on again and this time stayed on. Jon watched Naomi closely, going from room to room turning off light switches. As she came back into the sitting room there was a loud banging at the front door.

"I'll go!" Jon said, and dashed to the door. He was halfway down the hall when it was thrown open and a policeman in full body armour burst in.

"Jon Heath?" He snapped, flashing an identity card under his nose. He wore black sunshades, and carried a rifle at his side.

"Yes, this is him," said Naomi blocking the way behind him. "Are we ready to go?"

The policeman nodded. Jon turned round wildly. "Naomi? What does he want me for? Where are we going?"

She placed her arms gently round his neck. "I called the police, it is for the best. They will take us to a place of safety. They will need to talk to us about the Timescope, and we can help them fight it."

Dazed and far from reassured, Jon followed the police officer to an unmarked car. Another uniformed man was at the wheel, the engine running. "Am I under arrest?"

"Not yet," said the second policeman, "our orders are to take you to HQ for questioning. We will decide what to do when we have interviewed you both. Now get in."

Jon got in, Naomi settled next to him, her gaze fixed in middle distance. The car pulled away, its tyres squealing as it accelerated up the deserted streets.

"Na," Jon gently took her hand and squeezed it. "I'm so, so sorry. About George, and the Prof, I mean. I didn't know George went back for you."

Abruptly she seemed to snap out of her trance. "The codes! You said the Prof had the codes?"

"W…well yes! But he's dead, so we can't get them now. We're stuck!"

"He didn't tell you the codes?"

Jon was about to say, 'he was going to tell me at the hospital,' but by now he felt so uneasy with her, he bit his lip. She was so detached, indifferent to the situation around her. He glanced at her again, she was smiling!

"Naomi? What's funny? Naomi?" The pressure of the truth was starting to burst through his skull. Try as he might he could not keep it out. "Hannah?"

"I'm not Hannah!"

"Then who am I? Tell me Naomi!"

With terrible calmness she faced him. "You know who you are, don't you?"

"Tell me!" She regarded him impassively. Anger flared up in Jon; he seized her hand.

"You're hurting my fingers!"

"Say my name!" The police car rocketed towards the expressway. "Say it!" Jon demanded. "Say my name!"

She gave a cry, "You're hurting me!"

"Then say my name and I'll stop." Jon twisted his grip on her slender fingers; "Come on!"

"Yon! Stop, please!"

"Say my name properly!"

"Please, *Yon!"*

"You can't can you?"

The policeman in the front passenger seat twisted round. In a flash, Jon reached out and ripped the sunglasses from his face.

A pair of deep blue eyes stared back at him. Expressionless, dead blue eyes. Jon wrenched the door open and flung himself from the car.

He was lucky in many respects; the expressway was clear of traffic apart from a procession of army vehicles full of soldiers. The slow moving convoy forced the police car to slow down. Jon hurled himself from the car, then at the last moment made a grab for the door as it swung out. The driver slammed on the brakes and Jon was flung on to the grassy verge. He rolled a few metres then came to rest. He could see the man in the front seat fumbling with his seatbelt. Jon dashed into the cover of the low bushes that flanked the main road and scrabbled over a high wooden fence. He was in somebody's back garden; a child's swing and some toys were littered on the grass. He had a brief glimpse of a woman dragging a toddler through some French windows. Then with a crashing, splintering sound, a row of bullet holes peppered the fence.

Once again, Jon ran, blindly. Through the fence he could hear shouts, Hannah's voice, and a number of other men, soldiers from the convoy. As he fled down the neat tree-lined housing estate, once more the painful gasping for breath chafing his lungs raw, Jon tried to think through this latest twist.

Naomi was gone, or at least she was submerged under Hannah. Hannah was gone too, at least the Hannah he loved and admired. Instead there was this possessed thing, detached and soulless looking like her. And, as if that wasn't bad enough, Blue Eyes had replicated himself as a policeman armed with a semi-automatic rifle!

Jon's first thought was to distance himself from the Blue Eyed psychopath- what was it the Prof had said of him? *'Intelligence without compassion, greed without conscience.'* But where was safe? For all he knew the Timescope had the resources to trace his whereabouts anywhere in the country? And with the Prof dead the Timescope was now free to roam at large.

He stopped, sobbing for breath. A thought hammered his aching brain. Was the Prof dead? Naomi had told him so, but that meant nothing now. Perhaps there was still time to end this. Ahead the suburban street opened out on to an arterial road. The gantry sign read;

"HOSPITAL, ACCIDENT AND EMERGENCY- 4 MILES."

The car weaved crazily as Jon picked up speed. The wires to the ignition switch swung around by his knee. At least Roger Lord had taught him one useful thing in his life! The car had an automatic gearbox- Roger would have scorned an automatic, but it suited Jon fine, one less thing to worry about as he careered through the empty streets. On either side, buildings were burnt out, and a leisure complex that had opened only that Spring was wrecked and gutted. There were cars along the route, some smashed, others had been bulldozed on to the pavement to keep the streets clear, but very little signs of life, unless you counted the domestic dogs ranging around, lean and hungry. The electronic road signs were proclaiming; "CURFEW IN FORCE: LOOTERS WILL BE SHOT"

He was lucky in his choice of route. Roadblocks had been established on most of the city circular roads, and armed services were enforcing the curfew. Helicopters clattered overhead, but Jon's car was only spotted as he drew near to the hospital. He abandoned it close by a hedge, dived into the undergrowth and vaulted over a playground fence to where he knew the side entrance to the Chessington ward opened on to the small car park.

Once again luck favoured him. As he parted the bushes surrounding the playground to look at the car park, two soldiers ran from the door and towards the front of the building to where the helicopter was swooping low over the car. With his head down, Jon sprinted past his bike, still chained to the railings and dashed into the hospital.

It was anarchy! Medical staff were running in all directions, and patients on trolley-beds were taking up much of the corridor space. Phones were ringing, relatives were shouting and people were crying. A man with a bloodstained tee shirt staggered towards him, pointing at a wound in his chest and shouting and swearing freely.

It was almost as bad on the second floor. Gone was the decorum and expensive peace he had encountered on his previous visits. A general disorder and palpable panic suffused the atmosphere. A white coated figure was dashing around shouting "the power's back on!" as if nobody else knew. Unseen Jon slipped past the nurse's station where recently the treacherous Marsha had eavesdropped on him and into the room where the Prof lay.

"Prof?" The figure on the bed was still. Jon's heart plummeted. What Hannah had said was true. He was dead then.

But as he looked closer, Jon could see that a muscle quivered in his neck. He put out his finger and touched the flesh. It was still warm!

"Prof?" There was no answer. Below in the car park, Jon could hear shouts and the running of booted feet. He turned and locked the door. The figure on the bed did not stir.

"Prof!" Jon spoke as loudly as he dared, but there was no movement, no reaction.

"Prof, you said you'd be waiting for me. Please, it's me, Jon! Wake up will you?"

There was a screech of tyres, followed by a 'whumph! in the car park below' Jon dashed to the window; the police car he had recently exited at high speed was embedded in the side of a Range Rover. Khaki-clad figures were racing from all directions, guns raised; Naomi was crouched in the back seat. As he watched, one of the soldiers swung the rear door wide, one hand pulling her swiftly from the car, the other training his weapon on the driver. Naomi limped hurriedly across the car park and disappeared through the door.

Jon flashed a desperate glance around the room. A computer terminal was screwed to a shelf on the wall. He hit a key and the display came alive. It had one single blank message:

THIS TERMINAL HAS BEEN DISCONNECTED FROM THE NETWORK.

PLEASE CONTACT AN ADMINISTRATOR.

Jon slid to the floor gutted. It was so unfair! At this late stage to have such a simple hurdle! What were his chances of finding someone authorised to reconnect the terminal? Oh, please Mr Administrator, could you reconnect me so I can save the planet? As if!

Tired, aching and wretched he was dimly aware of the cacophony in the car park below. Even the sound of gunfire could not stir him. He was finished! Pipped at the final post by a dumb computer terminal! He slumped against the wall and waited for whatever it was that was coming. But at the sound of a gentle, insistent knocking at the door, he stood up.

"Are you alone, N...Hannah?" He swallowed hard. "Are you Hannah?" He looked into her eyes. The horrible impassiveness had gone.

She smiled and nodded slowly "Yes my lord. The cruel one has been delayed; he has left me alone for now." Below several more shots rang out. Jon pulled her into the room and relocked the door.

He looked at her. She was, if possible, more radiant than ever. Her glossy hair shimmered in the late afternoon light, and she moved seemingly without effort towards him. She gazed gravely at him, and Jon was aware of little else but her eyes.

He held her in his arms. He no longer cared about Blue Eyes, or whatever he had become. He no longer cared for the situation outside, the Timescope; the mounting death toll, the terrible chaos that had come out of the blue to the city he knew so well. He just wanted to hold this beautiful, beautiful girl in his arms and forget everything. And she too, relaxed in his embrace, soft, warm and with the unadulterated smell of the fields and vineyards of Carmel like an aura about her.

"My lord," she murmured. "My lord, shall we return to the slopes of the hill? There we can walk the fields and pastures of our homeland." She sighed. "Do you remember, *Yon*, the time when you lay with your head on my lap and I fed you the first-ripe grapes of Jokneam? The servants worked in the fields below, and there you first spoke to me of love?"

"Yes…I remember. Your brother chanced upon us when we kissed, and you were angry with him."

"My brother will not chance upon us here, my lord."

She tasted sweet, so, so sweet. Jon had kissed girls before; he tried to remember the first girl he had kissed…what was her name? Jenny? Jill? On the way home after school, or was it at lunch time? No, he thought languidly, it didn't matter and it was gone. Gone like the sounds of the gunfight below, gone like the sights, sounds and smells of the city of his childhood; gone along with Faris, and Roger whoever–he-was.

He remembered with pride afterwards returning home to the village by the river. His mother had scolded him for being late, but he didn't care. Hannah, the daughter of Obadiah had kissed him! He walked on air for days afterwards. The princess of Israel in love with the farmer's son!

The memories were flooding in thick and fast now. Every breath he took of hers inhaled a heady, intoxicating blend of experience and desire. He felt the grazed knees as he slid down the rocks of Carmel, shouting at Jacob, his lifelong friend who was pelting down the wooded track that led to the plain below. "She does love me, she said so." The words tasted like manna in his throat.

The canopy was decked with springtime flowers. They sat, cross-legged as village children ran round them, casting more of the meadow daisies upon them. Micah smiled benevolently at his cousin; "Take care of her, *Yon!*"

Take care of her? This flower of Carmel? What man in his right mind would want anything but to love, nourish and protect this dazzling creature? He was dizzy with love. "I would die for you, Hannah!"

There was his father, tall and bearded, taking down his great sword and preparing to answer the call of his king; his mother, her belly swollen with his sister, soon to be born; weeping as she held onto her husband; the wide, scared eyes of his little brother and after the terrible loneliness and heartache of loss that only Hannah could alleviate.

"You were always good at cheering me up, Hannah."

"He was an honourable man, *Yon.* He died a warrior's death. Many men of noble birth did not die as valiantly as he."

"Berechiah was so like him. It brought mother so much happiness to hold her first grandson in her arms."

"Oh, Berechiah!" She laughed lightly. "How he kicked! He struggled, he turned around within me! None of the others were as lively as him."

Memories, many sweet, many bitter, most just memories. Days and seasons, sons and daughters, springtime, harvest and winter. Quarrels and afterwards making up; new life and more death, laughter and tears; they flooded in; each one right, each one true, each one a tiny slice of their lives together.

"Jon!" The voice was distant, as if it were coming from the bottom of a well. Jon moved so he could see her eyes. "Hannah?"

A flicker crossed her face, as if she were battling a headache. "My lord, it is nothing."

"Jon!"

"You can say my name! Oh Hannah, say it again!"

"Yon?" Then again, distant but more urgent; "Jon! Don't leave me here, Jon!"

A fresh wave of memories bore down on him: times of war, times of peace, extremes of joy and depths of grief. And always her face, his Hannah central to the scene; older now, with the first lines of responsibility creasing her face; her stunning hair, tied back in a pigtail as she worked, or cascading freely down her back for him. Standing numbly by the small pile of freshly turned earth that marked the resting place of her father; placid, kind, self-effacing Obadiah for whom Jon's lowly background had been of no consequence.

He reeled from the burden of them. He tried to hold Hannah at arm's length to see her face, but she pulled him close, her hair washing around his shoulders.

"My lord, shall we journey to the sea again? Let us leave our family with the village and go together, just the two of us."

"Jon!"

"Naomi?"

"My lord, who are you calling?"

"Naomi?"

"Jon!" more distant now but more urgent, distressed. "Jon, I love you!"

Fields, meadows, vineyards, feast-days, journeys: children, friends, enemies, light and dark. They clamoured outside his skull, pouring in through the gaping holes torn in his personality, years upon years of memories.

"Naomi? Naomi! Please come to me!"

"No my lord, it is nothing. Push it away!" Hannah's jaw was set. She squeezed him, trying to force the intrusion away.

"Naomi!"

"Jon!

"Keep calling my name, Naomi. Don't stop."

"Jon, Jon, Jon, Jon, I love you Jon."

Slowly as if a radio were struggling to come into tune, the sounds of the outside world returned: men yelling and running across the car park. Helicopters overhead, their blades whupping the air. The vivid fields and vineyards of Carmel receded, the greens dwindling to greys and browns.

"Jon?" Her voice was close now. "Jon, where are we?"

"At the hospital. By your granddad's bed. Oh no!" The sudden realisation of what still remained to do hit him. "Naomi, we've got to get the codes into that computer."

"My lord? What are these codes?"

"Leave her alone Hannah! I love Naomi, not you!"

He heard her gasp, and the cruelty of it struck him like a body blow. "Hannah, I'm sorry, I didn't mean it like that."

"*Yon,* what did you mean?"

For a few seconds Jon thought. Outside in the corridor were crashing sounds, people screaming. "Hannah?"

"Yes my lord?"

"It's a lie! Hannah, I'm sorry, but all these things never existed. You died after Elijah showed Israel who was God on top of the mountain. You know that. You watched the rain coming down, then they had to carry you down the mountain…"

She was silent, digesting this. Jon whispered in her ear; "You remember the rain, Hannah?"

"The rain…yes I remember that; and you held my hand, *Yon*?"

"We carried you down the mountain…but…but you didn't make it."

"Yes, it was dark. And then…it went black."

She fell silent, just the sound of stifled sobs. Jon felt a tearing sensation under his rib cage. "Naomi? Are you there?"

"Yes, Jon. Right here." He could hear her breathing softly. "Jon?"

A shattering crash brought them back with a jolt. The door to the room was a sturdy, fireproof door. It bowed inwards as something heavy hit it, but held fast. They could hear muffled shouting.

"Hannah?"

"Yes my lord?"

"Hannah, can you help us?"

Silence… agonising silence. Finally;

"My lord, what do you want your servant to do?"

"Can you get us online? Can you log this computer on? It needs a password."

"You wish to destroy the Timescope, my lord? I will cease to be too."

"Hannah, I can't make you do this. But can you pretend to be something you weren't?"

There was another volley of blows on the door. "Please Hannah! There's no other way."

"My lord, it is done."

The screen showed a very dull web browser. "Shove the bed against the door!" Jon yelled. Naomi, still looking very dazed obeyed whilst Jon frantically tapped in the address the Professor had whispered to him. This website looked exceedingly dull. A few research links, bibliography, recent papers…Jon scanned the links…Nothing!

"Na! Do you know where he keeps Timescope stuff?"

She was locking the brakes on the bed with its sleeping occupant. "ALT and F6" she panted. "He usually has a hidden link or two there, failing that try F1 to F4 inclusive." The bed banged up against the door, just as the screen began loading something big.

"Come on…" Jon muttered. "Na, can you get anything out of him?"

Naomi threw her arms around the Professor's neck. "Granddad, can you hear me? Please speak, tell us…tell us what Jon?"

"The password! Whatever it takes to authorise changes to Timescope files. Or try your own if you think it'll work!"

"Shibboleth, my lord."

"Hannah? Or is that you, Naomi?"

"My lord, I know his password. He has used it many times."

"Hannah," Jon felt a huge surge of excitement; "can you tell us the codes?"

"No, my lord. The Timescope is laying siege to him as I speak. If he opens for me, the Timescope will get there first. You must ask him. Now *Yon* I must go. As long as I remain here, I distract Naomi from you and from the old man. Good bye, *Yon*."

Any chance Jon had to reply was drowned out in a shattering of glass as the windows overlooking the car park disappeared in a hail of gunfire. Jon dragged Naomi to the safety of the floor by the bed. The glass fragments crunched under their knees. She cried out in fear.

"Naomi!" Jon took her hands in his face. "Na, listen to me. We're going to get through this, d'ye hear? I love you. You're all I ever wanted, and whatever else the Timescope has done, I'm glad it brought us together. Got that?"

She nodded, the colour draining away from her face. Above them the bed shook with the force of the hammering on the door.

"Now get through to him!"

Together they faced the Professor on the bed. Glass fragments winked and sparkled. Naomi brushed them away. "Granddad! Please come back to me."

"Tell him our names! Like this!" Jon put his lips close to the Prof's ear; "Jon,Naomi,Jon,Naomi…"

"Jon,Naomi,Jon,Naomi…" she whispered from the other side. At the head of the bed the door was beginning to come away from the frame. Harsh sounds burst into the room.

"Jon,Naomi,Jon,Naomi…"

Louder now, urgent, insistent; "Jon,Naomi,Jon,Naomi…"

"Don't give up!"

She gave a sharp intake of breath. "Look!"

The Professor's lips were moving, picking up the chant; "Jon,Naomi,Jon,Naomi…"

"He's responding!" Jon yelled. There was a blast of gunfire in the corridor and the sound of more people running.

"Prof!" Jon screamed. "It's us. Jon and Naomi!"

"Granddad, tell us the codes!!"

The figure on the bed suddenly arched its back, almost leaping from the bed. He started shaking as if a heavy electric current were pouring through him. Every muscle jerked convulsively.

"What's happening to him?"

"The Timescope's trying to stop him!" Jon threw himself across his chest, pinning him to the bed.

"The codes!!" Naomi screamed .

"Eight!" the old man yelled, his voice angry.

It had been so long coming Jon was too stunned to move. Naomi hurled herself over the shattered glass to the keyboard. "Eight!" Immediately a text box appeared, and an asterisk flicked on and off.

"Six"

"Six!" she screamed the echo. Now there were two little asterisks side-by-side.

"Eight!" The Professor's body twisted and arched as if a giant hand were screwing him into a ball. Jon fought to hold him down.

This time the ceiling flew into fragments as the bullets raked across it. Scalding water poured onto the floor beside him. Jon jumped aside. "Three!" A strangled yell.

The door had resisted manfully, but now only the bed frame held it in place blocking the doorway and preventing the entrance of whoever it was out there. Four more numbers followed in quick succession.

"How many are there?"

"How should I know?" she yelled. "Probably room for one more!"

"Is that all?"

The shuddering figure, his nose pouring copious amounts of blood pursed his lips:

"One!"

The bed flew across the room, and the policeman stood in the doorway. The automatic rifle was pointed at Naomi, poised to enter the last number.

"Move away!" he gestured with the rifle. "Move away!"

Naomi hesitated.

"If you move so much as a muscle towards that keyboard, I shall fire." His eyes darted from her to Jon and back again. "Now move across to the window."

In a misery of indecision, Naomi obeyed. The cursor at the end of the line of asterisks winked agonisingly.

"Better," he said. "It would be a shame to kill you because the Timescope wants you alive. I want you alive. At least for now." He kicked the ruined door out into the corridor and planted himself between them and the keyboard.

"Jon! I'm glad I didn't finish it last time we met. I was going to then, but shall we say, my priorities have been rearranged?" He looked down at the figure on the bed.

Jon and Naomi watched him, hypnotised. It was like watching a snake rearing itself to strike.

"The old fool had no idea just how powerful this system was. He could not have foreseen program cells capable of multiplying a million times a second. He had no notion of just how quickly the Timescope would become cognisant." The humourless smile appeared like a ghost, then faded.

"Oh, how dumb he was! To give the Timescope such resource was like giving candy to an infant. It wanted more, Jon! Much more. And it could get it! As much power as it wanted. Within days it was global, requisitioning every satellite and mobile phone network it could in order to tap into the greatest unutilised programming reserve on the planet. Do you know what I mean?"

Receiving no answer he gloated on;

"Human intelligence! Those early programs were like pick and shovel compared to what the Timescope can do now! Now it is like dynamite! It can blast its way into your skull. Before you have chance to resist, your memory bank has been overwritten. You become Timescope! Those soldiers outside- it took five minutes before they started shooting each other. The Timescope has given me the power to control, command, deploy and destroy anything I please!"

"So why do you... does it, want us?" Naomi spoke at last.

"You're in love. Ha! Oh, forget romance, flowery hearts, that trash- you two are in love. The Timescope almost burnt itself out analysing you both. Such a dangerous emotion! So many examples of strong men brought down by it. Such a flaw is too deadly to be allowed to continue."

"I taught it to fight." His tone was matter-of fact. "I gave it strength to realise its potential, and cunning to protect itself. Oh, I have much more to give it yet, an ability to recognise weakness, and exterminate second-rate intellect. I can teach it to kill efficiently, and without remorse. I can give it all it needs to conquer. Between us we have the resources to infiltrate every mind on the planet. We can weed out the dross, and extract the silver. Human minds will bend to our needs and with a global network of linked intelligence; we can rise all the way to the stars! But first we must stamp out this conflicting concept of love."

"I think I'd rather be dead!" Naomi said dully.

"Oh you will be by then!" He said without humour. "This love thing- I don't understand it. Oh so vulnerable! So weak, so deadly! To see the risks you took for each other in the name of love. We can't have that virus in the Timescope any more. So we will download you both entirely, then dispose of you. And then, when we have the full problem on file, we can choke it at birth."

"However," keeping the gun trained on them both, he turned to the keyboard. "There is a more pressing weakness I must deal with. He has told you all the destruction codes and I see they have been entered, except one. The last number. Give it me now."

"One!" said Naomi, her voice faint and distant. Jon stared down the barrel of the gun to the man behind it. He felt defeat and failure wash over him again. The gunman was smiling triumphantly, as he reached out to the keyboard. Then he stopped. The line of asterisks had gone. In its place the words:

FORMATTING TIMESCOPE

"Jon, that was Hannah who said that; not me."

"Hannah... Hannah, are you still there? I thought you'd gone."

"*Yon?*" Her voice was faint now, "*Yon,* it hurts. Oh my lord, please stop this ..."

"Hannah...." Jon choked.

"Goodbye, my love."

"Down!!" Jon screamed, throwing himself against Naomi with such force that they both careered across the floor. Over their heads there was an ear-splitting roar as the weapon discharged. The whole clip was emptied into the wall where they had been standing, blasting holes in the plaster and brickwork and filling the room with acrid smoke and choking dust. It was fully a minute before the gun coughed and ceased firing.

The room was a ruin! Water continued to cascade down from the ceiling, damping down some of the smoke and dust, but mixing it into filthy puddles that ran from the bed to the floor. In the wall was a gaping hole through which a steady breeze was blowing. And above them the policeman, motionless as a statue.

Naomi picked herself up cautiously at first, and reached out to touch the uniformed man; every muscle was set hard, it was like touching marble. Jon rose too, his ears ringing and brushing the crumbs of glass from his knees. There was a groan from the bed.

"Granddad! It's me. Naomi. And Jon too!"

She threw her arms round his neck. For a few seconds he opened his eyes.

"Na...? Oh, you came back. Ahhh!"

"Mind his ribs!" Jon said, taking the old man's hand on the coverlet.

"What was that racket?"

"Jackman let off a few rounds;" Jon said. "But we got the codes into the Timescope."

"I know you did. Popping Candy."

"Popping what?"

"Na, do you remember when you were five? You came to stay and you bought some popping candy?"

Jon looked down at the Professor's face. He was hollow cheeked, and even under the layer of dust becoming very ashen. His breaths came infrequently, and were more of a spasm than an inhalation. He was dying in front of their eyes. But what a shame he should lose his sanity at this last moment.

"Yes, I remember. I found it really funny in my mouth."

He smiled, and with his free hand rubbed his forehead. "Popping candy, in there, in my brain. All the Timescope memories being burst open. It's like a head full of popping candy! That's how I know the Timescope is being destroyed."

Outside in the corridor feet were running. A burst of static on a walkie-talkie, then three soldiers stamped in, their weapons at the ready. The policeman did not move a muscle.

"Another one frozen here!" said one soldier into his radio. Then;

"Is one of you Jon Heath?"

"Me," said Jon, not taking his eyes off the Prof.

"Any ID? Oh never mind!" Then into his radio. "I think we've located him, send her over to the hospital; Chessington Ward." He walked around the bed. "Your mother, Mary Heath is on her way over. I've orders to detain you here until she arrives." He glanced at the fragile form of the Prof, then around the wreckage of the room. Summing up the situation, he barked at the other two men;

"Alright, I think we'd be fine waiting in the corridor!"

They were grateful for the respite, even more grateful when the petrified policeman was removed without ceremony from the room. They had experienced so much chaos, pain, suffering and death, not only here but also in the Timescope that their minds were shut down to anything but the present moment.

"Granddad?" Naomi put her face on the bedcovers, next to his. "Is this it? For us?"

He took another gulping breath before he replied; "for me; yes. I'm too much Timescope now. It goes, I go. Like that brave girl of yours, Jon. She knew the score, yet she had the guts to finish it."

They watched as his breaths became more spaced apart and finally less deep. He managed a few more words:

"But it's not it for you two…you've got plenty of time for each other. Don't fight too much!"

21

There were no tears from either of them. They left the room with the still form on the bed and were escorted down the stairs by the soldiers. In an office to the back of the hospital, Mary Heath was waiting.

"Ah, Jon, Naomi. I gather it's over, with the Professor. I'm sorry! I really am." Naomi nodded, a lump in her throat suffocating any reply. "That's alright, Lieutenant, I can deal with my own son without the need for armed guards."

When the door closed behind them, a dramatic change overcame her. She rushed across the room and threw her arms around them both crying hysterically. Then she yelled at them both, Jon in particular, before crying again. Finally calming down she said, wiping her eyes:

"You must excuse me. I've travelled non-stop from Koh Lanta. I touched down at RAF Lyneham two hours ago and I've been briefed with nothing but the most incredible stories.

She didn't want to hear their account, not then anyway. That was being left to qualified interviewers to piece the enormous jigsaw puzzle together. All she knew was that following Jon's phone call, their decision to abandon the diving expedition had led to a car-chase across the resort town, several shots being fired at them and then military police escorting herself and her husband to the British Embassy. From there they had arranged for anything that could get airborne to get them on a global hopscotch to the United Kingdom. What little she could then glean made her composure crumble: her son, Jon, (you do mean Jon Heath? Yes, ma'am, the one here in this photograph), had been at the centre of a conspiracy to corrupt communications that had very nearly catapulted the world economy back to the Middle Ages.

It was five days later that after endless hours of interviewing, checking, correlating and more interviewing, Jon was allowed to see her again.

"They've offered me the Home Office, Jon."

"Oh!" Jon was punch-drunk, having been pushed around from headquarters of some department here to military barracks somewhere else. If they had offered his mother the Monarchy he couldn't have cared. But nevertheless he listened as his mother outlined her part in resolving the crisis caused by the Professor's runaway toy.

"In other words, a complete cover-up!"

Mary had invested too much confidence in Jon to deny it. "Yes." She said.

Earlier that day Jon had met Naomi for the first time since the Prof had died. A lot had happened to them both, but they hugged each other in silence. Then she said;

"Did you see Granddad's house on the television?"

It had been blown up. Blown to little bits. But first there had been a staged gunfight between "Cyber-terrorists" and the SAS; the quiet neighbourhood had been further shattered by a dawn raid and hooded figures closing in on the property. Fabulous footage, a full camera crew just happened to be present! Two bodies had been recovered; a top-ranking civil servant and a local kid who, it was claimed, were hostages. Then as they endeavoured to retrieve the corpses of the terrorists, a series of huge booby trap explosions had demolished the property, scattering debris for miles around. All that remained was a crater.

Naomi didn't show any emotion. She was still in denial or shock, or both. Jon watched her closely to see how the reminders about George would affect her. But she remained stoical.

"So that's the cover story?"

"Yes," Mary agreed. Not entirely waterproof, but it would serve until some investigative journalist wanting to make a name for him or herself, started digging deeper into the story. Until then, the newspapers and media were publishing the obligatory grainy photographs of the conspirators, and faked CCTV footage showing their last movements.

"Why?"

"Jon, there comes a point when the truth no longer matters any more. If we could have done this before nuclear weapons were discovered, I think we would have. The Timescope, even in its infancy was too dangerous a tool to leave lying around. We have taken every measure to rip the pages out of the history book on this one. Nobody wants that level of surveillance. Our lives would not be worth living in a world where the Timescope was available, even to a limited clientele. And there's the matter of responsibility for this mess, Jon. We needed a shadowy, non-aligned organisation. No one country to blame. If it leaked out that we were the source of the virus, the compensation claims would ruin our economy for good. So we cooked up a story, and we are embroidering it to make it as plausible as we can. What's more we've destroyed the evidence. I'm sorry for Naomi, it was her home as well, but it had to be done."

"She's not bothered anyway."

"I'm sure she is, deep down." Mary looked at the clock on the wall. "I've got to go Jon, but spend time with her. Anyone can see she needs you around. We've got all we need from her and she's free to go. Spoil her; make her feel special, talk about it to her, she's a lovely girl Jon."

She paused, her hand on the door. "I don't need to remind you about secrecy do I?"

It was the umpteenth time that week somebody had reminded him. Jon didn't even manage a grunt.

Mary didn't tell Jon where she had to be that afternoon. Standing next to his ex-wife she watched in distaste as four sweating pallbearers carried the enormous coffin out of the parish church near his home; a full honourable send-off for a man who had long since lost sight of the meaning of honour. But the cover story came first. In death as well as in life, Prentice never ceased to amaze her with his ability to come up smelling of roses. All the same, she was curious to know what the coroner made of the cause of death of her private secretary: *asphyxiation due to drowning.* That was another piece of paper to bury as deep as possible!

She was a great deal more impressed with the Professor's funeral, and George Mere's, both of which were held on the same day a fortnight later. George's was simple. His parents bore up under their grief and confusion stoically, but the occasion served as a release for Naomi who howled inconsolably.

"He went back for me," she whispered; "even though he knew we were finished."

"One more bit of love for Jackman to cut out!" Jon replied bitterly. "Some world he'd have made."

The Professor's funeral service was almost a celebration. The simple church hall was packed, many more gathered outside to hear the commemoration of his remarkable life. Mary listened spellbound as tribute after tribute poured in; not wordy carefully-chosen phrases, but simple honest accolades to a man whose exceptional intelligence had not isolated him from his fellow human beings. But she had to smile as the reading, one of many chosen by the Professor himself boomed out of the loudspeakers:

"For now we see through a glass, darkly; but then face to face: now I know in part; but then shall I know even as also I am known. And now abides faith, hope, love, these three; but the greatest of these is love."

The death and injured toll was never satisfactorily reckoned. Across the world riots and civil unrest had erupted. Where there was order it was because it had been enforced by the military, elsewhere there had been, and still was anarchy.

Hard lessons had to be learnt. Huge, sprawling interconnected computer systems were all very well. They enabled financial transactions, the control of fuel and utility supplies, the rapid dissemination of information and news- in fact they were fundamental to the modern way of life. The Timescope had exposed the extreme danger of reliance on these networks, and efforts began to build systems that were proof against such attack. The new buzz-words were, *'iso-nets'* or *'disconnetworks'* and they were marketed not only on their capacity to pass data, but on their ability to sever themselves at a moment's notice, and if needs be disinfect any resident data. Further to this task, there were Timescope infections lurking in many places; networks where servers had been cut off, or network cards pulled- before these could be restored, they had to pass scrupulous inspection. It was months before electricity supplies across Europe could be said to be reliable. The Financial Times Share Index was only talked about in the hushed tones reserved for a terminally ill patient.

Life for Jon and Naomi was not straightforward either. Having their need for each other so comprehensively exposed by the Timescope, they had assumed that they would somehow live happily ever after. But the experiences had left deep scars. Hannah bath-Obadiah had departed; Jon had had no chance to grieve or say goodbye. In them both, especially in Naomi were a host of homeless memories; places that they could not possibly have visited, people they had never met but knew intimately. There was a life together that they had yet to live. At best it was confusing; at worst it was painful. Once Naomi found herself lifting the telephone to call her mother in the village by the river Kishon.

The sensation of these memories was like the ghost limb syndrome of someone who has had a leg or arm amputated. The tension they felt erupted often into rows, and Naomi thought wistfully of George who had been so placid compared to Jon, whilst Jon's thoughts strayed to Carmel.

"Jon, was the Timescope right about us?"

The directness of the question unsettled him. "What do you mean?"

"Jackman said we're in love, but it hasn't felt like that lately."

Jon had been musing this very question himself. He had talked it over with his mother, but surprisingly it was his Dad who put his finger on the problem:

"You haven't got any history to call your own. When I met your mother, we went places; we saw friends, held hands, we did silly things."

Jon tried to imagine his mother doing silly things, but gave up.

"It's those little things that stick; they're our experiences, things we did together, things we shared." He went on, clearly pleased with his sudden profundity.

"From what I understand, you've had all these false memories force-fed into you both. No wonder you're confused. You neither of you know for certain who you are any more. You've got to...well...overwrite that data, Jon. Take her out; spend time and all that holiday money we left you on her. Buy ice-creams, go boating on the lake, walk and talk, hold hands, kiss her..."

"Alright Dad, I get the message!"

"And above all, don't let her slip! You won't get another like her!"

They lay in the bottom of the boat, bobbing around on the lake; just watching the clouds in the early Autumn sky. Dad's advice had been sound. They had been shy with each other at first and several times it looked as though their relationship would falter; but now they saw each other most evenings, and were rarely apart at weekends.

"Look, there's an aircraft!"

"Where?"

She didn't need to, but she took his hand anyway and guided his finger. "There, it's a jumbo. Probably going to America." Regular scheduled flights had been slow to resume; not surprisingly passengers were unhappy at the prospect of being in the air should the 'Cyber-terrorist' attack recur.

"You still looking at going there? Your Granddad's old Uni?" An old friend of the Prof's had come across for the funeral. A few days afterwards, he had approached her with a proposal.

"Well they were happy to have me on the strength of his reputation. But it won't be for a couple of years yet."

"You're not answering my question. Are you going?"

"That depends on you! I... well... I need to know how things stand between us."

"You're shivering. Have my coat, Na."

"I'm not cold!" she pushed the coat aside. "I want some reassurance, Jon. It's bad enough all these memories that aren't mine. Our life at Carmel, having kids, growing old, you know."

"Go on Na." Jon sensed this was getting to something crucial between them.

"You were pretty smitten with Hannah weren't you? What was it you said to her? 'I would die for you.'"

"That was then, but Na…"

"Jon, is it me you love, or what the Timescope turned me into?"

And at that moment, Jon knew.

"Naomi Avery, you listen to me."

She sat up in the boat, taken aback by the intensity of his voice. "Hannah was amazing! Do you know why? She wasn't something the Timescope turned you into, she was a projection of you. She was what I felt about you, but didn't realise it! I should have known the moment she reappeared after I knew she was dead- she was everything I liked and admired about you. She knew what was right and stuck to it. She said what she thought and didn't mess around. And she was beautiful!"

Naomi felt her eyes prickling. She said nothing.

"And Hannah is dead, Na," he said fiercely. "And it hurt when she died. But I'm glad the Timescope showed her to me. Do you know why? 'Cause it was showing me what was right under my nose all the time. But I was too stupid to see it. It was showing me you."

"Hannah's dead," he repeated. "But you're alive, Na. You're alive, you're real and you're very beautiful."

Her only reply was to burst into tears.

Epilogue

Hannah was asleep. Or so Jon thought. As he rose gently from the bed and picked his way carefully across the room, treading softly to avoid stepping on any of her presents, he heard a rustle behind him. In the subdued light, a pair of dark eyes regarded him gravely from her pillow.

"Dad?"

"Go to sleep. You'll be tired for Living Word tomorrow."

"Is Mum happier now?" She had a frank way of speaking that made it impossible to lie to her.

"I think so. You make her happy."

That was true. Their daughter was ten today. No matter how hard they tried to gloss over them, the similarities were uncanny. Hannah resisted all attempts to have her hair shorn. She had a striking personality that even at her young age shone through. She possessed a remarkable, innate sense of justice that made her take the part of the bullied underdog many time in the school playground. Naomi loved Hannah to distraction, but she served as a constant reminder to them both of the events they had experienced in the Timescope. It was as if her Granddad's programs had reached even into their genes.

By contrast her younger brother, Rufus, named at his mother's insistence after the Professor, was a complete opposite. Loud, boisterous, impetuous and brimming with energy, Rufus took life at full tilt. He was at his Aunt Judith's house tonight. She loved having him round. And it gave them time for the new baby.

"Now go to sleep, Han."

As he climbed the stairs, Jon reflected on the last fifteen years. The Timescope had been right. Theirs had been a love capable of staying the course. In spite of the psychological damage inflicted on them both, the attraction that they had for each other had solidified into an unbreakable bond.

They still frequently struck sparks off each other; they were too alike in many respects and both unwilling to give ground on things they disagreed about. But they individually knew that there was nobody else who could give them what they needed from each other, and even now, all these years on, it only took a touch or a hug to resolve the dispute in progress.

Naomi had suffered badly from the postnatal depression after Gideon was born. In these horrible grey moments, the deep scars and bittersweet memories erupted as if they had happened yesterday. Hannah, with her incisive perceptiveness had felt her mother's hurt and done her best to heal.

As he crossed the landing, Jon could see that the baby's room was empty.

"Is he hungry again?" He put his head round the study door. In the soft light of the wallscreen, she was holding him close. It was one of his favourite sights, watching her feeding him. She could do this and work at the same time, which was just as well, because she was seemingly impervious to tiredness.

"Never stops feeding this one!" She wiped his chin gently and lifted him to her shoulder. Gideon's grey-blue eyes roved disjointedly around the room, then he emitted a soft belch. "I'll just change him, then I'll be along."

"Let me." Jon kicked the changing mat on to the floor and laid the baby flat. "Where's the wipes?" he wondered out loud. "Are they over by you, love?"

She made no reply. Jon glanced up from his task. She was staring at the computer screen, her jaw set rigid.

"Na? What's the matter? Have they refused our offer again?"

Still she made no reply. Jon stood up and followed her gaze.

In the corner of the wallscreen was a message box. Innocuous, inconspicuous and easy to miss. But it had punched through several layers of current tasks, through bombproof security systems that had been the product of the union of many brilliant minds, and through all the years of their history together.

HELP ME, MY LORD

About the Author

The Bible has always featured prominently in my life from early years when I was at the receiving end of Sunday school lessons. The pictures and actions always came across so vividly and it took only a little imagination to feel for myself the extraordinary events that fill its pages.

It was relatively recently, however, following a series of encounters with friends that the concept of Timescope took shape.

None of these ideas would have amounted to anything without a solid knowledge of the Scripture; a knowledge encouraged by the Christadelphian Church of which I have been a long term member.

As well as the names in the dedication I would like to thank the number of people in the church who knowingly or otherwise contributed to the store of knowledge of Bible times and customs without which I would have struggled to portray a convincing backdrop for the events in Timescope.

Selected chapters of the book in its current form were submitted to the Arts Council sponsored website Youwriteon.com, and I would like to acknowledge all those who reviewed and offered comments and advice which helped immensely in the final edit.

Printed in the United Kingdom by
Lightning Source UK Ltd., Milton Keynes
141512UK00001B/216/P